Acclaim for *Cecily* – an e
of the Wars o

'Masterful and majestic . . . England's unspoken history told by one
brilliant woman through the life of another. This important novel
blazes on every page from its brutal first scene to its glittering final act'
Chris Cleave

'Entirely absorbing and utterly compelling. Fifteenth-century England
leaps from the page, with all its political turmoil and bloodshed. I loved it'
Caroline Lea

'Cecily stalks the corridors of power like a female Thomas Cromwell.
A vividly female perspective on the Wars of the Roses – what a feat'
Imogen Hermes Gowar

'Masterfully written and wholly immersive, with characters that
live and breathe. *Cecily* is a tour de force. I loved every sentence'
Joanne Burn

'Annie Garthwaite writes about the past with the sort of intimacy,
immediacy and empathy that can only come from graft and craft'
Toby Clements

'BLOODY GREAT. So modern, so political, it could
almost be set in Downing Street'
Kate Sawyer

'An extraordinary achievement . . . I could touch and breathe
Cecily's world as if I were walking in her shadow'
Carol McGrath

'Impeccably researched, written with style and shot through with
energy, heart and power. A perfectly paced tale of intrigue, influence
and victory wrenched from defeat. Cecily has been overlooked for
centuries. Not any more'
A. J. West

'Utterly compelling, a phenomenal read'
Liz Hyder

Praise for Cecily, an epic feminist retelling of the Wars of the Roses

What Readers Say About *Cecily*

'High drama on an epic scale' ★★★★★

'It's impossible not to be caught up in this tale of intrigue,
love and ambition' ★★★★★

'I've been completely bowled over by this fierce
and feminist book' ★★★★★

'Encapsulates a woman of our time,
that time and every time' ★★★★★

'Sweeping, complex and brilliant' ★★★★★

'As many twists and turns as any
psychological thriller' ★★★★★

'Annie Garthwaite has produced a masterpiece' ★★★★★

'I was utterly absorbed and couldn't put it down' ★★★★★

'*Cecily* is historical fiction at its best' ★★★★★

'This novel has it all – a clever, considered, feisty female
lead plus emotion, peril and intrigue' ★★★★★

CECILY

ANNIE GARTHWAITE

PENGUIN BOOKS

PENGUIN BOOKS

UK | USA | Canada | Ireland | Australia
India | New Zealand | South Africa

Penguin Books is part of the Penguin Random House group of companies
whose addresses can be found at global.penguinrandomhouse.com.

Penguin
Random House
UK

First published by Viking 2021
Published in Penguin Books 2022
001

Copyright © Annie Garthwaite, 2021

The moral right of the author has been asserted

Typeset by Jouve (UK), Milton Keynes
Printed and bound in Great Britain by Clays Ltd, Elcograf S.p.A.

The authorized representative in the EEA is Penguin Random House Ireland,
Morrison Chambers, 32 Nassau Street, Dublin D02 YH68

A CIP catalogue record for this book is available from the British Library

ISBN: 978-0-241-99097-1

For my mother, who gave me time to read stories.
And for Caroline, who gives me time to write them.

Author's Note

Readers who wish to study in greater detail the family relation-
ships that fuel the dynastic allegiances and political rivalries
described in this novel will find genealogies at the back of the
book. These include an illustration of Richard Duke of York's
claim to the Crown.

Prologue

1431

Eight years ago, Cecily Neville's family gave her in marriage to Richard Plantagenet. It was a gamble. But the last of a dozen daughters must take her chances. Or make them.

Now, as Cecily turns sixteen, their life together begins. The son of a long-dead traitor, Richard's prospects are uncertain, his loyalties suspect. If he can win the young king's trust, he might regain his family's titles and make Cecily his Duchess of York. If not, he may be deemed too dangerous to let live.

The threat is inescapable and now they share it, for it is the blood in Richard's veins that he will pass on to their sons, the old royal blood his father died for. Cecily is undaunted. Together, she believes, they can do anything.

And besides, at some unseen future time, might not such blood as easily make their fortune as mar it?

I

30 May 1431
Rouen, France

It's no easy thing, to watch a woman burn. A young woman, who has seen only three more summers than yourself and claims the voice of God compels her actions. But there it is; the day's work. And she must harden herself to it.

So, on a May morning so fine its early sun has already chased Rouen's street dogs into shadows, Cecily has put on black velvet, sombre and rich. She has bound a rosary at her waist; a reminder to the French that God has answered the prayers of the English and delivered Joan of Arc into their hands. A reminder to her king that her loyalty is to him and to Heaven.

She waits now in the market square, her face to the pyre and sullen French anger at her back, for the signal that will tell her Joan is coming out to die. She raises her head when it comes, a trumpet call, high and vicious, and, beneath it, the crowd's murmur growing to a roar. Beside her, her husband Richard straightens his back, squares his feet. She swallows bile and does the same. The sun is hot enough, but that's nothing, she thinks, to the blaze to come. Have courage, her mother would say. Faith and courage can accomplish anything. Cecily wonders if Joan's mother told her the same. Likely someone did. In her glory days Joan put on armour and rode at the head of armies. With words alone she roused a fearful king and turned the tide of a war. Imagine. Now the tide runs all against her, and she must find only the courage to die. Though Joan is England's enemy, Cecily wishes courage for her now.

Soon the ring of metalled feet overwhelms the clarion, and the crowd parts for a wagon, its blade-bristling guard, and the prisoner bound upon it. It's the first time she's seen Joan and isn't sure what to expect. Just a pale, thin girl, it seems, head shorn and bloodied. It doesn't look like there's much fight left in her. The bright armour of Joan's soldiering days is long gone and today's thin shift, with the filth of a prison year upon it, is scant covering for a body that, some say, English soldiers have been allowed their way with. Though Richard says surely not, Cecily can believe it. The King's uncles have long wanted Joan dead. But they wanted her shamed, first.

Cecily sees Joan stumble as she's pulled from the wagon and thinks for a moment she will fall and knock herself senseless. And what then? But the guards press in to hold Joan upright, her body crushed between their bulk as they jostle towards the pyre, her arms pinioned behind her, her small breasts jutting.

The desperate parade passes close enough that Cecily can see Joan's eyes. One is closed by livid bruises, the other, white-rimmed and wide, is fixed on the crucifix borne high above her by a priest, leading the way to death and whatever might lie beyond it. Joan's lips are moving and Cecily recognizes the words of the Ave, falling stuttering and fast. She wonders what she prays for. Rescue? Or just an end to this?

I would pray for the death of every Englishman here, Cecily thinks. Then suddenly she is afraid, for no one can fathom the power of Joan's prayers, and Richard stands beside her, who has seen Joan tried and nodded his head at her sentence. Her breath catches and she pants, once, and he's holding out a hand to steady her. She raises a palm, shakes her head to signal no, then makes a fist to hide her fingers' trembling. He draws back, and she feels his gaze follow hers to where the guards are handing Joan into the reaching arms of men who wait to receive her. They draw her up, bare legs flailing, then bind her and bring more wood, so that she stands deep among a thicket of staves.

She can no longer hear Joan's prayers so, out of pity and to guard her own soul, she speaks them with her, as the men clamber down and reach for their torches. At last the fire is set and the flames lick like dogs at Joan's feet and thighs. Cecily feels their growing heat against her own cheek as Joan's voice, steady at the last, rings out above her head,

'All I have done was by God's order.' Then, urgent, as the priest's arms falter and his burden dips, 'Hold up the cross of Christ that I may see it as I die!'

Cecily narrows her eyes against livid sparks as Joan's prayers give way to hacking coughs and shrieks, then sudden silence. She sets herself to watch as flesh burns, blossoms and falls away. There's grit in her eyes, sweat runs the cleft of her shoulder blades and, beneath her clasped hands, her stomach shrivels. But she won't flinch. She knows this is a test.

It seems an age, but at last the fire is sated, and into the hush it leaves behind, Joan's body sags and falls with a soft sigh of ash.

Cecily looks down at last, swallows hard and blinks sore eyes.

Richard turns towards her. 'Come away now,' he says. 'It's done.' He moves to wrap an arm about her waist.

She stalls him, placing her fingers, still warm from the fire, on the back of his gloved hand. 'I stood firm.'

There's ash in his hair, his face is pinched and smutted, but he manages a wry smile. 'Firmer than your husband, I think.'

That morning she'd confessed to him her dread of it. He'd said she needn't go. That he himself did not relish the burning of women. She shook her head. No. We go together. It must be seen that we can watch the King's enemies die, and not falter.

And there, across the still-smoking fire, beyond the greasy stink of Joan's death, the child king's uncles, the Dukes of Bedford and Gloucester, stand shoulder to shoulder.

Watching.

She raises her chin, and then, having measured the depth of Bedford's slow bow, the slide of Gloucester's eyes, lets Richard raise her hand, turn her about, lead her away. The crowd parts for them and, as if their leaving is a signal, begins to disperse.

Englishmen murmur and pat each other's shoulders as they go, well done, well done.

Frenchmen, penned in to witness this defeat, slip between guards who part their pikes to let them pass and chide, 'Go home now, and take a lesson from this.'

Cecily watches them go. What lesson should she herself take? she wonders. Only that, if a woman takes up arms, she must be very sure of winning.

2

16 December 1431
Paris

With Joan dead, England's king can come to his French crowning. It's been a long wait. A hundred years of battling and scrapping, winning by inches, then losing again. The fifth Henry, this one's father, came close after Agincourt, but coughed up his guts on another battlefield before he could drag his bony arse to the throne. He handed the task to his brothers, Bedford and Gloucester. A deathbed promise wrested from them both: hold England, win France. Make my son king of both.

Now the day is come and the incense-drenched air above Notre Dame's high altar is riven by the Sanctus bell, calling God to come lay hands on his anointed. As the cathedral's vast spaces fall silent on the dying chime, Cecily dares raise her eyes to where, beyond a sea of bowed heads, her Uncle Beaufort, the towering scarlet cardinal, lowers the long-contested crown of France on to the child Henry's head.

Henry himself is a shimmer of white, his ten-year-old arms outstretched, his bare breast sheened with chrism, his face tear-swept and rapt. His mouth falls open in a small round 'oh' as the weight of a kingdom falls on him. She shivers at it. Dear God in Heaven, is this how kings are made? Henry raises his head in a shaft of sunlight, blinks in its dazzle. Her eyes, following his, are caught in the glare of a second crown, that of England. Henry's by right since he was six months old, now held aloft in Gloucester's arms.

The cardinal's voice rings out. 'Henry, the sixth of that name, King of England *and* of France.'

The glad words draw a tidal sigh of amens. When the cardinal turns to acknowledge them, Cecily knows herself seen, the only upturned face, watching holy mysteries as if she has a right to know God's business. She expects his look to be a chastisement. He is her mother's brother, after all, and no less sharp. But his eyes crease at the corners and, almost, he smiles, as if to say, there you are Cecily, bold as ever.

Among the slow-moving coronation procession, Cecily passes out through the cathedral's great west door, beneath the lofty tympanum, where Christ Triumphant, serene and indifferent, presides over the judgement of the dead. Emerging into winter sunlight, she feels the sanctity of the church fall away as the world, sharp with frost and conflict, rises up to meet her. She knows today's crowning marks no end to war. It's little more than a gesture, grand and provocative, tip for tap, for now France has two kings. Two years ago the mad king's son, last of the Valois line all thought finished at Agincourt, gave off licking his wounds and rode on the back of Joan's holy vision to his crowning in Rheims. He's down for now, but no one thinks he's finished.

Gloucester, stalking ahead of them, growls into his brother Bedford's ear. 'Today sends a message to Charles the Pretender, Charles the Bastard, Charles the thrice-cursed bane of our lives. England still has stomach for the fight, and the true heir of Agincourt comes to stake his claim.'

The dukes press on to be closer to their king, and Richard's face, when it turns to hers, is wry.

She takes his arm, leans close. 'The message might be more convincing if the heir of Agincourt was not a puling child who threw his insides up over the ship's rail an hour out from Dover. Or if he went to his weapons practice more enthusiastically, or more often, than to prayer.'

He threads her arm through his. 'We must hope Charles's spies don't hear of such things.' A smile. A wink.

Stepping into the carriage that will take them to the coronation feast, Cecily pauses a moment. Ahead of her the shimmering king, on a horse well chosen for a sovereign, but towering for a half-grown boy, steps out through a banner-waving crowd. All most splendid. Then she turns, looking back to where the business of the day reclaims the cathedral square. Beyond it and the encircling river lie the unfathomed byways of Paris. England's hold there, she knows, is tenuous and challenged. If she walked those narrow streets today, she'd hear low French voices, surly, resentful, biding their time. She wonders about Charles down there in Rheims. Is his courage burned to ash with Joan's bones, or does she walk his dreams now, urging him on?

She draws up the weighted velvet of her gown, steps inside the curtained carriage, takes a seat opposite her husband and folds her long white hands.

'So, it's done, Cecily. At last.'

'By God's will,' she answers.

Granting him a small smile, she leans back against the cushions and closes her eyes. In her private darkness she calculates the value of all she has learned since coming into France: that the will of God, which has called all things into being, might turn a child into a king, a girl into a warrior, or a body into ash. And that any man – or woman indeed – may, according to their courage, shape His will to their purpose.

That night the company dine listlessly on roast goose. No one's hungry, though they've barely eaten all day. They'd been too nervous to breakfast well that morning and the food at the coronation banquet, though impressive to look upon, had made poor eating. Pungent sauces masked fish dishes that were overcooked and cold when brought to table. Glistening

pastries hid meats grey with fat. The French lords had complained among themselves, muttering under their breath
about the incompetence of English cooks. 'All show and no
substance,' Cecily called it, sniffing. 'It wouldn't have happened at home.'

In her mother's household, the language of food spoke
through the senses to the heart: see what we have, how we
can sustain you. Don't you want to be one of us? It had spoken
to Richard, clearly enough. He's wanted very much to be one
of them ever since, in his twelfth year, eight years an orphan
and adrift, he was brought north through foul December weather into the warm brilliance of Raby's great hall at dinner.

The royal courier, who'd ridden graceless and hunched
ahead of him for the two-week journey, pushed him towards
Cecily's father, full of charm. 'Your new ward, my lord. I bring
him and the season's greetings from the Lord Protector, the
great Duke of Gloucester.'

Richard raised his eyes, ready to be resentful. Then his
vision was filled with the sight of Ralph, Earl of Westmorland,
rising from the table and striding towards him, tall and smiling, with his arms thrown wide. 'Ah, you're in out of the cold
now, Richard. Get that wet cloak off and come eat. Formal-
ities later.'

It was the first time he saw Cecily. From the space hastily
cleared for him, and with the blade of his hunger blunted, he
raised his eyes from the warm cup that soothed his chilblained
fingers. The earl was talking, bright and fast, down the table,
to men who seemed hungrier for his attention than for the
food before them. Nearer, a girl, no more than nine, stared
fixedly at him from beside the chair of a lady rich in silk who,
with her hand lying soft on the earl's sleeve, stared likewise, as
if measuring him for clothes. The girl blinked her grey eyes,
reached up to whisper into the lady's ear, then returned to her
staring.

The lady smiled softly down on the girl's head then turned another smile, less loving, more knowing, on him. 'You're welcome, Richard. My daughter Cecily says so.'

Richard came, in time, to idolize Cecily's father. Ralph Neville replaced the uncertainties of a childhood shadowed by treason with the reliable virtues of a well-governed household. Among the young men drawn together under Ralph's affinity, he found a place within a finely ordered discipline, where loyalty and good endeavour brought rewards he understood. The rules were simple. He could keep them.

He learned soon enough that he'd been brought into Ralph's household by a business transaction, but as time fostered his understanding of it, he found himself content with its terms. By the mercy of King Henry V, who brought the axe down on his father's traitorous neck, he retained rights of inheritance to the Earldom of Cambridge and the Dukedom of York. But only a royal affirmation at Richard's coming of age will turn those rights to reality, and that merciful king is long dead. His brothers, today's king's uncles, would have preferred the orphan tipped into a ditch with his father's headless corpse. Instead, he's spent his childhood between pillar and post, passed like baggage among men who despise him, unwanted, knocked about, scorned. Until Ralph said to Gloucester, let me have the boy. I'll make a king's man of him and give him to my girl.

Richard was married to Cecily within months of his arrival at Raby. He stood beside the grey-eyed girl in the castle's gilded chapel while the priest muttered and his bride, stiff in her finery, listened earnestly and repeated the words put to her.

'That's done then, Richard,' said Ralph, leaning down to look him in the eye and laying a steadying hand on his shoulder. 'Serve well, please the King, and you'll get a dukedom for my daughter.'

He watched over Ralph's shoulder as his young bride was

led away by her nurses. When she turned and smiled at him from the doorway, he felt his heart settle.

Richard has spent the last three years serving his king. Called to court and the King's company to have his loyalties tested. First in England, now in France.

'Traitor's get,' Gloucester had called him, that first day. 'Prove me wrong.'

Richard has made it his work to do so.

The dukes of Gloucester and Bedford sit opposite Cecily now, picking at the cooling carcass of the bird and passing a wine jug between them as they talk. Their wives have their heads together at the far end of the table. Cecily doesn't know if they're planning a skirmish or comparing the skills of their dressmakers, and doesn't much care. Like Richard, she's watching the dukes, wondering what their next move will be and what it might mean for them.

She's been Richard's wife for eight years now, but in truth their life together began when they boarded ship for Calais. These eighteen months in France they've been every day together, and the family that shaped them has shaped them to fit. They're natural allies. Watchers and listeners both. Thinkers, planners, weighers of words. They've seen their chance for a place in the world, and joined hands to grasp it.

From London to Calais, Rouen to Paris, Cecily has observed her husband's careful diplomacy, his ready ear for the boy king's prattling, his studied deference to Gloucester's barking plaints, his quiet conversations with Bedford, his readiness to be helpful, his aptitude for work. She's watched him wrack his conscience over Joan's trial and execution, troubled by its savagery but knowing it to be the price of royal approval.

'I don't like it,' he'd told her, that morning of the burning. 'I'd rather find the men who put her up to it.'

She'd shrugged. 'She's the woman in front of those men,

Richard. If French hopes live in a virgin maid, then a virgin maid must die.' A finger on his chest, chiding. 'King's man.'

She's smoothed his way, in so far as she could. She's courted the wives of both dukes, who now call her friend. She speaks with Gloucester of books and music; subjects he'd expect a woman to speak to him of. With Bedford she reminisces about her father and his; the loyal earl, his beloved king, now re-united in Heaven. He has softened at such times. He is a man who can be moved.

In Rouen, in the days after Joan's burning, Bedford's wife had come to her, threaded their arms as they walked the castle walls. 'I think they should be friends,' she said, 'your husband and mine.' That night they dined together, all four and no other. They talked of the young king's father, the greatness of his legacy, the preservation of his son.

'I will make it my life's work,' Richard told them, his voice earnest, his eyes steady and clear. He means he will forswear his own blood, flowing to him through his Mortimer ancestors from Edward III's second son; richer than young Henry's, descended from his third. Bedford had nodded and, when they parted, pressed a hand to Richard's shoulder, while Duchess Anne kissed Cecily's cheek, and smiled against it.

In the days since, Bedford has called Richard to him often, shown favour, talked to him of a campaign that will follow the King's crowning, as if he might have a part in it. He has introduced him to his captains, William de la Pole chief among them, who is between them in age and easy company. Bedford, who is inclined to be dour, laughs easily in William's company. Sometimes, now, all three laugh together. Her cardinal uncle, Cecily notes, is close by at such times, nodding, pleased. He's close now too, seemingly intent upon his dinner, pretending not to listen.

Now the wine jug comes to rest and Cecily's eyes are drawn

to Gloucester as he turns their way, pulls his napkin from his shoulder and clears his throat to speak. He's fourteen months Bedford's junior but it could be fourteen years at least. The urbane lord who spends his days managing Henry's English kingdom looks decidedly less careworn than weather-beaten Bedford, who has spent the last ten years and more fighting for his French one.

'Richard,' Gloucester says, 'once Christmas is done we leave Paris. Head back to Calais. My brother stays in France, of course, but you and I will have the King safe home before St George's Day.'

She glances at Richard, notes his caution and surprise. 'I'd thought,' he says, carefully, 'we'd stay longer in France. Let the King be seen in his kingdom?'

Cecily knew Bedford's hope had rested on Henry's continued presence, wonders why he's acquiesced. Perhaps he's concluded, just as she has during these months in Henry's company, that France wouldn't be much impressed by him.

'He's needed in England,' Gloucester growls. 'You've work there too,' and he turns away, down the table, to join his wife.

She feels in her own breast the sigh Bedford heaves as he draws his hands down the length of his face. He looks up at them with something attempting to be a smile. 'It's for the best,' he says. 'For all of us. For you, certainly.'

Richard watches Gloucester walk away then turns back to Bedford. His hopes, Cecily knows, had rested on staying here to serve with Bedford; to prove himself loyal beyond Joan's burning. 'I'd thought,' he says, 'to help you push Charles back from Rheims.'

Bedford shakes his head slowly, and sighs. 'Thank you. But what my brother means is that our king has decided to reward the good service you've already given. You're to wait no longer for your inheritance, Richard. Go back to England. Take possession of what's yours. Attend the King. Leave France to me a while. It will call you back soon enough.' He draws out his chair, pulls himself to his feet, then turns to them again with a final thought. 'I've convinced my brother you're a right-thinking man, Richard. Please don't prove me wrong.'

'I will not.'

Behind Bedford's retreating back, the cardinal raises a glass to his niece, taps his nose and then returns to his plate. His gesture signals both conspiracy and congratulation, and is as welcome to her as a dukedom. She turns her head to hide a grin, then collects herself, tightens her hold on Richard's hand, shakes it and leans close.

'Well, my lord. That was all very unexpected.'

He looks dazed, so she leans closer still.

'Now you are Duke of York at last, would you like to take your duchess to bed?'

His smile comes quickly then; the open one that only she ever sees.

They've learned each other's bodies here in France, as they've learned each other's minds, and find they are attuned. Cecily has discovered that, in loving, as in everything, boldness is rewarded. When Richard shakes beneath her hands and cannot speak but only reach for her; when he is buried in her and senseless with it, her heart exults and, in tenderness then, she draws him close, holds him till he calms. He tells her she has spelled him with love. She stretches her body beneath him, moonlit and pale, and says she has no need of witchcraft.

Tonight's love is exultant, the talk after, just the same; both set skin alight and leave them breathless. They're conjuring new futures, redrawing their lives with word and touch. They'll be home before winter ends, a summer before them in which to work.

'Two main administrative centres –' Richard pushes damp

hair from his eyes and raises his hands, expansive – 'Ludlow in the west, Fotheringhay in the east.'

She nods, slow. 'I see you've given this some thought.'

He sketches it out. To the Welsh border fortress of Ludlow the vast revenues of their Mortimer estates across Wales and Ireland will flow. From Fotheringhay, in the Nene's verdant valley, they'll manage their English holdings. 'And from there it's just a few days' ride to London and the court. What do you think?'

'Sensible. Fotheringhay, when we wish to be close to the King. Ludlow, when we want to escape him.'

He slaps her thigh, his touch light. 'Shush!'

'What?' She grins, stretches her own arms with languid ease. 'And in each place we will build a church. Great engines of prayer for the house of York. And, I suppose,' feigning prim, 'for the good of the realm and the health of our most sovereign lord.'

He laughs down at her as she throws off the covers to let the night air cool her body, then runs a hand between her breasts. 'Will it always be so with us, do you think?'

'What?'

'Oh . . . I don't know. Love and talk.'

'Business and pleasure?'

He nods.

'Yes. Providing I don't die of thirst.'

She's pleased, then, to watch the slide of muscle across his bare shoulder as he leans to pour wine from the flagon by the bed. She raises herself on her elbows and he lifts the cup to her lips. She sips, then watches as he drinks; follows the sinews of his throat as he swallows, sees the sheen of sweat in its hollow. The wine's redness glistens on his mouth and she kisses him, relishing its sweetness and his warmth. He smiles, drinks again, stretches beside her, resting the cup lazily on his breast.

Dawn isn't far off, and they are, at last, sated. All this talk of building.

'I wonder when we'll have our first child,' she says. Then laughs a little, hesitant. She's thinking of Gloucester's childless wife. And of Bedford's, who has been married eight years and never felt her womb quicken.

'We'd best be about it if we're to equal your parents. Your mother gave your father fourteen children.'

'Oh, did she? I thought my father gave them to her.'

'I expect you're right.' He's grinning. His free hand strokes her flank.

She takes it, threads his fingers with hers. 'I would hate to be barren.'

His voice turns soft, his face serious. 'It's not likely.'

'No. No, it is not.' She pulls herself upright again, leans in and grins. 'You will give me many children.'

'Well, I must do something, I suppose, to make up for my lack. I am only I, while you . . . well, you are most rich in relations.'

'I don't care. You're most rich in titles!' She's gleeful, straddling his waist, ready to love again.

But now he turns pensive.

'I think perhaps . . . I wonder sometimes if I might have had such a family. Had my father lived. Had he not been a traitor.'

'Or had he been a better one.'

He's shocked, and she sees it. She kisses his hand, smiles into his palm, then looks into his face, intent. 'A man is only a traitor if he doesn't win. My father, too, was one, if you choose to call him so.'

'Your father! Your father was loyal to Lancaster all his life.' Always Richard will defend Ralph against any slander. Even his daughter's.

'Yes, yes. But Lancaster wasn't always king. My father crowned Lancaster when he put young Henry's grandfather on the throne. But to do it he broke his oath of fealty to the king he helped depose.'

'Was it a sin, do you think?' Richard has made Ralph his lodestar, can't bear to think it's led him wrong.

She slides off and lies beside him. He turns to face her.

'No.' Cecily is emphatic. 'Ask my mother. She'll tell you. God might anoint kings and bring them to their thrones, but He can't keep them there.' Then she whispers, conspiratorial. 'Only nobles like yourself can do that.'

Richard laughs, but he can't look at her. He doesn't remember his own father, only the shame of him, and that Ralph called him a faithless dog. 'Then God save kings from rebellious nobles.'

'Yes, of course. Good kings. But if a king is weak, as that one was. If he's a fool and sets the country at odds.' When he looks away, grimacing, she reaches a finger, turns his face to hers again. 'It's simple. God's appointed order: king, nobles, the people, each ruled by the other in turn.'

'And if a king can't keep God's order, then the nobles must restore it. I know.' He shudders. 'But it's a desperate road . . .'

'That must be walked at times of great need. Or there's only chaos, and there the Devil reigns. There's duty in kingship, Richard. Not privilege alone.'

The boy king's grandfather knew that. He held the nobles in balance with a careful mixture of censure and reward, fear and patronage, for the fourteen years of his reign. Then he passed the banner to his son, the fifth Henry, who united them in conquest and gave them Agincourt.

They're quiet now, Cecily and Richard, side by side in the loving bed. They are both thinking the thing they cannot say yet; what of young Henry? Can he do it?

3

Bedford warned that France would draw them back. Daily now, Cecily hopes it won't. Since Henry came home from his crowning it's been a war of attrition across the Channel. Four years and both sides are exhausted. At last, an offer from Charles; England can keep its French territories if Henry will surrender his French crown. Gloucester spits and curses. Young Henry prays three days for guidance, before declaring that, though he craves peace above all things, God has made him king of France, so fight on. And Bedford does, till he falls from his horse to his sickbed.

While the good duke busies himself with dying, the cardinal goes to Arras for talks with the French king. Fruitless, of course. Charles says he won't come to the negotiating table until there's a crown for him to take away from it, so Cecily's uncle is quickly home again.

This morning he'll take his no-news to the King. But first, he walks with his niece and her husband in Westminster Gardens. It's late September, but summer is slow to give way to autumn and Cecily is chafed by the sun's heat, sullen on her back. She notices how tattered the flowers are. How the trees seem full of dust.

The cardinal's face matches his steady stride. He looks to her like a man who'd hoped for better but expected worse and so is sanguine. It's just one more move on the chessboard for him, she thinks. He's already planning the next. She wonders whether she and Richard are to be brought into the game. Why else has he called them to walk with him here, even before he goes to the King?

She frowns and kicks out a crease in her skirt. Then sighs and shakes herself, takes her uncle's arm. She knows well enough she's peevish and out of sorts, and it isn't all his fault. It's because of the other news he brought home with him. For John Duke of Bedford, at least, the long French game is over, and he died believing it lost.

'Did you see him,' she asks. 'Before the end?'

'I was in time to give him God's final office. I'd have brought his body home, but it was his last wish to remain in France.'

'Well,' says Richard. 'He fought for her long enough.' He shakes his head. 'Hard to imagine France without Bedford's hand upon it.'

'Indeed,' the cardinal sighs and nods. 'Or a better hand to send in his stead.'

Days later, more bad news comes billowing across the Channel.

England's ally, Burgundy's duke, has turned his coat, made peace with Charles and will fight no more for England.

It comes as little surprise to Cecily. But, for Henry, betrayal is new and painful, so when he hears of it he weeps and storms. His counsellors, usually so conspicuous, seem to merge with the tapestries so that, when the King's eye is casting around for a lieutenant to replace Bedford and do his bidding in France, it alights upon Richard who, with the cardinal, stands quietly by.

It's their first real fight. Or, at least, Cecily fights. Richard will not, which makes her madder still. He stands steady while she storms, speaks quietly when she rails. He holds tight to her hand when she raises it against him, lowers his eyes, turns his head. She pulls away, sheathing in fists the nails that want to rake his face.

'And what exactly do you think to do in France?' she spits.

'The King's will, I imagine. My duty.'

'The King's will,' she mocks. 'Does he have one? Are you sure it isn't Gloucester's will you do? Or the cardinal's? It surely isn't mine.'

She can hardly bear to look at him and, instead, paces the length of the hall to slam its doors against the wagging ears of servants who, having seen their master alight from the river and enter the house, have waited for orders and heard only shouts.

As she storms again, skirts flying, she hears his voice, low and steady.

'Are you not glad that I am given such an office? I thought it would please your pride. The last man to hold this trust stood second only to Henry for the throne.'

'And that man is dead!' She stops before him, hands clenched.

Richard looks down and away from her. 'I will not die, Cecily.'

She paces again, circling. 'You'll do yourself and us no good. England is losing in France, did you not know?'

'I will not lose.'

'You'll come back a beaten dog. The man who lost France. What fame!' Her raised arms mock him and her hand itches to slap.

'I am more than you think me, Cecily.'

'How will you win? You won't even fight me!'

He has the gall to wink at her. 'I would never fight you, Cecily. I'm saving myself for the French.'

She is stilled. Almost she laughs, but draws up anger to stifle it. She circles him once more, then stops. He's smiling still. She stares, takes a breath, taps her fingers, light against the bodice of her gown, her foot against the rushes of the floor. 'And what resources does the King give?'

'Not enough, I suppose. But we are not without coin our-selves, Cecily.'

She throws up her hands again. 'Oh yes, we are richer than any in England!' Rage turns to pain and bites her. Tears threaten, but she won't let him have them. Instead, she breathes deep, turns and walks away. At the door she pauses, a shaking hand on her flat belly. 'But my body's purse is empty, and will not be filled while you are in France.'

'It's only a year,' the cardinal shrugs when she confronts him next morning. She has waylaid him on the river walk at West-minster, and from the way he squares his shoulders at the sight of her she knows she is expected.

'He should be in England building his power, not in France squandering it.'

'Niece, niece, he squanders nothing. Do I not have your best interests at heart?'

'Only when they match yours.'

He pulls her from the path, where listening courtiers walk, into the shadow of a tree. Once secreted, he speaks low and plain. 'Cecily, he may be Duke of York, but his father's treason follows him like a dog.'

'What? Is he not loyal?'

'I'm very sure he is. But when Gloucester sees him he's reminded that the last of his royal brothers has just died and that your husband's father tried to kill the best of them. Then he recalls that, with Bedford dead, he is himself the King's only remaining family and heir to his throne, but that he's old and his pizzle won't rise and, besides, his wife's an old stick. And the King's still a boy and childless. And look! Who's next in line after him but the young Duke of York? Well, he looks lusty enough. Men like him. They listen when he speaks.'

'So, my husband goes to France because he speaks sense?'

'Cecily, you were never stupid. Your husband goes to France

so Gloucester might forget him for a while. He goes to prove himself a good servant of the Crown.'

'And I suppose it would be no bad thing if he died there?'

'A man may die anywhere.'

Almost, she spits.

'Come now, Cecily. It's a year. Then he'll be back in your arms, high in the King's love. Even Gloucester won't dare gainsay him then. All he need do is hold Normandy.'

'Really?' Her look calls him a liar.

'Well. Hold Normandy . . . and push a little. Just enough to give Charles pause and the English something to cheer about.'

'That's all?'

'Nobody expects more.' His spread arms proclaim him innocent of all guile.

She thinks of all the things a year in France might cost a man: his life, his purse, his reputation. 'The King will expect more.'

'The King will expect what I tell him to expect.'

Winter and spring have passed in preparation. Tonight they lie at an inn in Southampton. Tomorrow Richard takes ship for Honfleur. From there on to Rouen. Not to Paris. That's lost already. Traitors opened its gates to a French army one starlit night in April. Before the sun had scaled the rooftops, the English garrison was tossed out on its raggedy arse to tread the hungry road to Rouen, with its tail between its legs. Normandy is in chaos. Calais holding on. Just.

And this is what he goes to, thinks Cecily, wakeful and bitter.

He doesn't go alone. She takes comfort in that. The Earl of Suffolk goes too, and John Talbot, who the French fear more than hellfire. Even her own brother, Richard, Earl of Salisbury, is called down from his keeping of Scotland's borders. Most welcome is their old friend William de la Pole, who has been back in England a year now and much in her cardinal uncle's company, and the King's. They are seasoned commanders all, and Richard – untried in battle, but a strategist of her father's training – will lead them and a force of three thousand.

They've made love, and it's made her angry again. For Richard had looked for passion, while she could offer only a determined striving that bruised his flesh, wore on her nerves and gave no pleasure to either. She doesn't believe a child can take hold while her heart is so disquiet and so fears that, for another year at least, her womb will lie empty. She rubs a hand across her belly, digs a fist into the empty cradle of her hips. She miscarried their first child the year they returned from France. Then another. Not three months ago she bled away a third, lying ill and listless at Fotheringhay while Richard was in the south, recruiting soldiers, calling up ordnance and organizing the thousand details necessary when men must cross the sea to fight.

He lies stone-still beside her, but she knows by his breath he doesn't sleep. She turns her head and sees the shine of his eyes in the light of candles they'd had no time to extinguish as they fell into bed, ripping at each other. He turns too. His face is sad and the fire of her rage is, at last, dampened.

'I will miss you,' she confesses.

'As I will miss you. How will I know what to do with a sea between us?'

'Write, and I will tell you.' She smiles and so does he, then reaches out and pulls her close. From her place at his side she draws it out for him. 'Be a little less reckless than Talbot, a little bolder than Suffolk and you'll do well enough. Keep my brother close. He has less reason than either of them to hate the French, and only fights battles he knows he can win.'

'Good advice. I'll take it.'

She sleeps a little and, when she wakes, the dawn light is

sneaking, all unwelcome, through the shutters. Richard is pulling on a robe and padding across the bare floor to the next room, where his squires wait to dress him. She listens to their voices a moment; his softly spoken orders, their steady replies, a splash of water, a chink of steel.

Time to be up.

They take mass together, make confession, then walk down to the port and their parting, where she must bear the sight of Talbot's wife dandling a new baby daughter on her knee and all the children farewelling fathers from the quayside. She watches Richard stride across the ship's deck, laughing with William de la Pole, then looking sail-ward while he quizzes the captain for wind direction and crossing times.

He's gone already, she thinks. And so must I be.

Before the ropes are cast off she's walking back to the inn, where her wagons are packed and her horses ready.

From Southampton she goes north. Raby is a quieter place now, with its family out in the world and her father ten years dead. She hasn't seen her mother in the five years since she went to France, but finds her undiminished. There are many who petition for Joan's good ladyship, and she is as much about her papers as among her women. They have little time together, but in the warm evenings they walk the garden's gravel paths, or climb the castle's walls to watch the swans glide on the encircling water. Then, when the sun dips, they retire to Joan's chamber to play chess by a low fire. Cecily comes close to winning several times, never quite. It would not be wise.

'Your game has improved since I saw you last.' Joan's long fingers reset the pieces for another match.

'I play with my husband.'

The slide of a smile. 'Oh? There, I'm sure, you win.'

'As often as he does.'

'And does that make for a happy marriage?'

'I am content.'

'Content with your husband? That must be why I never see you.'

'We're busy,' Cecily tells her. 'Our inheritance didn't come to us in a tidy bundle.'

'Did it not?'

Cecily shrugs. 'Oh, just that it was subject to the usual petty corruptions that come about when a great estate is managed many years by stewards. The work of it has had Richard scouring the country, knocking heads together, laying down the law.'

'You can't complain. It's made Richard one of the richest men in England. And you, one of its greatest ladies.' Joan's smile is a true one now, satisfied and smug. 'I made good marriages for my children. Yours best of all.'

Cecily knows how much it matters to her. Joan was born a bastard. Her own mother bore four children for John of Gaunt, old King Edward's third son, before he made her his wife. It was fortunate for those children that Gaunt's nephew, the young King Richard, loved a romance as much as he loved his uncle, and was pleased to work with Pope and Parliament to have the burden of bastardy lifted. One day they went to bed the shameful by-blows of an infamous adulterer. Next morning they rose up the legitimate offspring of a royal duke. Joan has buried that early shame deep beneath the edifice of the family she has built, one of the finest in England. Her children are dukes and duchesses, earls, countesses and bishops. Well married, well made. And now her youngest daughter, Cecily, is first among them.

She leans across the board, squeezes her mother's hand. 'You did well for me. And I love you for it.' Then sits back, prim. 'But you mustn't take all the credit. You gave me only the hope of a dukedom. Richard brought the prize home.'

Her mother arches a brow. 'I am chastised. Yet my cardinal brother says you played some part in it yourself.'

'Perhaps I did. A little.' She gives a sly smile and sees it returned.

Joan laughs, waves a hand to signal the new game's beginning.

Cecily shakes her head and moves her first pawn. 'Anyway, I do not complain of being busy, mother. I am only explaining. We are never still.'

'And you travel with your husband, do you?'

She knows where this is going. Twenty-one this summer, five years bedding with Richard, and her cradle still empty. 'When I can.'

'When you've not had to take to your bed, you mean?'

Cecily doesn't answer, but watches, intent, her mother's first move on the board.

'How many have you lost?'

Cecily had written only of the first. Her mother's reply had been terse. It urged her to endurance, and recommended prayer; reminded Cecily that she herself had miscarried, lost four children in infancy, but seen ten live on and thrive.

Cecily has kept silent on the subject since. 'Must we talk about this?'

'Why should we not?'

'Because you tolerate failure no better than I do.'

So they talk instead of politics; the foolishness of France, the competence of the King's ministers. Until Cecily sacrifices her king to let her mother win.

Joan takes the captured king in her hand, holds it before her eyes in the firelight. 'And what of young Henry?'

'He cannot play chess.'

'Then you had better give your husband a son. There might be more to play for, one day.'

Joan is thinking, Cecily knows, of the thing Richard will

not speak of, other than to curse: the old royal blood his father died for. She has been gathering the game's pieces and now takes the king from her mother's hand and puts it in its box. 'It must be dizzying, mother, to plan so many moves ahead.'

'Indeed, it is.' Joan rises, smooths her skirts and sighs. 'And often pointless. The game may never be played, nor the board ever set.' She takes the box from Cecily's lap, closes it and sets it aside. 'But it's wise to keep in practice.'

When a fortnight is done Cecily moves south again to Fotheringhay, where her household awaits her orders and the walls of her church grow.

On her first day home she surveys the work with master mason Hanwood. While the air rings with hammers and men teeter on scaffolds, he points out progress here, a detail there. He explains how a stairway will rise just so and how, one day, sunlight will pour through windows high in the lantern tower to focus all eyes on the sanctuary, where her priests will summon God to earth. The church is dedicated to the Virgin, but its creation is all about York. What they make here will challenge even the chapels of Westminster and Windsor for glory.

Striding ahead of the mason, deaf to his prattle, she sees it as it will one day be: a shimmering tower of limestone, an arching nave, a high-vaulted choir. She hears the high, pure voices of the canon and choristers she'll bring here to keep the endless offices, from lauds to terce, vespers to compline, as the seasons turn, and on for ever; an inexhaustible engine of prayer. Here God will be reminded, every hour, of Richard, of Cecily, of the family He must bless them with.

'Press on with God's house, Master Hanwood,' she urges. 'We have need of its prayers.'

At Fotheringhay news of France can reach her quickly. Every letter is a cause for reluctant pride. Fécamp and Saint-Germain are retaken, Rouen secured. The Pays de Caux settled. While he lets Talbot lead the fighting, Richard gathers the remains of Bedford's competent council about him and, under his steady hand, they bring good order back to Normandy. The ravages of famine are alleviated, banditry subdued.

The cardinal is crowing. 'Your lord is a Colossus,' he writes.

'Call him home that I might tell him,' Cecily replies.

'The King says he will relieve him himself, when he takes up his strength.'

'Then am I never to see my husband again?'

So amused is her uncle at this that he sends her a cask of his best Burgundian wine. The accompanying note tells her to drink deep of the blood of Richard's enemies.

4

Cecily takes no wine in Lent but, when its privations are over, she has chance to share her uncle's gift with unlooked-for visitors. Bedford's widow comes to Fotheringhay. Not the gentle duchess Anne she'd come to care for in France, but pretty young Jacquetta, who took that lady's place after plague demanded she vacate it.

In truth, of course, she'd met Jacquetta too, that time in Paris.

It was the morning after Henry's crowning and she and Richard had been staying in the Bedfords' household. Their new good fortune had made them more hungry for excitement than sleep, so they stole out in the cold dawn light, planning to take horses and race each other over the frost-hard fields beyond the city. They were laughing as they came, thinking themselves alone, until they turned a corner into the mews and saw Jacquetta, daughter of Bedford's ally the Count of St Pol, leaning down from a fine grey mare and kissing John of Bedford hard on the mouth.

They brazened it out. Jacquetta smiled boldly, gave brief farewells and was gone. Bedford, dismissive, bade them take whichever of his horses they fancied and enjoy their morning.

Richard thanked him warmly, but couldn't look him in the eye.

Cecily could. 'I believe it was Jacquetta's uncle who captured the peasant Joan when the English could not and sold her to you for ten thousand *livres*,' she said, pulling on her gloves. 'I suppose that, for such service, you owe her much.'

Enough for him to marry her, it seems. Duchess Anne died the winter after Cecily returned from France. By spring the Duke of Bedford had dried his tears in Jacquetta's lap and taken her to wife. Cecily had grieved for it but, in truth, who could blame him? Jacquetta was sixteen, untouched by grief and, likely, fertile. He was forty years old and lonely; the King's heir and childless. After the wedding he'd brought his new wife briefly to England and had grace enough to look shamefaced when he'd asked Cecily to be a friend to her. 'She knows no one here, you see. And I must be busy, so . . .'

He'd come to make pleas to the council for more money and more men. They begrudged giving either to a man who kept losing. Even then, he'd looked ill; whip thin and hollow. She'd told him so.

'I'm just tired, Cecily,' he'd shrugged. 'This endless war.'

So, out of pity, and because, in truth, he'd been a maker of her fortune, she'd taken Jacquetta into her company, tolerated her French gossip; her vanity and foolishness.

Now, as she pours wine for her, she wishes the season were not so early, and that she had tansy or belladonna to sink into the drink's red depths, for she would like to take the smile from Jacquetta's lips, and the gentle swelling of the child from under her heart. She would not, of course, but just to think of it gives her a satisfaction that's worth the confession she'll have to make for it later.

She schools her face and passes the wine. First to Jacquetta and then to the golden-haired knight who now calls Bedford's widow his wife. He takes it, toasts them both, drinks deep and grins. Jacquetta, as if she's never seen anything so marvellous, laughs and looks to Cecily. Isn't he a wonder? her bright eyes ask. Isn't he an angel set loose from Heaven?

Cecily doesn't know quite what he is other than lucky.

Richard Woodville has had a good year. Last spring, tender Henry sent him to France to bring succour to Bedford's grieving widow and escort her home. That he has given her more than comfort is very evident. That he has gained greatly by it, even more so, for Bedford in his time was generous and Jacquetta's dower lands are rich and extensive. The Woodvilles are good enough knightly stock: soldiers, sheriffs, justices of the peace. This golden boy's father was body esquire to the fifth Henry once. The golden boy himself was in service to Bedford's household when the good duke brought Jacquetta home as wife. Was the seed planted even then? Cecily wonders. Were there late-night dalliances while Bedford sickened? Favours in the tilt yard, kisses in corners? Jacquetta is practised at that, after all.

I could have saved the wine, she thinks. He's drunk on his own good fortune.

She despises unequal marriages. Thinks women fools who make them. Marriage to her mother had been the old King's gift to her father, a reward for helping him to his throne, for she was that king's half-sister, even though a bastard. Cecily had understood the bargain from childhood: her father's legitimate blood and title for her mother's closeness to the King. It had enriched them both, as marriage should. On the day she began her life with Richard, as she packed her bags for France, her mother took her aside to remind her that she would now bring each of those gifts to her own marriage. 'Value them,' she'd said, 'they are a prize equal to your belly.'

True enough, she thinks, looking deep into the wine's depths. Though they must compensate for her belly just now.

That Woodville gains greatly from this marriage is plain to see, but what he offers Jacquetta surely isn't something she had to marry him to get. Cecily lifts her head, shakes away the thought of that. 'So you're making a home at Grafton?'

'Yes,' Jacquetta nods, shining. 'Your neighbours, Cecily. Not two days' ride. Imagine.'

Cecily imagines.

'We'll be there often enough, I think,' says the golden boy. 'I hope, lady, you'll come visit us. When your noble lord returns, perhaps?'

'May that be soon.' She watches Woodville lay a broad square hand on Jacquetta's shoulder and squeeze. His wife looks up at him, wide-eyed, bewitched. Cecily takes a drink to hide her smile. Indeed, it is laughable. But she can't help but admire his boldness; to aim so high and win home. She recovers herself. 'And all is well now, with the King?'

'Oh, yes. We are good friends.' Jacquetta takes her hand. 'We're in debt to you for that.'

'There's no debt,' Cecily assures her.

Not quite the truth. Enamoured of new love, Jacquetta had quite forgotten that she held her dower rights by grace of the King and needed his permission to take a fresh husband. Henry, when he found his uncle had been so soon supplanted in her heart and bed, had threatened to take them back, which, Cecily imagines, must have caused the golden Woodville some sleepless nights.

Knowing few others in England, Jacquetta applied to her for help. Cecily had surprised herself by giving it. She wrote to the King, reminding him that Jacquetta had nursed his uncle tenderly in his final illness, though she'd no idea if she had. Henry, mollified, accepted her suggestion of an affordable fine.

'You were kind to her,' Richard wrote when she told him of it.

'Wasn't I? I'm not sure why.'

'Perhaps it pleases you more to see her the wife of a knight than a duke?'

'I think that must be it. Still, he is very handsome. Which is well. It must console her for his being so little else.'

★

Richard's letters are rarely so light-hearted. Mostly they ask for money, which Cecily, resignedly, sends. The King keeps him short of funds.

'He thinks his prayers salary enough for soldiers,' Cecily complains.

So they pay their army from their own purse. They both know they're outspending the King to make sure more of France isn't lost on Richard's watch. But they can't do it for ever. A year they've signed for, but a year has come and gone.

And still, Richard writes. And still, Cecily sends, until another summer gives up the coin of its brightness, until the wind-torn colours of autumn fly from Fotheringhay's river valley, and the first frosts come shivering in to gild its trees in counterfeit silver.

5

At last Richard's successor is appointed, Dick Beauchamp, an old warhorse who has fought for England more than thirty years. The fifth Henry named him tutor to his son soon after the boy's birth – hoping, no doubt, he'd make a soldier and leader of men out of him.

Let's hope he has better luck in this post, Cecily writes to her uncle when he sends news of it.

It's deep winter when Cecily and Richard meet again. Eighteen months have passed since they parted. One month since she heard that a smug Jacquetta has been delivered of a daughter. Cecily sent a teething ring in silver, but not the prayers the new mother had petitioned for. It seems to have made little difference: gilt-haired Elizabeth, she is assured, thrives.

Advised of Richard's coming, she travels down from Fotheringhay to Westminster, is there three days before his ship docks and two more before he rides up from Southampton. She watches him swing down from his horse, shake snow from his cloak and stride smiling towards her.

She returns the smile and stands her ground. Let him come to her.

'Well, Cecily,' he says, as his mount is led away. 'It seems I am not dead.'

'You look most healthful, my lord.'

'And I have not lost.'

'With my prayers, how could you?'

He steals, she grants, a kiss, brief and public. His face is cold, his mouth warm and full of hunger. She grins against it and is glad.

'We're to go straight to the King,' she tells him.

'Ah,' he says, falling into step beside her. 'And how is our dread sovereign?'

She ponders, looks about her. In such bitter weather the pathways to the palace are empty of all but a handful of servants and messengers, who go about their business with hats pulled down and cloaks drawn up.

She draws him close, leans in to confide. 'Unpredictable? Capricious? You must ask my uncle, who studies every day how to manage his moods and sulks.' She smiles as Richard grimaces. 'The King's opinions, you must understand, are typically those of the last man to speak with him, so his counsellors are constantly jostling. My uncle will tell you it makes the business of running a country hard work and encourages vain men to seek power through influence.'

'Lord, Cecily,' Richard sighs. 'You make me wish I were back in France.'

'Oh, and still he is dressed like a scarecrow –' a mock shudder – 'albeit a very rich one.'

The King, before all the court, greets Richard like a long-lost brother, walking him about with an arm across his shoulder. His eyes, pale as rabbit fur, blink and skitter as he talks. He nods and nods and gazes all about him, as if to say, look at this fine man I walk beside, as if, by pressing his thin frame close, he hopes to draw into himself something of Richard's breadth and colour. He wants to know everything of France, from its battlefields to its wine harvests and the state of its sewers. 'I would be for France myself, you know,' he declares. 'But I am so needed here at home, and Beauchamp did so wish to go.'

Gloucester flutters, swears England couldn't do without

him, and the King, delighted, smiles his pale-lipped smile. But when Richard turns to the weakness of Normandy's defences, the lack of cannon and the need for cash, he grows listless, taps his feet, fidgets with the silver laces of his sleeve. 'You must speak with Uncle Gloucester of such things,' he says.

'Of course, Your Grace, but . . .'

'Or the cardinal here, who, as you know, is a godly man of business. But now, I must . . . it's time . . .' His gaze flits to the chamber entrance where, Cecily has noticed, a huddle of priests has been waiting.

The chapel bell has set up its call and its pull on the King's mind is obvious. There's a sigh of silk as the company makes haste to bow, but already Henry has stepped beyond them.

As Richard bends his knee, Cecily falls into a deep curtsey. 'Remember us in your prayers, Your Grace.'

The King, who is vain about his conversations with God, turns back, holds out a ring-weighted hand. Its skin is dry and soft beneath her kiss.

He hesitates, then signals to them both. 'Walk with me.'

In the long corridor, Cecily and Richard step either side of their king and wait for him to speak, while the priests pace slow behind them.

'My Lord of York, you've been married long.'

'And happily, Your Grace.' Richard's eyes flicker towards her, cautious.

She wonders where this is going.

The King falls silent a while, walks slowly. 'My Uncle Gloucester would see me wed. And the cardinal. And all the council. They do . . . press . . . upon me.'

'It must surely be your wish too, Your Grace. England needs an heir and . . . and a wife is a great comfort—'

'Is she not a great distraction? Your wife?' His voice suddenly sharp. 'From duty? From prayer?'

Cecily feels her cheeks flush.

'No, indeed, she is my trusted helpmeet in both.'

'And yet, it was through a woman that sin came into the world.'

'And through a woman, also, that Christ came to redeem it.'

The King halts, tilts his head as if the thought is wholly new to him. 'God love you, Richard, you speak truth. In time then, perhaps. If such a woman can be found as you have been blessed with.' He taps a finger on Richard's breast. 'I will seek His will on it.' Almost, he turns away. 'And yet,' he holds up the finger, enquiring. 'You have got no child on her.'

Richard's voice is level. 'God gives His gifts in His own good time, Your Grace.'

Henry laughs, shakes his head. 'Yes, of course. In His good time. And so will I marry.' Sobered in an instant, he makes the sign of the cross before them, more priest than king. This time the dismissal is final, and he walks on to his prayers.

Left behind in the quiet corridor, Cecily fights to subdue her rage. She unclenches her fists, smooths her sleeves to hide her hands' trembling. 'I don't know how my uncle bears it,' she hisses. 'About him . . . day in, day out. His childishness . . . I pity the poor woman he . . .' She leans close. 'God's blood, could he even—'

Richard's hand on her arm is immediate and constraining. 'No more. Let's away.'

That night, they dine with the cardinal and compare notes on the passing of a year and more in England and France. The mood is sombre. Richard has done more than the cardinal might have hoped, but he has merely stemmed the tide, not turned it. For years France has crippled the exchequer and, with Burgundy now an enemy, the cost of garrisoning every English-held town is beyond sense.

'We bleed money,' Richard reminds the cardinal, who needs no such reminding. 'Surely even the King must see—'

'The King sees what I show him. And begins to understand.'

'But Gloucester?'

'Ah yes, Gloucester. A dog gnawing on old bones. Fighting Agincourt every morning before breakfast. I wish he would –' waving a be-ringed finger towards the window – 'go away.'

'He remembers the promises he made after Agincourt,' says Cecily. 'Keep England. Win France. They wear on him.'

'They wear on us all,' the cardinal sighs.

Richard steeples his fingers, taps nails on teeth. For a moment it's the only sound. Then his voice, very low. 'The King spoke to us today of his marrying.'

The cardinal barks a laugh. 'Marrying? He has not the taste for that.'

'What about a French marriage? Make Charles's daughter Henry's queen. Their son will be a prince of England and of France. A pathway to peace?'

'Only if they have one. The girl's what, nine years old? It would be a long wait. Besides,' the cardinal rolls his eyes. 'When I suggested such an alliance, the King reminded me that the French royal house is tainted by madness.'

'He should know,' says Cecily. 'Given that his mother was the French king's sister. That lady's father believed himself made of glass and feared assassination by smashing.'

The cardinal smiles, grim. 'He has also turned down brides from Portugal, Spain and Austria.'

'On what grounds?' Richard asks.

'It seems that although we speak often to Henry of marriage, God remains silent on the subject.'

'Not much we can do there, then.'

'Perhaps your good example will inspire him?' He pulls himself upright, opens his hands. 'I need you here in Westminster a while, Richard. On the King's Council. It's yours for the asking now, after all you've done in France.'

'I'm already on the council.'

'I mean the inner council. Day to day. In case you haven't noticed, we're ruled now by a fifteen-year-old who needs help wiping his arse.'

Cecily smiles. And Richard too, reluctantly.

'Not this year,' he says. 'Uncle Gloucester loves me no better because I kept France safe. Besides, I must be about my own business for a while. This time in France has cost half the income of our Mortimer estates, which is falling, by the way. I'm in Wales and Ireland this coming time, putting things to rights. Send for me there if you need me for something more important than arse wiping.'

And so, within the week, they're gone. First to Fotheringhay, where they keep Christmas, then to Ludlow and, as the spring comes on, into Wales. A year passes easily; they are almost always together, and constantly busy. When Christmas is come and gone again, and Richard is called to Westminster to take counsel with the King, Cecily goes with him.

She makes sure she is much seen about court, and commissions, in fabrics so rich they threaten York's economy only a little less than his time in France, several of the new-style Burgundian gowns. Caught up high beneath her breast, their rising skirts show off the growing roundness of her belly, upon which she rests a long white hand as she walks and talks and smiles under Richard's shining eyes.

6

Her whole life, Cecily has chafed against confinement. Now, in the third week of her lying-in, she wants nothing more than to wait out these long summer days in the sheltered half-light of this curtained room. She was brought here straight from the church. Shriven, blessed, absolved of sin. They led her back over summer fields, where the ring of scythes in the hay crop played counterpoint to the murmuring of priests, who paced beside her, fore and aft, lining her way with prayer. Then under Fotheringhay's towering barbican they brought her, through the halls, passages and stairways of the castle to this room, which is her world now, till the child comes. At the threshold she hesitated, the priests fell back and only Richard stood beside her. His face was pale, his gaze tender, but his fingers grasped hers tightly and she knew it would hurt him to let her go. She looked to where her feet must take her, where her waiting women moved like shadows in the dim, and at the bed where she will labour, pillow-laden, canopied and wide.

'Wait,' he said, and turned to take from waiting arms a drape of soft white wool. His hands unfolded it and there, harnessed with silver and seeded with pearl, was a girdle, corded, thin with age. 'I begged loan of it from Westminster, from the Abbey. For you.'

She knew then what it was.

He gave into her hands the girdle Christ's mother wore

when she delivered; that fell from her hips as she ascended to Heaven; that was caught in the waiting arms of Thomas, the disciple who doubted. It has rested in England a thousand years. It is the comfort of queens in childbed. It is his prayer for her preservation.

She wondered how he had convinced the monks to lend it, how long he had petitioned, how rich had been his gift of alms. She held it against her face and breathed its age.

'I will come back to you,' she told him.

His lips were firm upon her brow. 'I will wait.'

Beyond the tapestried walls of this room, she knows, the sun is burning its way through the month. The servants, who bring all that is necessary and take away all that is not, whisper at the door of the days' warmth, of the lack of rain, the weight of work. She knows that the business of the world goes on without her. Men ride into Fotheringhay with news in their satchels and sweat on their backs. Her stewards sit at trestles collecting Lammas Day rents from tenants who begrudge the time it takes to pay them, when the sheep clamour for shearing and the first corn stands up to the cut. Somewhere out there is Richard, ordering it all. Directing his will and hers through the arteries of England, easy in the exercise of power.

She pushes the sleep-damp sheet away from her, draws a hand over the drum of her belly, tests the ache in the hollow of her back and sighs.

The maid, Kate this time, leans to her. 'Lady, will you drink?'

She closes her eyes again and doesn't answer. The world seems so far away and of so little import.

Her sister is here now. Anne, who has borne four children and lost none. Who placed a child in her husband's arms within a year of going to his bed. Who Cecily has envied to the point of loathing. She holds Anne's hand now and is glad of her. She's been floating, these days, and needs Anne's presence to anchor her to the world. Anne speaks with the other women. Sometimes Cecily listens. They speak of their own birthings. Of children come early. Of children come late. Of the foolish things some women do. The risks they should never take.

'My mother rode horseback till her seventh month and took no harm.'

'My aunt's maid ate the meat of a ewe lamb and her son was born a crouch back.'

'A black cat crossed me at the foot of the stairs, but I prayed all night to St Margaret and the child lived.'

Cecily hears all these things. Eat nothing too salt, nothing too sweet, no beer but well-watered, no bull flesh or chitterlings or river fish. Keep the fire burning always, in case the Devil comes down the chimney to feed on the unborn soul. They do not speak of stillborns, or breech births; of milk fever, or of women who die and have their children cut from them. But these things are there in the room, she knows. In the shadows beyond the candlelight, in the space beneath the bed.

It's dark now and all but Anne have gone to their sleep. Her sister sits by her pillow and sews in a pool of candlelight, familiar. It takes her back to the long ago of Raby, where Anne taught her to sew, the last of her sisters to leave her for marriage, badly missed when she was gone. Lying on her side, Cecily watches the needle dart, while the child rolls slow and heavy within her, like the dull-eyed carp whose backs break the dark surface of Fotheringhay's fish pools, before disappearing again into the deep. She reaches out and stills Anne's needle, grasps her hand and draws it under the cover to rest against her belly. She watches Anne's smile grow as the weight rolls beneath her fingers, as the tight flesh stretches and subsides.

'Let me rub you with the rose oil. It will send the child to sleep so you can rest.'

So she turns on her back, pillow-propped, and Anne brings the scent of summer in a slick of oil.

'Soon the head will settle low between your hips,' Anne says. 'And then, well, then it will be only a few days at most.'

Cecily is sure this is right. She knows the child is coming, swimming towards her through the dark. She closes her eyes again, opens, and lets them rest upon the girdle, where it hangs on the wall before her bed. 'Is it true, do you think, that the Virgin suffered no birth pains?'

' 'Tis certain, for she was without sin.'

'My confessor says they were kept for her till Golgotha, and there she felt their terror a thousand fold.'

She has thought much on this since the child quickened and came alive for her. She doesn't much fear pain. She has tested it; held a finger against the candle flame, pricked her arms with needles, twisted the flesh of her thighs in her fists till her breath came short and fast. 'Take the greatest of these pains and imagine them doubled. Then double them again. If you can bear that, you can bear a child.' Her mother's advice is always practical.

No. Her greatest fear is loss. For to leave this room with nothing will break her. Or if at some other time, however far distant, someone takes this child's life from her, she will tear out their heart and devour it warm. She will dig out their tongue by its root. She will blind their eyes. Break their bones. She will drink their blood. She sees herself doing these things in her dreams and wakes in horror. She prays to St Margaret, who was eaten by a dragon and cast up again alive, who intercedes for all women in childbirth that they may be delivered, just as she was.

Three days later and the child is low in her belly. She wants to walk but her legs are splayed and the weight presses till she thinks she will fall, so instead she crouches on the carpeted floor and lets the heft of her body hang suspended from her spine. All day the ache in her back grows. Then, as night comes, the ache becomes pain that rises in her like a wave, as if the oceans of the world are caught up within her.

The midwives are urgent with advice. Walk now. Sit a while. Come back to the bed.

She wants to strike them. She shakes off their hands. Her mother has sent a stone of pain-easing green jasper banded with white like the flesh of her thigh. They rub it against her flanks, then tie it in a bag and cord it about her waist. They take down the girdle from its wall and lay it against her body. They send word out into the world of the castle that the duchess's time is come, and the priests in the chapel and the canons of the Church must keep vigil.

By morning she is all animal. Slick with sweat and beyond all words. A tide of pain has driven her deep inside, to where the strength of her will has its wellspring.

'*Push!*'

She hears the midwife's cry from a world away and she drags herself, clawing at the arms of she knows not who, scrabbling with her heels to raise herself, so she can push harder, deeper, meeting pain with frenzied effort.

'Open, open!' The women cry as they tear around the room.

She hears cupboards thrown open, drawers pulled out. She feels fingers fumble to take down her hair.

'All about you is open now . . .' She feels her sister's breath in her ear. 'It's time, Cecily, push!'

She hears her own roar like a demon set loose, before her body turns to liquid and a new cry comes, high and plangent, a blade of longing twisted in her heart. She clambers up towards the sound and sees, between her blood-streaked legs, the midwife bent over something red and writhing that glistens in her hands. Then a flash of steel.

'Mine,' she cries. 'Give me mine!'

And her hands grasp as the midwife surrenders and she has the child at last in her arms. And her eyes cannot see enough, her hands cannot feel, her body trembles and falls back among the pillows, but that lovely weight comes with her, pummelling against her breast, and that hungry cry is against her ear and she feels exultant joy rising. She lays back her head and laughs.

7

Within an hour the room is quiet, though Cecily's heart is unsteady. They keep taking the child from her, to wash it, to swaddle it, to rub its limbs with salt and its gums with honey. She wishes them all gone, for the child to be hers alone again. Instead, she lies anchored to the bed, her eyes fixed on the curve of her baby's head, cradled like an egg in the broad hand of the wet nurse. She listens to the murmuring suck of its feeding, while her own breasts ache.

The nurse, her face round and milk-white, looks up at her and smiles. 'Your daughter feeds strongly, my lady. She's hungry for life.'

Cecily holds out her hand and the nurse takes it, lays it along the baby's back. She closes her eyes and rests.

A while later, Anne wakes her. 'Richard is coming.'

They help her to sit, stack pillows at her back, gather her hair and braid it, wipe her face with rosewater. They lay the child in her arms, parcelled and sleeping. There's a little sunlight now. The window hangings have been drawn aside for the first time in a month to take away the smell of blood and the afterbirth's burning. Then a tap at the door. Anne squeezes her hand, crosses the room, opens it wide.

And there he is.

Cecily raises her chin. 'God has given us a daughter.' She scans his face for disappointment and sees none. Only a growing smile as he comes forward, sits beside her on the bed and lowers his head to gaze.

He's silent a moment while the women, gazing back over

their shoulders, edge from the room. When they're gone, he speaks. 'So, this is little Anne, then?'

'For your mother.'

'And your sister.'

'And for the Holy Virgin's mother, who was so long barren then blessed with so great a daughter.'

She hears his breath catch. 'What a world we will make for her, Cecily.'

'She is the first of our house.' She means there will be more.

They talk a while and in minutes have brought their newborn to womanhood, drawn out her beauty, married her to greatness, blessed her with brothers.

They laugh at themselves and, when Richard looks at her, his eyes are soft with joy. But beneath his smile he too looks tired. She wonders if he slept while she laboured. Probably not. But it's good that he should learn the art of waiting. She leans across the child and lays a hand against his cheek, touches her lips to his. He draws her fingers to his mouth and kisses them.

'They say a month for the churching,' she tells him.

He closes his eyes, resigned. Nods.

She draws her thumb along his lips, a promise. 'It will be less.'

True to her word, not three weeks pass before she demands to be taken back across the fields to receive the Church's blessing, to light candles before the Virgin's altar and give thanks for her deliverance. The unfinished nave, still open to the skies, is bathed in golden sunlight and the masons, now in their seventh year of building, down tools to marvel at the sight of the proud duchess on her knees. As the choristers send up their song she gazes skyward to where swallows, already dreaming of an autumn departure, dart and chitter. Like them she's been impatient to be away. Within days of the birth, the room that had been her sanctuary had become a cage. As her milk dried she found herself glad to hand little Anne to the wet nurse when she fretted. She's tired of nursery talk and the unleavened company of women. She's happy enough when they tell her the child feeds well and sleeps soundly; reassured that it has been baptized and received into God's grace. She can see for herself its limbs are strong and growing, that the child is cared for, body and soul. Now she wants only to return to the world.

Richard, who waited patiently for her coming, is elated as they leave. He walks before her, laughing, turning to look at her with dancing eyes as he casts silver pennies into the sunlight, picked up in handfuls from a deep bowl carried in the arms of his esquire. The poor of the town, accustomed to their lord's generous alms-giving, have come in crowds to scrabble for his money among the grass, while young girls in festival dresses throw white rose petals at his lady's feet. That's Richard's work, she knows, for they have taken the white rose as the emblem of their house, for its purity and glory and because it is the flower of the Virgin, who brought God into the world. She shakes her head at him, indulgent, pleased, for it's late in the season and he must have sent far and paid much to find so many.

More roses bedeck Fotheringhay's great hall, where the feast is laid ready for their arrival, and where maids and serving men scatter to attend them as they enter amid music and song. Richard takes her hand and guides her up the hall to the board, where she takes her seat at his side after so long an absence. The child is brought. Richard takes his daughter in his arms, holds her up to the room's adoration, kisses her soundly and hands her back to her nurses, who scurry away with her to the nursery.

Cecily smooths the sleeves of her gown, white damask, silver-shot, and accepts greedily the wine Richard offers her in toast. She has trained herself to eat frugally in these weeks since the birth and already her body is recovering its slenderness. Her mirror, this morning, told her she was beautiful; a rich purse, of proven worth. Today she will drink deep and eat heartily. She looks along the tables to where the good families of Northamptonshire feast on her bounty. Beside her at board, two of her sisters, Katherine and Anne, keep company with their noble husbands, Norfolk and Buckingham, and her brother Edward, the only child her mother bore after her, is solicitous to his wife, who gave him a fine first son at last year's turning. Today she doesn't mind even that, she tells herself. She has only good will towards everyone, even Jacquetta, who has added a second daughter to her tally and confided to Cecily that she expects to be brought to bed again next spring. She smiles as she watches her make love eyes at the golden Woodville who, it seems, dotes on her still and feeds her sugared almonds from his hands.

Beside her, she realizes, Richard is deep in conversation with her cardinal uncle, who has escaped the court's clutches to bring the King's greetings to them both. They're speaking of France; of who will take up the lieutenancy made vacant by Richard Beauchamp who, last spring, escaped the demands of the post by dying in it.

'There's only one man in England who can be sent without enraging Gloucester or disappointing me,' says the cardinal.

'I don't want it,' Richard is saying. 'I give good service. I hold the Welsh Marches for the King and I bring rich revenues to the Crown. Let that be enough. Besides, since when have you scrupled to enrage Gloucester?'

'I can get nothing done for the noise of his barking. I need a man in France who can work for peace.'

Cecily listens while watching the room. In her head she's listing those who have come to witness her triumph. She's warmed by the sight of her mother's eldest son, Salisbury, taller by a head than most men, broad like her father, come striding into hall. His hand rests on the shoulder of his eldest boy. At eleven the boy is growing into his sire's handsome image. Where's my brother's wife? she wonders. At home, probably, fat with yet another child. She's surprised to find she doesn't mind that so much either. Her brother has noticed her watching him, so she acknowledges him with a nod. He stops as if arrow-struck, then sketches an elaborate, laughing bow before coming up to join them at the board. A space is made for him and he sits beside her, his son taking the esquire's place behind his chair. She's so pleased he's here. Like most of her siblings he was well out in the world before she was born, so she's learned to love him as a man, not a boy. And she's grateful, too, for his love of Richard. While most of her brothers spurned his traitor's blood, he's been a friend to him, and they've worked well together lately, in France.

'What's your husband speaking of that makes his face so serious, today of all days?' he asks her, reaching for a cup.

'Of France. What else?' She turns from him to the cardinal. 'If no one wants peace, uncle, your work will be fruitless, whoever you send.' She smiles. Politics. How she's missed it.

'Your uncle the cardinal believes he has a way to make peace palatable.' Richard acknowledges his brother-in-law, then takes her hand, drawing her into the conversation.

'I say we free the Duke of Orléans.' The cardinal catches her gaze and winks.

Salisbury laughs and calls for wine.

Cecily too can't help but scoff. 'It seems I've been away too long and the wise have turned witless. That will never be.'

Charles Duke of Orléans has been England's prisoner more than twenty years, ever since he was pulled like a boot from the sucking mud of Agincourt. The fifth Henry swore he would never be released and laid the same oath on his brothers, Bedford and Gloucester, for Orléans is too fine a soldier and stands too close to the French Crown.

The cardinal shrugs. 'He's a natural enemy to the Duke of Burgundy, whose father murdered his. His release will win us favour with the French nobility and with Charles the King.' His be-ringed hand describes a pathway before him. 'It will open a road for diplomacy.'

She can see the sense in what he says. It's audacious. But her uncle was ever so, and she admires him for it, but still. 'To return to France one of her greatest fighters . . .?'

'A fighter still, you think?' He rubs his nose and shrugs. 'Perhaps. I visited him in Pontefract this summer. He tends more to poetry these days. His hands are soft and ink-stained. And his English is better than his French.'

'That doesn't make him an ally.'

'It may make him amenable.'

Cecily's expression is sceptical.

'What are you thinking?' Richard asks her.

'I'm wondering how amenable I would feel towards the people who kept me a prisoner twenty years.'

The cardinal's sly smile takes mastery of his face. 'Think instead how grateful you'd feel towards those who set you free.'

Richard lays his hand on her arm. 'Orléans told me himself he thinks it's time to find a diplomatic solution.'

'Oh, so you too have been visiting poets in Pontefract?' She looks around. 'Please tell me, brother, that you have not been embroiled in this.'

Salisbury drinks deep. 'Not I, sister. I've had enough of France for now. Beware our uncle, and what he might talk you into.'

'Have you ever known me talked into anything?'

Her brother shakes his head and addresses himself to his wine cup.

She turns again to Richard. 'And anyway, husband, won't a man who hopes to barter for release tell his gaolers what they want to hear?'

'Perhaps, but—'

The cardinal interrupts him. 'At this stage, Cecily, I hardly care. If he'll work for peace, that's a blessing. If not –' he spreads his hands – 'if he drives a wedge between France and Burgundy, that will content me. And if his return sets the French bickering between themselves about who should lead them, better still. We need the distraction.'

'Does Charles still sicken?' Before she was immured Cecily had heard rumours that the French king was ill and, almost as promising, running out of money.

'Our spies say so.'

'I'm sure you pray avidly for his everlasting rest. But, has it not occurred to you that Orléans would make a formidable regent for the dauphin, little Louis?'

'Of course. But little Louis is sixteen now. He may feel he doesn't need a regent. On the other hand, the French may not want a child king again. Perhaps its nobles would prefer a proven fighter.'

'A one-time fighter, uncle. A poet now, you say.'

The cardinal waves his fingers, concedes the point.

Richard holds up his hands between them, placating. 'Or a one-time fighter with an appetite for peace? Whatever, we go before our horse to market. We hear Charles is sick, not dying. But it could be useful to bring Orléans back into play.'

'Ah, yes, a forward play.' Cecily raises her empty glass as her tow-haired nephew steps forward to refill it. 'French chess.'

'The long game.' The cardinal drinks deep, and smiles.

*

Before bed Cecily and Richard visit the nursery. Little Anne is sleeping. Her nurses, soft-footed, lead them to her cradle, then withdraw. When she bends to kiss her daughter's shadowed head Cecily scents milk and the faint tang of salt. This smell was a constant in her cloistered time and, she realizes, she misses it. She's relieved to be free, to be in the thick of things again. But she would return to that room a thousand times for such a gift as this.

'So, my cardinal uncle wants you in France?' she asks, still gazing on the child.

Behind her Richard sighs. 'He does.'

'And will you go?'

'I don't know. I don't want to. But if a diplomat is needed, I'm a better choice than your cousin Somerset, who nurse-maids the post for now.'

'Somerset?'

'He's a figurehead,' Richard assures her. 'Talbot does the real work.'

She nods. Until his ransom last year, John Beaufort, Earl of Somerset, had been a prisoner of war in France, taken in his first battle, little more than a lad. It's been eighteen years all told, almost as long as Orléans has been in England. It's hard to imagine the experience could have prepared him for the complex leadership of England's most challenged governance. Cecily imagines him, a mole, blinking in sunlight.

'And Gloucester will accept me,' Richard says with a low, wry laugh. 'Which makes me a rare creature indeed.'

'And so you will keep the peace in England and make a peace in France? Now that would be a thing.'

He shrugs. 'I've no wish to go but . . .'

She begins to think it could be done. She looks again at little Anne sleeping, imagines her married into the French royal house, then smiles at her own foolishness. Better a boy child for that. Now it's her turn to sigh. 'Well, if you go, I go with you.' She feels him squeeze her hand and, turning, sees that he's pleased.

'I hoped you would.'

She raises an eyebrow. 'Well, I will get no brothers for this one with the sea spread wide between us.'

8

November 1440

Cecily knew death was coming for her mother even before the seed of this second child was set. Word confirming that great lady's passing comes as new life quickens, and as preparations for the move to France gather pace. One morning she halts on the stair to cup a hand against that first trembling movement. At the same moment she hears, through a window open on to Fotheringhay's courtyard, a messenger's horse being reined in tight. She guesses the news its rider carries before his boots strike the cobbles.

Richard frets. Worried that grief will consume her strength and weaken the child. He need not. Cecily is, after all, her mother's daughter.

The old lady had prepared for death as thoroughly as for any of life's inevitabilities. Years since, her husband established a chantry in tiny Staindrop church, where, within view of Raby's towering walls, he has lain waiting for her full fifteen years. She herself founded a second chantry in Lincoln, where her own mother is buried. In both, she has ordered masses to be said in perpetuity for Ralph's soul and hers, for the souls of her parents, and for the kings whose causes they made their own. Last Christmas, along with gifts for little Anne, Joan sent a letter, telling Cecily that the cancer could not be halted and she was ready to go to God. In May, she wrote her will. There was news in it that surprised all but Cecily, for Joan's letter had told her already that Ralph's long wait would be in vain.

'My mother will be buried in Lincoln,' Cecily told Richard, folding the letter in her hands. 'Beside my grandmother.' She smiled at his amazement and then, remembering his love for Ralph, touched a finger to his cheek. 'She wishes to remind the world who she was first. Before Westmorland's wife, she was Gaunt's daughter, half-sister to a king.'

Cecily's mother was the youngest of the four children John of Gaunt got on his mistress. The only one still living is Henry. For twenty-one years he was a bastard brat, a struggling churchman. Then his father married his mother and he found himself a bishop. Today he is Cardinal Beaufort, England's foremost churchman and the King's most trusted counsellor; a patron of art and learning so rich that even the exchequer comes to him for loans. Once, Cecily remarked how high fortune's wheel had raised him. He concurred, smiled his sly old smile, and ventured she'd no idea how hard he'd had to push.

He turns the wheel for all of us now, she thinks, and, for the first time, the thought makes her uncomfortable. She looks up at him, wonders if he grieves. His brothers have died and he has seen them buried, and today, his breath misting in the cathedral's cold air, he reads his sister's funeral office. On her knees, hands clasped over the sleeping child in her belly, Cecily speaks each word with him in her heart and knows he will not falter. He looks tired. But his voice is firm as it always is, and his hand steady, as he raises it to sign God's cross over the body and the open tomb that receives it.

As sudden as sunrise, the chancel fills with song. The waiting masons chafe their hands and take up the ropes.

They lift the heavy stone sheet into place and Joan is gone.

Cecily looks up at the cardinal and he down at her. Joan's burial has given the world one message. Cecily has another for him. I am Beaufort, too, her eyes say. I am my mother's daughter and Richard's wife both; royal dukes on both sides.

Don't forget.

She holds his gaze.

He nods.

At the funeral feast Cecily finds she cannot eat. The frost was hard this morning and the fenland wind blew bitterly through the town. After two hours in the cathedral's pinching cold, she now finds herself stifled. Here in the priory hall, which was once her grandmother's home, the fires burn hot and the smell of meat has her stomach roiling. So, instead of feasting, she watches. Across the hall she spies her cousin, John Beaufort, Earl of Somerset, newly returned from France. She suspects his presence brings cold comfort to the cardinal. Comfort because, after eighteen long years a prisoner, he is at least here. Cold because he brings so little love with him.

She watches him eat. She had imagined him a mole; knows now he is nothing so sightless nor so soft. She leans towards Richard, lays a finger on his arm, nods towards the earl and keeps her voice low. 'He takes his knife to that chicken as if he wishes it were a Frenchman.'

Richard's eyes follow hers, his frown disparaging. 'A habit with him, no doubt.'

Somerset is a challenge where they had not looked for one. She knows it. He was taken prisoner in the chaos of his first battle, lately a boy, barely a man. He's spent the months since he was ransomed laying waste to French towns, making it clear just how much he hates the country and people that stole his youth from him. The cardinal, who loved the boy's father, his own brother, has spent that time trying to win his affection, with grants and funds and petitions to the King for new estates and honours. The more the earl disdains him for not securing his freedom earlier, the more the cardinal spends. There was even talk at the start of the year that the cardinal had wanted to take back Richard's lieutenancy of France and give it to his nephew. Richard shrugged and said, let him have it. Cecily said, over my dead body. Gloucester, enraged, threatened to take charge in France himself rather than see a Beaufort lead England's second kingdom. The cardinal had laughed at the idea of that, but was sobered enough to ensure that Richard was confirmed in the role.

Now, thinks Cecily, it's our turn to call the tune. With the appointment made, both cardinal and king are keen for them to be off to France. Richard has said they will not sail until the child is born. Cecily that they will not go until the King confirms their stipend. She knows how much one year cost them. This time they go for five. She had not said she must first bury her mother, yet here they are. Across the room she watches John Beaufort's teeth tear flesh while, beside him, his younger brother, Edmund, eyes shot, chin jutting, drinks hard and sullen.

She leans again to speak to Richard. 'Poor Edmund Beaufort,' she mocks, smiling thinly.

'Why poor?'

'He thought he had only to sit on his hands and wait for his father's earldom to fall into his lap. Now he's the second son again, dragging around like an afterthought in his brother's angry train.' She hears Richard humph beside her; watches Edmund smear a sleeve across his mouth. Suddenly disgusted and impatient with it all, she draws her napkin from her shoulder, casts it to the table and attempts to stretch her back, which aches wickedly. 'Oh, how tedious this is.'

Richard takes her hand beneath the table. 'Are you well?' he asks her. 'Do you need to leave?'

She shakes her head, which sets it throbbing, then leans past him to address her uncle.

'One more thing, my lord cardinal, before we leave for France . . .'

'Cecily, you will have the income from the Rouen exchequer

and twenty thousand pounds a year from England. It's more than Bedford or Beauchamp had. What more do you want?'

'Not money. Only your assurance that, while we are in France, your nephews will not be.'

'They are good soldiers.'

'Edmund, perhaps. John is a child lately given his sword back. He wields it with more petulance than skill.'

'Yet in the last year, while you've been dallying, they've captured Folleville and Lihons, and retaken Harfleur.'

'I know, but . . .'

She holds back reluctantly as Richard lays down his knife, flexes his hand and raises it between wife and cardinal. Across the table she sees that John Beaufort, as if sensing a conversation he can't possibly hear, has raised his eyes from his plate to meet Richard's. He bares his teeth in an approximation of a smile, his lips flecked with grease, then nudges Edmund who looks up too. John whispers, Edmund shrugs and reaches for more wine.

Richard grimaces and turns to the cardinal. 'And in Lihons they torched the church where three hundred townsfolk had claimed sanctuary. You're a man of God, can you condone it?'

The cardinal is stony-faced. 'It's war, Richard.'

'It's war, my lord, indeed. But you wish me to make a peace. To do that I will fight only when I must – and when I do, I will do it honourably.' Then with a final nod towards the sullen brothers across the hall, 'And I would have you kennel your dogs in England while it's done.'

Cecily lays a hand on his sleeve, feels the anger thrum in him and knows that the cardinal feels it too. For she sees her uncle's face register surprise, and then smother it with an effort of will. She follows his eyes as they gaze across the room, stop a moment, blink, then turn back to Richard and to her.

His diplomat's smile stretches his lips and his voice is cold.

'Very well. I will keep them here. I have lost a sister. It will do me good to have family about me.'

That night, Richard's anger is gone and he is all tender care. He has sent her ladies away and himself undresses her. His practised fingers loosen laces and draw the heavy fabric of her gown from her shoulders. When she's bare she stands before him and pretends she is not tired. When he kisses her, she can believe she no longer is. She lets her weight rest on him and knows he will hold. 'You were angry today.'

He nods, a slow agreement. 'I was.'

'With me, a little, I think.'

He kisses her neck. 'No, love, not with you.'

'Just a little.'

'With your uncle for playing games. With Beauforts who look after their own. I'm as happy to stay in England as go to France but, if I go—'

'If *we* go, we go on our terms.'

'On our terms. Yes.'

She leans into the warmth of his hand as he lays it across her face, and feels, too, the cool hardness of his ring with its bull's blood ruby. She can't remember ever seeing his hand without it; knows it to be his only talisman of the father he never knew. It was kept for him by the kindness of a servant, who had been there at the end, sent to him when still a boy, before he came to Raby. An uncommon kindness. He told her, once, that it had still had his father's blood upon it, dark and dry about the stone, when he unwrapped it from its shred of cloth. He had not cleaned it, but, soon enough, under the world's rubbing, the stain had fallen away.

She thinks, now, that she knows the real root of his anger. He's remembering her father, who he knew and loved, lying alone in the little church at Staindrop.

'I go with you, Richard.'

'And when we are dead, Cecily, where will you go then?'

His eyes when she looks into them are sad and full of questions.

'With you, Richard. Do you not know? We are a new thing, you and I. We are York.' She takes his face in her hands, kisses his mouth, careful and soft. 'Alive or dead, I lie only with you.'

9

Little Anne, excited by the rush of wind in sailcloth, turns in her nurse's arms and, with the lung-bursting squeal of an almost two-year-old, reaches for her mother with grasping fingers.

Cecily turns her shoulder. The sound of her daughter's pleasure tears a strip from patience already worn thin. 'Will you take that child away and stop its screeching.' The disdain in her voice pains her, but really, she cannot bear the child about her just now.

She watches the nurse, who is inured by now to her black moods, draw Anne's disappointed face under her cloak and bundle unsteadily along the ship's deck to the steps that lead below. Cecily sighs, stretches her shoulders, then looks up to the forecastle, where Richard stands and his officers gather. She should be with him, she knows. She will go in a moment. For now she wants only to look back; at Portsmouth disappearing from sight, the Solent stretching its silver finger deep into England's green heart.

A long tail of ships follows in wake of theirs. Each is filled with archers and infantry, their horses and ordnance, their lords and commanders. Together they carry the largest army England has sent to France since the fifth Henry's day. No one expects them to do as he did. Their task is compromise, not conquest. No one thinks England can win in France any more.

But they want peace without shame. So here we come, striding up to the negotiating table, bristling with blades, thinks Cecily. The image is so foolish she almost laughs, but her mouth won't quite stretch to it. Instead, she closes a fist on the wooden rail and examines the whiteness of her fingers, the tightness of her grip.

Well. Peace, no less than war, calls for strength of arm.

You still have to win it.

To win is the promise they made at Windsor, three weeks past, when they farewelled king and court.

'Good Duke Richard will win the peace for us,' the smiling cardinal said to the slowly nodding King, an encouraging arm around her husband's shoulder.

Cecily noted Richard's self-deprecating smile, smooth as silk, yet his eyes were careful, as she knew her own to be.

Behind him Gloucester glowered. 'Peace, not capitulation, mind. We must hold what's ours.'

The King nodded and Cecily was almost surprised to hear him speak. Most often of late he listens, and with only half an ear. 'Dear uncle, I'm sure we can rely on my Lord of York to do that.'

Let's hope so. No one else has managed it.

Gloucester blustered and frowned as if the thought of peace with France ground like glass in his gut.

The King rose from his seat, came close. 'We are Christian men, Richard, are we not?' He reached out a milk-pale hand, laid it upon Richard's silk-clad breast, where beats his Christian heart.

Richard bowed his head, acknowledging the favour of the royal touch. 'So I do trust, Your Grace.'

'Then surely, like I, you wish no more English blood spilt in France?'

'No more than necessary, Your Grace.'

Good. He did not say none.

Henry turned his hand to tap a narrow finger against rich silk. 'There must be friendship between kings, Richard. Between us and France. But we must give not an inch more land. Uncle Gloucester is right. Normandy, Gascony, Calais, all ours.' He dropped his hand, turned away. 'I will pray for you daily. For a conclusion that will honour my father's memory and enrich England.'

'Your prayers will be a tower of strength to us, Your Grace.'

We'll need them to be, she thinks now, as she watches the birds that have been following in their wake wheel and turn inland. It will be no small thing to find a conclusion that satisfies everyone: the cardinal's appetite for peace, and Gloucester's revulsion at it.

And what about the King? What does he actually want?

It depends what time of day you're asking. And who spoke to him last.

The wind rises and it seems the ship leaps forward. Cecily shakes herself, looks up, stretches her eyes into distance and is surprised to see only sea and sunlight and the following ships. England is gone already. The court and its sand-shifting king. Fotheringhay and all she left behind there.

It was hard to leave. It would have been harder to stay.

No less than the King, she has put questions to God that await answers. They built the church at Fotheringhay as an engine of prayer for York. It has become, already, a mausoleum for their house. Their son is buried there. Born while the snow fell in the coldest days of February, dead while it still lay thick upon the ground. They were a week from the churching and Cecily had been dreaming of the world beyond the walls when a scream woke her. She leapt up, pushing sheets and blankets away to reach the crib. There was the wet nurse, her face horror-struck and fingers trembling, tearing at the swaddling. And the pale body emerging, limp in her hands, its lips tinged blue as if it had lain in snow. She remembers slapping the woman, grasping the child, its skin still warm and with sweat upon it. She remembers shaking him, calling him, letting no one near, slapping away hands that reached to take him from her. They took hold of her at last and made her drink something vile. She spat at them and cursed. A slamming door. Then darkness. And when she woke, the curtains were down from the windows, the crib was gone, winter sunlight draining colour from the room and Richard, sitting beside her, as pale as his son and no less deathlike.

No walk across the meadow. No churching in the sun. Only a sad funeral and talks with master mason Hanwood about the carving of a tomb. It would be quickly done, he told her. So small a grave. So few words to put upon it.

A month into their mourning came a letter from the King, expressing regret for the little one that had been named for him and for whom he had stood as godfather. And a question. Why were they not in France yet?

Cecily had squared her shoulders and said they must be about it.

She squares them again now, turns and walks the length of the ship, head high and skirts swinging. She climbs the steps to where Richard stands with his officers about him. Among them, leaning against a post while Richard talks, is the golden Woodville. He sees her first, bows and smiles.

Seeing it, Richard turns and his eyes light. 'Cecily. Come join us. We're planning our first moves.'

As she steps forward the men stand aside to make room for her beside her lord. She looks about at the circle of faces that wait for his words. She wonders how many of them wish she would just stay below with the women and children. Let them wish. Richard has never wanted that, even now with this failure upon her. It has saved her, these past weeks, to be at the centre of his stratagems, poring over maps, drawing up plans, deciding the appointments of officers and captains; weighing up men's competence and ambition, where they will serve best and how far they can be trusted. She has poured her energy into it to quench her grief. So, yes, let them wish.

'My lord, I cannot imagine but that your first move will be to ride to Pontoise, relieve its garrison, and knock the French king back on his garlicky arse.'

The men bark surprised laughter. They swagger a little as she smiles at them, and she knows she has bought her welcome.

Pontoise will be their first test. Both Cecily and Richard know it. Charles, clearly cured of whatever illness assailed him, has been pounding the walls of the English-held town for a month and more. It must not be lost. For it sits on the confluence of the Seine and Oise, and beside it runs the straight road the Caesars built to link Paris to the coast. Without Pontoise, both river and road will be open to Richard's enemies and, even with this mighty force, he will struggle to hold Normandy.

'That is what we are about, indeed,' Richard confirms.

'And with these bold men around you, surely you cannot fail.' Her head is high and she looks a challenge at them.

Richard turns from his men to face her, kisses her hand, secretly winks. It is rehearsed, for they both know how the fear of a proud woman's scorn can put heart in a man.

It is needed. There are seasoned veterans of the wars here. They know how hard the fight will be and they fear death. There are new men with careers to make, who fear humiliation even more. Most have not fought under Richard before. All know this to be his biggest military command. They want to trust him. Wonder if they should. A show of bravado helps.

Looking about her, Cecily sees each man pull himself up to stand a little taller.

'I am most sure of it.' Richard turns back to the men. 'My lady's word is good. Tomorrow we land in Honfleur, then up the river to Rouen, straight. We stay there no longer than it takes to say a mass and seek God's blessing for our enterprise. He will most assuredly give it. Two days, no more. Be ready, we ride for Pontoise. Now . . .'

Cecily listens as the plans they have made together are laid out.

All eyes are on Richard. Except those of the golden Woodville, who is leaning against his post again, eyes dancing and lit on her.

She allows herself to imagine a crossbow bolt slamming between them, and smiles.

He thinks it a kindness, and flashes his teeth in return.

Below decks, Cecily knows, Jacquetta sits crooning over their son, Antony, born while Cecily still carried the child who now lies coldly cradled. She sighs, looks up at the sails, wind-swollen and carrying them forward. Skirting around the earnest group, she walks to the ship's prow and fixes her eyes ahead where she fancies she can see, sunlit and far distant, the coast of France.

10

July 1441
Rouen

'Is that bastard John Beaufort with you?'

The first question out of John Talbot's mouth is for Richard as, not sparing her a glance, he reaches out a sword-callused hand to guide Cecily on to Rouen's crowded quayside. When Richard steps down beside her and confirms that Somerset is not, she sees the old soldier's face break into a brown-toothed grin, before he turns aside to hawk yellow phlegm on to the filthy cobbles.

'Good. God curse him. Anyway, what took you so long? How many men have you got? We're up to our arseholes in French shit over here, in case you hadn't noticed.'

If Cecily is surprised to see Richard laugh and clap a hand to Talbot's shoulder, she doesn't show it. She simply redeems her hand, rubs thumb against fingertips, then wipes both against the silk of her sleeve.

'We have six thousand, my lord,' she tells him. 'Get us out of this crowd and we'll see what might be done to relieve the threat to your arsehole.'

Talbot looks at her for the first time, wiping his mouth against the sleeve of what was once a fine brocade surcoat, then back to Richard, still grinning. 'You said she'd turned out well.' He laughs, pulls a sweat-rimed hat from dung-dull hair and stumps a bow. 'And my wife? She's with you too?'

'And Eleanor, your daughter. Yes.' Cecily looks behind her

to where the golden Woodville, ever solicitous, escorts both his own wife and Talbot's along the jostling deck.

Jacquetta, as ever, is all smiles, waving at the crowd as if she thinks it pleased to see her. Beside her, Margaret Talbot scans the quay for only one face. Seeing it, she points, then leans down to speak quickly into the ear of the thin-faced girl before her, whose dark eyes follow nervously the line of her mother's finger. When they come to rest on Talbot's face there is no bolt of recognition.

The girl stares and her father squints, then looks to his wife.

'Margaret?' shouts Talbot.

He has seen neither wife nor daughter in five years. He has enough trouble to recognize the first. For the second there's no hope.

And now here they come, Cecily thinks.

While the women come ashore with the children and their nurses, Richard gives brief, quiet orders that set men scurrying. The disembarkation will take the rest of the day, but they needn't stay for it. Cecily is keen to be away from the ship, with its cramped quarters, and the oil-laden fish smell of the port. She, with Richard beside her, is the first to fall in and follow Talbot's rolling gait. Richard's noble captains, their wives and families follow. She hears little Anne crying against her nurse's shoulder, and frowns.

Ten years have passed since she was here last. That summer when she was little more than a girl herself and Joan burned in the warm May sunshine. The air smells no better, she thinks. Worse, in fact. And the sky is unseasonably grey. Where once there was vibrant colour and prosperous trading, now there's only peeling paint and unswept streets. People and horses wear their bones too close to their skin and, when she glances up at gabled windows, the faces that look down at her are hostile. It's to be expected. It's been ten long years of war and the tide set strong against England most of the way. If the people of Rouen are starting to think they've backed the wrong horse, it would be hard to blame them.

'I don't know how we'll reach a peace.'

Old soldier Talbot is resisting the temptation to put his feet on the table. Instead, he plants them wide among the floor rushes and rests ham fists on his thighs. Cecily watches as he stretches to take a crick from his neck, and hears a series of quiet clinks. Even here, in the security of the Lord Lieutenant's apartments, he goes so conspicuously armed that he rattles with every movement. He must be nearly sixty now and has barely been out of France for fifteen years. Before that he did time in Ireland, fighting rebels who called themselves princes. He's used to hard places and doesn't much expect to be liked. Richard likes him, though. And he likes Richard. They've worked together before, of course.

'Not our problem, old friend.' Richard leans towards him across the table. 'We've only to create an atmosphere in which peace might one day flourish.'

'Spoken like a politician. Does creating that atmosphere include kicking the French king's arse out of Pontoise?'

'Well, that's certainly my wife's plan,' laughs Richard.

Talbot looks askance, as if the idea of a woman with a plan is no less a miracle than the loaves and fishes.

'My Lord Talbot –' Cecily is all quiet charm – 'I am sure you know very well how that is to be done and have only been waiting for us to bring men and armaments to make it easy.'

Talbot isn't used to being complimented, either, and he is, for the moment, silenced.

Cecily folds her hands and endeavours to look as demure as he would expect her to be. 'It is my lord's first order in France to name you as his lieutenant general for the conduct of war. The role you had when last he was here and you achieved so much together.'

'That Beaufort brat took it from me.'

'And I give it back,' says Richard. 'It will be as it was before, John. You fight, I'll govern. Between us we'll bring Normandy back into shape, get revenues flowing again. Buy some time until the real politicians can find a way to let England hold on to its French territories without having to kiss the French king's arse for them.'

'Is that the best we hope for, then?' Talbot's wide mouth turns down in disappointment. He's old enough to remember Agincourt. He drank himself foolish on the night of its victory and carries the wine-fuelled dream with him still. Despite the evidence of his waking eyes, he finds it hard to believe it's over.

Cecily keeps her voice low. 'Normandy, Gascony, Maine. Calais. If we can.'

'Without fealty to the French king?'

'Under England's sovereignty. Just so.'

He rubs a hand across a stubbled chin, scratches and looks to Richard for an answer. 'And young Henry will settle for that, will he? King of England and Duke of Normandy. No more?'

Cecily watches Richard's face, curious to know how much he will say.

His eyes move from Talbot's clouded face to her own, then down to his fingers, which are threaded on the table before him. 'He's not his father, John.'

It's a small treason but, even here, a sea away from Westminster, it's best to whisper it.

II

'Cecily, they come!' With this news Jacquetta's bright face is, for once, unequivocally welcome. Seven days have crawled by since a messenger, who could barely stand for weariness, nor speak for joy, brought news that the siege of Pontoise was broken; that the French king and his dauphin had fled before York's forces and were even now licking their wounds in Poissy.

'Your lord bids you make ready,' the messenger told her, smilingly. 'He returns in triumph right soon.'

Then a triumph we will give him, she promised herself.

It's a good victory, it's come as early as she could have wished, and, since there is no telling when there will be another, she will use it to send clear messages. To England: York is delivering on its promise. To France: get used to not having it all your own way.

She has spent her days well. The streets that lead to the cathedral are clean and flag-lined, the bishop has been told what his welcoming sermon should say and, in the castle's great hall, the banners of York hang waiting to be lifted high on the wind of Richard's arrival. And now the watchers she set upon the wall two nights ago have marked the army's approach and sent word. Within the hour Richard will reach the city gate through which, even now, her own messenger stretches his horse's neck to carry her instruction. 'Put on your armour. Shine. The world is watching. On the cathedral's steps I will greet you.'

The next hour is a busy one. She sends heralds into the streets to tell Rouen's citizenry that their duke brings victory home. They're given flags to wave, roses to throw – and pennies to ensure they do so. She sends messages to the cathedral and to Rouen's many churches to set their bells pealing. The bishop and his priests, his canons and his choristers are called from their waiting to make ready. All this she does while maids swarm like flies to dress her in cloth of silver, to catch up her hair in its cage of gauze-veiled gilt, to lay in her hands the bible that tells the world she is pious, about her neck the jewels that say she is rich.

Now down the stairs to her carriage. She arrives at the cathedral and takes up her place at its door as the first cheers ring out from Rouen's southern gate. She breathes deep, ignores the trickle of sweat in the valley of her shoulder blades and raises her head to catch the rays of early evening sunshine against the closed lids of her eyes.

When she opens them again she makes no effort to contain her pleasure, for here he comes, emerging from the gabled streets into the cathedral square. The sun brightens his armour but, bare-headed, his dark hair is tailed by sweat and weighted with dust. The men that follow him are Talbot's veterans, grateful to have been relieved by Richard's fresh troops. Though they smile and wave, they do so with pinched, hungry faces; beneath sweat-slick horse hide, bones slide, sharp as sword edges. Richard's back is straight, though, and in his dusty face his teeth flash white.

She takes a step towards him as he dismounts, then falls into a low obeisance.

'Cecily.' He looks down as if she were a cup of wine he thirsts for.

She sees elation beneath the grime. It's the first time he has come home to her fresh from a fight and she feels the heat of it running from his fingers as he draws her up. Her heart jolts and a laugh breaks from her throat.

Watching him through the thanksgiving mass, she sees he cannot subdue his pleasure. Nor, at the feast that follows, his appetite. He revels in the praise poured upon him when the golden Woodville is called forth to regale the company with an account of York's victory.

Cecily heard it seven days ago from the messenger. Already she's had it written down, despatched to the court in England, posted to every garrison in Normandy. But she's glad to hear it told again, with Woodville flourish.

'When we arrived,' Woodville swaggers, golden, 'there was the French king and his whelp holed up in Abbey St Martin. And would not come out to fight us!'

'Too scared!' The room roars.

Cecily watches Richard, who leans behind him and signals for drink.

Woodville, getting into his stride, raises his hands to quiet them. 'So, after too many days of this lily-livered shivering, we take pity on them and bring a swift end to it.'

More laughter.

He tells, then, how Talbot led a feint to draw the main part of the French force downriver while Richard, under cover of a moonless night, led men across the water on a bridge of boats to pierce the unguarded heart of the French camp.

Hearing the tale afresh, Cecily senses the darkness of sky and water. The shallow pitching of the boats beneath men's steps. They would have blacked their faces, she knows. Put off their harness lest it betray them by a glint or a chink. She sees Richard, his dark hair a curtain. In her own breast she feels the tripping of his heart. Then, coming to ground, the swift race, the drawing of swords and the staggering panic of the waking camp. His blade in her hand is weightless. Her head rings with the exhilaration of risk.

'Our fearless duke gets close enough to the dauphin to smell his –' Woodville turns, pokes out his arse and points at it – 'before father and son take to their heels and run.'

Richard shakes his head, self-deprecating but pleased.

Cecily takes his hand, kisses its knuckles. Woodville has embellished the tale, she knows. But Richard had come close indeed. Close enough to kill the dauphin's squire before a French relief force arrived, horses were brought up, and his quarry was away. Richard and his men gave chase, then returned to pick over the royal spoils, left behind in the hurry of escape.

At this point in the tale Richard gets to his feet, drawing Cecily up beside him.

'What?' she laughs.

He grins, then takes from his purse a golden lily set with pearls. He holds it up for the room's admiration, then turns to fasten it to the shimmer of her dress. 'The King of France once wore this in his hat,' he announces. 'Now the Duchess of York wears it upon her breast.'

He moves to kiss her, but they're both grinning, so that their teeth clash. They laugh, and the hall erupts.

The next morning, on the ebb tide of love, he tells her the real story. What Woodville painted as a daring attack had actually been a desperate gamble. Less colourful, more roughly drawn. Talbot had proposed it because they both knew they couldn't survive a long stand-off before the walls of Pontoise. Since Cecily was last here, Normandy has been devastated by war, and the land around Pontoise even more so, since the King of France has burned every ear of corn, speared every pig and throttled every chicken left living, to ensure the English fight on empty bellies. The fresh troops Richard had brought to the siege were soon hungry. They saw their unhappy future in the eyes of the men they'd come to relieve; dead on their feet, most of them. Or losing their guts to dysentery.

'So you took your chance . . .' Cecily, loose haired and bare shouldered, shrugs.

'And fumbled it.'

'How so? Pontoise is ours.' She pulls back the covers and, grinning, straddles his waist. 'If ever I meet the French king I shall wear his bauble, to remind him how my husband trounced him.'

As she leans down to kiss him out of this dark mood he raises his hands to her shoulders, to hold her back. 'There was more at stake than a bauble, Cecily.'

She sits back against his raised thighs. 'Then, if we must be serious, tell me.'

He slides his hands down her arms. 'We had Charles on the run in the days after the siege broke. Talbot came up with a plan to drive him out of his hiding place in Poissy. I'd take up a position just north, intercept him as he made a break for Paris.'

He doesn't have to tell her that, with the French king and his son captive, England would have its best negotiating position for two decades or more. 'And?'

'Talbot raided Poissy, Charles ran and . . .' They're looking hard at each other. It seems he wants to look away, but will not. 'I misread the road. Too far east. He got past me and on to St Denis.'

'You had set scouts?'

'Too few. And not far enough ahead. He's back in Paris by now.'

She has always told him there is nothing he can tell her that she will not want to hear. This morning she wishes she had not. Or that he had not taken her at her word. She wonders how angry Talbot had been, and whether disappointment tasted as sour in his mouth as it does now in hers.

'Talbot is still in the field. Will you rejoin him?'

Richard's eyes are still fixed on hers. 'No. He has military command. I'll stay in Rouen for now. I'm here to govern, Cecily.'

Well, she thinks. Here is a man who knows himself, at least. But she remembers how she had exulted under his hand last night. How her body had answered the heat of battle in him. She dismounts, lies back, closes her eyes. She feels him rise up on his elbow, knows he is seeking her face again. A word from her could crush him now. 'If you want absolution you should have gone to your confessor.'

She counts fully three breaths before he speaks again. 'What penance might he have set me, do you think?'

She opens her eyes and there is his face, full of trouble. And she relents. 'None. For there is no fault.' She will make light of this. To strike at him is to strike at herself. At York. 'You misjudged a moment. What soldier has not?'

She feels him lie down again beside her, his long breath moves in her hair, and his heart, which was hammering, slows. His hand has come to rest on her belly. She takes it in her own and squeezes. She, who usually rails against any goal not reached, decides this will not matter. The French have been humbled and, for now, that's enough. She has her own goal to aim for. She believes a child was begun last night and nests now beneath their joined hands. This one, she thinks, conceived in heat, will live. Tempered by fire, it will thrive.

12

April 1442

Conceived in heat and born in it, too. Cecily is slathered in sweat. She has laboured from sunrise into the dead of night and now a final, flesh-tearing heave ends in a rush of pain and noise. This child is born shouting. When it's lifted up to her, red-faced and screaming, she falls back in hollowed-out relief. She sees she has birthed a son. And the size of him! When they lay him across her breast, she can hardly believe the weight.

'He's a giant, Cecily!' she hears Jacquetta exclaim. 'A mighty man!'

The relieved laughter of her women is almost drowned out by his cries. When they stop, sudden, on a moment, the laughter stumbles to silence and the midwife's satisfied smile disappears into creases as she lifts the child again. Cecily sees the thrusting limbs fall still and the head sink, round-mouthed and soundless against a white sleeve, before the woman turns away and her view is broken.

'What's wrong? What's happening?'

'Nothing, Cecily, I'm sure.' But she feels a tremble in Jacquetta's hand as it pushes sweat-slick hair from her face.

She screws her eyes shut, stinging and salt-blind, and tries to rise. But the pain is searing and her strength, when she reaches for it, is gone. They've taken her child and she hates them for it.

What are they doing?

There is only Jacquetta, fussing, useless, hardly worth hating.

'My son!'

Then a figure turns from the huddle of women that has formed about the midwife, steps with certainty to the bed, kneels beside her, takes her flailing hands in one that does not tremble, and lays another against her cheek to turn her face. Cecily looks into eyes that are clear and steady. It's Annette, the widow she has taken into her household to be this new child's nurse.

'Be still, lady. Wait. I have seen this before and the good wife knows what to do. Pray with me now. Pray to the Virgin. Still your soul. Ave Maria . . .' She taps her cheek. 'Come now. Ave Maria . . .'

Cecily has never looked for an anchor before, but here is one and she clings to it, for this bed is a sea of grief that will pull her down if another child dies. She tries to pray, but the tide has taken her voice already, so she follows Annette's words, first one then another, as certain as rosary beads, as familiar as her name. 'Blessed be the fruit of thy womb . . .'

Before the second Ave is done, there is a whimper, then a full-blooded cry.

Annette looks up. 'Is it well, good wife?'

And the answer comes. 'It is well.'

And Cecily feels her breath come, all in a rush, as the sea gives her up into life.

When Richard is sent for at last the child is swaddled, sleeping, breathing sure and steady against Cecily's breast. She knows he's been told he has a son; that there was fear for a moment, but all is well now. That his wife is weary. Weary! She heard them tell him so, damn them.

His face is elation veiled with concern.

She strives for patience but has to make him see. 'Richard, he must be baptized.'

'Of course, of course. We will fill the cathedral. All of Normandy will come to welcome York's son.'

'No.' She shakes her head. Dear God, why does he not see? 'Now. Don't wait.' She reaches out a hand, grasps his sleeve, curses the weakness of her grip. She knows her son's soul to be in peril. In the dark of night she has seen demons prowl this very room, red-clawed and ravenous. 'We have thwarted the Devil once, but he waits.'

He tries to hush her. To hush her, for Heaven's sake! Will he not just listen?

'Richard, you saw how Henry was torn from us. This one too, almost. Please. Just do it.'

She sees his mind change and knows he has heard her. 'Yes,' he nods. 'Alright.'

And then he's about it.

She lies back and rests against the calm of his voice. His steady orders will have candles lit in the chapel, the priest pulled from his bed. At the last, Annette lifts the child from her arms, smiles and steps away. She lets him go. Knowing him safe in the nurse's hands.

Cecily's son is named, not for the King, who has had his due, but for York. For Richard's uncle, from whom the dukedom came and, perhaps, for his long-dead grandfather, the third King Edward. And, while Henry faltered and is gone from her, this Edward thrives and stays. All the days Cecily lies healing, knitting flesh, she watches him. He feeds so hungrily he needs two wet nurses, sleeps deep, cries fiercely. And grows. The astrologers make much of the virile spring sun he has been born under and the preponderance of fire in his chart. They say it almost burned him up when he entered the world but is banked within him now. He will be bold, they tell her. Forward, lusty and strong.

'He will rule us all then!' laughs Annette, who washes him, wraps him, carries him to his wet nurse, then lays him replete in his mother's arms.

As Cecily watches him, it seems he watches back, commanding her attention, matching his heat to hers. She has given him life. Secured his soul. He is all hers. And, for now at least, her hungry heart is sated.

After the churching, she enters Rouen's great hall with a son in her arms. As the assembled nobles of Normandy raise the rafters with cheers, she looks out over their heads, unflinching. Before them all she places her son in Richard's arms, sweeps an obeisance, then rises to stand beside him.

Richard smiles and waves gladly at the shouts of congratulation. He is all joy.

She is all relief. She cannot say why, but this feels like salvation.

When her son begins his shouting again, Annette steps forward – steady Annette, with her powerful prayers – and Cecily hands him to her care. It pains her to part with him as it never does with her daughter.

They sit to eat. She reaches for the wine set before her and sees her knuckles, white about the glass. She sets it down, shakes the stiffness from her hand, shifts her head to stretch her spine.

Richard smiles at her, eyebrow raised.

She picks up the glass again, toasts him and drinks. 'I wish we were at Westminster,' she whispers. 'Or Windsor. Wherever King Henry is, with my cardinal uncle and his hell-spawned nephews.'

He drinks with quiet relish. 'I'm rather glad we're not.'

'I want them to see the son I've given you. To know that York is strong and will not be set aside.'

'Oh, Cecily. Not today. We are the King's good servants and he knows it. Drink your wine.' He nudges her, apes a grin.

She gives up, laughs and drinks.

And now the food is come, towering dishes, and the music strikes. She remembers she is hungry and decides, for now at least, to be happy.

But later, alone, they return to it. She has retired to her rooms and when business is done, he follows her there. They've been too long apart, but they won't love yet. She's sore still, and tired. It's enough just to talk. First of their son, which delights them, and then of France, which does not. Pontoise, the glory of last summer, was lost again by winter. Charles returned to besiege it with a force of arms so great it could not stand. He marched its English citizens to Paris, bound them hand and foot, then pushed them from the city's bridges to find new lodging in the Seine.

Militarily, they're under pressure. The promised support from England, both money and men, is late. Richard has sent Talbot to England, to challenge the council. Cecily thinks he should have gone himself, but Richard would not. He says he would not be abroad when this child came, but she wonders if that was his only reason and, anyway, thinks it a bad one.

'So, what do we hear from Talbot then?' she asks.

They are seated with a fire between them, though outside the high window the birds are sending the last of their songs into a warm May twilight.

'All good things. He's raising men, with the council's blessing.'

'And what of naval support? We won't retake Dieppe without it.'

'Ah, well. Of that no news yet.'

'It is no good thing to be so far from the King, while other men make up his mind for him,' she complains.

'Do you not trust your cardinal uncle?'

'I trust him to know the way the world turns. And to turn it to his advantage.'

Richard grimaces, but does not speak.

'Has Talbot seen Gloucester?'

He shakes his head slowly, stretches his long legs before him. 'He has not.'

'What does he hear of him then?'

'No single tale. That he is broken by the loss of his wife. That he cast her aside gladly to save his own skin. That he gives thanks to God he is free of her sorcery. Who can say which, if any, of these things are true?' He nets his fingers, stretches his arms as if to push rumour away.

'He's not at court?'

'No. He has left both court and King's Council. He keeps to his home and sees no one. And . . .'

'And?'

'And the King will not hear his name spoken.'

'Dear God, he is England's heir still! And likely to be so for ever, while Henry scorns women too much to marry.' She does not say, 'And you, Richard, are next in line,' though his knowledge of that – and its danger – is there in the way he twists his ring about his finger, its bull's blood ruby catching light from the fire.

All through last summer and then autumn, as Cecily's belly began to grow, the scandal had fattened. It was long known, of course, that the Gloucesters kept astrologers in their household. What man does not who wants to understand his times? Nor did it surprise Cecily to learn that the duke's childless wife had taken potions and bought witches' spells to make her fruitful. She herself did that in the eight years she was barren. But when those astrologers were accused of predicting the King's death they were brought before King's Council, where Cecily's cardinal uncle holds sway. Suddenly they had not only predicted death, but divined it, with dark masses and damnable acts. And they named Eleanor, Gloucester's wife, as their patron in it all.

And a witch was brought to trial too, Marjory Jourdemayne, who said that Eleanor came to her for spells that would kill the King, bring her husband to the throne and give him an heir of her body to succeed him. When asked if she knew the witch, Eleanor admitted, yes, but said she has bought from her only simples to aid conception. Of all other crimes, she protested herself innocent.

Before winter, all were condemned. The witch burned, the astrologers quartered or dead in the Tower. And Eleanor solemnly divorced from her husband by a commission of bishops that the cardinal heads. She has been sent barefoot through London in penance, walking from church to church, into perpetual imprisonment.

'And what of my uncle? What does Talbot say of him?'

Richard shrugs. 'That he has never looked so well. Nor ridden so high in the King's favour.'

The cardinal and Gloucester. Gloucester and the cardinal. So long rivals for the heart of the King. And now Gloucester is down. The balance of power that has rested on the fulcrum of Henry's love, all upset. Cecily looks into the fire and thinks of her uncle, of his burning ambition and his hungry love for his brother's son, John Beaufort. His letters, which have for so many years amused her and kept her close to court news, have been sparse since their coming into France. 'We should be back in England.'

'We do the King's will here in France, Cecily.'

'We are out of England while the King does my uncle's will, you mean.'

'If you say so. But we're getting the men we asked for. And more.' He looks sideways at her, raises a brow to tease a smile she won't give.

'What?'

'I wrote to ask the King to reward Talbot's long good service.'

'And?'

'Do you think you can bear to welcome back the Earl of Shrewsbury?'

'Ha! An Earldom for Talbot? And you mock me for valuing baubles too highly?'

'It is an honour, given at my request, to the man who executes our policy in France. I choose to see it as reassurance of the King's continuing favour – and your uncle's. You may see it as you will.'

She sees his fist, curled around the arm of his chair, while a long finger rubs back and forth against a tight frown. The distance between them is suddenly too great.

She rises to cross it, lays a hand against his cheek. 'I am too tired to fight. Come, I'll write the King and thank him for his favour. And my uncle. Let's to bed.'

But first they go to the nursery to look once more upon their sleeping son.

The widow Annette is there beside the crib, stitching and watching in a pool of candlelight. She rises, and steps quietly aside as they approach.

There's a shadow of golden hair on Edward's head that Cecily cannot help but kiss.

Richard gazes at his son. 'He is the greatest gift you have ever given me, Cecily.'

'I have drawn the sun to earth for you.'

He smiles at her and she feigns a laugh, as if she believes her words to be only a mother's fondness and not gospel truth.

That night she lies beside her sleeping husband thinking only of her son, remembering the weight of him in her arms, the warmth of his breath, the prayers that banked his fire and made him safe.

When sleep comes, it brings Gloucester to her mind,

spinning and adrift. And then Eleanor, stepping taper-lit through the grey London dawn while men laugh and women sneer. Cecily feels in her feet the cold of the cobbles and the jeers of the crowd that fall like blows about her head. She watches the lady's penitent back disappearing into mist, the damp hem of a thin shift clinging to bruised heels.

Poor Eleanor. Cecily will not bludgeon her with pity. She will take her as a lesson and rest.

Edward sleeps soft and safe on Annette's careful watch. She nests her body against Richard's curled back. If any man should rise now to threaten York, they cannot do it through her empty belly.

13

January–April 1443
Dijon, Burgundy

Burgundy's Duchess Isabella is not a beautiful woman. Her features are too sharp, her lips too thin and, if diplomacy did not matter, Cecily would say the lady plucks her brow too high. And for all she bathes her face in lemon juice and camomile, her Portuguese blood robs her skin of the moon-pale lustre with which Cecily can light a room. It hardly matters. If Isabella's flesh doesn't sparkle, her jewels do, and Cecily has never seen any woman dress so richly or so fine.

For their first meeting, in Dijon's gilded palace, Cecily has prepared carefully. She wears her wealth in muted colours, rich but plain, to let the older woman shine. Isabella is not blind to the compliment and, when her hooded eyes have valued the depth of her visitor's velvet and the quality of her furs, she smiles and speaks and is transformed. Isabella's ability to captivate, Cecily quickly learns, lies in her intelligence and is embellished by her power.

If Isabella's husband was ever disappointed by his third wife's looks, thirteen years of marriage have taught him to value her mind, which even he would admit is a sharper blade than his own. He married her to get a son. Since that was achieved ten years ago they've not shared a bed, but when the duke is out of his domain, fighting wars or getting bastards, she rules in his stead as regent. It's a state of affairs, she admits to Cecily, with which she is entirely content. Richard, who is no stranger to the keenness of a woman's wit, she finds charming.

They are here, Cecily and Richard, because Duke Philip has at last remembered that he does not love the French and has set his wife the task of rebuilding his old friendship with England. The Duke of Orléans, prisoner turned poet, has paved their diplomatic path to her door. He knows the way well enough. When released from his English captivity three years ago, he turned his back on France, declared himself Isabella's happy prisoner and made marriage with Burgundy's niece.

At their first dinner together, Isabella does not scruple to mock the French king: his fleshy lips, his dripping nose. She laughs, shivering her shoulders, looking sly at Cecily, then turning to Richard, mock serious, brows arched.

'He daily undermines my lord's authority.' She leans in, lowers her voice. 'I believe he envies our wealth and suspects our ambition.' Her eyes widen as if scandalized while, across the table, Orléans smiles, languid in his chair, turning the glass in his hand to catch candlelight.

Cecily taps a finger to her lip and speculates that France has, perhaps, grounds for suspicion. 'Since Burgundy has nested so firmly in her breast a man who could, should he choose, challenge for its throne.'

Orléans' smile broadens further still. 'Ah, but I have no interests these days beyond poetry. And to bring about peace among my friends.'

Isabella, eyes shining, laughs and leans to lay a hand on Richard's arm. 'What delightful company. You are fortunate, my lord. Few men's wives have even half an eye for policy.'

Richard raises a glass to the ladies and confesses himself blessed indeed.

For policy's sake Isabella sets a high price on Burgundy's friendship, understanding that Richard will pay much to have only one enemy to fight instead of two. But she deals honestly and speaks plain. When he reminds her how well it suits Burgundy to have the eye of France distracted from her borders by squabbles with England, she has the good grace to concede the point.

Not all of their time is taken up with politics. Evenings are given over to poetry and music, and the measured steps of the *basse danse*, whose slow turns set jewels shining and bring a candlelit shimmer to silk. By day they walk in Dijon's vast interiors, where stitched huntsmen, lanced with gold, ride endlessly through tapestried forests, and silver unicorns lie down to sleep in the laps of virgins. In shadowed corridors they are introduced to Isabella's painted family: fine-nosed Philip and the boy Charles, his ten-year-old curls a riot about his head. They are no more than oil and colour laid on board, but Philip's face thrums with impatience and his son's sensuous mouth is moistened, ready to speak. And there, in her gilded frame, is Isabella, half smiling, all knowing, eyes hooded. Then, turning, Cecily sees the lady herself, a breath away – and smiling, just the same.

Cecily has never seen such verisimilitude and cannot help but touch. 'Your artists tame colour to capture the soul. There's nothing like this in England.'

Isabella slides past her, a sigh of silk. 'We should have them set down your beauty, perhaps?'

'Yes!' Richard turns on his heel, suddenly delighted.

Cecily smiles, then shakes her head and steps on. She cannot say why, but the thought that men might gaze upon her painted face and thereby divine her thoughts makes her heart trip and her breath come short.

By the end of their visit they are much pleased with one another. Orléans is dedicating verses to three duchesses, only one of them his wife, and the tentative seeds of peace have been sown.

*

In the four months that follow, those seeds are watered with frequent despatches, addressed always both to York's duke and his duchess, and responded to in kind.

With each courier comes also a personal packet for Cecily. They exchange elaborate jewels. A musician is loaned, advice on fashions exchanged. But the best gift of all is a book given by Isabella, *The City of Ladies*. In it, Christine de Pisan – that rare creature, the female scholar – argues women to be men's equals and peoples a world with those of her sex who, across long ages, have proved her right. Within its gilded pages, rich in cobalt and vermillion, women walk untrammelled, knowing their will, speaking it and seeing it done. Cecily is entranced and, in the weeks that follow, their letters to each other extol the virtues of their favourites. Isabella champions Penthesilea, the Amazonian queen who fought at Troy to avenge the death of Hector. Cecily applauds the barbarian Lilia, whose valiant heart inspired her son's conquest of Italy, and Judith, the noble widow who slew a tyrant to save Israel. In her last letter, Isabella, in playful mood no doubt, commends to her Sappho, the philosopher-poet who had no need of men.

'Poetry must console me too, a while,' Cecily then writes. 'For I am heavy with child again and my husband will come to you alone this time. But you know my heart and all the wishes in it for peace between us.'

14

May 1443

Richard is gone all of April at Isabella's court. When May Day comes it brings a promise of summer's heat that might have raised Cecily's spirits had it not increased her body's burden. She itches to ride on a day like this, to be in the air, but her belly will not let her. Besides, her hours have been spent with an ill-tempered Talbot and his lady, searching for sense in the news from England's king.

'As well to seek chastity in a brothel,' Talbot complains. 'Or mercy in Hell.'

This may be true, but is unhelpful. Little wonder her nerves are on edge.

Then, with a soft-coloured twilight, comes Richard's squire, sent to say that his master has entered the city and is coming home.

Cecily looks up from the sweat-curled head of the kneeling boy to where her steward hovers, expecting orders. 'Go greet my lord husband and tell him I await him. If he would come to me here, straight, I will be most glad.' The steward is halfway to the chamber door before she calls him back, finger pointing, imperious. 'To me straight, mind. He speaks with me before any other.'

The man nods and goes.

She turns now, smoothing her sleeves and ignoring the ache in her back, to the squire, still kneeling before her. 'So. Is my lord merry?'

He looks up at her, perplexed.

She sighs. 'Has he concluded our business with Burgundy happily?'

Understanding dawns on him and he finds courage to reply. 'Most happily, my lady. Yes. The ink is dry on a perpetual truce between Burgundy and England.' His smile invites her congratulation, but is disappointed.

'Good. Now get you gone.' Before the door has closed behind him she has turned her frowning face to Talbot.

His sullen glare sets her foot tapping.

'You should sit down, lady.' He gestures vaguely at her belly. 'Surely . . .' He finds it hard to look at her and thinks she should not be here.

She agrees. Though Edward is barely a year old, she expects to be brought to bed with a new babe any day. She should have gone to her lying-in already; had been of a mind to do so a fortnight since, when her plans had been upset by the clattering arrival of King Henry's herald. He'd swaggered and said his news was for York's ears only. She had pinned him with a stare and asked him who he thought she was.

'My lady, you are York's wife. Will you tell me where the duke is so I might ride there and give him the King's message?'

'You can give your message to me and I will tell you if it's worth the sweat of your horse to carry it.'

She had kept him on his feet until he understood that his duty was to give the King's letter into her hands. It greeted Richard as a dear and well-beloved cousin, but carried barbs that would pierce his heart. Though anger burned her eyes and scorched her throat, she swallowed it, for the herald watched her intently and would, she knew, report back.

Her eyes never left him while she rolled the letter in brisk hands, placed it among others on her table. 'The duke my husband is deep in negotiations with Burgundy's duchess that we pray will further the King's cause in France. I'm sure you don't wish to distract that enterprise. Your message can wait.'

Give him credit, he'd tried to stand his ground. 'Will you tell me where he is, lady?'

'I will not.'

And she has made it hard for him to find out, too. Her household either don't know or are forbidden to say. And she has forgone her seclusion to keep him under her eye. She's watched him skulking about corridors, hoping to catch a whisper and wondering, no doubt, how it is that a woman has come to stand between himself and his will.

Certainly Richard's return will not escape his notice. Time to act.

'My Lord Talbot, you should go and inform the King's herald of the duke's return. Tell him we will summon him right soon.'

His red face reddens further. 'Am I your page, lady?'

'You are the Earl of Shrewsbury, my lord. A man with authority to prevent the King's lackey from spilling his news on our doorstep and taking tales of my husband's rage at it back to his master.'

Cecily can't remember exactly when Talbot started accepting her orders or seeing the sense in her strategies, but she is glad to see the habit established. Off he goes, with no further complaint.

His wife, too, rises, squeezes Cecily's hand. 'You'll want to be alone with him. I'll be with Talbot. We'll come when you call.'

Cecily nods, thankful. The three of them have been much together these last days, arranging, as the King has demanded, a redoubling of Normandy's defences against a renewed French threat; a threat they've seen no evidence of and she suspects is in the King's head only. She has written, with discretion, to her cardinal uncle, to understand his mind. But no reply yet.

She's at the window, watching shadows grow across the

garden, when she hears a catch of spurs on the stair and knows it's Richard. She sighs in relief. It isn't, in fact, her husband's rage that Cecily wishes hidden from the King's messenger. Richard isn't a man given to rage. It's the disappointment; the shock he won't immediately be able to hide. She turns to the door as it opens and here he is, all smiles.

'I'd thought not to see you; that I'd be too late. Are you well?' His eyes move to where her hand rests, high on her belly.

'I've waited for you—'

His smile widens and, almost, she loses her hard-won patience. 'No, no. I've waited because there's news from England you must hear at once, and from me.' They are alone, so she decides it's best to wield the knife quickly. She walks to him, lays a hand on each shoulder and speaks. 'The King is sending John Beaufort here with an army. And has named him Captain General of France.'

And there it is: the wound to his heart, written on his face.

To hide it he turns from her, removes himself a step or two, takes off his gloves, runs his hand through his hair. It will be a moment, she imagines, till he can trust his voice. 'Captain of France?'

'Well. Of those territories in France, at least, where we ourselves do not hold sway.'

He throws down the gloves, shakes his head, walks to the window and back again. 'Which means, in fact, those areas of France still in French hands. Is this war then? And, if so, against whom? Charles or me?'

While he walks, she talks.

'Not war. Just nonsense. The King writes that his spies have discovered plans for a combined French offensive against Normandy and Aquitaine.' She's disparaging. 'We've seen nothing of it. And it's hard to imagine Henry's spies are better than our own. In any case, we're given to understand that Beaufort is ordered not to enter our lands, but to set himself between that offensive and us. We're told it's for our aid.'

He barks a harsh laugh.

'You are reminded of the King's very great love for you.'

'Indeed?' He walks still, to the window again, then to the table. He draws out a chair and slumps into it, eases his neck, pours wine, drains it and sets down the cup. 'And how is this –' he waves his hand, searching for the word – 'foray into France to be financed? Given that our king is so laggardly in his payments that we currently hold Normandy from our own purse.'

She sees that he's guessed it, that she need hardly tell him. 'The King's messenger told me that my cardinal uncle has given a loan.'

His head dips, shakes from side to side. 'Your uncle. Of course he has.'

She crosses the room. Takes a seat opposite him. 'And, regarding our own funds, the King bids York to be patient a while.'

Now his face turns very dark and the ring on his finger is turning and turning. 'I have secured peace with Burgundy. I have made Brittany our ally. I was asked, by your uncle, and when no other man of sense would take the commission, to pave the way for peace with France. And, against odds that even I found daunting, I've done it.' His voice is thick in his throat and his lips curl back from his teeth. 'I have emptied my purse and risked my reputation to prove my loyalty to the King and my good use to your uncle. And now they send John Beaufort to do . . . what? To make war? Or something so like war I can't tell the difference.'

She takes his shaking hands to still them. 'Richard. We must face it. We've been out-played. There are men on the council who would sooner murder their children than have peace in France. John Beaufort's hungry for nothing but fame in England and revenge here, so they've made him their champion. And together they've swayed the King. Which is not difficult.'

'And your uncle?'

She shrugs, shakes her head. For this betrayal makes less sense and hurts more. 'Well, I suppose he wants John's love.' And that pains her; that when her uncle weighed his love for his sister's daughter against his love for his brother's son, she came up light. 'And whatever else he is, he is a servant of the King.'

Richard stares at her, incredulous. 'You don't believe that.'

She throws up her hands, sits back in her chair. 'Oh, Richard, it's family. It's always family. John is Beaufort and we . . . we are York.'

'The chance to lead an army into the mess of France is hardly a prize I would covet for my family! God knows, my own service here is thankless enough. What does Beaufort expect to gain from it?'

'Ah. On that point I pressed the messenger a little further. It seems the terms of Beaufort's coming into France are . . .' How to describe it? 'Unusual.'

'Indeed. How so?'

She wills her voice to steadiness as she tells him. 'Whatever spoils he wins are to be his own, not the Crown's. And he is no longer Earl of Somerset but Duke.' Richard's look is disbelieving. Now even she must look away. 'My uncle made it a condition of the loan.'

Richard nets his hands, taps his thumbs against his teeth. 'Let me understand. He is richly funded, with money that should be mine, to impose on my jurisdiction. And he keeps all the profit?'

'It's best you know it all. I've taken counsel with Talbot, and he with his captains. There's no evidence of a renewed offensive, things are much as they have been—'

'Of course there's not! This is nothing more than an excuse for a raiding party that lets John Beaufort slake his resentment and line his pockets at our expense.' His voice lowers. 'And it puts at risk everything we've strived for these two years.'

'I know.'

He lays his hands, palms down, on the table. 'I'm going to England.'

She lays her own atop them. 'That you should not do.'

'You've always said that to influence the King you need to be near the King. So, well and good, I will go to the King.'

'And leave your post? And give John Beaufort the excuse he needs to walk into Normandy too? No. We should send Talbot. In any case, if the council is for war again, better an old soldier tells them it's madness than the Duke of York. We must stay here and deal with whatever nonsense Beaufort brings. And Richard,' she binds her fingers with his, tight. 'I am sorry, but now I must be about the business of making this child.'

He nods, lowers his head on to their joined hands, and sighs.

15

When Cecily's second French-born son is welcomed into
Christ's Church there is no lack of grandeur. Or of purpose.
His solemn task, on the first morning of his life, is to remind
the world that, in Normandy at least, the reins of power lie in
York's hands and no one else's. It's Cecily's idea, but Annette
inspires it, with tales and histories told to distract her mistress
during the impatient days of her lying-in. Normandy's first
duke, she tells her, was the Viking warrior Rollo. He was so
huge no horse could carry him. So strong no man could best
him. So fearsome that the king who ruled France then – 'He
was called Charles the Simple, you know' – ceded him this
rich land in return for being left alone. 'So, from Rollo's loins
have come all the Dukes of Normandy. Including William, of
course, the conqueror of England.'

'So Normandy belongs naturally to England,' Cecily
concludes.

She watches Annette still her needle, quirk a brow and think.

'Or England to Normandy, I think?' A provoking smile, and
back to her sewing.

Annette claims not to be political; a Frenchwoman who
married an Englishman. Buried him too, and the little one
that toddled after him into the grave. She has decided to love
other women's children. It hurts less when they die.

'There is a font, still,' Annette remembers, 'here in our own
cathedral. Rollo ordered it made for the baptism of his sons

only. No other man's child. Empty now five hundred years or more. They say,' she confides, 'that any boy baptized in it will have all that Rollo had: his greatness and his power.'

Cecily, who has been short of smiles lately, grins. 'And, hopefully, a bigger horse.' Then she takes Annette's hand. 'Go to my husband and tell him your story. He'll know what to do.'

And, of course, he does. Despite the blustering protests of Rouen's archbishop, Rollo's dry stone holds water again and the newborn Edmund, once doused in it, cries powerfully in his father's arms. Afterwards Annette, who carried this boy to his baptism, just as she carried his brother, makes a fine tale of it for Cecily. How the noses of the good men of Rouen scraped the floor with bows so deep she thought their backs might snap, as she followed Richard's arrow-straight back down the flower-strewn nave and out into midday sunlight.

'Your husband knows how to impress, lady. Never a ceremony so fine.' Annette smirks. 'You would have thought a king had come to Rouen and Christ himself leaned down from Heaven to bless him.'

'A king? Nonsense, Annette. You make too much of it.' But Cecily, pleased as a cat, kisses her baby's head, tells him well done and takes from Annette's lips the loving caress Richard has sent for her.

It's petty, of course, she knows it; a slap across the face that John Beaufort will never feel. But the pleasure of giving it sets her fingers tingling and has her smiling for an hour or more.

By the time she's churched and returned to the world there's further cause for glee. Talbot's first letter from home tells them that John Beaufort is late leaving England for France and that the King's patience with him wears thin.

'All to the good,' says Cecily, smug as she scrutinizes the flatness of her belly in the glass.

'There's more.' Richard raises a brow, as he reads from the

page. 'Talbot writes that the fat wife Beaufort took for himself last year has given him a child.'

Cecily turns her shoulder to look the inevitable question at him.

He can't help but smile. 'A puling girl, Talbot says. Named Margaret, for its mother.'

Cecily throws back her head and laughs.

He puts the letter aside. 'But I have even better news than Talbot's. Of more import. It seems the French king is of a mood to talk peace again.'

Now Cecily is impressed, and leaves her mirror to sit close at Richard's side. 'Perhaps our truce with Burgundy has given him pause?'

Richard shrugs. 'Or, it may be intended to blind us to the offensive Henry's spies speak of . . .' He laughs when Cecily frowns. 'Who can guess? Besides, it may come to nothing. We've seen feints enough in this long French game.'

Nevertheless, at Richard's request, Brittany's Duke Francis has offered himself as mediator and sent his brother to England to understand whether, if Charles will talk, Henry will listen. Richard gives his hands into Cecily's. 'And so I have done what the King asked of me. I have opened a window through which peace might enter, if the warmongers on his council don't bar the way.'

Cecily's scowl betrays her opinion of a king who cannot bend his council's will to his own. 'We shall see. It may, at the very least, be enough to make him kennel John Beaufort again.'

It's not. In August, John's unwelcome army lands in Cherbourg; in Normandy, where he has been ordered not to set foot. Richard's captain there rides to Rouen with news of the arrival, but can say nothing of the duke's plans.

'All I can tell you is that he rides south. Towards Maine, I suppose. And that he pays nothing for the supplies he demands from Norman towns and villages to feed his army.'

Cecily watches as the poor captain twists his hat in his hands, anticipating censure from his pacing lord. She narrows her eyes as, imploringly, the man holds out his hat to Richard's retreating back.

'He is the Duke of Somerset, my lord! He carries the King's warrant. I could hardly stop him.'

When she sees how his eyes range about the chamber, marking the ear-wagging servants and Richard's inky secretary, bent over his letters, she steps in. Clapping her hands for attention, she empties the room of all but the three of them and, with a low voice, pitched to soothe, bids Cherbourg's captain speak his mind.

He addresses himself to Richard. 'My lord, as I love and serve you, can I ask? Is the Duke of Somerset mad?'

Richard, who till now has thought John Beaufort only vicious, stops his pacing and turns. 'You may ask. But why would you think it?'

And then the man tells how John Beaufort came to Cherbourg and left without a word to its captain or a courtesy to his office. 'I sent my man to his camp to greet him and understand his intentions. He was back within the hour, barred from the camp on the duke's order and his eye blacked for his pains. I went then myself. He kept me waiting four hours and more. It was dark midnight before I was admitted to his tent.' He shakes his head.

'And what did you see there?' Cecily prompts him.

'I saw a man very deep in his cups. And looking like he'd been there a long time. His captains were about him, like a swaggering mob. Like a dog pack. It was a warm night but he had a fire roaring. It was hotter than hell in there and he but half dressed, sweating like a horse and shivering. I told him I came as your representative.'

'And how did he answer you?' Richard asks.

The man's voice stumbles, he averts his head. 'He cursed then, and his captains laughed. I asked how I might assist him, and what I might say to my Lord of York of his intentions in France. He came to his feet then, like a fury. He . . . he put his dagger to my throat and told me straight that his strategy was his secret and he would tell it to no one; that he would skewer any man who tried to discover it. Then he plucked at his clothes as if they scorched him and said that if even his shirt guessed his secret, he would burn it. Then he tore the shirt off and threw it in the fire. And his dagger across the floor after it. "Tell that to the Duke of York," he said. And he laughed.' The man shrugs, shakes his head. 'He was still laughing when I left.'

The room is quiet now.

Cecily looks at Richard. Sees that he's not shocked to the core as she is. He nods slowly, then goes to his secretary's desk, rifles among papers, picks up a quill and starts to write.

The captain can bear it no longer. 'What should I do, my lord?'

'Do nothing. And nor will I. We will not engage him, we will not support him and we will not stand in his way. Whatever madness he pursues we stand aloof from him. Go home. Go quietly to our towns and villages he has robbed, and make reparation. Draw the funds from my steward.' He puts down the quill, folds the note and seals it. 'Here is my authority.'

'Not from Rouen's treasury?'

Richard's smile is wry. 'No. This comes from my purse, so keep a careful accounting.'

And they do stand aloof, while Beaufort passes from Normandy into French-held land, leaving a trail of fire: burned villages, scorched earth, French corpses. When Talbot returns from England with no good answers and less money, Richard nods and holds his peace. When England's last bastion in Dieppe falls, and old soldier Talbot weeps for its captain, his bastard son, among the dead, he folds his hands and thins his lips.

'What are we doing, Richard?' Cecily implores him. 'With only half John Beaufort's men and money we could have taken Dieppe for the King, and Talbot's son would still be living.'

'We are waiting out the storm, Cecily. John Beaufort will burn himself out eventually. The King will come to his senses.'

'Will he? I see little sign of it.' She feels at the end of her patience. 'Does it not make you mad?'

He bows his head. 'It irks me to see our purpose here endangered by this foolishness of policy, but . . .'

'But?'

'But we cannot oppose Beaufort without opposing the King.'

She throws up her hands.

'Nor need we,' he soothes her. 'Beaufort will destroy himself. And, when he is gone, the King will remember York. We will speak sense to him, and he will listen.'

She wonders how hard it must be for him to keep believing this. But because she has no alternative strategy to offer, and because she has no wish to quarrel without purpose, she nods and holds her peace.

Then, at last, Beaufort's firestorm does end. In shame and ignominy and withdrawal.

In the first days of winter he burns through snow as he slips across the border from Anjou to Brittany, where England's ally, Duke Francis, holds sway. Bent on plunder, he lays siege to the rich town of La Guerche, where his men run through the town like dogs, tearing out hearts. Citizens are dragged from sanctuary churches and Beaufort, raving, tells Francis he must ransom them or see them dangle from the town's battered walls.

Francis's brother, white-faced with rage at Henry's court, asks why England has betrayed its alliance. The King, casting about, remembers only that he wanted peace and that his cardinal has bankrolled war. And so, all in a moment, John Beaufort's burning star is falling, and the men who helped set it in the sky run from its destruction. He is recalled to England, exiled from court and his purse emptied to pay the reparation that will smooth Brittany's hackles. He storms home to his estates, where his fat wife turns her back on him and he sits, still drinking, still sweating, still cursing, while the fire in his blood turns to ice. By springtime he is dead, whether from shame or sickness or by his own hand none can say.

The cardinal sends news of it in a letter, cold and stark. Then writes, 'As for you, the King commends your patient work in France, and bids you redouble your efforts. Now ask me no more of John Beaufort. I know of no such man.'

And so their careful work begins; the rebuilding of their diplomacy, their holding of England's line.

'You were right,' Cecily tells Richard.

'I take no pleasure in it.'

And she finds she cannot either. The world no longer knows John Beaufort, but she cannot quell the feeling that his fallen star has scorched the earth in some unseen way and that, at a future step, she will feel the heat of it.

16

She has looked forward to seeing their old friend again but, as
he walks towards her along the ice-slick quayside of Pontoise,
it seems to Cecily that William de la Pole is not a happy man.
On the face of it, he has every cause for gladness. He has in his
pocket a truce with France and, on his arm, a wife for his king.
But to Cecily's eyes he looks stretched and she's sure that,
when she saw him last, there had been less silver in his hair.
That was a year ago. He'd been on his way to Tours then, high
in King Henry's favour, and sent by him in haste to talk peace
with King Charles. More than that, he had confided, mellowed
by the good dinner they gave him and not a little wine, a peace
marked by a marriage.

'A marriage for the King?' She had spoken low, to hide her
incredulity.

He nodded slow. 'Between the royal houses of England and
France.'

'Well,' she had smiled into her cup. 'He must want peace
very much.'

'Since John Beaufort died it is all he thinks of.'

'Peace, William? Or marriage?'

His turn to smile. 'Well, is one not a blessing upon the
other?'

But William isn't smiling now. And the young girl who
walks beside him, and whose pale hand lies rigid on his sleeve,

looks no happier than he. Arguably, Marguerite of Anjou's joy should be unalloyed, for she, against all expectation, is to be England's queen.

'Is that the best he could do, do you think?' Cecily had asked Richard when William wrote that he was returning with the King's bride. 'She's . . . what? The French queen's niece?'

'On her father's side.'

'Do you think any man in England has ever heard of her?'

'If they have, they've probably forgotten. But honestly, Cecily. I don't care if Henry marries the queen's niece or the queen's spaniel, if it can bring us to an honourable peace.'

'Well,' she had conceded with a grin, 'a spaniel. It's not quite as bad as that.'

Now, as the girl approaches, Cecily stares shamelessly. She's been warned that Marguerite brings no dowry save her looks, so is keen to value them. They're good, she concludes, but could be much improved by smiling.

Cecily sweeps into her deepest bow as William leans to tell the King's bride that this is the Duchess of York, most noble of all English ladies, who will be her hostess in Rouen for Easter. 'And here is her lord, the Duke of York, the King's cousin and good friend.'

Cecily stays low, head bent, until a thin voice bids her welcome and a small bare hand is reached out for her kiss. Bringing it to her lips, Cecily finds it stiff with cold but not shivering. Looking up into Marguerite's face she sees tension behind fine dark eyes. The smile, when at last it comes, is fleeting and brittle. She feels an unexpected stab of sympathy. Marguerite is five days short of her fifteenth birthday. Three days ago, in Paris, she bade her world goodbye and gave herself into the hands of strangers to be taken to a man, already her husband in the eyes of law and the Church, who she has never met and cannot know. That in itself is nothing, of course, but when Cecily thinks of who that man is, that blade of sympathy twists a little.

So she puts a welcome into her own smile, takes William's place at Marguerite's side, and speaks. 'We are most happy to receive Your Grace. Will you come aboard where warmth and comfort await you? This quayside is bitter.'

Indicating the way forward, Cecily keeps a careful half-step behind the young Queen, who raises her chin, fixes her eyes forward and walks, poised and steady, towards the ship. Observers might call her progress haughty, despite the plainness of her dress, the paucity of her jewels and the single French waiting woman who falls in behind her. Cecily knows that the price of such hauteur is a self-control so fierce it twists the sinews of the neck into ropes. She finds some respect for the girl and resolves to show her, if she can, a little friendship.

Once aboard, Cecily decides the first kindness she can give Marguerite is a reprieve from observation, so she takes her to the cabin that has been reserved for her. It's the ship's best, of course, but small still. Even here the smell of tar is pungent and the afternoon light from its riverward window begs help from a lantern. Marguerite's nostrils flare. But wine and sweet almond cakes are laid out ready and, upon the narrow bed, are gifts with little notes that Cecily has placed but does not mention: a fair copy of *The City of Ladies* is among them, for she has been told Marguerite is a scholar; a jade rosary, because she assumes her to be devout; and a ruby set in gold that will flatter both the darkness of her hair and the pallor of her skin. The ruby's value, Cecily calculates, is greater than everything the girl stands up in today.

The waiting woman excuses herself to give directions to the porters about which of her mistress's things must be brought here to the cabin and which can be stored in the hold. There should be others to do that, but Marguerite brings no household either. When the woman is gone, Cecily watches as the girl looks carefully about, hands clasped before her. Her dark eyes widen only a fraction as the sailors' shouts penetrate the walls and Cecily feels, under her feet, the first lurch of the ship as it pulls away from the quay. A swift departure this; no fond farewells, no loved voices calling *bonne chance* across the water. Though Marguerite must journey to the mouth of the Seine and cross the Channel to find her new home, she is, in truth, already in England: a country her own has been at war with for a hundred years and she has heard named enemy all her life.

Cecily takes pity. 'I will leave you alone a while, Your Grace. I'm sure you must wish for some rest. We will dine in an hour or two, but quietly. Just my lord and I. Suffolk and his wife, Alice, who you already know. Friendly company, I hope. I will send an escort for you.'

Marguerite nods, once.

'Should I send a maid, to help you . . .?'

'Please no.' A palm is raised, a step forward almost taken. 'Marie will return and can do all I need for now.'

Cecily concedes with a nod and turns to leave. As she closes the door soft behind her, she hears a low sough of silk and smiles to know that the girl has, at least, unbent enough to take a seat upon the bed.

Their dinner is, indeed, a quiet one. Marguerite eats little. She has changed her dress and wears the ruby, which suits her well. She thanks Cecily with careful courtesy and looks pleased when all admire its effect. She is, Cecily realizes, quite lovely when she smiles. Richard's low voice seems to soothe her as he speaks of Rouen, its great cathedral and many churches, the slow glide of river that will bring them into view.

She asks questions about London; its own holy places and the palaces that will be home to her. She ventures a few words in English, cautious, painfully correct. You're practising, thinks Cecily. Well done. The English court is fluent in both languages, of course, but it is wisdom to make sure men cannot speak their secrets in your presence, or use words you don't know to trick you. In the comfort of her own tongue Marguerite speaks warmly of the French queen who, she reminds them, is her father's sister, and of her father himself who, as they must know, is king both of Naples and Jerusalem, as well as Count of Anjou. They know these titles to be empty, but they nod and speak admiringly of his influence within France and beyond it. They do not point out what all know: that Spain rules in Naples, the Holy Land is held by the Infidel, and Anjou is currently an English possession.

Watching Marguerite smile and accept their compliments, Cecily concedes that she plays a poor hand well. And though her heritage is a tarnished jewel, she has polished it to a lustre. It is the skill of making much with little. Marguerite will need it in England.

When, after an hour or two, the patina of conversation turns dull, the girl begs pardon. The journey, she says, has tired her and she will sleep now. The page pulls back her chair and, clumsy in the cramped space, the company rises. Cecily herself offers to escort her.

Outside, the cold-pinched squire who waits to escort them warns them to watch their footing. The deck has been sanded, but ropes and rails are rimed with frost and the moon is a cold blade of silver above them. They follow the mist of his breath and the pale glow of his lantern to Marguerite's door.

When they arrive there, the girl's hand reaches for the latch, then falters. She turns to Cecily as if she has made a decision. 'Your king, I am given to understand, is a man most devout, whose wish for peace with France is most earnest?'

Cecily feels surprise, a little, but schools it. 'I believe it to be his most heartfelt desire.' At least it is now, since John Beaufort's flame went out.

The girl nods. 'Good. It will be my happy duty to help him

secure it. And to change the hearts of any among his nobles who oppose that great enterprise.'

Cecily draws a breath to speak, but the door is open before she can do so. She has barely time to sketch a curtsey before it closes again and Marguerite is gone. She blinks, shakes her head and feels her eyes widen. Has this chit of a girl, not half her age, just issued a warning? She acknowledges the hit with a release of breath, turns on her heel and makes her lantern-lit way back to the warmth, where Richard, William and Alice still pick at carcasses; the new Queen and the terms that bring her to England.

In those terms Cecily finds good cause for the grey hairs on William's head and the lines that draw his mouth into a frown. He has spent a year and more, he complains, securing a deal that damns him both ways. Those in England who want an end to fighting say he has given too much for too little; that a truce is not a peace and he has sold his king into an impoverished marriage for little more than a reprieve. Those few with a will to fight on despise him utterly and spit through their teeth at the idea of a Frenchwoman bearing heirs for England.

'Have they forgotten that the King's own mother was French?' asks Richard.

'Certainly not,' Alice informs him. 'But dying was the only thing she did that ever pleased the English.'

'Either way, Marguerite's welcome will be a cold one,' says Cecily. She leans forward. 'But anyway, now you can tell us, William, why Marguerite? Would the King of France not at least offer one of his own daughters?'

'Charles would not offer a daughter, and Henry would not take one from his hands,' says William. 'He says, if Charles wants to marry a daughter to England, let him have one of York's sons. He himself will have none of them. He says, in fact, that you should make an offer.'

Richard shakes his head and Cecily laughs. 'Ha! If Charles

won't give a daughter to England's king, he certainly won't give one to York's heir. What folly.' Too foolish to think of. 'But why not for himself, does he still fear the old family madness?'

He shrugs. It seems that's not a subject he's willing to be drawn on.

'Well,' she concedes, 'Marguerite is the Queen's kin, so is free of it.'

'And as his wife's kin, much loved and valued by Charles.'

'Not so very much valued, it seems, since he sends her to England so unprovided for and ill attended. She brings little enough that our countrymen will value.'

It's not an observation meant to spike William. But it seems it does.

'Our king is well satisfied,' he retorts. 'She brings hope of peace between England and France. Is that not enough?'

Cecily smiles, conciliatory, though she thinks hope to be a poor dowry. 'For my lord and I, it is more than enough. And certainly she is very fair.' Then, beneath her breath, 'And by no means a fool.'

'It's a good marriage. The best I could make.' William runs his hands through his hair, fists them on the table before him. He's been drinking steadily all evening and has, it seems to Cecily, speeded up since Marguerite went to her bed. 'If England isn't pleased with her, it won't be my fault. I do the King's bidding. "Do what you must to bring home a peace," he said. "Stop at nothing. Concede what you have to." Concede, concede.'

His wife lays a calming hand on his arm, her voice low. 'William . . .'

He falls quiet then. Reaches to pour another drink. He looks so miserable that Cecily takes the jug and pours it for him. 'Then it's good you've held as much as you have. We at least keep territory: Normandy, Gascony and Anjou.'

'At least that,' he nods, though his face could sour milk and he looks into his wine cup rather than her eyes. Even Alice averts her gaze. Then he pulls back his shoulders, draws his hands down his face and rubs red eyes with the heels of his thumbs. 'But the truce has only a year to run, and I must turn it, in that time, into a lasting peace.'

'A year is a short time to master alchemy,' Cecily acknowledges.

It's an attempt at humour that earns her a grimace.

'Indeed. And while I am here, playing pander to girls, Gloucester has crawled out of his hiding place to whisper into Henry's ear of the glories of Agincourt and how this truce defiles the memory of all who fought there. And there are men aplenty with practised voices ready to sing descant to that song.'

Richard seeks to buoy his spirits. 'Gloucester is a spent force. The King won't listen. He's wanted peace for years. Since Beaufort's madness never more so. He'll love the man who gives it to him, William. You're safe.'

William is exasperated. 'Richard, the King listens best to the man standing closest to him, whether duke, earl or pot washer. Every hour I'm out of England I risk the tide of his will being turned against me.'

Cecily can understand that fear. They've felt it often enough, she and Richard. 'But what of my cardinal uncle?' she asks. 'Surely he is bulwark against Gloucester?'

William looks away and Alice's hand reaches across the table to rest now on Cecily's arm. 'Your uncle is little seen at court, these days.' She shakes her head. 'They say his will is written. He's old, Cecily. And since John Beaufort died . . .'

Cecily has suspected, but it is a blow to have it confirmed. For good or ill the cardinal has been at her world's centre all her life. She's rarely sought his advice, never trusted it when given, but has asked herself, many times and at critical junctures: what would my uncle do now? Of all people, she thinks, he should die at the height of his powers, not grieving alone for John Beaufort's wreckage. Who would have thought he'd turn foolish in the end?

Into the room's new quiet, where only the creak of rigging can be heard, William speaks. 'How I do miss John Bedford.'

Yes, Cecily remembers. They were friends, of course. Clearheaded John of Bedford and his loyal captain, William de la Pole.

'Aye,' Richard smiles. 'Bedford here in France, Gloucester in England and the cardinal straddling the sea to keep the peace between them both.' His voice has longing in it, as if he speaks of a simpler time.

Simpler, yes. And safer too. Power had been knotted tight between those three, and the child king bound up safe somewhere inside it. Now the King is grown, the knot is loosed and, in her mind's eye, Cecily sees Henry's pale, dry fingers fumbling at the threads. William is right to worry. He has placed himself very close to the King since Bedford died. He's done well enough by it. A marquess now, King's Councillor and a rich man. But it's hard to say no to the man who owns you. If that man says pay any price for peace, you will do it. Even if you think it's too much. Even if he might change his mind. She finds her eyes narrowing as she watches him turn the empty wine cup in his hand. She remembers how he looked away when they spoke of territories and wonders if he has paid a higher price than he admits to.

When William speaks, his voice is bitter. 'And we're left with nothing but a weathervane king. And Gloucester, blustering in his ear.'

Cecily pours him a little more wine. 'Perhaps the Queen will keep him on the straight and narrow path to peace you have set.'

He takes a gulp, nods as if the idea is new and worth thinking of. 'She's a sharp little thing, that one.'

Cecily remembers Marguerite's firm hand, her stiff neck, her resolution and her warning. 'I would make her my friend, if I were you.'

17

March–April 1445
Rouen

Velvet on velvet. It is the richest fabric in the world. Cecily
holds the heavy white weight of it against her face and
breathes. It seems the scents of an Italian summer are trapped
in its folds, or that, by some magic, the tiny marguerites pat-
terned in its alternating depths carry the perfume of true
flowers. It is the best, the finest. Months in the making, with
wealth in every thread. For its sake the weavers of Lucca are
made prisoner, forbidden to leave their city lest they sell their
skills to rival silk houses in Florence or Milan. At Cecily's
order it has been crafted into the most beautiful gown she has
ever seen, lined with ermine, threaded with silver, edged
with a hundred pearls. She takes a last breath of its glory; lets
it go with a sigh of regret. This was for Marguerite, for her
arrival into Rouen. And beside it lies its sister in crimson,
which she, Cecily herself, would have worn. Now the crimson must be packed away and Alice, William's wife, stands
waiting in her shift for the ocean of white to be lapped about
her shoulders.

'She is fifteen, I am forty,' Alice complains, holding out her
arms as waiting women approach with the gown in their
arms. 'No one will ever believe me to be her. I'm ten years
older even than you! You should be doing this.'

Cecily is unmoved. 'You are dark-haired and her equal for
height. I am a hand's breadth taller, and fair. You'll be seen

from a distance. All you need do is smile –' she shows her how, demure first, then sly – 'and look fertile.' She turns for the door. So much to do. 'And let down your hair, Alice. You are a virgin queen for the day.'

Down the stairs with brisk steps, Cecily leaves the merchant's house that's been commandeered for their preparations and finds Richard, hovering on the doorstep. 'Will she be ready?' he asks.

'Alice? Yes.'

'Alice then.' He nods. He knows her plan and is ready to carry it out.

They look together along the quayside, where the gold-bedecked chariot Henry has sent from England awaits his queen, and nervous groomsmen trim the harness of the six white palfreys sent to draw it. She can hear Talbot's booming voice lining up the honour guard, the scrape of steel as they come into line. The air is thick with anticipation and noise, the strike of metal-clad feet against cobbles, the snap of banners in a cold wind from the river and all the bustle of a boat's unloading.

A groom struggles to bring up Richard's new black stallion. It's skittering and nervous, dancing on hoof tips and shaking out its polished mane from a short, arched neck.

'Showy,' says Cecily. 'Don't fall off it.'

He winks at her, smiling, as he pulls on his gloves. 'Not as showy as that crimson gown of yours. I'm sorry not to see you in it.'

'Ah well. A check to my pride, perhaps.'

He leans in to kiss her cheek. 'You will always outshine her you know. She is a queen and very lovely, but you are York's royal duchess. The mother of my sons.'

She lays a hand against his shoulder, drawing him towards her to confide. 'She's not very lovely this morning,' she whispers. 'Grey as a fish and sick as a dog. Anyway –' she pushes him away now to her arm's length – 'get on with you, there's much to do.'

Then she's on the move again, on to the ship and across the deck to the Queen's cabin, to the bed Marguerite has not risen from since their dinner together two nights ago.

Yesterday, Cecily had decided that her advice to William, to make Marguerite his friend, was so good she should follow it herself. But the hour for breakfast had passed and the Queen's door remained resolutely closed. It was almost noon before the little French waiting lady, Marie, squeezed timidly around the door jamb clutching a covered pot and, with face averted, tipped it over the ship's side.

'You know, we have people to do such things.' Cecily had been waiting. 'You should not be expected to . . .' She waved a hand in the direction of the pot, which the woman tried to hide within the curve of her body. Cecily noticed hair escaping from her coif, dark smudges under her eyes and the smell about her of something worse than night soil. 'Is your mistress sick?' Cecily stepped to the door and placed her own hand upon the latch.

'My lady, my mistress wishes none to wait upon her but myself for the moment. If you would . . .' She tried to pass.

'I asked if your mistress was sick.'

'It's the movement of the river, my lady, it has unsettled her stomach. And it is the bleeding time with her, I . . .'

'Then I must attend her.'

'No, please . . .'

'Indeed yes. Tomorrow she comes to Rouen as England's queen. She must ride through the city and be seen by her people. Now I must see her to know if she can do that. Or to understand what can be done to make her able.'

When she opened the door the smell of sickness was heavy, tinged with the copper tang of blood.

The young Queen, ashen upon the bed, had heard her. 'I will be ready, Duchess Cecily, when the time comes, to do whatever is required of me.'

But the time has come, and she is not ready. Though they've dosed her for a day and a night with willow bark and lemon balm, her stomach still betrays her and her shivering legs won't bear her weight. Cecily herself has barely slept for tending her.

Coming in now from the cold quayside, Cecily sighs to see the girl struggle to stand upright, pushing Marie aside with gritted teeth, furious tears threatening her eyes.

Two steps take Cecily to the girl's side. 'Lie down, Your Grace. Please.'

'It is required that I enter Rouen as England's Queen . . .'

'I think you cannot.'

The girl is clinging to the bedpost. Cecily dares to put hands under her elbows; to ease her down to sitting on the bed. She holds her by the shoulders and looks, direct, into her face. 'Listen. I know very well the things you must do. None better. And I commend the strength of your will to do them. But, sometimes, another way has to be found.'

The girl screws her eyes, turns away.

'Your Grace, look at me. If you ride into Rouen today and faint in its streets, they will say you are a weak woman, not fit to be Queen. And you may be sure the news of that will cross to England faster than a gull can fly. Marguerite, you must always appear strong, even when you are not.'

She sobs in frustration. 'Then what am I to do?'

'Trust me. Alice will take your place. It is already arranged.'

'Alice?' The girl is not so sick she cannot be incredulous.

Cecily shrugs. 'The people will see what they expect to see: a dark-haired lady, richly dressed. She will applaud their pageants, blush at their compliments and, when they fall down drunk, she'll pretend not to notice. Nothing more is required. Then, when the fanfare is over, you and I, and Marie here, will be carried through quiet streets to a comfortable bed, where you can rest till you are well.'

The girl shakes her head, cautious of the pain in it. 'Surely the escort will know.'

'They are my people. They know what I tell them to know.' She tightens her grip on the girl's shoulders. 'Your Grace. Marguerite. Listen to me. I give you a good lesson, learn it. When it is impossible to do a thing, you must simply find a way to make it appear to be done.'

They wait a secret hour in the dim-lit cabin, intent on the quayside bustle and noise until, at last, a hush. Marguerite's hand snakes from the sheets. Cecily takes it on to her lap, holds it close between her own and looks down into the girl's pale face, her wide eyes. 'Trust me.'

Then comes the sergeant's call; a clarion of trumpets and a clattering of hooves as the procession moves off.

Cecily leans closer. 'Wait.'

The first cheers seem low, hesitant, then they rise, jubilant and soaring, drowning all other sound. Cecily imagines Alice, resplendent, waving from her chariot as she passes through the gates and into the city streets.

Marguerite sighs and lets her eyes fall closed.

Cecily smiles down on her, gives her hand a single squeeze. 'There. You see?'

In three days Marguerite is back on her feet. By Good Friday, well enough to tread, barefoot and solemn, to the castle's chapel for Tenebrae where, in the cold dark before dawn, Christ's passion is remembered.

Kneeling beside her, Cecily curls icy toes into the furred lining of her gown and watches from beneath lowered lashes. Marguerite's feet, she imagines, do not scorn cold stone as hers do, nor does she seem distracted from her prayers. Perhaps Henry will find in her a match for his own fervour. An anchor for his wandering will.

That would be a blessing.

She hides a grin in her cloak's collar, helped by a growing darkness. The service is ending. The choir's voices, and the chapel's many candles, are extinguished, one by one. Nothing remains but a single flame, cupped in the priest's hands; reminder to a sorrowing world that even the darkest times can be lived through.

'Thanks be to God for his mercy,' Marguerite whispers in her sibilant French.

Cecily reins in her thoughts and adds, 'Amen.'

Save for the feasts of Easter, when Marguerite is shown to the city and introduced to its lords, the days that follow are spent quietly. No ostentatious celebrations, no formal audiences. 'You'll have more than you'll ever want of all that when you get to England,' Cecily tells her. 'Take time now to gather your strength.'

The girl seems content to do so. In the mornings they ride the riverbanks, where the trees are hung with hoar frost and long winter grasses splinter against their horses' legs. They visit the white-painted abbeys of Saint Ouen and Saint George, where Marguerite asks time alone to pray. Cecily does not know how she herself should speak to God of Marguerite. What she should ask for. Happiness would be conventional, she supposes. Fertility. But the word that comes most readily to her lips is endurance.

In the afternoons the cold drives them indoors. Marguerite talks fashion with Jacquetta and poetry with Alice and, with Cecily, she views the wealthy trousseau that awaited her in Rouen. King Henry, who baulked at the price required to save Dieppe, has stinted nothing to enrich his bride with all that will make her queenly. Cecily had the choosing of it all. Gowns and jewels, velvets and furs, towering hennins, and linens so sheer a nun could read scripture through them. The white gown with its silver girdle Cecily keeps till last, and even Marguerite's well-schooled face cannot hide her wonder. When she is dressed in it, and turns from the mirror to be admired, when she takes off her smile and puts on her imperious face, even Cecily is impressed.

'You are every inch a queen.'

'I am sorry I lost the chance to wear it.'

'It will come again. Wear it in London, when you are welcomed to the city.'

Jacquetta steps forward, fussy, to adjust the line of a fold, to smooth the nap of white fur at Marguerite's shoulder. 'Yes, wear it then, of course. King Henry will swoon for love of you,' she laughs into her ear, 'and all the men of England will lay their hearts at your feet.'

Marguerite's sigh is rueful, as if she sets as little store by that fairy tale as Cecily herself does. But she turns again to the mirror, raises her chin and courts her own reflection.

Their last day together is come. Tomorrow Marguerite will take ship for England with William and Alice. Jacquetta and her golden Woodville, too, who have petitioned Richard for release. With peace at hand, Woodville claims, his warlike captaincy is no longer needed, and it is time to take his family home.

When Richard tells her this, Cecily arches her brow. 'It's more that the bee scents a richer honeypot,' she tells him. 'There's better fortune to be made in England now, buzzing about the Queen.' But she'll miss Jacquetta, in truth. A daily irritation, a whetstone for her wit.

And their children will miss each other. She and Jacquetta each have four now, though Jacquetta has another coming.

Cecily's youngest, little Elizabeth, was the gift of last year's autumn, red-cheeked and healthful as an apple. Jacquetta herself and Talbot stood godparents. Cecily would not have given either of them a son.

Jacquetta is making herself useful, fussing about the packing of Marguerite's bags and chests; supervising Cecily's servants, who are so well trained they need no supervision.

Cecily takes the opportunity to escape and invites the Queen to walk with her in the gardens. Though the cold is bitter, a weak sun draws out what little colour remains; beech leaves, mostly, bronze and tenacious, clinging to branches like hope. It seems to Cecily that Marguerite welcomes the stillness of it.

They step along gravelled walkways between herb beds that will live again, in a month or two.

'I'm sorry not to see it in summer,' says Marguerite.

'Summer will come to you in England,' Cecily tells her. 'And there are better gardens there, for certain. At Windsor and especially at Greenwich, by the river.'

'And are we likely to see you in England soon?'

'As the King wills it. Richard's term of office here is up before the year's end.'

'Does he wish for home?'

Cecily thinks hard before she answers. Marguerite's questions are never idle. 'Your coming has been the crowning glory of all he has achieved here.' She smiles. 'But I think he'd like to stay a while. It would be a very different thing to govern here in peacetime and would suit his talents better. Richard is not a warlike man.'

'Yet he wishes to govern still. England in France, as ever. My countrymen suffer for it. My father himself is Count of Anjou, though he is kept from it by an English garrison that answers to your husband.'

'Who governs it on your husband's behalf.' She takes a

breath and dares. 'Your Grace, if I may. When we marry we must balance new loyalties with old.'

When Marguerite stops and looks thoughtful at her, Cecily turns and holds her gaze.

After a breath, two, three, Marguerite nods and walks on. 'It is good advice.' Then, moments later, 'Ah. We are no longer alone.'

From beyond the hedge that borders the herb garden come childish squeals and the sound of women's voices. They pass through an arch to a terrace and look down on to a lawn. Annette, who has rule of all Cecily's nursery now, has bundled her charges in warm clothes and brought them into the air. Five-year-old Anne paces quietly, clutching the skirt of a young attendant in whose arms her baby sister is parcelled. Edmund toddles along, holding determinedly to his nurse's fingers and the encouragement of her words. Edward, brighter than the sun in Cecily's eyes, runs squealing between them, brandishing two-handed a miniature sword.

Cecily laughs. 'Shall we go down and join them?'

'No, let's just watch.'

Marguerite has kept her distance from the children in the time she has been here. They've been shown to her, of course, but she did not pet them or coo as other young women might. It's understandable perhaps. Like Cecily, Marguerite is the youngest of a brood. Babes that came after, and too many that came before, died early. Such things will weigh on any woman's mind, especially as she goes to her wedding.

'Your son is very tall.' Edward is attacking a newly planted apple tree that shivers at his blows. 'And, unlike his father, seems very warlike.'

18

On the night before her daughter's wedding, Cecily dreams of her mother. They walk together, soft-shoed and silent, towards the door of Raby's chapel where Richard, who sleeps beside her now, waits with her father. She gazes up along the length of her brocaded arm to where her small hand disappears among her mother's fingers. She knows this is the day she will be given to her future. Her mother looks down at her, nods once. Ready? Yes. She awakes and her hand is her own again. The dream's passing leaves a cold space in her breast.

Lying in the dark now she thinks of little Anne, six years old. She will take her by the hand tomorrow, lead her to the chapel here in Hatfield, and give her to young Henry Holland. She dislikes the boy already. This morning, when his father introduced groom to bride, and Anne made her carefully schooled curtsey, Henry's lips had curled before they smiled. While the parents admired the bride-to-be, he had shown more interest in his dogs: Alaunt hounds, broad-headed fighters that stood taller than Anne, had foul breath and pissed against the tapestries.

'He's fifteen and she's a child.' Richard soothed her concerns when she spoke of them. 'He'll warm to her as she grows.'

'You never looked so at me.'

'I would not have dared.' When she did not return his smile he put it away, took her hands instead. 'Look, it will be well enough. John Holland is a good man. He'll take care of her till she comes of age and his son comes to his senses.'

'Let's not scruple to name our purpose, Richard. John Holland is fifty years old and ailing. When he dies the boy will be Duke of Exeter and Anne his duchess.'

And for that reason she will put aside her doubts and give Anne to Henry Holland. She will send her into the household of the boy's father and his third wife, who is not Henry's mother and doesn't much look as if she likes him either. She will do it for a dukedom and for ever-closer ties to the old royal house, for the network of affinity that will keep York strong. John Holland traces his descent, as she does – and Richard – from the third Edward and calls the King his cousin.

On that long-gone morning when she was taken to Richard, her mother had knelt down, looked deep into her face and asked, 'Do you like him well enough?' Five years later, when she had reached the age of knowing, before she spoke her vows again to make them firm, her mother asked once more, 'Are you content?'

Cecily's answer had been a certain, 'Yes.'

In the time between, she had studied him and seen her own nature mirrored in his. She trusted his careful watchfulness, admired his certain actions. She knew that, like her, he read people as if they were books, and that he would return to her pages, again and again. He had taught her chess till she could beat all her brothers, and did not laugh when she asked why the queen was the only lady on the board. Lying here, though, in the dark while he sleeps, she wonders what would have happened had she told her mother no. She believes it would have made no difference. So, tomorrow, with Anne, she will not ask. Better not to know that she is giving her daughter to a man she cannot like.

The King comes to the wedding. And Marguerite, of course. They arrive in royal state at the Bishop of Ely's residence at

Hatfield, which has provided near-to-London lodgings for the Yorks since they returned from France before Christmas, their term of office there ended. As dusk falls, the King and Queen are drawn into the candlelit hall, shedding furs and frost.

King Henry wraps Richard in his arms and calls him brother, his partner in peace, and thanks him for all he has done to build amity with France.

Cecily smiles and holds her tongue. We might have done more, had you paid us better.

William de la Pole, who travels as a limpet on the royal keel, stands watching, chafing his hands, but does not smile until the King claps him on the shoulder too, and calls him friend.

When Cecily bows to Marguerite, the young Queen draws her up and kisses her on the cheek with winter-cold lips. 'You give away one child today, but another is coming I see.'

Cecily runs a hand across the swollen silk of her dress, pleased. 'A spring baby.' She has noted that the Queen, who was slender last winter, is slender still.

Marguerite, too quick to miss the slide of Cecily's eyes, is rueful. 'No such blessing for me yet. Though all your English court watch for it. But a child is not the only font of joy. She smiles at William. My Lord of Suffolk is lately back from France. He does much to please me there. And his king, of course.' She places a hand on her husband's sleeve.

He turns to her, blinking, as if surprised to see her.

Marguerite takes back her hand, shakes her head. 'You will learn all in good time, Duchess Cecily. But we will have peace. And your king and I will go into France soon.'

'And you will come with us, Richard,' says Henry, beaming. 'And William here, too. You are our partners in this peace you know.'

Richard bows.

Only Cecily marks his pleasure. No doubt he sees in this

the confirmation he has hoped for, that his lieutenancy will be renewed.

'I will return to France whenever your order sends me there, Your Grace.'

The servants have brought up wine, and Cecily smiles as she hands a cup to Marguerite. 'We both will, of course.' She hands another to William, who will not catch her eye.

'Good, good,' says Henry, taking his own cup from Richard's hand. 'Now to loving business. We are here to see your daughter wed.'

So Cecily goes and fetches little Anne to the gilded chapel, bare of flowers in this winter season, shivering with candlelight.

As the door opens for them, all faces but one turn towards them, palely shining. Then the groom, nudged by his father, raises his sullen head.

'Are you ready?' she asks her daughter.

And Anne nods.

So she leads her by the hand to Henry Holland, who hurries his vows and pets his dogs that have followed him to church.

When it's done she brings the child back to her nurse. But before her daughter is led away, she kneels and looks deep into the small, stern face. 'It is well done, Anne. I am pleased.'

A little colour comes to the bone-pale cheeks and, almost, the girl smiles.

The next day dawns colder still, with sheets of pink cast against a silver sky and beads of frost glimmering on the muzzles of the Alaunt hounds. They make big-pawed nuisances of themselves, snuffling the ground between the horses' legs. Their master is mounted already, downing cup after cup of the warmed wine handed out by grooms to keep sluggish blood from freezing. Anne is little more than a parcel of furs when the nurse lifts her from her mother's side into the carriage, then draws herself heavily in beside her.

Cecily watches a small white hand worm from the furry bundle and wrap itself tight about the nurse's chapped finger. 'Has she no gloves?'

The nurse loosens the child's grip and plunges Anne's empty fist back beneath the furs. Opposite her, John Holland's wife reaches down for one of the wool-wrapped hot stones placed there for their comfort, and lays it in Anne's lap. 'Here. Hold this for heat.' Then to Cecily, with a shrug, 'She looks well enough wrapped.'

Cecily nods and looks about her. The escort is ready, its horses breathing smoke into sharp air. She's impatient, now, for them to be away. She has her own journey to make. While Anne travels to a new life in Devon, she goes to Cambridge with the King. She wants to see what he does with the money he will not spend on his French garrisons.

At last, here comes John Holland, pulling his cloak about him, and Richard hurrying him down the steps, speaking fast. This weather will do the old duke no good. She wonders if Richard reminds him to have a care for his own health, or for their daughter's who is now in his charge. She sighs. A little late for that now.

They ride towards Cambridge along a swollen River Cam, on a path that skirts its sodden water meadows, sheened by a low sun. The day is bright at least and, if she keeps her chin dipped in her cloak's furred collar, Cecily is not cold. By noon, she can hear the sound of building over the suck of hooves in mud; the ring of hammers growing steadily louder, until she can find men's voices among them, calling out to one another as they work. At last the teetering scaffolds come into view. She raises a hand to shield her eyes and squints. Yes, it is every bit as ambitious as she has heard.

At the entrance to the site Edmund Beaufort waits to greet the King and to court the Queen with smiles. He is Somerset now. Watching him, Cecily decides that, if ever his heart had burned with grief for his fiery brother, then the gift of John's earldom has quenched the flames.

'He's quite handsome now that he has less cause to be sullen,' Cecily whispers to Richard as they step behind the King, between stones that await the mason's hammer. 'But why is he here?'

'He came a day early to make sure all was ready for the King.'

'Lest the royal boots be sullied by builders' dust?'

'Cecily, you may always be sure of one thing. Wherever the King comes, Edmund Beaufort will be there already, or arrive soon. He gives service like a Southwark strumpet; with energy and in expectation of payment.'

'Well, he is a poor man, Richard.' Cecily laughs quietly. 'He got his brother's earldom but little of its land. And most of the money is in Brittany's pockets. He has little choice but to play the whore.'

She's not surprised to hear Richard so bitter. He's spent most of the past month in Parliament, watching Edmund Beaufort play for the King's attention and get it, while William de la Pole holds sway in the cardinal's empty spaces. Meanwhile his own pleas, that money should not be diverted from England's French defences, have gone unheeded.

She has heard of Edmund's needling, on dark nights when her husband has ridden home for respite.

'My Lord of York, we are at peace with France. Have you who were so lately there, forgotten?' Edmund had smiled at the watching King.

And the King had smiled back.

Richard had addressed himself to the man he thought mattered. 'Your Grace, you know I work for peace as hard as any man, but our truce is not yet a treaty. And while we starve our garrisons of funds and men, Charles is building a standing army. If we want to bring him to a peace we must at least make him believe we're willing to fight for what's ours.'

'Indeed,' Cecily shrugged. 'Or what need Charles to come to terms at all?'

Richard held out his hands. 'Exact.'

'So, what did the King say then?'

'That I should have more faith in his dear wife's uncle.'

'Can he really be so simple?'

Richard grimaced, shrugged his shoulders. 'And then, of course, Gloucester was on his feet, spitting and snarling with his usual tirade: that Henry is giving away his father's legacy; that England must fight on in France. That the Queen is Charles's spy in the King's bed.'

'Perhaps he's right. About the Queen anyway. But dare he really accuse the King so openly?'

'Oh, he's sense at least to blame Suffolk and Beaufort for leading Henry by the nose.'

She laughed. 'Right again!' Then more serious, 'But he should have a care. He courts powerful enemies.' She did not say, as might you. And the Queen among them.

'And he prevents my voice from being heard. I find myself playing Edmund's game, vying like a doxy for time with the King, for only when I can get him alone can I talk sense to him. And every other moment of the day I'm wondering what foolishness is being poured into his ears by others.'

'Last summer, William de la Pole was on your side, telling the King to spend money in France.'

'Well, he is very silent on the subject now.'

'Why do you think that is?'

Richard turned the bull's blood ruby ring about his finger three more times before answering her. 'Because the King told him he sounded like the Duke of Gloucester.' He turned from the fire then, and looked into Cecily's eyes. 'William says, when you start to sound like Gloucester, it's probably time to shut up.'

'My Lady Cecily,' the king's voice calls to her now, from ahead.

She gives Richard a rueful smile and strides forward to where Henry and Marguerite stand, and where Edmund Beaufort and William de la Pole strut like peacocks amid a clutch of clerics.

'Lady Cecily –' the King welcomes her as she approaches, and Richard, who has fallen in behind her – 'you, more than any, must see what we do here.'

They have moved through the low foundation walls of the college buildings and here, opening out before her, is the cloister, its pathways pegged, and the chapel sketched beyond it. The space is vast, and the stacks of pearl-white stone at its perimeter promise towering height. Men swarm everywhere about it, measuring, moving, hammering and shaping.

The noise of it is suddenly deafening. Henry grimaces.

Edmund Beaufort is immediately solicitous. 'We could halt the work while you tour . . .'

Henry holds up a hand and smiles. 'I would not have them lose an hour for my comfort,' he says. 'It is the Lord's work they do. Lady Cecily, Richard . . .' He draws them forward. 'You, who have given Fotheringhay to God, will understand. This is our gift to Him, a palace of faith and learning that will outshine any in England.'

She follows his eyes as they look up, sparkling and light-filled. It's as if he sees into another world, where the work is finished already; where traceried windows finger the heavens and the sound of hammers is translated into song.

She answers him honestly, that Fotheringhay is nothing to this. That none but God's anointed could give so rich a gift. She knows the cost of Fotheringhay and imagines what is being spent here. She knows, too, that it is doubled. Twin colleges at Cambridge and Eton; twin mouths sucking and gulping at the withered teat of the royal exchequer.

'And surely it will be rewarded,' he smiles, serene. 'In return for our gift He will give us peace. Peace with France and with all men of honour.' The royal finger extends, ring-freighted, to rest on Richard's breast. 'Better we spend our money here, Richard, eh? Give this to God and trust His strength to defend our garrisons in France.'

Beside her husband, Marguerite speaks, soft. 'Quite so, Your Grace.'

19

January–February 1447
   Fotheringhay

Merlin meets skylark in bone-shattering collision. Locked in their wing-clattering fall, the birds spiral down and the falconer's boy lumbers through snow to retrieve the prey.

Cecily raises her glove to recall her hawk, lifts a brow to Richard and grins. 'I've bested you.' There are a dozen larks in her basket.

Richard's groom has a brace of rabbits slung at his saddle's pommel.

'Do you intend to leave any alive?' he asks her. Then, with a nod, he guides her eyes along the river to a rising bank of cloud. 'Best beat that weather home, I think.'

Riding into Fotheringhay's bailey, they encounter a melee. Men, grooms and horses battle rising snow flurries and a freshening wind. At the centre of it, William de la Pole, swiping ice from his shoulders and a dewdrop from his nose.

'Epiphany eve, William,' Cecily calls out to him. 'Are you a wise man bringing gifts?'

He smiles up at them. 'Wise enough to arrive at your homecoming, it seems.' He rubs his gloved hands together, looks a little shamefaced at the bustle about him, smiles again. 'I should have sent word that I was coming but . . . well, here I am.'

And twenty of your followers I've now to find room for, thinks Cecily. 'You're welcome, of course. We've been hawking, along the river. The sky was clear for it, before this weather blew up.'

Richard is on the ground already, stepping forward with a laughing embrace. 'We needed the air. And a break from the feasting.' With his arms about William's winter-wrapped bulk, he looks over his shoulder to Cecily. His smile gone.

What now? his eyes ask her.

She shrugs.

If the King's limpet has prised himself from court at Christmas, it's not likely he brings good news. She hands her hooded merlin to the falconer's waiting glove, puts cold-numbed feet to the mounting block and slides from the saddle.

A waiting woman steps forward to straighten her skirts, but Cecily has no patience for it. She ignores her, kicks them into order herself and makes for the steps. 'Let's out of this weather before we freeze.'

Good or not, any news will be welcome after a year of uncertainty and second-guessing. Richard's council still administers Normandy in his name, but the renewal of his lieutenancy is not yet confirmed. The King still speaks of going to France and bringing home a treaty, but the date of departure is never fixed and no one believes, anyway, that he will go – or that he should. There have been delegations from the French court, but Richard hasn't been invited to them or told of their conclusions. They know the French king still demands lands for peace, so the stalemate holds.

If any know Henry's mind, William does. But he's been an opaque window into it. He's done little more than urge patience and complain of being much put upon by Henry's fickle nature.

By autumn they'd had enough and Richard brought them back to Fotheringhay. 'I've business of my own to tend,' he'd said. 'If they want me they can send for me.'

But they haven't sent.

And now here is William, fidgeting and smiling too much, and slow to the point. He's brought gifts from the King and Queen. 'Reminders of their love,' he calls them. He's drunk their wine, eaten their Twelfth Night feast and laughed at the antics of their Lord of Misrule. He has chucked the chin of May-born baby Margaret, exclaimed how tall the boys have grown and applauded Elizabeth's teetering steps. He's alone with them now, in Richard's chamber at the dog end of the evening, turning a half-empty wine glass in his hand.

And so, because he is yet to tell them why he is here, Cecily asks.

He puts down the glass, rubs the side of his nose and clasps his hands before him. 'The Bastard of Orléans came to the King before Christmas.'

'A welcome sight he must have been,' remarks Richard.

Jean of Orléans is the French king's natural cousin and no lover of the English. He led the assault that robbed them of Paris and, before that, rode in Joan of Arc's vanguard. More warrior than diplomat.

'Aye, well. He was sent to say that Charles will not extend the truce beyond April.' He stops, draws a breath. 'Unless we surrender Anjou and Maine.'

Richard's gaze is steady. 'If you were smiling now, William, I'd assume you're about to tell me that the King has released funds to defend these territories.'

'I am not smiling, Richard.' He takes up the glass again, drinks, turns it in his hand and sets it down. 'Henry has agreed it. Anjou and Maine. Gone.'

Cecily watches Richard's face and sees the lines deepen between mouth and jaw.

'A gambit, William, surely?' His voice is low; he has turned his eyes to the fire and the bull's blood ruby turns and turns.

William's head sways, side to side. 'It is certain fact,

Richard. The King offered them to Charles last winter –' he looks up at them both – 'Anjou and Maine for a twenty-year truce. I carried the letter myself.'

Of course. Cecily remembers Marguerite's pleasure in it. 'My Lord of Suffolk is lately back from France,' she'd said at Anne's wedding. 'He does much to please me there.'

'But William, there are a good many English settlers to think of. How are they to be moved or recompensed in a quarter year?' she asks.

'We'll play for time, of course. But it will be done.'

Richard is up and pacing. From the end of the room he speaks. 'William, how could he . . . how could you . . .?'

William, too, now rises to his feet. 'What choice, Richard? What choice? I have said, again and again, the policy I pursue in France is the King's. Not my own.'

'And the Queen's, perhaps,' says Cecily.

William shrugs. 'Since her father is Count of Anjou, I dare say.'

Well played, Marguerite, Cecily concedes. But how badly England's own hand has been bungled. There's a sour taste in her mouth, born of disgust rather than the wine she's drunk. She scorns to look at William, his red face, his shot eyes. The shame in him. The bluster. How pitiable to be so spineless. No, she corrects. How pitiable to be so tethered to a weak king's will.

She sighs. Let's to the point. 'William,' she asks. 'Are you come to ask for our support?'

'I am here to say –' he takes a drink – 'that the King urges you to welcome this peace.'

'This you say for the King, William.' Richard's voice is colder than Cecily has ever heard it. 'What say you for yourself?'

William sets down the glass and spreads his hands. 'That we cannot hold France if the King will not fight. And since the

137

King will not fight, we must have a peace. We will play for time to surrender Anjou and Maine. We will manage it . . . somehow. But, Richard. In all truth, what's the alternative?'

Richard comes back to the fire, snatches a glass from the table as he passes and folds into a chair. 'I only wonder what the Duke of Gloucester must make of this.'

William sits too. 'I am sure that, when he knows of it, he will make his views known to any who will listen.'

Richard grunts. 'Nor do I think your friend Edmund Beaufort will be easily convinced. Or the cardinal. Their interests in Maine are vast and Edmund its governor.'

William's fists are clenched, thumbs tight against his lips. 'They are to be compensated.'

Richard's eyebrow begs the question.

William swallows, blinks slowly, fixes his eye on Richard and speaks. 'Edmund is named Governor of Normandy. Lieutenant of France. Whatever remains of it.' He shrugs. 'It was done at Christmas. I thought it best you hear it from me.'

Richard's shock is an explosion of breath that fills the room. She feels it as he does; a sword in his belly, a blow to his breast. But, as William's gaze intensifies, her head is alight with certain knowledge: William has come to sound them. And they will be fools if they trust him.

She feels Richard rising beside her, hears him draw a breath to speak. She is on her feet, her hand flat against his breast before she knows it. 'Say nothing, Richard. Say nothing now.' She looks into his face, holds his eyes with her own, waits for him to blink, give a shadow of a nod. 'Goodnight, William. It is much to hear and all unexpected. It is kind of you, to have come so far in such weather with such news. Let's speak again in the morning. If this is peace, then we take joy in it.'

She hears William rise behind her; moments later, his voice from the door. 'The King loves you, Richard. He will make good your loss, trust me. Only have patience. Only keep with us.'

She feels the rise and fall of breath in Richard's breast. Then the door clicks and William is gone.

Next noon they ride with William to the Great North Road and see him on his way.

At the crossroads he leans from his horse, takes Richard's hand, looks full in his face. 'King's men, Richard?'

Cecily is proud of the firm answer Richard is able to give him.

'King's men, William.'

They've told him they will be patient. They are the King's loyal subjects. They will not oppose any peace bought with the surrender of Anjou and Maine. Richard will not add his voice to Gloucester's or any other party's, either in condemnation of policy or in a call for war. Nor will he contest Beaufort's appointment to the post he had made his own and in which he achieved so much. They will meet again in February, and with the King, at the New Year's Parliament.

They have made William sure of them, but they are less sure of themselves.

In the dark shelter of last night's bed they loosed thoughts long caged. That the King is not fit to rule. That he is ruled himself by whoever's voice speaks loudest in his ear. God's, presumably.

The Beauforts', always.

The Queen's, too, now.

'Then our choices are stark, Richard,' said Cecily. 'Either we seek to rule him ourselves . . .'

'I will not play whore to him as Edmund Beaufort does.'

'. . . or we oppose him.'

He was silent three breaths. 'Rebellion?'

The word is a spark. They could start a fire with it, or smother it now in their fingertips.

She put her lips to his shoulder.

'My father died a traitor,' he reminded her.

'But you are only a traitor if you lose.'

He drew her hand to his breast then. Held it there a long time in silence.

He was examining his heart, she knew. She was remembering the clarity of a frost-bright morning. Throwing her merlin after skylarks. Relishing the speed of the hawk's climb; the cleanness of its strike.

'No,' he said at last. 'Endanger body and soul to put Gloucester on the throne? An old man, and childless? It would be madness.'

That had not been her thought, exactly, but she did not say so.

'Then what?'

'We bide. We wait and see. I will be the King's man still. But we look to our own . . .'

'And we build our power?'

He kissed her fingers, still clenched in his. 'That has never been a question.'

By February's end there is no longer a childless old man for whom Richard might endanger anything.

So often excluded, Gloucester must have been surprised by a summons to the Parliament in Bury. More so when he arrives and finds William de la Pole and Edmund Beaufort waiting to arrest him. They tell him he has plotted treason. That, like his wife, he has sought the King's death, coveted his throne. The next morning, he suffers an apoplexy and, two days later, dies of it. So the official report reads. Only brave men or fools would question it, when William de la Pole is firing out arrest orders for Gloucester's retainers as fast as an archer looses arrows. There are enough, though, that the old man's body, naked and white as a candle, is laid out in Bury's cathedral, where any man might seek in it the secret of his end.

Richard forbids Cecily to go. She is with child again. Such a thing could blight a babe in the womb.

'No mark on him,' he tells her when he returns to their lodging; when he has closed the door and checked they are alone.

'Of course not. When a man's heart is old and tired you don't need a sword to pierce it.'

He nods, throws his gloves on to the bed. 'No, indeed.'

She comes to him. Hands him a paper. 'A note from William. You are summoned to the King.'

He reads, sighs. Rubs his face. Picks up his gloves again. 'Then I'd best be about it.' He hesitates a moment as she, too, rises to go.

'What?' she asks. 'Am I not York too?'

The King wears black and his eyes are red-rimmed, as if he has wept. He rises to greet them, accepts their obeisance. 'Cousin –' he lays a hand on Richard's arm – 'Lady Cecily, how do you bear it? I am sure, like us, you deeply grieve the loss of our dear uncle.'

Behind him, black as crows, William de la Pole, Beaufort and the Queen have not been weeping. Though their faces are solemn, there is the shadow of a smirk about Beaufort's lips and William is fidgeting with his cuffs as if fascinated by them. The Queen's face is unreadable, locked on Richard.

'He gave Your Grace good service for many years,' Richard acknowledges. 'And if he has lately turned from that . . .'

'In my youth, Richard.' The King raises a finger, suddenly imperious. 'In my youth he served me well and I loved him.' Fresh tears spill from his eyes. 'It is bitter to believe that, now I am a man, he could wish me dead.'

William steps to the King's side, his eyes on Richard. 'And we grieve, Your Grace, that death has robbed him of the chance to prove his innocence.'

That imperious finger, trembling now, comes to rest on

Richard's breast. The tears are gone and his eyes blink and dart. 'Do you think him innocent, Richard?'

How to answer?

'If he is,' says Cecily, 'then God will surely comfort him. As He will Your Grace. If not, then . . .'

'How wise is your wife, Richard.' The King nods, slow. 'How precious a helpmeet.'

'And blessed with so many children.' Behind her husband, the Queen's French voice is soft.

'Yes.' The King's finger is now a closed fist, tapping lightly on Richard's breast. 'Yes.' A bite to the lip, a shake of the head, a sudden turning away.

'To business, Your Grace?' suggests William, holding out a paper in his hand.

'Yes, yes.' The King takes it, turns to them again, stands close but averts his eyes, speaks low. 'There are some who might call you our heir now, Richard, with Gloucester gone. Till we have a son.'

'Your loyal subject, Your Grace.'

'Of course.' He nods, fast and shallow. 'And we want you near us. And yet you have no London home?' He takes Richard's hand in his own and lays the paper in it. 'Baynard's Castle. My uncle's house. The best on the Thames, I've always thought. Yours now. And various –' he waves his pale hand, losing interest – 'manors and such that were his. Lordship of the Isle of Wight. Hmm?' He smiles.

Cecily watches Richard's jaw tighten as he looks at the paper in his hand. Just as she despairs of him accepting it, he nods. 'Your Grace is generous.'

'And for your loss of France. I understand.' He pats Richard's sleeve. 'We will think on it a while.'

That night, Richard sleeps ill beside her and keeps her wakeful.

She counts the hours by the sergeant's bell, imagining a

future lived close to a king whose love is so mercurial, whose mind seems barely his own.

Suddenly the bed feels stifling.

She throws back the covers and relishes the room's cold air; lets it take her back to that frost-bright January morning, throwing her merlin up into open skies.

20

May 1449
  London

'So, they take away France and give you Ireland? I hope God loves you, Richard, for it seems the King does not.' Cecily's brother, Salisbury's earl, is grinning. He lifts the flagon himself, the page being too slow, and pours for them all. Then leans back in his seat and raises a glass. 'Here's to you.'

Richard returns the nod. 'King or counsellors, would you say?'

'Same thing. None of them love you.'

Richard smiles and shrugs. 'Oh, I don't know.'

It's long past midnight. They're drinking because there's nothing else to do. The servants are yawning behind their hands. There were five hundred in the hall of Salisbury's London home tonight, and only at the King's table could they have eaten better. The guests have long since gone, or are asleep under the tables. Their host left them to it hours ago. 'We've shown ourselves off and spent enough to be talked about,' Salisbury had said, signalling to his family. 'Let's to ourselves.' He drew them aside to this private chamber, where they could feast without an audience. Talk and not be overheard.

It's to be Cecily's last night in London for a while. The King has named Richard Lord Lieutenant of Ireland, England's most troublesome conquest after France. Tomorrow the long journey begins. West from London. A week or two in Ludlow to put affairs in order. Then through Wales and across the narrow straits to Anglesey where, long ago, the wild Britons made their last stand against Rome. From there, over the treacherous sea that stood as a western wall to even those most ambitious of empire builders.

They hope to be in Dublin by early July, in time for a summer progress before that rain-sodden land hems them in. Cecily is trying not to think of it. Either the destination or the journey.

'It's a fair exchange.' Richard pushes his empty plate away, clearing a space for his glass among the table's debris. 'There's work to be done there.' A shrug. 'It might as well be me who does it.'

Cecily pulls the napkin from her shoulder, lays it down. 'You see, brother. My husband is most sanguine.'

Richard raises a brow, but his eyes are still on the table; his fingers turn his brimming cup. 'I am no less keen than the Crown that Ireland doesn't go the way of France.'

That's true enough. From his uncle, Richard holds the earldom of Cork. From his mother that of Ulster and the rich lordships of Trim and Leix. He's left the management of them to deputies in the past, good men who've played fair. More than can be said for most English lords in Ireland. He's visited, once or twice, and liked it. Cecily herself has never ventured so far.

'Never been. What's it like?' asks Salisbury.

Cecily lays her knife across her plate and signals a page to remove it. 'It is a very long way from Westminster.'

'It's a very long way from everywhere,' Richard smiles, takes her fingers in his, kisses them. 'Which is perhaps its sweetest attraction.'

Salisbury laughs. 'Aye. If you must serve a king, best do it from a distance.'

He lives by his own advice, Salisbury. Rules the distant north, as her father did. Holds the Scottish border and keeps a lid on the fermenting rivalries of northern magnates. Problems he can solve with a poleaxe. He comes to court when he has to, smiles a lot and keeps his nose clean.

'But brother,' Cecily's smile is sly and slow. 'Does this policy not rob you of the glorious spectacle of our most noble court?'

'What? Of Suffolk licking the King's arse, while his own is kicked by all and sundry? Of Edmund Beaufort sniffing the Queen's tail and pilfering the treasury?'

Cecily laughs into her cup. 'News does reach you up north then?'

'Enough.'

Richard holds up a hand between them. 'Well, for this last year at least Beaufort's been out of the way in Rouen. And, for my sake, he can stay there.' It's brave talk. The thought of it still smarts.

'He'll be back soon enough.' Salisbury elbows the table, leans to Richard's ear. 'My prediction? Rouen falls before Christmas.' He taps his nose. 'I need no astrologer to tell me that. England is finished in France. You're well out of it.'

Richard shrugs. 'Perhaps.'

It's a year now since Anjou and Maine were handed to the French. William played for time, but couldn't play for ever. In the end, Charles pitched his army outside Le Mans and said, hand it over or I'll take it. Just like that. Now England's full of grumblers: settlers dispossessed of land and livelihood; unpaid soldiers who scratch their itch to fight in London's streets. In every shire there are knights and nobles looking for new troughs to stick their snouts into now the French one is snatched away; angry lords who, though their enthusiasm for the old French game has faded, seem outraged to find it lost.

Salisbury's right. Normandy is all but indefensible; its garrisons depleted, nothing much now between it and Charles's ambition to have his kingdom back. In private Cecily and Richard tired of speaking of it months ago; the wasted effort, the might-have-beens, the possibilities that slipped from their grasp, or were snatched from it. In public they do not speak of it at all. Closed lips, clean hands. For two years they've lived quietly, done the King's bidding in small things, looked to their own. They've kept well away from William de la Pole, who, like a magnet, draws the anger of every discontent in England. Let him. William's only friend these days is his king. And his queen perhaps, who, people complain, has brought nothing to England in four years of marriage. Not even a son.

If Marguerite has not borne a son, at least she has lost none. Cecily has buried two since they came home from France. Days old, each of them; well at evening, dead at dawn. Just like the first. Henry, William and John now. Three small tombs hemmed within Fotheringhay's white walls; three prayer-swept souls, fledged too soon from their nests of bone. She's heard the Queen smiled when told of the last. Jacquetta whispered it in confidence, eyes shining with outrage, pausing to see if Cecily would curse, if there would be gossip to carry back.

'I pray she never suffers so,' Cecily told her.

Most of all, she abhors the waste of it. And now her belly is set to swell again. Last night Richard asked if she would rather stay behind in England, for the child's sake, and follow later. Though the journey will be dreadful, she sees little point in that. Tears push against the backs of her eyes as the talk moves on without her. She blinks and chides herself. Foolishness. She is done with crying.

'For Heaven's sake, let's not speak of France,' she says. 'Or of Ireland.'

Richard pulls himself up, blinks. 'Indeed. Surely we have better subjects?'

The weight of finding one falls on Salisbury's shoulders. He hesitates. Then, drawing on the laugh that seems never far from his throat, he reaches a sword-callused hand to tousle the bright hair of the young man opposite him. 'Well, I suppose we could toast once again the very great good fortune of my son and heir?'

That'll do. She nods agreement as the page, keen not to be caught dallying a second time, steps forward to charge glasses and young Richard Neville bats his father's hand away, smilingly. He's a man past twenty, could best her brother in a fight if he wanted to, but they're each as pleased with the other as with themselves. And so alike. And like her father. Don't think of that either. A generation gone. Father and mother; all of Gaunt's children. Even the cardinal. He barely outlived Gloucester long enough to crow over his corpse. Dying, he'd said that, were he not certain of God's mercy, he would be in anguish. Or so his confessor wrote to her. He betrayed no secrets, he said, for her uncle had felt this so keenly he commanded it inscribed upon his tomb.

Was he sorry then, she wonders, in the end? Hard to imagine. She holds her glass to the candle; its light doesn't penetrate. What does it matter anyway?

Stay with the living, Cecily. So they drink the health of her brother's son, just as they've done all evening. He's the reason they're here, after all, the lever that prised her brother from the North like a cockle from its shell.

She holds up her dark-filled glass. 'To your handsome son.'

'To my very rich, handsome son.'

Handsomely the rich son drinks, and smiles, red wine glistening on strong white teeth. He is Earl of Warwick. Worthy of a toast. Newly made today, when the King fastened the sword of that honour to his steel-clad hip. It's come to him through his wife who, thanks to untimely deaths among her brothers, has made her husband her father's heir. Old Warwick's daughter she was, now new Warwick's wife. Another Anne. She sits at his side, looking a little surprised at it all. No looks to commend her, and nothing to say, but that hardly matters.

Cecily looks about the room, at loved faces now sated and soft. They are none of them sober. The candles are all but burned down and the hovering steward is wondering, no doubt, whether to set more. She'll save him the bother. She catches Richard's eye.

He blinks and stretches and comes to his feet, but before he can do so, her nephew, the new earl, rises to draw out her chair. Handsome, rich – and courteous, too. No end to his qualities, it seems. While Richard and her brother fall in behind, he walks with her to the inner ward, where their escort shakes itself alert and fumbles for sconces to light their way home, down through the darkness of Thames Street to Baynard's Castle. Her brother embraces her. His son kisses her hand and wishes her safe travels.

'And where next for you, young lord?'

He shrugs. 'North, with my father.'

'To pull faces at the Scots?'

His smile is dazzling. Pity his enemies. If he can't beat them in a fair fight, surely he'll charm them to death.

He reminds her of Edward a little; though, of course, her own son's fiery brightness puts even this one in the shade. He sleeps now at Baynard's Castle beside Edmund, safe under Annette's powerful watch. She wants, suddenly and very badly, to be with them.

They come towards Ludlow as the month ends. The Teme still has the spring's fast run upon it, but the valley is tiered with new green and the billowing white of may blossom. As the weather has warmed she's abandoned the carriage to her daughters and their nurses, and ridden each day at Richard's side. Little Edward, playing the man, pushes his piebald pony to keep pace with their tall horses and, when tired of the effort of it, is happy to perch astride his father's saddle and have all the sights of the road explained for him. From time to time Edmund, who follows his brother in all things, demands to ride likewise and Cecily takes him up, but it's Edward's voice she listens for and, when he grows quiet, she reaches out to touch his face, coaxing him to speak again.

As they cross the river at Ludford Bridge, she looks up, following the keening of a fork-tailed kite. She squints her eye against the castle's crenellated bulk, set alight by a lowering sun. The bird wheels against a sky that's been blue and cloudless all day and is fingered now with pink and gold. Though her back aches and the sweat clings beneath her arms and breasts, she feels a lightening within herself. She looks across and sees that Richard, too, is looking up, his long hand shielding his view. When he turns to her, she's surprised how easy it is to return his smile.

He taps the golden head before him. 'Look, Edward . . .' His finger points the way. 'Ludlow.'

The nave is so newly finished that the smell of paint and fresh carved wood is headier even than the incense that clouds her view. Here too, as at Fotheringhay, they are building a gift to God. Not alone this time, for the churches of the western March are built on the backs of sheep, by merchants rich in wool. But they've given generous alms to rebuild Ludlow's church and make it the finest in the March. The nave and chancel are all but finished, though the bell tower still rings to the sound of hammers.

They have come, at the request of the town's aldermen and council, to a service of thanks; thanks for Richard's good lordship and for the new charter that will protect Ludlow's wealth and rights while its duke labours for the King in the wild lands to the west.

'Do they think you're unlikely to come back?' Cecily had teased him.

'I suspect they believe we will be spirited away by water sprites.'

'More likely murdered in our beds by the native Irish. Or drowned in a rainy bog.'

Richard had grinned at that. 'I think you will like it more than you imagine.'

He has spoken to her of his hopes. They can do good work in Ireland; work that will be profitable and raise revenues for the royal exchequer. There is no rival king there as in France, just petty lords too busy fighting among themselves to seriously threaten the Crown. So what if the Irish begin to look across the Channel and think they can do as the French have done? He will nip it in the bud. He will knock their heads together. He will give them sound administration, strong justice, and they will be content.

'Let's live as your brother does. As your father did. Doing good work for the King, far from court, in our own lands.' And he is in earnest.

When she looks out from Ludlow's castle, around the silvered curve of the river to the rising hills of Wales, where church-building sheep bleat sweeter than courtiers, she wants very much to believe it can be as he says. But her father was not the king's heir with a claim to England's throne as good as the man's who sits upon it. He was not, as Richard is, envied by Edmund Beaufort or suspected by William de la Pole. His sons were not resented by a childless queen.

'They have put you in Ireland to get you out of the way.'

He'd shrugged. 'I suppose.'

The service is over now and the people gone, but they have lingered. The warden of Ludlow's Palmers' Guild, who has directed the rebuilding, is showing off the work. He explains the raising of the roof, how it has swelled the hallowed space, and the glory of its painted sky, lit by stars and held aloft by angels. He prices for them the tall windows dedicated to God by the town's rich guilds: the merchants, the fullers, the tailors, smiths and dyers.

At last Richard brings her back to the chancel.

'You can see these, now everyone's gone. Look . . .' He points to the stalls, where every misericord, against which tired choristers will lean when worn with song, is a work of art in oak. He kneels, turns, draws her eyes to look. 'I commissioned some of these myself.'

She leans beside him and the first he shows her bears King Henry's antelope, necked with a crown. Another, the second Richard's white hart. The next, the royal feathers, brought to England by the third Edward's heir. Symbols of kingship, present and past, the rule of England lending strength to prayer.

His fine fingers run across the grain of them. 'From my present duty to my long heritage.' He turns on his heels. 'Now, look here.' He points her to another stall, where a sharp-eyed falcon tests its wings within a fetterlock. It is power and patience combined, the true cognizance of York since the first duke's day. Here it stands, holding its own among kings.

'I know who I am, Cecily. I am not bound. I may choose to sit quiet to the glove for now, yet I have talons. I will strike, if I must.'

21

October 1449
  Dublin, Ireland

A long labour, and painful, but the child is come at last. And, day by day, he lives. They have bought prayers for his life in every church in Dublin. But, while the faithful hold him before God's face, Cecily holds him before her own. She watches with him, breathes for him, binds him to this world by the strength of her will. She will not lose another. Angel or demon, she will fight any who dares come for this one. After three days she is feverish, her vision blurred and the shaking in her hands constant. Her women grow fearful and beg her to sleep. She snarls at them, pinches herself to wakefulness, watches and breathes.

Annette, who has crossed the sea to be with her in Ireland, has the good sense to say little. Instead, she brings broth and makes her drink. Cecily tastes salt and blood in it. She is hungry for both. The child feeds and sleeps, cries and grows.

When a week is gone, he has outlived his dead brothers and she is sure of him at last. She gives him into Annette's arms, turns her face to her pillow, sleeps like the dead, wakes hungry and asks for news.

'Your son thrives. And the duke your husband has all the lords of Ireland at his feet,' Annette tells her.

She smiles and sleeps again.

Each evening, now, Annette leaves her for an hour and returns with word from Richard; a note, usually, in his own hand.

Sometimes, if business presses, just a word or two. While Cecily has laboured, he has worked. His notes list the lords who have ridden to his first Parliament; tell how they have accepted his new laws, applauded his judgements and put their men at his call. Postscripts say he misses her.

She frowns. He should be too busy for that. Never mind. The plans they have laid are unfolding, neat as linen on a table.

Ireland has been under English rule three hundred years, though its native chieftains are minded to forget. Even among the English lords long settled here, old allegiances have worn thin. So they fight among themselves for Ireland's wealth and neglect to pay Crown taxes. Westminster is a world away, after all. Lord Lieutenants come and go; best smile to their faces, tell them what they want to hear, and wait for them to leave.

'We must come as one of their own,' Cecily had said, back in England, as they laid their plans. 'You'll get more done as Earl of Ulster than Duke of York.'

'As Welsh Mortimer rather than English Plantagenet?'

'Just so. Fortunately, you are both.'

His hand had run thoughtful along her flank. Even after so many years, they still do their best talking in bed. 'Mmm. Make them think we're on their side?'

'Perhaps we are. If they are on ours.' His hand had travelled lower then and she'd captured it in her own. 'And we must sow the seed early.'

So Richard had laid out money to put his Irish affinity to work. It became profitable for his deputies, captains and stewards to talk up his native heritage, his good lordship, his even hand.

'Tell them I am a man they can do business with,' Richard instructed. 'Tell them I am one of them.'

'And more,' says Cecily. 'In private, when the doors are

closed, let them say you are a man of your own mind. No puppet of the King's.'

A chosen few received more than general assurances. So in July, when they landed at the port of Howth, the Earls of Ormond and Desmond, foremost among the English lords in Ireland, were watching for them, squinting into the sun and grinning. Assured of preference and a place in Richard's government, they had surrendered to his authority most publicly. They rode into Dublin together under Richard's banners; the lions of England and the black dragon of Ulster snapping at each other in the air above their heads. From Dublin, they went shoulder to shoulder, west through the English Pale, to the great Mortimer castle of Trim, then turned north towards Ulster.

'I am come home,' Richard told all who came to meet him. 'And glad to be among you.'

Under the iron eyes of Desmond and Ormond, lords both English and Irish swore fealty, had their voices heard and their concerns noted. Cecily paid court to their ladies, her full belly carried high, and told them how proud she would be to bear a son for Ireland.

But the O'Byrnes, prideful descendants of the ancient kings of Leinster, calling themselves rulers of Wicklow, refused to kneel.

'Good,' said Cecily. 'We needed one.'

So the cavalcade turned again to Dublin and from there Richard led an army that fell upon Wicklow like a hammer. The Chieftain O'Byrne and his sons, brought bloody into Richard's presence, were granted mercy.

'But only after he had sworn submission and allegiance?' Cecily, leaning into Richard's homecoming tale, wanted to be sure.

He nodded, slow and smiling. 'Yes, of course. To me. And to the King of England.'

'Well, yes, of course,' she said, sly. 'To him.'

And so, before autumn, and before the door was closed on Cecily's confinement, the message had been sent. Richard of Ulster is a man you can do business with. Just don't expect to be given a choice about it.

Her son is four weeks old when Cecily comes to her churching. By no accident it is the last day of Richard's Parliament and the priory church of St Saviour's is packed tight as a herring barrel. She kneels to the priest who meets her at the church door, holds out her taper for his light and waits while the slow rub of his thumb marks the cross upon her brow.

When she rises again, there is Richard. He leans beyond her to lay a loving hand against the face of his son, held safe in the crook of Annette's arm. He looks younger, fit, and his face hasn't quite lost its summer colour. The fine lines about his eyes still show white. He's had some time from business to squint into the sun, then. She takes his hand and squeezes it.

'Come,' she whispers, 'let's remind these people you have sons to follow you.'

'And a wife still young enough to give me more,' he smiles. 'And fair enough for me to want her to.'

She tuts and pinches his wrist. She has carried twenty-seven of the last thirty-six months and still feels, sometimes, that she grieves the sons lost in that time more than she rejoices in the one gained. It seems shameful, she'd confessed one night to Annette in the secrecy of the quiet nursery.

The nurse looked thoughtfully down at George, asleep and heedless in his crib. 'Surely grief and love are bedfellows,' she pondered. 'Is there not room in the heart for both?' Then she turned her gaze on Cecily. 'When I think how fiercely you fought for this one, I cannot doubt his dearness to you.'

'Of course, you're right.' It seemed suddenly important to make light of it. 'Certainly he was hard work.'

To Richard, now, she only says, 'Perhaps I'd like a little respite?'

At the last, he falls back and she walks on alone into God's
space. Before the altar she lights nine candles; one for the souls
of each of her children. There's much to be grateful for; six yet
live. She kneels, breathes deep to still her thoughts and bring
her heart to God. From beside her comes the baby's low murmur, Annette's gentle hushing. But from within herself,
nothing. No answering tug of affection, no welcoming
warmth. And that deep well of thankfulness, which has always
overflown at these moments, is dry. Staring into its darkness,
a thought comes unbidden: God has taken three from me and,
if this one lives, the credit is mine. She feels a cold flutter in her
breast, as if her heart has stumbled. This is blasphemy, surely.

And then she is praying in earnest; for forgiveness, for
humility, for a grateful heart. She brings her children to God,
one by one, and begs protection. For her daughters, who are
with her in Ireland. Margaret and Elizabeth, and little Anne,
who came back hollow-eyed from Henry Holland when that
wretch's father died, but must go to him again when she's of
age. For this new babe, who has done no wrong and surely
warrants her love. For Edward and Edmund, left behind in
Ludlow with their own household now, their training begun
in earnest, learning to be men. She sees Edward's open face
turned to his father as they crossed Ludford Bridge in the
evening; feels the bold grasp of his hand about her fingers.
And then, then her heart overflows and she prostrates herself among the candle flames, washed in love, contrite and
thankful.

In the celebration after, that fearful moment is all but forgotten. The food is good, the wine better and the noise of many
men, all vying for her husband's attention, drowns out the
musicians set to play for them. From his side, Cecily watches

as Richard moves easily among the crowd, a word here, a hand on a shoulder there; acknowledgements that will matter, that will make a difference. Not a gesture wasted. But the most important moment of all they have planned together.

At the appointed time, after the meats are gone and before the confections and marchpanes are brought, she looks down the hall and sees Annette, handing the child to its god-fathers, the Earls of Ormond and Desmond. For a moment they seem to fumble over which should have the honour of carrying him while the other walks beside him and waves. Ormond wins out. A trumpet sounds and a hush falls as they set out on their slow way. When they reach the dais, and lay their charge in its father's arms, the child sets up a great cry.

Richard looks up, smiling, and a low thrum of laughter ripples down the hall. 'Meet my strong-lunged son!' he invites them. 'We have named him for St George, the dragon slayer. He is a son of Ireland. Like his father he will live to be a strong defender of your rights and privileges here under God.'

The people's cheers threaten the roof.

'And under England's king, of course,' Richard adds more quietly.

Cecily smiles under his kiss.

Later, there is dancing. Richard leads her in slow turns. She is showing off the crimson that was for Marguerite's arrival into Rouen and thinks it put to better use here. At her breast is a diamond dragon, its claws gory with rubies, Richard's gift of thanks for this new son. As one dance ends she turns, and there is Richard's ally the Earl of Ormond, begging for the honour, brimming with charm. She likes him; he's clever, keeps a good library, she's told, so she says yes, and they step out.

'I am the most envied man in the hall,' he tells her.

'Because you dance with the Duke of York's wife?'

'Because I dance with you.'

'What nonsense. Don't be a courtier.'

He feigns surprise. 'But am I not at court? The court of Richard, King of Ireland?'

She puts a finger to her lips. 'I would have to consult my lawyers, but I think that might be treason.'

'Don't worry,' he says, leaning to her ear, 'there are no courtiers to hear us.'

She laughs and likes him even more.

And as they turn about the hall in a crush of couples her eyes follow Richard. They mark his easy confidence, his ready smile. She sees how men come to him, how they lean into his words as once they did to her father's. How they nod or laugh or turn thoughtful when he speaks. She knows he has the measure of all; that he has in mind what must be said to each man to secure his good faith, to make the achievements of this Parliament last. He's good at this, she thinks. He looks happy.

Ormond's voice breaks into her thoughts again. 'It's a good start you've made. By Christmas you'll be able to write King Henry that every wild man in Ireland has sworn himself English.'

'Well, for that I will sharpen my pen.'

And here comes Richard, shining and easy, holding out his hand to take her back.

They winter in Trim on the edge of the English Pale, in the castle that looks out over the Boyne into the unruly heartlands of Ireland, where English authority barely reaches.

They have come because it is beautiful. They want to hawk its riverbanks, visit its abbeys and hunt in the thick forests that edge the river plain to the Hill of Tara. But they've come also to send a message; they will extend their power beyond the river. Their work has just begun.

Though it rains a good deal, the sunlight, when it comes, is dazzling and drowns their eyes in green. As Christmas approaches, Cecily finds herself, for the first time, glad not to be in England. Even more so, not to be in France. She looks ahead ten years and thinks they could be well spent here.

She lets that belief take root in her until the day William Oldhall arrives to tear it out.

He comes to tell them that King Charles has declared war in Normandy, and that Edmund Beaufort has surrendered Rouen into his hands.

22

January–May 1450

They get dry clothes on him, set him by a fire, feed him and let him talk. He's hale enough for his age, William Oldhall, but it's a hard journey over the Irish Sea in the teeth of winter. Still, Cecily supposes, he's endured worse.

He can't but speak of the old French game, at which he is an accomplished player. One of Richard's best administrators in his time. Bedford's before that. In it since he was a lad, in fact, before the glory days of Agincourt. He first saw Rouen back in '18, when the old King Henry sat his army down at its gates to starve the French out. They exercised their arses through summer to winter, while hunger did its work. By Christmas, there couldn't have been a cat or dog uneaten in the city, so its commanders expelled the citizens in their thousands, thinking, no doubt, that the soldiery might eke out a little longer on the rats and the mice.

'They thought we'd give them safe passage, I suppose,' says William. 'Not Henry. Had us barricade them into the defence ditches. "Let the fuckers on the walls watch them die," he said.' William Oldhall sniffs. 'We had to watch it too, mind. Saving the French a job, Henry called it. Said they'd be glad not to have the bother of digging graves for the poor bastards after the surrender.'

So young William Oldhall, his belly not much fuller than a Frenchman's, had tightened his belt and shivered in the mud another month, until the crying stopped, the bodies stilled and the snow came to cover them. Only then had the gates opened, and he'd ridden with Henry's army into Rouen's iron-cold streets. He's a man past sixty now. He understands the price of things.

'I'm not proud, Richard. I'm not proud.' He eyes the half-eaten chicken breast on his knife as if it were a French child on a spit, then drops it to the empty plate before him. 'Wasn't then. Am not now.'

It's an old story. Cecily's heard it before. He's telling it again because, grim as it is, it's easier than the new one, the one he told them all in a rush when he rode in from the rain two hours ago. How Edmund Beaufort handed Rouen back to the French without a fight and after a full supper. Then bargained his own safety by giving good men as hostage. Their friend, old soldier Talbot, among them.

Cecily looks across the table's corner to where Richard sits, the long fingers of his right hand wrapped about his chin, the bull's blood ruby lifeless and still and, above it, his eyes, blacker than she's ever seen them. They sent the servants away when William started in on his tale. Now the fire's burned almost to nothing, dusk has cast the room in shadow, and still she doesn't know why Oldhall is here.

She stands, sets candles, kicks life into the hearth for a taper to light them. As a little warmth comes back, both men pull themselves up, stretch chilled fingers.

'William.' She puts a fresh glass before him, pours. 'We are most glad to see you and, though your news is bitter, we're grateful for it. But I wonder. It could have been put in a letter. What is it that you would not trust to paper?'

Richard's voice is dead calm. 'I imagine William has come to tell us why, though Rouen fell in October, we've heard no news of it yet from England.'

The old man nods. 'Aye. That. Exactly so.' He sits back, takes a breath. 'My lord, you're the best man we had in France since Bedford's day and, were you there still, I think it would not have come to this—'

Richard holds up a hand. 'Yet I was not opposed to the peace, William. Providing it's honourably won. You know that.'

'But we haven't got peace, have we? We've got war. And we're staring defeat in the face, thanks to that money-grabbing bastard Somerset.'

Richard's eyes find Cecily's and hold them. 'Now that's a charge, William.'

'Aye,' Oldhall shrugs, defensive. 'And I don't hold back from it.' He counts Edmund Beaufort's sins on swollen fingers. 'First he blackmails the King; says he won't honour the truce and surrender Anjou and Maine until he's paid compensation. Which Henry gives him. Then you'd think he'd spend that on the defence of Rouen? No chance. He's pocketed the lot. And, along with it, half of what was meant for the people who lost their livelihoods.'

She watches Richard's frown twist in his face and knows his thoughts. He's remembering how much of their own money was spent propping up Rouen's rickety defences. Of the soldiers' wages paid, quarter day after quarter day, from his own purse. He's reckoning up plate and property they've mortgaged in England to pay for the King's work in Ireland. And yet, there are the Beauforts, first John and now Edmund, gaping maws that princes seem ever ready to pour coin into. One of the richest men in England now, Edmund Beaufort, since the cardinal died and left him everything. Still hungry for more, though. Still gobbling.

'Nor is there a man in our army that's had pay for the last twelvemonth.' It's the last of Oldhall's charges.

And Richard bows his head at it.

'Where is Beaufort now?' Cecily asks.

'Caen. But not for long, I think. We can't hold it. We've

nothing to throw at Charles's army. Even if we had a leader with balls for a fight. He sent me as messenger boy back to England when we pulled out of Rouen. I think because he couldn't stand the sight of my miserable face any longer.'

'To ask for more money and men, no doubt.' Richard's voice is cold.

Oldhall nods.

'And they were sent?'

He nods again, grudging. 'Too little. Too late. The money straight into Somerset's pocket, I expect.'

She watches Richard's knuckles flex and whiten, his throat rise as he closes his teeth on resentment. She wonders how he bears it so silently. 'Richard. We—'

He holds up a hand, frowns. 'I think William has more to tell us.'

'Aye. I do.' The old man spreads his hands, as if the cause might be in them. They come up empty and he sighs. 'France is bad enough, God knows. But what I saw at home . . .' He looks away.

She sees that Richard's eyes are on her still. 'Go on,' he says.

'My lord, I hardly recognize England, or the men about the King. But I know them to be no friends of yours. They're keeping you in the dark.'

'Who? Exactly.'

He shuffles. It's hard to say it. 'For a start, one who should be a friend. Captain under John of Bedford when first we knew him. Duke of Suffolk now.' He is not the first to marvel at this change in fortune. 'William de la Pole. William de la Pole and his lickspittle cronies.'

She watches Richard's bitter smile, the slow shake of his head. 'You've been too long out of England if that surprises you, old friend,' he says.

'Well, I have. It does. He whispers in the King's ear against you.'

'How so?' she asks, and sees Oldhall almost startle at the sharpness in her voice.

'When I came to court with my begging bowl –' he allows himself a snarl – 'the King turned straight to Suffolk and asked, what could be sent. As if Suffolk directed England's armies, not him. Then he asked Suffolk if York should be recalled from Ireland and sent to France. Never a better man for France, the King says. No, no, says Suffolk. Too busy in Ireland, says Suffolk. Too much a friend of the King of France. Ah, well, says the King. But we shall write and ask for his counsel. And he calls a scribe and has him write away, and me standing there. And he gives the letter to Suffolk. And I'll wager you've never seen it.'

Richard's head still shakes, slowly, side to side. 'No.'

'William de la Pole has the King in his pocket, Richard.'

'Aye. And to Edmund Beaufort he opens that pocket. And to me, not at all.'

Oldhall slumps a little. 'I see I tell you nothing you don't already know.'

'You must not think so, William.' Cecily lays a hand on his arm. 'You tell us much we need to hear.'

'But tell me,' asks Richard, 'why might I be believed to be the French king's special friend?'

'Because, before he went to war against us, the King of France was not averse to comparing you to our current lieutenant in ways most unfavourable to Edmund Beaufort. He sent his herald to Henry to complain of it. You, he said, were a man France could do business with, while Beaufort . . . well, Beaufort couldn't have done more to offend the French if he'd tried.'

Richard's laugh is like ice cracking. 'That's Charles making trouble. No doubt a belligerent Beaufort suited him well enough. Gave him the excuse he needed to break the truce.'

She hears her own voice, waspish with impatience. 'So, the

best we can say of Beaufort is that he sharpens the King of France's sword for him? What's the worst? I wonder.'

'That he has given away Rouen, and all we fought for in France,' says Oldhall. 'And meanwhile, de la Pole whispers in the King's ear that you take friendship too far, Richard. He reminds him that you offered your son to the King of France for marriage with his daughter, and wonders what you meant by it.'

Cecily's voice is incredulous. 'What? That? Is he mad? We did that because the King asked it of us. And the request was carried by Suffolk himself. It was all part of the King's great love fever when he married Marguerite – he was all for everybody marrying everyone then.'

And if Henry was fool enough not to realize that marrying one of his most powerful dukes into the French royal house was a dangerous idea, she hadn't been. 'He can't be serious,' Cecily had said then to Suffolk, who'd held up his hands, exasperated, and said, 'Just write a few letters, Richard. Look keen for a month or two, then let the matter drop.'

'William de la Pole's memory of events is most politic,' says Richard now, reaching for the wine jug.

Aye, thinks Cecily. A vicious mind playing on a simple one.

'The point is this, Richard,' says Oldhall. 'He whispers that you fancy yourself England's heir and harbour ambitions.'

She watches her husband pour the wine into his cup. Calm, precise. As if it commanded his attention entirely.

'He's right, on the first point at least,' he says. He offers the jug to Oldhall and pours when the old man nods.

'Well. By the by. But Richard, you have powerful enemies at court and, God knows, Edmund Beaufort hates you. I come to put you on your guard.'

'You have, William. And I thank you for it.' He takes the man's hand in both of his and holds it. Then shakes it loose and sits back. 'And what now for you?'

He shrugs. 'To England, if you've nothing for me here.' He looks hopeful.

She waits as Richard leans his head, thinks and speaks. 'You could serve me better in England, I think. Do the Commons still mutter against Suffolk in Parliament?'

'In Parliament and on every street corner. But the King won't listen. I think Suffolk is the most hated man in England.'

Richard leans forward. 'I think so, too. And England will only bear him so long. Go home, William. Be about the court.' Another thought occurs. 'You've land enough in the shires to get yourself appointed to Parliament, I'd say?'

He shrugs and nods.

'I'll lay out the funds. I need a man among the Commons to tell me what's about. Will you do it?'

'Become a politician?'

She sees what Richard is thinking. 'A voice of the people,' she says. 'An ear for York.'

Richard steeples his hands. 'Just so.'

As winter moves towards spring, the flow of news from England to Ireland is much eased. Oldhall's good at picking men he can trust. Men who travel fast, and come and go in darkness.

Cecily is all expectation the night the first of them arrives. She paces as Richard reads the letter he brings, then sits across the desk from him and threatens him with stares. 'Well?'

At last he looks up with that slow smile of his and hands her the paper. 'Read it yourself.'

She snatches it and finds herself smiling with him. 'At the demand of the Commons, and of the Lords, the King, though most unwillingly, has agreed the arrest of William de la Pole. Well.'

He signals her to read on, and there are the charges, itemized in Oldhall's good administrator's hand. They are incoherent, ludicrous and vicious. The gist of them is that Suffolk has played traitor to two kings. That he has plotted to put the Duke of Orléans on the French throne and then, with that lord's grateful help, to put his own son on England's. That he has given away one of Henry's crowns and sought to rob him of the other. They are wild enough, almost, to set her laughing.

'None of it true, of course,' says Richard, crossing the room to lean his back against the warm hearthside. 'But it doesn't have to be.'

'Will it stick?'

He shrugs. 'There's enough in it to make it plausible, if people want to believe it. Orléans has always been a challenge to Charles. And William argued hard for his release from England's prison.'

'As did my uncle. As did you.'

He smiles. 'Perhaps you should ask Isabella what her pet poet has been up to.'

She laughs.

England freed Orléans, but Burgundy made a tool of him, a stick to beat France with; a burr beneath Charles's saddle.

She widens her eyes further still. 'And William de la Pole's son on the throne?'

'You'll not forget he took John Beaufort's daughter into wardship when her father died? He meant her for his boy.'

'He wanted her money.'

'Of course. But the Beauforts would claim the blood in their veins to be no less royal than mine.'

She is incredulous. 'Tainted by bastardy. As I know better than anyone.'

He laughs, pushes his shoulder from the wall and comes to sit beside her. 'I know it, too. It doesn't matter.' He takes her hands, shakes them lightly. 'None of it's true.'

'But will Henry indict him?'

'What do you think?'

She knows he's right, that Henry will. The charges say, in short, that England's disastrous policies in France, its terrible losses, are all the work of William de la Pole. Henry believes himself God's anointed, a channel for the divine will. That will, he believes, cannot but run true in him, but its course may be diverted by treason. And there is precedent in scripture, after all; if your right hand offends you, cut it off.

She remembers William, miserable in Pontoise with Marguerite on his arm, shamefaced in Fotheringhay, admitting Anjou and Maine promised away. She remembers how hard it had become for Alice to look her in the eye. 'The policy I pursue in France is the King's,' he'd said then. 'Never, never my own.'

'Poor William. Do you think he knew?'

'That the King would cut him loose? If he didn't, after Gloucester, he's a fool far beyond our pity.'

So Cecily feels little surprise when, a month later, Oldhall writes that William de la Pole is exiled from England and must quit the country before May Day.

And only a little more when it is confirmed that his headless corpse, sword-hacked and sea-bloated, had washed up at the foot of Dover's bare-faced cliffs the day after his ship sailed.

23

Impossible, now, to imagine a quiet life in Ireland. Surely they must return home. Leave Ormond here as deputy and take de la Pole's place at the King's side.

'Put my head in that noose?' says Richard. 'I don't think so.'

His back is to her, his attention all before him; on the armour that will go with him tomorrow when he rides out against the traitor MacGeoghegan. It hangs empty on its stand, a silvered ghost of him. Already it has been sanded and oiled, polished by his armourer. All three of his body squires have, in their duty, checked every buckle, rivet and joint. But Richard is meticulous, so here he is, as the slow summer evening softens the light in his chamber, tugging at straps, feeling for flaws, testing in his hands the slide of plate he will rely on for safety and speed.

She is all impatience. 'Will you let it be? I checked it myself this afternoon.'

He looks over his shoulder, gives a smile she doesn't return.

'And you know better than to ask what women know of such things.'

'I'm sure you were very thorough.'

'I was.' She does not say that, her inspection done, she'd signed the cross at every known weak point; where helm and gorget meet at the neck, where pauldron, couter and poleyn shelter shoulder, elbow and knee. He needn't know that she had set her lips against the arced breastplate and whispered the Ave, to put his heart in the Queen of Heaven's keeping.

'You seem ready enough to put your neck in MacGeoghegan's noose.'

'I'm rather hoping to put his in mine. I cannot deal so forthrightly with the King of England.'

'The king who has yet to pay us and doesn't reply to our letters?'

It has become pressing this last month, the lack of money. There's insurrection in Meath. The native chief MacGeoghegan has torched the town of Ramor and the villages about it. It is banditry and must be snuffed out. But you need coin to put men on the march, and the English lords of Ireland, who Richard has called on for a levy, begin to whisper that their Lord Lieutenant may have boasted of royal support he doesn't have. Some of them have a taste for banditry themselves.

He has written to Lord Saye, England's Treasurer, to remind him of payments overdue. He has written to the King. Cecily herself has deigned to respectfully ask the Queen to intercede with her husband the King on their behalf.

They've received assurances of good faith – of love, even – but no money.

Richard takes up his sword, runs an oiled cloth down its steel. But he does not speak.

'We'll get nothing from Henry until we stand before him with our hands out,' she complains. There is tension in every line of his body, but she chooses to ignore it. 'I wonder you still believe, after so many years and against all the evidence, that your good service will be rewarded.'

Her irritable fingers have been testing the seams of his mailing shirt. She's done with it and throws it aside. Richard's blade gleams in the window's light as he eyes the weapon along its savage edge.

'It's a mercy you inherited such wealth, Richard. Your delusions run expensive.'

There is a sudden screech of steel as the sword is plunged into its ring. 'What would you have me do, Cecily? Please, don't hold back. Tell me what your foolish, deluded husband must do to content you.'

He has turned, and now she has all his attention. His face is pale and his lips thin, but she is no less angry than he is, and so, 'If William de la Pole can stand by the King and rule through him, I do not see why you cannot. Sure you would do so with more skill – and to better purpose.'

He stands so close his breath assaults her face. 'And that is what you'd have me be, is it? Puppet master to a dithering king. Tugging at his strings, smiling at his whims. Insinuating my thoughts into his empty head, hoping I'll still find them there tomorrow.'

She walks away not to look at him.

He keeps talking. 'Or is it just the money you want? Shall I play the beggar for you? Hold out my bowl like any petty lordling who'd gladly pander his wife for this title or that estate or even a paltry purse of coin.'

She comes to a halt; throws up her hands. 'I would not fear for my honour. I think the King barely inclined to bed his own wife, never mind anyone else's!'

She hears him curse behind her and, turning, sees hurt chase anger across his face. She comes to lay her hands against his cheeks, to force him to look at her.

'Richard, do you not see? He is barely a man and yet, every day, he wrongs you.'

His hands come up to cover hers. He draws them from his face, wraps them in his fingers. 'And you would make me less of a man even than he is. Cecily, I am the Crown's loyal servant. I give good service. I look to my own. If he doesn't see that. If that's not enough . . .'

Her heart is a hammer striking sparks from her throat. 'God's blood, Richard, that will never be enough!'

She pulls her hands from his, gains the door and slams it behind her.

His angry cry follows her as she strides the corridor's length. 'I will not be William de la Pole!'

Fine, she thinks. But if you won't, someone else will.

That night, she keeps to her own rooms and, for the first time in a long while, he does not come to her, either for sleep or love. She is woken by the sound of swallows chattering at her window, of men gathering in the bailey, and her women, tip-toeing about her dressing room, whispering, no doubt, about where her lord is.

She is up and out early. At the foot of the castle steps, she stops.

He's there already, standing with his captains at the head of his force. They hang on his words. From the slide of his eyes she knows he's seen her, but he carries on talking. One of the men laughs. Then they're nodding and moving away to the front of their units, where sergeants are shouting to bring men into marching order. It would take twenty steps to reach him, but she'll not take them. Now here are the grooms bringing his horse up, that showy stallion he brought with him from France. One of them has his hands netted to boost him to the saddle. He's about to put his boot in them, but hesitates. A word to the groom, who steps back to wait. He's coming towards her.

She raises her chin.

He stops a stride away and looks at her. Raises a brow.

She puts out her hand.

He shakes his head, kisses her fingers and smiles, guarded. 'Still angry?'

'Still sulking?'

Then they're both smiling.

'We'll speak of it when you get back,' she tells him.

He squints into the sunlight, pulls on his gloves. 'Now there's something to look forward to.'

He's back within a fortnight. MacGeoghegan brought to heel. But only just.

'Why wasn't our intelligence better?' Cecily wants to know.

Richard is evasive. He'll look to it. But, in truth, no one had imagined his adversary able to field so many men. Reports had spoken of raiding parties hundreds strong. Not an organized force of two thousand. When Richard and MacGeoghegan squared up to each other on the borders of Meath, they'd found themselves almost equal for numbers. Both men had spat in the dust and settled into their saddles to think. When Richard offered pardon in exchange for an end to banditry, an oath of allegiance and recompense for the burned villages, MacGeoghegan agreed and dispersed his men. Richard set up a commission to administer the reparations and stayed to see the first payments made before riding for home.

It's a desultory return. Nothing much to celebrate, except that nobody's dead.

'I'd rather you'd put his head in a noose,' says Cecily.

'I only kill when I have to,' he reminds her. 'And I prefer to fight when the odds are better.'

He's an old-fashioned soldier, Richard. He believes men who have sworn their lives to him have the right to expect he won't waste them.

'But if you don't kill your enemies, they oft times get up and fight you again.'

'Then I will improve the odds. Next time I'll take four thousand.'

'Then we'd better find a way to pay for them.'

*

So they write to her brother Salisbury, who is with the King's Parliament in Leicester. Richard hopes his is one of the reasonable voices that the King will listen to now de la Pole is gone.

'Don't hold back,' says Cecily.

He does not. He asks for the money he is owed, so that he can wage men to put down insurrection. He exaggerates a little when he suggests the threat is great enough that Ireland may otherwise be lost. Less so, when he says he'd rather die than see that happen.

They wait a month for a response and, when it comes, it changes everything. Letters from Salisbury and Oldhall arrive within a week, each with the same tale to tell.

'You'll get no money now, Richard,' writes Salisbury. 'The violence that took down de la Pole has become a contagion. The men of Kent have risen.'

'Jack Cade's mob was fifteen thousand strong when he brought it to Blackheath,' says Oldhall. 'God knows who he is, but men follow him. He swears no quarrel with the King, but denounces his evil counsellors; those who sold off France, who oppress poor men and set aside law and order for gain. According to Cade, de la Pole was the first of them, but not the last. Though they swear they did not kill him.'

'I rode with Henry to Blackheath,' says Salisbury. 'We were twenty thousand when we got there, Henry swearing he'd see every rebel dead. Cade backs off into Kent and we think we've got him on the run. But when the men Henry sends after them don't come back, and their bodies start showing up in ditches and trees, he takes fright and buggers off to Kenilworth. And he takes half the army with him. The half he's left behind thinks Cade to be much in the right and seems of a mind to join him.'

'Now Cade's back, with a rebel army,' says Oldhall. 'They came up through Southwark. The sneaky bugger had the bridge ropes cut in the night so it couldn't be raised against them, so they clopped over it and were in the city straight. There's been no looting, mind. It's the King's men they're after – and who can blame them? Corrupt bastards to a man. But you'll get no money, Richard, for Treasurer Saye is pulled from the Tower and his head rolls down Cheapside. They say Lord Scales will lead a force against the rebels tomorrow and drive them out of Southwark.'

'Richard,' says Salisbury, 'get yourself home. Cade is calling for the lords of the old royal blood to be given the reins of England under the King. He's named you chief among them. And he's taken to calling himself Mortimer. And don't imagine anyone's forgotten for a moment that it was Mortimer blood your father died for. Anyway, no one knows who the bugger is, but those with little cause to love you whisper that, since he comes in your name, you must have sent him. I pray you did not.'

And a week later, another letter from Oldhall. 'Get yourself home, Richard, for Cade is dead and Caen is fallen. Edmund Beaufort's back in England. He's asking how Jack Cade became John Mortimer and wondering where you are in all this. He's swearing he'll set the world to rights. And Henry has been fool enough to believe him and name him Constable of England.'

Impossible, now, to stay.

'You were right,' says Richard. 'We should have gone when de la Pole was killed.'

She says nothing. What would be the point? Besides, there's too much to do.

It's well into August before they're ready. Richard refused to go until all was in order. Ormond is named deputy and has been at his shoulder day and night; meetings and conferences, orders and plans; harassed scribes massaging sore fingers, and fast-horsed messengers sending up dust every hour of the day. She's seen the letter Richard has written to the King saying that he is coming, explaining the good order in which he leaves Ireland, promising to wait on him on his return. It should be in Henry's hands by now. She wonders if it is in Edmund Beaufort's.

But today is their last day. Tomorrow they'll ride out of Trim, and she cannot imagine they will ever return. But the sun is warm, the sky blessedly empty of rain, so when she looks into Richard's tired morning face and sees the sadness in it, she tells him they will have one last day of pleasure. They will fly their hawks on the banks of the Boyne and ride to Tara; to the hill's top, this time, from where, they've been told, all the counties of Ireland will be given to their sight.

'Ormond must come too, then,' says Richard, 'for there's much still to speak of. Besides,' he tells her, when her smile falls, 'he's promised, many times, to tell us the hill's history, and has not yet.'

It's a good morning's hawking. Rabbits mostly, though Richard has brought down a hare. Its muscled hind legs are crossed in a hitch at the falconer's shoulder and its head falls almost to his knees. A thing built for an arrow's speed, now bouncing, quiverless and dull, against a servant's greasy jerkin.

They send the birds and their kill back to the castle and ride on to Tara, up through its wooded slopes, where flies are drawn to the sweat of their horses. She feels her palfrey's muscles bunch with the effort of the climb and her hand comes away wet from its hide. As they come out of the trees, into the light of the open heath, it tosses its head and sets its harness jangling. They've not come so far before. Ormond rides ahead of them, heralded by skylarks rising from the grass. I should have brought the hawk, she thinks.

'There was a great fort here,' Ormond shouts back, circling

his hand above his head to describe it. 'The fort of the pagan kings. And from it ran five roads, broad and clear, carrying royal authority to every corner of Ireland.'

On foot they trace the great circular ditch that, he says, marked the fort's boundaries. A fold of green that, Cecily thinks, could be anything.

'It was here St Patrick brought the gospel when first he came to Ireland,' Ormond calls back, striding. 'The pagan Laoghaire, who was king then, wouldn't bow to him. But God had his way with him, and the old kingship is gone now for ever.' He turns then and laughs. 'Especially since we came.'

At the hill's bare centre stands a stone, smooth and white, almost as tall as a man.

'What's that?' asks Cecily, shielding her eyes and pointing.

'Ah,' says Ormond. He leans in and leers. 'Don't go near.' Then he takes her arm and draws her to it, Richard following, kicking at shamrocks in the grass.

When they stand before it, Ormond reaches out a hand, but doesn't touch. 'It is the *Lia Fáil*. Destiny's Stone.' He holds up his arms about it, playing the druid. 'The Maker of Kings.'

In the days before Patrick, he tells them, kingship didn't pass from father to son. It was given by the gods to the man of most merit. 'The one who had the temerity to ask, and courage to face the test.' He looks at them and grins.

'Well, yes,' says Richard. 'There would be a test.'

'First he must win to his bed Maeve, Queen of the World.' He sketches a bow to Cecily. 'You've done that already, Richard. Then he must drink her mead and not die.'

'I breathe yet,' says Richard, warming to the game.

'And gallop his horse at a stone wall and trust it will fall before him.'

'Now that's just not sensible.'

Cecily laughs.

'Then he must lay his hand on this stone and, if the gods

approve him, it will sing out his name.' Ormond holds his hand an inch from the stone's top. 'Richard, Richard, Richard!'

He's laughing, then looks round at the sound of voices drifting up to them from the treeline. It's the followers. They've struggled up the hill with baskets and boxes and a great rolled canopy for shade. Good, thinks Cecily, I'm hungry. And there goes Ormond, striding down the hill to meet them, waving a welcome.

She turns to Richard, who stands before the stone, his chin in his hand.

'I dare you,' she says.

He turns his head, smiles slow, lays his testing fingers against the white stone, cocks his head to listen. There's nothing. Just the voices below them, and the skylarks sending up their song.

He frowns at her, mock rueful.

She steps to him, turns his frown back to a smile with a kiss. 'It's only a story,' she whispers in his ear.

She threads her arm through his, and they set off down the hill.

24

September 1450
  Wales

They've made no secret of their coming. No reason why they should. Rounding the northern tip of Anglesey then sailing down its eastern coast, ever in sight of land and flying the blue and murrey of York. No surprise, then, that William Bulkeley has had word of it. He keeps Beaumaris Castle, across the narrow straits from Wales. He should be preparing a welcome. But here he stands on castle dock, with armed men at his back, shouting across the water that they cannot land.

Cecily narrows her eyes in the evening light and lays a hand on her husband's sleeve.

'What are you saying, man?' Richard shouts from the prow, but the offshore wind takes his voice away.

Bulkeley leans forward, cups his ear. As if that will help.

'King's orders, my lord,' he calls back. Then his hand is in the air and he's signalling, 'I'll come to you.'

Along the dock he runs, down narrow steps to a skiff, whose oarsmen have their muscles warm and ready for him. In the boat and here he comes, ducking low under the chain cast across the dock to bar their entry. When he looks up again, Cecily sees that shame has painted his face crimson. As well it might, she thinks. You were glad enough to feast us on our way to Ireland. Bowing and scraping and grateful for the honour.

When the little boat comes alongside, Richard orders a ladder be thrown down but, though Bulkeley struggles to stand in the bobbing craft, forcing the oarsmen to grab for the gunwales to steady it, he shouts up that he'd best not board.

'Why not?' Richard's voice is grim.

Bulkeley looks nervously over his shoulder across the stretch of water that separates him from his men, then back again. 'What force do you come with, my lord?'

'What force do I need, are you set to fight me? I come with no force, man. I am the Duke of York, the King's heir come home.'

That has Bulkeley tottering, and turning his hat in his hands. 'My lord, the King has named you traitor.' The hat is near torn in two. 'A watch has been set to bar you from all ports.'

Dear God. She watches Richard's knuckles wrap white about the ship's rail and hears him curse God's blood beneath his breath. The rough crossing of the Irish Sea has threatened her stomach more than once, but now bile stings her throat and there is a pitch beneath her feet that has nothing to do with the tide. She locks her knees, takes a breath and holds it.

'I don't believe it, my lord, of course,' Bulkeley calls up. 'But if you try to land, I'm ordered to arrest you. To take you to Conwy Castle to await the King's justice.' Another look over his shoulder, as if he fears he'll be heard onshore. 'I've no wish to do it, my lord. But the King's officers are here and if you try to land they'll give me no choice in the matter. Or you.' He looks up, wrings his hands. 'Sail on to Denbighshire, my lord, where your own loyal men are,' he urges. 'Come ashore there.'

When the ship turns about at his order, it's Richard who loses his stomach. He staggers across the deck like a drunkard, half stumbling down the steps to their cabin. Eager to follow him, Cecily looks behind her at the milk-white faces of her children and their nurses. Thank God for Annette. That good woman is already bundling her charges back below decks and, though her eyes are as shock-widened as anyone's, she nods a hasty assurance over her shoulder as she goes.

When Cecily reaches him, Richard is already on his knees and heaving. She grabs a basin, holds his head till he's done. When he looks up at her, his brow sweat-beaded and his lips white, she hardly knows him. His fingers are fisted in her skirts as if, without her, he might fall.

'A traitor, Cecily. He has named me traitor. Sweet Christ.'

She joins him on the floor, pulling his head to her shoulder, while her own mind grasps for purchase on that word; the word that made his father meat for the headsman and is come now to threaten the neck beneath her hand. Beyond the cabin's thin wall baby George sets up a cry. A sharp tug draws her heart across the many miles to Ludlow, where Edward is, and Edmund, a traitor's sons now, and far beyond the reach of her arm.

'Dear God, Richard,' she says. 'We need an army.'

She feels the intake of breath, the tensing of muscle as he steadies himself.

'Yes.'

They sail on into a late summer twilight and a blessedly moon-lit night, to land at the Clwyd's wide mouth; they clamber up the beach at dawn, children and nurses and a meagre guard of thirty men, and other boats of their flotilla to follow. They pull themselves on to horses that are wet to their flanks and nervous from the offloading, and set off for Denbigh, a twenty-mile ride into their own Welsh heartlands. They send a messenger ahead, to prepare the castle's steward for their arrival, and to sound the call for Welshmen of York's affinity to come to his aid.

When they arrive, salt-slapped and road-weary, towards day's end, the first men to answer the summons are already straggling into the town and an encampment is forming on castle green. Riding in, Cecily looks about her.

Please God, more will come.

*

By the time they ride into Ludlow, three days beyond Denbigh, they have the makings of an army. Fifteen hundred march behind them under the castle's towering barbican. Eight-year-old Edward seems more excited at the sight of it than of his parents, though he bows neatly to his father and doesn't resist when Cecily pulls him into her arms. He is grown so much taller. His head rests now just below her breast when she bends to kiss it. His hair is spun gold between her fingers, warm, new-washed and scented with rosemary. Edmund, as ever, hovers just behind him, so she pulls him in too. But she can't hold them long. Servants clatter all about them, Annette shepherds fretful children and George is crying again. From behind comes the bark of sergeants, as hard-marched men are ordered to make camp in the outer bailey. Edward is on his toes, trying to see it all. There's no time.

'Inside,' she says. 'Now.'

'So many men, father! Are you for war?' Edward dances backwards before them up the steps, at risk of falling.

His father takes his shoulders, turns him about.

'I am not. I am for the King's justice. I ride to Westminster tomorrow to meet with him.'

'Let me go with you!'

Inside, men wait for them. Some are of their affinity and have been summoned, others have themselves sought the safety of Ludlow's stout walls. They have much to say. Cade may be dead, they complain, but there's violence across the country. King's men everywhere. Royal officers and administrators live in fear of uprisings, riots or murder. Petty nobles mass private armies to settle personal scores. They each want to know what Richard's intentions are, why he has returned.

'To bring sense to all of this,' he tells them. 'To restore the King's justice.'

Alone at last, they plan their way through night's darkness;

steal fitful sleep in the early hours, then rise with the dawn to ready Richard for the road.

As she strides beside him to their leave-taking, he says he will leave half his force in her command, to defend Ludlow, should it come to that.

She tells him he is a fool and should take them all.

'I go to swear allegiance to my king,' he says. 'Not to fight him.'

She stops.

He walks on a step or two then turns, squares his shoulders, ready.

'I dare say Gloucester said the same. Remember him? He was the King's heir, just as you are, but he feeds worms now.'

'I remember. But I am not an old man.' He pats his chest, pulls a smile from somewhere. 'And my heart is strong.'

She strikes his shoulder, almost hard. 'Men can still put a blade through it.'

They have neither of them forgotten Gloucester. His ghost has ridden beside them all the way from the Clwyd. King's heir and uncle, loyal and loving all his life. Yet, at need, de la Pole taught Henry to fear and hate him. It's easy to make Henry do things when you stand by his side. Edmund Beaufort stands there now. And, while Gloucester was childless and old, Richard is a man in his prime and has all the sons the King lacks. Cecily knows that, if Beaufort is looking for reasons for Henry to fear her husband, Jack Cade and his rebels have given him one. But her womb has given him three more.

'Just promise me you won't go into the King's presence without a sword at your hip and a guard at your back.'

25

In the end he rides with eight hundred. They look like nothing more than the lordly escort any great man might take when he rides into the world on a fine September morning. But under every fine cloak lies a close coat of mail, every man has a blade at his side, and the long-legged coursers they ride are as fit for battle as swift travel. It's enough, he says, to make a showing. To defend himself, at need.

Pray God a show is all that's needed.

She watches from the walls as he rides out down Broad Street towards Ludford Bridge and the roads that lead east and south to London. Outpacing him speeds a lone messenger, his horse throwing up dust and carrying to the King the letter they've composed together. I am your true liege man and servant, it says. If any say otherwise, they lie. Call them, and I, to your presence, let them charge me and I will answer.

At last, even the noise of his going is over. She bows her head and feels the risen sun beat upon it. She's nauseous, and there's a taste on her tongue like old coins. She knows what it means. Her hands find their way to her belly. She's with child again. Conceived in a green Irish summer when the sun's heat was still a blessing. God's blood. What need has she now of another babe to pull on her? She steps down from the wall and finds her boys behind her. Edmund, tow-headed beside his brother's gold, stands quiet, but Edward is surly, throwing his weight and kicking his heels.

'I wanted to go with him,' he accuses. 'You should have let me.'

Her hand strikes his head faster than a snake. 'Would you were a man that you could be of such use!'

Striding past him to the tower stair, she hears his scream of shock and outrage, then his tutor's hushing.

Let him shout, she thinks. Stoke the fire in him. Better angry than weeping.

She is not kept short of news. Every second or third day a messenger comes from Richard. Each is given food, a fresh horse, then sent back with her reply. It is some comfort to hear that, as he rides, more men of his affinity come to swell his numbers.

'I am thankful for that,' she writes him.

He replies that, in the towns he passes through, knights and burghers complain of the loss of Normandy – and of the King's favourites, who ride roughshod over their rights. They are glad he is come and petition him to take up the reins of government, as Cade said he should. 'It will not make Edmund Beaufort love me,' he confides.

'He hates you already,' she reminds him. 'And you must wrest him from the King's side.'

Richard writes that several nobles and not a few royal officers have come. 'They want to know what I'm about,' he says. 'To serve the King's justice, I tell them, and to clear my name. And, yes, you may send word to the King of that intent.'

Among those who come is her sister Anne's husband, the Duke of Buckingham.

'Your sister keeps a good table,' Richard writes. 'I am their guest at Maxstoke tonight. I've learned much from them of Cade's rebellion, for Buckingham led Henry's forces against it and put the rebel's head on a spike. He confirms that Cade called himself Mortimer. I have assured him I was no part of it.'

Cecily spits venom. The husband of her sister should have known that without asking.

He sends her fair copy of the letter Buckingham encouraged him to write to the King. It repeats his loyal assurances and says he comes only to serve and prove his honour. 'Buckingham will send it under cover with his own,' he tells her. 'I am grateful for that.'

Cecily has already heard from Anne herself. She has written to all her family in the time he's been gone. To Anne, of course. To Salisbury and his shining son, Warwick. To Katherine, whose son is Norfolk's duke, and Eleanor, who is wife to Northumberland's earl. To George Baron Latimer and Edward Baron Bergavenny. To Robert, who is Bishop of Durham.

They all say the same: Richard must build bridges. His golden chance is lost.

She reads the shrug of shoulders in their pages. De la Pole's death left a space at Henry's side. Edmund Beaufort won the race to fill it. They don't say whether, should it come to a fight, they'll stand with Richard.

She had known better than to ask. Why should they? They are in calm waters and will not brave a storm for her.

Two weeks pass, the weather gives way to autumn, and still Richard has not completed his cautious progress to London. Every morning she rises, sick to her stomach; through every day she fears news of ambush, attack or arrest on his way. None comes.

At last, she opens a letter addressed from the capital and in Richard's hand. She orders the room emptied. When all are gone and the door closed behind them, she takes a seat by the fire, lays a hand on the early swell of her belly, and reads.

He came to the city with three thousand men, left most of them outside the walls and rode in with two hundred. At the door to the King's presence chamber he was met with crossed pikes, forbidden entry until his guard of twenty stood down their weapons. She hears the steel in his voice, calling in to the King from the threshold, and her heart beats tabor-fast with his.

'Your Grace, gladly will I surrender my sword to you, but my enemies have spoken against me to my king and, until I know who they are, you must excuse that I come armed.'

The tumult of the room rises in her own ears, and then comes the King's querulous voice.

'Let him come in. I have nothing to fear from my cousin of York.'

26

The gates open to Richard's messenger as she leads her household to vespers. In Ludlow going to prayer means braving the weather, for the castle's chapel stands alone in the bailey. It was built to honour crusader knights, who fought their way to salvation through blood and heat. Its loneliness mirrors Jerusalem's Holy Sepulchre and the life of the Magdalene to whom it is dedicated. Today's weather has been vicious, with tearing winds driving sleet and rain down off the western hills. To walk out in it is a prayer in itself, a sacrifice of comfort, a dedication of cold feet. Cecily accepts it, though the wild air threatens the torches that light her way, and the slick cobbles are treacherous underfoot. She looks up from watching her step when she hears the heavy pull of wood and a skid of hooves. She squints to see the gate-keep, hunched against the weather, pointing the way for a messenger, who throws his reins to a shivering groom and sets off on his buffeted way towards her.

'Your Lord has passed the priory at Bromfield,' he tells her. 'He will be home within the hour.'

His news makes it unclear what she should pray for, so she sends everyone to the chapel ahead of her and turns on her heel to make ready.

She has ordered it that, at the close of each day of Richard's absence, all of her people should come together to pray for his safe return. She herself, of course, has prayed for it at every office, from matins through to compline, and her canons have kept vigil day and night.

Now, standing in his chambers before a hastily made up fire, watching him wring rainwater from his hair while his valet peels wet layers off him, she is less than glad of it. Not of his safety, of course, or his weathering of the journey, but that he is returned at all. He should be in London, sticking like a burr to the King.

'Richard, I can by no means imagine why you are here.'

Behind her, clattering servants carry pails of water up the stairs for his bath. Good, that'll warm him. And they've brought meat at least, for look how lean he is. He lowers his head for his man to draw off his sodden shirt. Free of it, he shakes more water from his hair, points a chin at her stomach.

'And I can by no means imagine why you did not tell me you are with child.'

'Because you had more important things to concern yourself with.' She knows how fragile the peace is. 'Are you at odds with the King?'

'Hard to say. I am no longer called traitor if that's what you mean.' He shrugs. 'I am his dear cousin.'

The valet reaches to untie the points of his hose.

Richard's hand bars him. 'I'll manage this, see to the bath.' Then he thrusts his chin again, to Cecily. 'When?'

She watches the valet pick up armfuls of sodden cloth and make his way to the antechamber where, in a low voice, he starts ordering his lord's comfort.

'An Easter baby, perhaps.'

'Mmm.' He nods, loosening the cords at his thigh, then looking up at her. 'I am home because I want your counsel.'

'Do you not read my letters?'

'Alright. Because I missed you.'

'That's not a good reason.'

He holds out a hand. When she relents and takes it, he pulls her towards him and tries for a kiss.

She turns a shoulder. 'Phew, you stink of wet wool and horseflesh.' She pushes his hands from her and makes for the door, then takes pity and looks back. 'You may come to me when you are clean. And worthy of my nose.'

An hour later, he appears at her room's threshold. She's guessed right that he's ripe for bed, and her women know well enough to welcome him and leave. They love before they talk. He's tired, but not too tired for that and, as ever, it puts life in him. When they're done he's hungry, so they make a warm tent of the blankets and feast on the soft white manchet bread that is left by her bed nightly, and which she never eats. Now, like his son, he smells of rosemary. Of the wine they've drunk. And of her.

'I hope now you will tell me truly why you are here.'

He looks a little shamefaced. 'For this. For love and talk.' He pulls himself up to lean his back against the headboard.

She rises to stir the fire and then returns. It's hard to be patient.

'If you'd asked my advice, I'd have said stay by the King. I dare say that's where Edmund Beaufort is.'

He sighs. 'It's where he always is. Or with the Queen. Or they are all three together.'

There are things he has scrupled to write of. His letters have told her, of course, of that first meeting with Henry, how Beaufort bristled and the Queen scowled when the King put an arm about his shoulder and said it had all been a misunderstanding. That, though he'd feared him coming as an enemy, he was glad to welcome him as a friend. That he'd wept for joy on receiving Richard's letter. Till the ink ran from the page, he said.

'Did I not, Marguerite?' Henry turned to his wife.

'Sure the Duke of York has given you cause for tears.'

Then turning back to Richard, 'You see, the general whispering against you was so strong. That you would come and take my throne from me.'

But Henry would not say who had whispered, except Cade who was dead and, in truth, had said no such thing. When Richard begged the right to answer his accusers, face-to-face before his king, Henry waved it away.

'It doesn't matter now,' he said. 'Just the general crowd. My kingdom is full of violence and so many wish me ill. Ask Beaufort here, he'll tell you. He watches them all.'

'It's why I am come to you out of Ireland,' Richard told him. 'To stand by your side. To oppose your enemies and restore your justice.'

Then Beaufort broke his silence. 'Is that Jack Cade's idea or your own?'

'It's hard for me to know Cade's purpose, for I never knew the man.'

'Go ask him. His head was still on London Bridge when last I passed.'

'Then he will give me scant answer. But if he stood before us now and spoke against my king, then I would have his head again.'

He turned back then to Henry, who was smiling and whose eyes had never left him. 'I've heard the rumours, Your Grace. That I stood behind Jack Cade and spurred him on—'

Henry held up a hand. 'That he was your man, Richard, and did all he did at your order.'

'I swear to you, on my honour, he did not.'

Henry leaned to him then, close to his ear. 'I believe you, cousin.' Then the King's hand was upon his breast, and the smile was gone. 'For to believe otherwise would grieve me bitterly.'

'Did he believe you, do you think?' Cecily asks now, lying

beside him, while the candles waver and the fire shifts in its grate.

Richard takes her hand and pulls it to his breast. 'I truly have no idea.' He shakes his head as though puzzled. 'In that instant? Yes. Perhaps. But the next?'

'Pah! He is playing games with you.'

'And sometimes I believe him cunning enough to do that, to cajole, to flatter, to threaten with intent. But at others . . .' He shakes his head again. 'It's as if he is a child that others play upon. From one moment to the next I never know.'

'Sure Beaufort plays upon him.'

'And the Queen. I know well enough it is they who rule England now. Not Henry.'

'They still keep close then, Beaufort and the Queen?'

'Like snakes in a basket. Do you know he's now in her pay, too, as well as the King's? For his especial good counsel, I'm told. She pays him a salary.'

She is incredulous. 'For his counsel? I wonder what other services he offers for a salary.'

'Ha!' He squeezes her hand.

'The Queen is not with child?'

'No.'

'Does the King go often to her bed?'

'God's blood, Cecily, ask her women!'

'Were I there, I would.' She stares at him, wide-eyed.

'Yes, I'm sure you would.' He dips his head. 'Men say he sleeps most nights alone. And that he prays much.'

She can't help but smile. 'Then I'll wager she prays too.'

Whether he was believed or not, Cecily knows Richard has sworn his oath of fealty before the court and that, when he did so, the King kissed him on both cheeks. With tears in his eyes, so Richard had written her. After, when Richard asked for speech, he was invited to walk with Henry to his chambers. He told the King that, now all was well between them, he would attend the next Parliament, as was his right, and asked for authority there.

'We should not ignore the Commons' calls for reform,' he told his king. 'They think England ill governed, taxes too high, bread too dear. Well, let me hear and judge what is reasonable.'

'You think they have cause?'

'I don't know. I need to hear.'

'They mew always about the loss of France. Don't they understand the benefits of peace?'

'Perhaps they've not felt them yet.'

Henry, flanked by the inevitable Beaufort and the ever-present Queen, drew to a halt at his words. 'I want all my people to feel them, in their hearts and in their purses.'

Cecily had laughed when she read that.

'Then let me hear what they have to say,' Richard said. 'And let's have a Speaker they can respect, one who understands France and fought for it. William Oldhall is a good man.'

Henry looked hard at him. 'He is your man.'

'He is his own. That's why he's good.'

Beaufort bristled, but the King laughed, clapped Richard on the shoulder, and granted it full willing.

'Well done,' Cecily had whispered on reading of it, folding the page.

Richard's next letters, though, had not come from London. They told her he rode with her nephew Norfolk into East Anglia to see how tempers were in what was once Suffolk's heartland. He found them ill, as elsewhere. Cade may be dead, but in every county the unrest that birthed his rebellion still simmers beneath the surface. He went briefly to Fothering-hay, to visit his sons under stone. She has no wish to speak of that. She'd imagined he'd then return to London, stay by the King until Parliament opened. But here he is, in her bed.

She asks him again. 'Why?'

He shrugs. 'My journey east was at Henry's bidding but, most surely, at Beaufort's prompting. To get me out of the way. Out of his way.'

'And you've played into his hands very readily.'

He grimaces, slides down the bed to lie flat.

Impossible, now, to hide the irritation in her voice. 'Why would you do that? And then why come here?'

'Because I hate it, Cecily.' He will not look at her, and throws an arm over his eyes. Now he tells her what he did not write, but she has long guessed. That the voice raised against him had been Beaufort's, that the watch on the ports was set at his order. That, in London, the man's spies dogged his steps, so that he could barely walk for tripping over them and never got to see the King alone. 'It's intolerable.'

She looks at him, stern. 'Do you believe yourself the King's heir?'

'Yes, of course.'

'And first among England's dukes, well worthy of a king's attention, and—'

'Yes, yes, yes. Of course.'

She waits a long moment, then dares. 'Do you remember? We spoke once, very long ago, about a nobleman's duty when a king is unfit to rule.'

He is quiet a long while. She watches him breathe. It is a test that has her own heart hammering.

'I have not forgot. Cecily –' his hand sweeps up through his hair – 'we wouldn't get the support. The Commons, perhaps. The likes of Cade and his men. But, without noble support, that's more danger to me than blessing. And our fellow dukes and earls are either snout in the trough with Beaufort or, like your brother Salisbury, keeping their noses clean and getting on with business. A weak king isn't always a bad thing, providing no one calls you his enemy. I'm not the king for them,' he grimaces. 'They wouldn't like the changes I'd make.'

Her heart trips, as it does when she slips the leash to set a hound running, or looses the jess from her fingers to let a hawk rise to its kill. A tight-reined excitement, a held breath. The idea is in his head, and she did not have to put it there. They can speak of it now, as they do of all things. It's not a thing to be done today, he has the truth of that. It may never be. But one day, if the need is great and a chance at hand, she can believe, now, that he will not baulk at it.

She lays her fingers across his brow, irons out the lines that have deepened there since Trim. 'Then what will you do now?'

He sighs beneath her touch. 'Go back to London. Push for reform. I've got Oldhall in place now, and others. Work around Beaufort. Find ways to get Henry alone and talk to him.'

'You must wrest Beaufort from his side.'

'Aye. And put myself there.' He looks so miserable.

She leans down and kisses his closed eyes. 'We must speak of all of this. Of how it can be done.'

He smiles, wry. 'See. I do need your counsel. We must speak of it all. But I'm so tired, Cecily. Let me sleep now.' He turns on his side.

She rises to quench the candles and bank the fire. By its light she turns back to the bed, then stops at the window, leans by it to listen. Beyond the glass, the curtain and the warmth of this room, the untrammelled wind still hurtles knives of rain against the night.

27

December 1450–September 1451

When Richard writes that Edmund Beaufort is not only removed from the King's side but constrained within the Tower, Cecily wonders whether to salute her husband's ingenuity or thank God for a miracle. Either way, the news lightens her days. She imagines her enemy circling a bare cell like an angry dog, gnawing at the bars with bloody teeth. It's an indulgence, she knows. The reality is less colourful. Beaufort is comfortable enough, rescued from an angry mob that beset him at Blackfriars, and taken to the Tower for his own protection. The rescue, if not the assault, was Richard's work. He had friends fortuitously on hand to beat off the attackers, spirit Beaufort to safety, and despatch a swift-heeled messenger to tell Richard to make his way to the King.

'Where I plan to stay for as long as I can manage it,' he writes.

Well done, she smiles.

Next day, when two more of the King's close advisers were bloodied in similar attacks, Richard had no difficulty convincing Henry that his favourite was safest, for now, behind the Tower's stout walls. He then set himself the task of restoring the King's order in the city. His is a voice that angry men listen to, who they do not blame for injuries at home or abroad. That done, he rode with Henry through the streets, shoulder to shoulder, and with a force. He set his herald to cry out before him that any who threatened the King's peace would answer for it to the Duke of York. It made for a good show, his letter says.

Well done indeed.

Before he left Ludlow for London last month, they'd agreed their intent. Get Beaufort out of the way by whatever means. Convince the King of their loyalty and strength. Both, mind you, Cecily insisted, for one is security for the other. Then push for reforms that will stabilize government, with Richard at its heart. The first two he's achieved. The third will be more difficult.

She leans back and stretches a foot to the fire, strokes a hand over her swelling belly. Her fingers are stained with ink and ache from the slow work of writing. Her letters to Richard are of love and strategy; twin subjects she will not trust to a secretary. The parchment is sealed and will be on its way to him at first light. Now is the moment to push for reform, it tells him, and to turn Beaufort's sanctuary into imprisonment. 'My heart is with you, and my prayers line your path. I wish I were beside you. I am of more use among events than at home awaiting news of them.'

She'd wanted to go, but Richard would have none of it. Travelling in winter with a child in her belly and the country so unsettled would be madness, he said. She spat like a cat and let him go without her blessing, but sent enough after him to make amends.

She blinks sore eyes now and eases her back to standing. The maid, Katherine, silent enough to be forgotten, appears at her side, solicitous.

'Tell my women we go to compline,' she orders, and the girl is gone.

Cecily follows slowly, taking the long way through Ludlow's draught-ridden corridors to lay a hand on each of the doors that guard her children's sleep. Soon enough she hears feet pattering towards her and the swish of hurrying silks as her women catch her up. They wrap her in a cloak, put pattens on her feet and walk with her into the frosty night, drawn to the prayerful flicker of the chapel's windows. She shuns the icy wind, turns up her collar and nests her hands within her sleeves. She will give thanks for the day's news, for Beaufort's incarceration, for Richard's safety, for this step forward. She will beg another step, a certain path through the morass.

Today's news was good. Tomorrow's may be otherwise.

Richard walks on a sword's edge and, since she cannot be with him, prayer must be her labour.

The reform bill Richard presents to Parliament was drafted by him and Cecily together. It says the country is ill governed, to the detriment of its people. That English interests have been betrayed in France. That the King is misled by corrupt counsel. It lists those who must be held responsible. It is a list not dissimilar to Cade's, and Beaufort's name tops it. It calls for them to be imprisoned, forbidden the King's presence until they can be brought to trial.

'It reads like an ultimatum,' Richard had said as the ink dried.

'It is a trial of strength,' Cecily told him, folding its pages. 'But you must get Parliament to say it first, so that your voice can be its echo, not its clarion.'

With Oldhall in place that's easily done. But when Parliament speaks, the King dithers. Says he will. Says he won't.

'Until the Queen makes up his mind for him,' writes Richard. 'I told him, he must be seen to judge fairly. To listen to his people's petitions as God listens to his.'

'You sound like Jack Cade,' Marguerite had said. 'These men are our friends and we do not see that they have wronged us. Should we punish them to satisfy peasants who rose in rebellion against God's anointed? Who, by the way, my Lord of York, called on your name, when they did so.'

Cecily grimaces as she reads.

The King smiled. 'My queen has the right of it, of course. What good Christian man would so betray his friends?'

I should have thrown that chit of a girl into the Seine when I had the chance, thinks Cecily, tapping her finger against the page. But Marguerite is a girl no longer. She is a queen now, French and childless. She too steps on swords.

'It doesn't help that men still call out for me,' Richard writes. 'In London, Kent and across the country. Never have voices raised in support done a man such harm.'

Christmas comes, but brings little cheer. Richard's gift of news is that Edmund Beaufort struts like a cock through Westminster once again.

'The Queen,' he writes, 'argued that, since I have quelled the city's riots, it was safe for him to return. She is all smiles, of course, and the King ever in their company.'

If the Queen is happy, no one else is. Parliament is slighted no less than Richard, and men who'd hoped for justice with Beaufort gone are outraged by his return. By January, cries of discontent sound louder than ever. From Kent comes the threat of fresh rebellion.

'Let me ride out to quell it,' said Richard.

'That would hardly do,' responded the Queen. 'Since the rebels call out to you as to their saviour.'

So Beaufort rode into Kent to reap a harvest of heads. And the King went with him to see it done.

'That young bastard Henry Holland, too,' writes Richard. 'God grant our daughter grows to be a woman strong enough to curb him. She's yours, so I must believe she will.'

Through the misery of February and March, as Cecily's belly swells and her head aches, Richard's letters bring only agitation. He is isolated again, watched, spied upon, suspected. He prowls the fringes of the court, waiting in corridors, hoping for a turn in a tide that runs against him.

The King reopens Parliament in May.

'He needs it to grant taxes to prop up his teetering treasury,' Richard writes. Flexing its muscles, Parliament refuses to do so, unless the Duke of York is formally recognized as the King's heir, and given the pre-eminence in Government that such a title demands. 'Beaufort, of course, says I put them up to it.'

Parliament is dissolved on an angry instant, and Richard is called before a king in high temper, who snarls and snaps in circles about him. 'Then he raises his arm and I think, for a moment, that he'll strike me, Cecily. Then his arm's about my shoulder and there's tears on his cheeks and, sometimes, sometimes, I'd swear he's not right.'

That should not be news to you, she thinks.

'You're my cousin,' Henry told him, whining like a child denied. 'And I love you, well enough . . .' Then snarling again, 'But I will not raise above all others a man called upon by so many in challenge to myself.'

He means he will not raise him above Beaufort.

'I am loyal, Your Grace,' Richard said as the King turned his back on him. He cannot help but say it. 'And I am your heir.'

'God will bless us with a son.' Thrown over the King's shoulder as he stalked away.

You'd need to do something about that, Henry, thinks Cecily, folding the page.

Before Richard writes that he is coming home, another child is lost. Quiet Thomas, whose blue-tinged lips never opened in a cry. He is delivered two weeks after Easter, despaired of in his first hour, but holds until Ascension. Then, in his mercy, the risen Christ looses the tethers that bind body to soul, that he might rise with him to Paradise. So says her confessor.

Attempting more earthly consolation, Annette whispers it must surely be a relief to let him go, for the sight of his birdcage breast straining for air was enough to break a heart. Cecily finds strength enough to slap her, for she had not let him go and would have fought to keep him with her however long. She nurses her anger another week, then rises. She has other sons.

When Richard rides into Ludlow, at May's end, she takes care to have his children about her to welcome him. The girls in their finest making careful curtseys, George in her arms, and the boys racing across the castle yard, waving their practice swords and crying, 'Ai, for York!' then throwing themselves against him. She sees him note their new-gained height, for both have celebrated birthdays this last month; eight now and nine, a promise of the men they will become. It is meant to lighten his heart, but seems only to sadden him.

'They have a poor father,' he tells her.

'We will have no self-pity,' she says, with a soft slap to his shoulder. 'This was a skirmish. Nothing more. We pull back. We regroup. Remember what my uncle the cardinal used to say. The wheel turns. We'll catch it again as it rises.'

He nods, but they both know it was more than that. He is Edmund Beaufort's declared enemy now, and that is a danger to them all.

She takes him to bed, though it's the middle of the day, and lets him love her, though her body is sore still and she takes no pleasure in it. After, he is shamefaced and sorry, so it seems it did no good at all.

The summer is hot, weighted with loss. For want of something to spend it on, she wastes her time. She watches the river that was a torrent in winter turn sluggish, its listless course shaped only by the banks that hold it. She wishes it would storm and fill again.

Richard will not speak of their future. He spends much time with his growing sons. She believes it is because they are interested only in today; in whether he will ride with them or set them at the quintain, or drill their sword play. There is some pleasure in watching them. Edmund so attentive, emulating his father in all things, glowing quietly when praised, dipping his buff-coloured head when corrected and trying harder still. Edward listens with half an ear, argues back, does everything his own way till he finds a way that works, makes his father laugh, and revels in it.

When the boys go to their lessons, Richard calls his own arms master and trains with him, hours on end, as he never has before.

'What are you preparing for?' she asks him.

He only shrugs and squints into the sun.

'You're better at thinking than fighting.'

Yet what is there to think of, except how long this summer will last and what will end it?

In August she has an excuse to be on the move. Her nephew, the shining Warwick, has done his duty by his wife. He says the child is expected at summer's end and asks her to come. She has set her women to packing. Richard is sullen and getting in their way.

'She miscarried her first last year and fears for this one,' she tells him. 'Well, I know what that's like. She has no mother. I'll be a help to her, I'm sure.'

'I'd have thought it's the last thing you'd want. Cooped up with women talking about . . . whatever it is you talk about.'

'Don't sulk. We talk about you. Idiot. About what our men are doing. And how to get them to do what we want.' He shudders and she smiles. 'Have you forgotten that Edmund Beaufort is married to her half-sister? Who knows what I might learn?'

She learns a good deal. Her experience of childbed loss and gain make her indispensable to Warwick's Anne, whose other companions are young, little more than girls really, with a baby or two in their cradles at best. Cecily's the eldest of them, with three sons and three daughters, and all the learning that's come from bringing them into the world. She takes care not to speak of those she's buried and what she learned from them. She is practical, unsentimental and, when Anne confesses her fear of the pain, she shares her mother's trick.

'Give me your forearm,' she says. And, when Anne does, she wraps her hands around it, grips and twists, one hand forward, one hand back.

The girl's eyes widen.

'Don't cry out,' she warns, and twists harder. She has strong hands from hard riding on horses Richard picks himself to challenge her. When Anne's breath comes short, and her eyes close and water, she twists harder still, then lets go. 'You bore it.'

'Yes,' says Anne, rubbing the redness of her skin.

'Were it twice as hard, could you bear it still?'

'Yes.' Defiant.

'Good,' says Cecily. 'It's only pain. And your will is stronger.'

Later, she sees the girl examining the bruises her fingers have made on her, and smiles to see the pride in her face.

She becomes a confidante and, since the days of confinement are long and tedious, the talk can't always be of children. In the quiet watches she learns that Anne's anxiety to put a living child into her husband's arms is born, in part, from fear that much else she has brought to him is under threat. Cecily can see why she'd worry. It's surely not her looks or wit he values. Anne's three half-sisters have long contested her inheritance of the Warwick lands. One of them is married to Beaufort and, on her behalf, he threatens to press their case.

'If he does, we could lose so much . . .' says Anne.

'But sure, you need not fear; the King has confirmed the inheritance.'

'Yes, but you know he is changeable.'

'And Beaufort persuasive,' Cecily concedes. 'Yes.'

'To be at odds with Edmund Beaufort is to be at odds with the King. I would not have us so.'

I would, thinks Cecily. It would make you our ally. It's time my nephew gave me more than smiles. I would greet an unhappy Warwick with open arms. Better yet if he brought his father, my brother, with him. 'Well, if anything comes of Beaufort's efforts, you can always turn to York for support.'

When the mood turns to gossip there's learning there, too. Anne can at least laugh at Beaufort as much as she fears him. Beaufort the lecher. Beaufort the fornicator. Beaufort the old goat.

'Don't call him old, ladies, please,' laughs Cecily. 'He has only a handful more years than my husband.'

'Oh, but he's not handsome like your lord,' says Anne, and her women nod, roll their eyes and sigh.

'I've little to say of the Duke of Somerset, but he is not unhandsome.' It is the single concession she will make for Edmund Beaufort.

They consider his legs. Whether he is tall enough or too tall. They concede that he has kept his hair, that his eyes are large and fine, and that the beard upon his jutting chin is not yet full grey.

'Sure there must be something that makes queens love him,' says Maud, the catty one.

'Our queen?' asks Cecily, mock surprised.

'Certain! You've seen how he walks behind her with his tongue hanging out?' Maud demonstrates. 'Or more than his tongue!'

Gales of laughter.

'More than his tongue with the old queen, I'm sure,' says Anne.

This is a scandal so old that Cecily had almost forgotten it;

that, in his youth, Edmund Beaufort made a harlot of Dowager Queen Katherine after her royal husband died and before she married that Welsh nobody, Owen Tudor.

'They say,' Anne whispers, 'that she was already carrying Beaufort's child when she gave Owen her vows.'

'Who told you that?'

'My mother, on her honour!' Hand on heart and eyes heavenward.

'Sure you were a young maid for such a tale.' Anne's mother is ten years dead. 'You think Edmund Tudor, the King's halfbrother, is Edmund Beaufort's son?'

'You see, he even bears his name.' Anne's eyes are wide with gleeful horror.

Cecily remembers Edmund Tudor and laughs; a tall man, diffident and handsome, to whom the King shows some favour, but Edmund Beaufort shows none. 'He has a younger brother, Jasper . . .?'

'Who looks so different,' says Anne.

Cecily concedes that he does.

'Short, dark and very, very Welsh.' Sly cat Maud.

More laughter, falling to sighs and shaking of heads.

'Oh, I don't know if it's true,' says Anne, surrendering breathless into her pillows. 'But it's a fine tale.'

'Well, I'm certain of one thing.' Maud is determined to bring the laughter back.

'What?' asks Anne.

'That Edmund Beaufort would not scruple to fuck a queen.'

And away they go again, tears in their eyes, hands shielding their blushes, shoulders shaking.

Cecily watches and smiles. She wonders when she became too old to laugh at such things.

28

September 1451–March 1452

Anne's labour begins on the third day of September. It ends on the fifth, in the small hours before the matins bell, when only priests and women work. The new mother is so tired she can greet her child's first cry with nothing more than a whimper and trembling fingers that reach out, but have no strength to hold.

'A girl,' Cecily whispers into Anne's ear as she lays the swaddled babe on her breast. 'Well done. A fine start. Boys will surely follow.'

But such consolation is needless. The mother's disappointment is stillborn the moment the red-faced bundle is placed in her arms. In her pale, weary face, eyes startle and widen. It awakens in Cecily an aching envy, the realization that other women feel, no less intensely than she did, that shock of love for the firstborn. That blade that comes from nowhere and sheathes itself in the heart.

Cecily is to be godmother. Later that morning, when she has slept an hour and drowned a raging thirst in watered beer, she takes the child to its father. He looks so pleased you'd swear he'd done the hard work himself. They step to the font together.

'She wants Isabel,' she tells him. 'For her mother.'

Warwick only grins and shrugs. 'Yes. Isabel,' he tells the priest.

It would have been Richard, for a boy. It seems not to matter so much, the name you give a girl.

When she returns to Ludlow, she finds her husband gone from home. She calls his marshal and steward to her and is told he's taken a thousand men into Somerset to quell a dispute between Thomas Courtney, who is Earl of Devon, and William Baron Bonville. Bonville is holed up in Taunton Castle, where Courtney has him under belligerent siege.

'He went there on the King's order?' she asks.

They shuffle their feet and say they believe not.

She has a week to brood on it; then he's back.

There's a looseness of limb about him as he strides into hall, like a muscle that's had the kinks worked out of it. Like a man who wouldn't say no to another fight. So, when they're alone, she gives him one.

He's walking around the table, pretending to take an interest in the food that's been brought, too restless to sit and sate his appetite.

She looks up from a measured smoothing of her sleeves. 'I am given to understand that, while I've been fostering our alliances, you've been making war? This is most unlike you.'

'Is it? I've been making the King's peace, Cecily. I seem to be the only man in England that wants to do it.'

'God knows why you must.'

He shrugs. 'Duty, perhaps. It's a lonely calling.'

'And what profit in it for us?' she barks, walking about the table to come face-to-face with him. 'Tell me how it adds to our peace to be embroiled in a dispute in the heart of Edmund Beaufort's dukedom?' She cocks her head. 'You do recall he's Duke of Somerset?'

He doesn't look at her. 'The dispute was *in* Somerset. It was *about* Cornwall.'

'Oh, I see. That makes all the difference.'

'It is in my jurisdiction. I'm still steward of royal justice south of the Trent, remember. I had good right.'

When he's like this she could slap him. 'Good right is not good reason.'

'Alright. I was showing the King that I can do what Edmund Beaufort cannot.'

'I'm sure he'll be grateful for the lesson. What was the dispute?'

He sets down a pheasant breast uneaten, wipes his hands on the tablecloth.

'Henry's incompetent government has somehow granted the stewardship of Cornwall to both Devon and Bonville. It's a rich office, so they're fighting over it. It's been rumbling on for months. Beaufort's done nothing about it, so now it's come to blows. I went down to Somerset to talk some sense into them both.' He stretches his neck. 'Look, disputes like this are springing up all over the country. If men can't get good judgement, they'll resort to violence.'

'And will you resolve them all?'

'Tom Courtney is an old friend. I'm trying to keep him out of trouble.'

'By putting us in it. Bah! You've been itching for a fight all summer.'

The pheasant and its platter crash to the floor.

'God's blood, Cecily, I don't itch for a fight. I itch for satisfaction, for work worthy of me, for recognition of what I am. What do you want? That I should sit here, idle, till I die?'

And he's off, striding the length of the hall and slamming the door behind him.

Two days later comes a summons from the King; Richard is invited to attend a council meeting, to explain his usurpation of authority in the West Country.

'Did you honestly think he'd thank you?' Cecily asks.

It seems he did.

Richard sulks and says he will not go. Nor will he speak of it. He sends a messenger to say he has not the leisure to wait upon his cousin the King, but confirms his commitment to peace and to royal justice.

Two sullen weeks pass, then comes a letter from William Oldhall that tells them just how angry Beaufort is. 'He speaks against you everywhere and to everyone,' he writes. 'And is more than ever in favour with the King.'

'Beaufort is made Captain of Calais,' Richard tells her, laying Oldhall's letter down and netting his hands over it. 'A reward for his fruitful service. His exertion in war and wise counsel in peace.' He speaks as if the words hold a knife to his throat.

Calais is almost England's last bastion in France. A trading port mostly. Its customs duties make up a third of the country's revenues, and the captain's cut is a rich one. Cecily fixes her eye on the bull's blood ruby twisting on Richard's finger. Last month they mortgaged more land to subsidize their deputy in Ireland. No point thinking about that.

'Calais,' she says, 'is not a bauble that should be worn on Edmund Beaufort's hat.'

'If the French move on it, as they threaten to, sure we can rely on him to lose it.'

She shrugs. 'His interest will be in its income more than its defence, for sure. But the one depends on the other, so perhaps he'll shift himself.'

They sit across the table from each other, the paper between them and the air thick with discontent. That damn ruby is still turning and Richard's frown is dark and deep. He's thinking, she knows, of all that has been given to Beaufort and taken from him. Of Henry's incompetence and Beaufort's abuse, the injustice of it and the danger. Perhaps, like her, he is counting allies in his head. They are too few. And they are keeping their heads down.

'What do we do, Cecily?'

She sighs. He won't like her answer. She despises it herself. 'We must bide our time.'

He nods, screws the paper in his hand. 'I'm going riding,' he says, gets up and walks away.

He doesn't say, come with me.

She doesn't say, I'll come.

Before Christmas, Oldhall writes again. And from a new address. He'd had word that there were moves planned against him, so had set lads outside his house, watching. When they broke in on his supper to say King's men were coming armed up the street, he grabbed the bag he'd packed a week ago, slipped out the back way and took his ready-harnessed horse up through the snow and shit of Cheapside, to the great abbey church of St Martin's Le Grand. He's paid enough in alms over the years. More, recently, just in case. So was sure of sanctuary.

'Beaufort's decided it was me that clonked him on the head at Blackfriars last year,' William writes. 'On your good orders, of course. Now, Richard, do nothing. He's hoping you will, so don't. He'll find no evidence, and the King has cause to love me. I fought beside his father. He'll not forget that.'

Richard sits pale, swallowing anger like cannon balls. Cecily watches him do it. They both know that men die without evidence every day, and that what the King remembers cannot be depended upon. Is this how it must be, she thinks. We sit and watch while Beaufort the terrier rips out the throats of our friends?

It makes for a miserable Christmas. They put on a show, invite men they hope to influence. Few of them come. Old Talbot does, though, bless him. Newly back from Rome, paying God with pilgrimage for his ransom from the French. He brings his wife, Margaret, who Cecily hasn't seen since Rouen, and dark-eyed Eleanor, fifteen years old now and as fair as her father is ugly. She has a husband, twice her age and paying her little notice. Another soldier, cut from the old cloth. His father a friend to hers. Cecily watches her strike up a quiet friendship with her own daughter, Anne, who must go to her own disinterested husband soon enough. Perhaps they speak of their marriages.

'Christ's balls but Beaufort hates you, Richard.' The old soldier has finally drunk enough of their good wine to say things he wouldn't say sober. It's Epiphany evening, a good time for truths to be revealed, Cecily supposes. The hall is half empty and the servants are clearing the boards. The children have long gone to bed, and even Eleanor has trailed sadly off after her husband.

Richard is sober as a stone. 'I've no love for him. Nor had you or I for his brother. You know what they are, John.'

'Bootless bastards both, and I hate one no less than the other. Look, none love Edmund Beaufort but those that live off him. But I call him friend because the King does. You know how it goes, Richard.'

'I know. But mine is not the only voice raised against him.'

'No, but it's the only voice that matters. Who are the rest? Knights in the shires with their noses out of joint, sour-bellied soldiers, the hard-up home from France . . .'

'They've had rough justice, John.'

His shrug says he knows this better than anyone. 'Well, the world's a rough place.' He leans across the table, lays a meaty fist on Cecily's arm. 'Lady, tell your fool of a husband. While the King loves Edmund Beaufort he can't afford to be his enemy.'

'It's good advice,' she tells him. 'But it comes too late. Besides, I'm Beaufort's enemy, too.' She smiles at Richard and he smiles back. The first time in a long time. 'But we are loyal to the King, John. You must know that.'

'Beaufort tells the King you intend to rise against him.'

'He's been saying so for over a year now, John.' She spreads her hands. 'Yet here we sit.'

He nods and frowns. 'What do you want of me, Richard? I love you, but I'll not stand against Beaufort for you, I've too strong a wish to keep my head on my shoulders.'

'I don't ask it.' Richard is sudden and vehement. 'Only make the King see I am loyal.' He looks up from the table. 'Is the Bishop of Hereford still here?' he shouts. 'Bishop Boulers?'

There he is, halfway down the hall and deep in his cups, a typical churchman. He looks up, baffled.

'Come here, man.' Richard has them up on their feet, Bishop Boulers and soldier Talbot, out from the hall and across the corridor.

Cecily picks up her skirts and follows them to an anteroom, ill lit and bare, piled with soiled linen and plate from the feasting. Richard closes the door behind him, sets his back to it.

'I am in earnest now,' he says, holding John's blinking eyes with his own. 'Give me your cross, Father,' his hand out, peremptory.

The bishop fumbles, gives it over.

'I have one enemy, John. Edmund Beaufort. None other. And by his making, not mine.' He's on his knees now, the cross in his hands before him. 'I am the King's true man. Am now. Ever have been. Will be till death. Loyal. Tell him, John. Tell him what I have pledged before you tonight.'

An hour later, the last of the company abed, Cecily goes to her room and finds her maids sent away and Richard, waiting.

'Well,' she says, the closed door to her back. 'That was a show. Oaths sworn on the cross. Churchmen called as witness. You on your knees calling on God. Everything Henry's fervent spirit will like.'

Richard smiles. 'And Talbot will relay it faithfully. He wasn't that drunk. Are you coming to bed?'

She comes, and the loving is like food after famine.

★

Richard writes to his king. Tells him of the oath he swore to Talbot. Offers to come to London to swear it before his face. He hears nothing. A council is called at Westminster. He's not invited. Beaufort, he hears, has had Oldhall dragged from sanctuary and imprisoned. Only the Dean's pleas to the King have saved him, and he's back in St Martin's with nothing more than bruises. It is not to be borne.

In the dark days of February, when the Teme is trammelled by ice and its banks hang heavy under hoar frost, Richard says he's done with it all, and sits down with his secretary.

'Can I say nothing that will stop you?' Cecily asks.

They have argued themselves to exhaustion, up and down the ladder of reasons for and against this madness. They are tired of themselves and of each other. Even their dogs slink away when they meet.

Richard's face is a sheet of stone. 'I will say in the open what all say in secret. That England will have no peace until Beaufort is removed from the King's side.'

'Words won't do it. Can you fight Edmund Beaufort without fighting the King?'

'The time is not right to fight the King.'

'Then the time is not right for this.'

'Then what's the alternative? To be harassed and harried till our enemy is strong enough to pull us down?'

'Think what will happen to our children if you lose. To our boys. You know better than any what it is to grow up the son of a dead traitor.'

He pales at that and turns away as if she'd struck him. Then he recovers himself, squares his shoulders, turns his face to her again. 'Cecily,' he asks, 'do you ever think what will happen to them if I do nothing?'

So he writes a declaration to his affinity across England. To towns within his purview, to those who look for justice. It says how England suffers, how France has been lost. It names

Beaufort a traitor in Normandy, a threat to Calais, a blight on the realm. It spells out how his own efforts to restore good government have been set at nothing. Beaufort's power over the King, it says, will bring England to ruin. He must be removed. 'Send men to me, good men, who know their duty, and I will do it. And all that I will do,' it says, 'will be born out of my duty and my allegiance to the King.'

He hands it to her and she reads. 'It won't come to a fight,' he tells her. 'Half the nobles of England know what Beaufort is. I will give them heart to say so. And the King will listen.'

She hands it back to him, wraps cold hands in the fur of her sleeves, nods. Well, in the end you can't lock your husband up in his own tower. His declaration is copied. The copies are sealed. They are sent.

A week later, he's ready to ride. Three thousand have come to him in Ludlow. Men muster across the country and will join him on the way. He expects to reach London with twenty thousand or more.

The night before he leaves, she lies awake, his living heart beneath her hand. They are gambling. Their wager is that the nobles will see Richard in his power and find courage in that sight to condemn the King's favourite. Their stake is all they have.

She sees the whites of his eyes in dawn's half-light and knows he, too, has not slept. She will not keep it from him. 'There's another child coming.'

He takes her hand in his and kisses it. 'I will not leave him fatherless.' But the smile he gives her is a sad thing, as poor in substance as his promise.

As he travels he sets up messenger posts with changes of horse, so news can be carried to her quickly.

Two weeks and he's outside Northampton, his force all but assembled. 'I've written to the King,' he tells her. 'I've told him I'm coming, and why. Everything in the open.'

Two days later. 'I've received an embassy from Henry. They ask my motives for insurrection. There is no insurrection, I tell them. I serve the King. I come for justice against a traitor, no more.'

He reaches London at month's end. Its gates are closed against him, by order of the King. 'Henry's been in the Midlands,' he writes, 'but is coming south now and gathering men. Your brother Salisbury is with him. And Warwick. Talbot, too. Everyone, pretty much. Edmund Beaufort, of course, and the Queen. I'll circle around to Dartford, camp there and let him come to me.'

Then his letters, which have come almost daily, stop.

Through four age-long days, she prays. The morning the news comes, she's in her chamber, her confessor is with her and her women. She has taken mass and is still on her knees. The silence is broken by the racket of heavy boots on the stairs, of harness jangling. She's up and turning to the door as it opens.

Her chamberlain barely makes it through before the messenger, pale-faced and mud-spattered, pushes past him to come to his knees at her feet.

'Lady, the duke your husband is taken.'

29

'I did not expect this betrayal, sister. Believe me.' Her brother Salisbury's words are hastily written, barely readable as they race across the page. They tell her that Beaufort walks free as air and Richard is the King's prisoner. 'They're taking him to London. I go too, and will do what I can to keep him alive. Do nothing, sister. Wait.'

The King had come to Dartford with equal force and, when Richard requested parley, sent a royal delegation with Salisbury at its head, with his son Warwick and a bevy of lords and bishops. Men, carefully chosen, Cecily realizes. Men Richard would trust.

'Is it a fight you've come for, brother?' Salisbury asked him.

Richard told him, 'No, it is as I have written, I want only peace and justice.'

'Aye, you look peaceable enough. With twenty thousand bristling at your back.'

'My enemy is strong. And my good faith spent.'

Salisbury asked him to name his demands.

There was only one. That Beaufort be arrested on charges Richard has drawn up. That he be removed from the King's side and Richard restored to it.

'Only that?' Salisbury asked.

'Only that. I to be the King's chief Councillor. Beaufort to be tried before Lords and Commons. I will even step aside from the trial. I will leave it to others. And on the King's promise of this, for I know him to be a man faithful to God, I will disperse my force and come on my knees before him.'

'And if not, you will fight?'

'I will fight Beaufort.'

'You can't fight Beaufort without fighting the King.'

'So my wife tells me.' They stood a while and looked at each other. Then, 'You know you want this no less than I do.'

Salisbury nodded slow, sucked his teeth and returned to his king.

'I went back to Richard that evening,' continues her brother's hectic message. 'With the King's sworn assurances and promises of love. Told him I myself had seen Beaufort led away under guard. I swear to you, Cecily, I did see it. I supervised the dispersal of your husband's army, so I could tell Henry I'd seen it done. Next day, I took Richard to the King. We found him at table, damn him, with Beaufort and the Queen. Right and left of him, grinning like cats. Then I knew your husband betrayed, and I their tool in it.'

'Benighted idiot!' Cecily's body curls on itself in rage, like parchment in a fire, painful and reflexive. Then she's up on her feet and moving, striding fast about the room. 'Where is his army?'

The messenger doesn't know – how could he? Dispersed, scattered, making its way to its several homes, he supposes, in counties across England and Wales. She knows where those homes are and the roads they'll take to get to them. She calls up her secretaries, starts dictating her own messages, demanding her husband's freedom, rallying Richard's dissipated force, calling up more men from Wales.

'Lady, you cannot march an army on London!' Reynold, Ludlow's marshal, keeper of its garrison. She had sent for him first. He's a man who's known her in her right mind and is bold enough to speak plain.

'You think I should follow my brother's advice? Do nothing?'

'Who would lead such a force?'

She's desperate, there's no one to hand. 'I will! You will come with me. Call up your captains.'

'Forgive me, lady, as I serve you, but you cannot lead an army.' He dares to lay a hand on her.

She shrugs it off like a scald, screams her frustration. She launches herself at the nearest of the secretaries, a young man, who can barely still his trembling to scribble, spills his ink in his fright. 'Write the King. Tell him Edward of March comes. Edward Earl of March and his mother. I will show that barren queen of bitches that I have a son!'

Then there is a new voice, a woman's, strong hands on her wrists, pushing against her, and a face inches from hers. 'You have three sons, lady. Would you see them dead at your feet?' It's Annette. Annette, who must have heard the news and come running. Who has been with her in the worst of times. Who knows all about dead children.

She feels the pulse drumming in her throat and temples, her breath sawing through blown lungs. And there is Annette's face, hard, resolute, clear. She looks as I do when I'm not mad, she thinks. 'Annette, my husband has put his head into a noose.'

'Then let us not put your sons' there.' Good advice.

She lets the madness drain from her and when Annette leads her to a chair and lets go her wrists, she sits.

'Shall we send these men away, so we can think?'

Cecily nods and listens to them go, footsteps disappearing, fair scampering to be gone. And her women too, white-faced, and with good reason. Most of them have husbands in Richard's company.

'Don't go far, Marshal Reynold,' she hears Annette say. 'I am sure my lady will have need of you.'

There's relief in his mumbled, 'Aye.' She should laugh at it. A soldier taking orders from a nurse.

Annette puts a cup of wine in her hands and she drinks it. Unwatered, sharp and cold from the jug, it sears her mouth and clears her head.

She rubs the back of her hand across her lips. 'No army would follow me. And Edward is not ten years old.'

'And, if your husband dies, he is the King's heir.'

'And the Queen's enemy. And Beaufort's.'

'Which is a dangerous thing. Lady, I don't know what you should do. But I think you should not put your sons in Beaufort's way till they are men.'

Cecily nods, closes her eyes against a spinning world, takes a rasping breath, then opens them again. She must look at it, spin as it might. A world without Richard. The days beyond his death. She sees her hands lying loose in her lap, her fingers bloodless and cold. She clasps them and, when she feels the unforgiving metal of her rings grind against bone, tightens her grip till it grows painful. It is something to focus upon while her heart slows and her breath evens. 'Forgive me, Annette. I was mad for a moment. I am well enough now.'

'What can I do for you?'

'Nothing. I must think. Go to the children. Keep them together.'

'Shall I send your women to you?'

She shakes her head. 'What use are they? But if messengers arrive they're to be sent to me straight. No one else, mind. Stay with the children. Tell them all will be well.'

But she knows it will be far from well. Don't put your sons in harm's way, Annette has said. Too late. That's done. If Richard dies a traitor they'll be taken from her, their wardships sold to men the King owes favours to, or wants to reward. Edmund Beaufort and others like him. Her daughters sold down in marriage to men of ambition, who'll pay good money for the richness of their blood. And the child now in her womb? Dear God, better it were lost now.

At the end of a hunt, when the stag is dead, all men, according to their station, are gifted a share of the kill, till there's nothing left but bone and scrag, and then the dogs fight over that. So it will be for all that she and Richard have built together and been. Their children. Their affinity. Their titles and estates. All will be meted out, gobbled up and slathered over. Even Fotheringhay, and the dead that lie there. And what of her? Her dower lands are rich enough. They'll want those, too. Will they name her traitor to get them? Women, too, can be condemned. She remembers Gloucester's Eleanor, her bruised feet stepping into darkness, and Joan, who she watched burn.

All day she sits alone, growing colder as the fire dies. When it is nothing but ash, and the room shadowed by dusk, she pulls herself to her feet, rubs blood back into icy fingers, kicks the fire. There's no life in it, but no matter. She is decided. Tomorrow she will ride to London, to the King. Not to fight or threaten. To sue for mercy. To beg for her husband's life. And if it is too late for that, for her children's, and her own.

Stiff legs stilt her to the door. She lays her head against the wood. They will demand that you denounce him, she counsels herself. At the very least they will want that. She has never betrayed him. His cause has been hers, always. But the thought of her children, the rich coin of them in other men's purses, is unbearable. She will save him if she can, denounce him if she must. Sure, he has been a fool. And now she must be about it. Her hand finds the cold metal of the door's latch and lifts it. She steps out into the world of the castle where, subdued and silent, her people wait to know her will.

She leaves Ludlow in driving rain and travels five days through its foulness, crossing a broiling Severn at Worcester and pushing on through Tewkesbury. From there the torrent eases, though the skies stay leaden, and for some hours of the day, she gives up the carriage to tire her body and mind on horseback. Marshal Reynold has indeed come with her, leading two hundred men to guard her honour. He rides ahead to scout the way. As they come towards Woodstock, with its royal hunting lodge, she looks up from her saddle's pommel at the labouring sound of a horse ridden fast over wet ground.

She sees it is Reynold, coming back towards her, raising his arm for a halt. Dear God, what?

He pulls up beside her, his face split by a smile. 'Lady, a company under the falcon and fetterlock is not a half-mile off, and your lord rides at the head of it.'

She pushes her horse up the low rise, and from its top she sees him. There's open ground between them, falling softly down. She could cross it in moments. But she waits, and lets him labour up the slope towards her. She needs the time to still her heart. Her men have held back. She sees him order his to do the same.

He stops his horse a yard away and looks at her. His face is grey, thinner than she's ever seen it. Shamed.

'You still have your head on your shoulders then?'

He twists in the saddle, draws a gloved hand across an unshaven jaw. There is no jest in him, not even a bitter one.

She closes the distance and reaches across to him, feels moving muscle beneath his rain-damp sleeve before his hand turns, grasps hers and holds. She cannot breathe but say his name, 'Richard.' And the question, the only one that matters. 'Are we safe?'

His bowed head nods. 'Aye. For now.'

30

Last Epiphany night Richard offered an oath. Now his king has taken it from him. In public at St Paul's. On God's word and the body of the crucified Christ. Before all the court and a goggling London crowd. Loyalty until death, and so much more. Obedience, humility, surrender. On the long road home to Ludlow, he tells her of the words he has given to purchase his life, and how their future will be bound by them. He will never again raise a force for any purpose but at the King's command. He will come to his king whenever and wherever he is called upon to do so. Should he feel himself grieved, by any party, he will seek no remedy for it but from his king. And, if called upon to explain his actions at any time or place, he will; not only to his king, but to his peers, the nobles of England.

Cecily's eyes narrow at the last. 'That would include Edmund Beaufort, I suppose.'

'Most surely. He penned the oath.'

'Then you are his dog now.'

She waits for his answer, while leather creaks and hooves fall soft on grass.

'Chained and kennelled,' he admits.

Nor is the humiliation over. Through spring and summer the carcass of Richard's pride is picked to the bone, as titles and offices are taken from him. Lordship of the Isle of Wight goes to Beaufort, the earldom of Pembroke to young Jasper Tudor, the King's half-brother. His lieutenancy of Ireland is given to Ormond's son, who is Earl of Wiltshire, friend of Beaufort, licker of the King's arse, who despises the Irish and his newly dead father, and will not muddy his boots in their soggy fields.

And honour, too, is besmirched. Richard traded his oath, not only for his own pardon, but for the men of his affinity who came at his call and followed him in good faith to Dartford. Now they're made to beg for it. There are show trials and questions, delays and prevarications. They must make a defence, they must come on their knees. They must be truly penitent. They are toyed with and teased and gloated over. And Richard can do nothing. For Oldhall there is no pardon at all. He's in sanctuary still, harassed and harried, and his wife sick with the grief of it.

Cecily, too, is sick. Sick of watching Richard submit to every blow. Of his crippling shame and hidden rage. He abides by his oath, does his duty, busies himself with work. Keeps from her bed. She's glad of that at least, for she can hardly bear to touch him. Nor he her, she thinks. He spars with the boys still, and sometimes she watches, for the joy of seeing Edward, mostly. To be out of doors.

Edward comes almost to his father's shoulder already, moves fast and scores points you'd commend in a much older boy. He must know his father is out of favour. Children have ears and servants will talk, but he never speaks of it. Until one day, he puts his sword beyond his father's guard with such efficiency its dull blade strikes hard against Richard's hip.

'Ouch!' Richard feigns an injury worse than it is.

Edward rushes about him, dancing in circles, triumphant at his own prowess.

And there it is for a moment, Richard's smile, so long unseen, his hand stretched out to his son's bright head. 'Well done, lad. You've fair taken my leg off.'

Edward's heart is proud but generous. He raises his weapon high. 'When next the King offends you, father, send him to me. I will beat him bloody!'

She cannot help but laugh, though she turns her head to hide it.

'That's treachery, son,' she hears Richard say and, when she turns back, his face is pale and bitter and angry. He's putting up his sword, then walking away.

Edward watches after him a moment, then turns to her and shrugs. Then his arms master steps into the breach and he's moving again.

Suddenly, the day is too hot. She goes inside, dismisses her women and lies down on her bed, grimacing while the child inside her kicks and pushes.

When September comes, she goes to her confinement. They've moved on to Fotheringhay, a change they've been restless for, but which in fact changes nothing. When all is ready, Richard leads her to the threshold, hands her silently in. But suddenly it seems too painful a parting. Halfway across the room she turns to him, his slender height framed in the doorway.

'Will you pray for me?' she asks.

'With all my strength,' he tells her. 'Such as it is.'

And now that she cannot, she longs to touch him. To mend the breach.

She thinks a moment. 'You know, we have named all of our children for policy. To please one person or honour another. If this one's a boy. And if he lives. And since there is only you and I now, I would name him Richard.'

He cocks his head and his eyes soften. 'That would be a gift, Cecily.'

She nods. Then turns her side to him, runs her hands over her swollen belly, quirks a brow and smiles a little. 'I've work to do. Stay out of trouble.'

He laughs once, shakes his head and, softly, closes the door.

31

The baby came in October, a boy, named, as she had promised, for his father. Born in Fotheringhay as the first gales of autumn shredded the valley's trees and swelled its river with rain. He was sickly at first, but is thriving well enough now. That aside, there's no good news to speak of, only bad, and today she must be its bearer.

Cecily never waits to be admitted to her husband's presence, even when he's busy with his steward and his door closed to all but those he sends for. The talking stops as she enters the room; secretaries cease their scribbling and look nervously to their lord. She doesn't blame them. Her moods have been perilous of late.

'Gentlemen.' Richard raises his arm towards the door, which she stands beside and holds open.

When all are gone, the door closed behind them, she moves to the fire and waits for him to follow. She takes the time to seat herself, to smooth her skirts. Then, when he has stretched his long legs towards the heat, she speaks.

'Our daughter, I am informed, is not to be Duchess of Burgundy.'

'Ah.'

'You will tell me we should be inured to such disappointments.'

'We've had practice, of late.'

She nods. True enough. But this one bites. It's been talked of for so long: apple-cheeked Elizabeth for Isabella's chestnut-haired boy; an alliance for York with the richest court in Europe. It is for such marriages she has had daughters. 'Isabella writes that, though she wishes no one more than Elizabeth for her son, her husband now favours a French princess. He has opened negotiations for Isabella of Bourbon.'

Richard purses a finger against his lip. 'His own niece?'

'And a very distant cousin of the King of France. But even that outranks us, these days.'

'Ripe for marriage?'

'Eighteen years old. Sickly, though.'

'Then there's hope. Young Charles may outlast her, and live to choose again.'

She leans behind her, towards his secretary's desk. 'There is an inkwell here. Shall I throw it at you?'

His lips widen in a placatory smile and, for a moment, his eyes dance as they used to. 'Please don't.' Then his face turns serious, as befits the times. 'Tell me instead all that Isabella has said.'

'What she doesn't say speaks loudest. Ask yourself, how often does she submit to her husband's will?'

'About as often as you do to mine, I imagine. No, this is her decision, I would think.'

'Our Elizabeth was the daughter of England's lieutenant in France when Isabella and I first compassed this marriage. Now she's the daughter of a man who holds paltry office and is shunned by his king. Isabella won't give her only son for that. I wouldn't.'

When his face falls, she reaches across, lays a hand on his knee. 'I don't blame you. Only it's the truth. And we must face it.'

They've been friends again since the new baby came in October. Little Richard, whose very name was a reconciliation; who, on first sight, was welcomed by his father with the grateful love a man feels when hellfire licks his heels and God reaches a hand to save him. Cecily remembers that much about the birth, but little more. It had been bloody, and she ill after, nauseous and fevered and unable to eat. It had been Christmas, almost, till she was fit for churching.

Their first night reunited she'd looked naked into the mirror and been shocked by the sight. Hip bones jutting above spindled legs, breasts gone flat and belly sunken, gaunt as a corpse. 'I'm hideous,' she said.

He wrapped her in his arms as she wept and told her she was beautiful; that no queen could hold a candle to her.

She's better now, but even so, sometimes her heart beats very fast and her breath comes short on the stairs. And now, she knows, there is a journey ahead of her, and it is yet winter.

He takes her hand. 'Elizabeth is young. We have time to think again.'

'She will be nine in September. I was married to you by that age.'

He kisses her fingers. 'I bless the day.'

Such nonsense. She pulls away, sits back in her chair. 'Well, if there are to be such days for our daughters, something must be done.'

He too sits back, looks at her over netted fingers, and waits.

'I had another letter today, beside Isabella's,' she tells him. 'From Jacquetta. She's with child again.'

He raises an eyebrow. 'Is it a competition between you?'

'That's not the news. The news is that the Queen visits the Virgin's shrine at Walsingham next month. Jacquetta will keep her company.' The quirk of his lips tells her he doesn't know what he should make of this. 'Richard, a woman goes to Walsingham for one of two reasons. To pray she be given a child, or delivered safe of one she already carries.'

'You think the Queen . . .?'

'My confessor tells me we live in an age of miracles.' A thin smile. 'And Jacquetta writes that the Queen has never looked so healthsome.'

His eyes widen. 'Now, that might change things.'

'You would no longer be Henry's heir.'

'I would welcome that, even if you would not.'

She would not, entirely. But will make of it what she can. 'Well, it would depend rather, on whether Henry and Marguerite can cobble together a son better than his father.' She sighs. 'But if you were no longer Henry's heir, if Marguerite had a son, there may be, well, what should we say? A softening, perhaps, in her attitude to us.' She folds her hands in her lap, rubs her white, cold fingers. 'So. I will go to the Queen at Walsingham. I will play the wife, and entreat her to return my lord to her lord's good favour.'

He looks doubtful. 'Do you think her moveable?'

'I don't know. They say it can soften a woman's heart, having a child in her belly. She will feel safer.'

His eyes soften as he looks at her, but the doubt hasn't left him. 'I've never seen you entreat.'

'Well,' she concedes, ' 'tis rare.'

To visit Walsingham is to make a pilgrimage to the Holy Land, for here is Nazareth in Albion. At its heart stands the humble house in which redemption began. Where an angel spread his wings to a peasant girl and told her she would bear God's son. In humility, she surrendered to him and is Queen of Heaven now. See how a boy may raise his mother. Cecily has made the journey many times. First, to beg that her own womb be made fruitful. Later, to give thanks for children living, or pray repose for those dead. The last mile is walked barefoot. It is a reminder that God's way is rarely easy and that sin is sanctified through pain.

Today, two wet weeks after Easter, the path has been churned to mud by the press of pilgrims' feet. The rain has abated overnight, but the wind from the sea carries knives. The prayers of the faithful are lost to the keening of gulls thrown inland and the mewing of scraggy lambs that muzzle their sodden mothers and find no warmth.

Cecily awaits her queen's arrival at the mile mark, in the tiny slipper chapel where pilgrims give up their shoes for faith. If Marguerite is surprised to find her there, she gives no sign of it. And, indeed, she does look well. No swell to her belly yet, but her face lit, in the way a young woman's can be when new life is kindled. Cecily's obeisance is the lowest she has ever made, and she waits, head bowed and unmoving, until bidden to rise.

'I imagine,' says the Queen, 'that you are here to give thanks for yet another son.'

'And in supplication, Your Grace. A child's life is tenuous and I've buried as many as I've cradled.' She has no wish to appear too blessed.

'I had heard it was your health feared for, not the child's.'

'But, by God's grace, I live yet.'

'Then that, too, is cause for thanks. For those who love you.'

Into the silence that follows steps Jacquetta to clasp her hand and kiss her cheek. 'Cecily, how good to see you. A long time since we three were together in France.' Then, turning to the Queen, 'Your Grace, should we not relive those happy days and make our pilgrimage together?'

Marguerite, testing her bare white feet on the chapel's cold tiled floor, concedes.

Bless you, Jacquetta, thinks Cecily.

Making their muddy way towards the town and its towering abbey, Cecily pits her will against pain that fists from cold-numbed feet into the muscles of her calves, and watches Jacquetta's determined back, ahead of her in procession. Her old companion looks to be around five months gone. The road must be hard on her. She's lost her youthful slimness, but prettiness remains. Cecily wonders if the golden Woodville still dotes on her and admits he'd have good cause. As they pass the first low-roofed houses of the town and the shelter of the friary's wall, that pretty head turns to throw a smile at her. She surprises herself by returning it, though she knows it to be born, not from the pleasure of a good turn done, but from this rich opportunity to flaunt her closeness to the Queen.

Ah well. Jacquetta is a welcome irritation. A reminder of better days.

A pathway has been opened for them across the crowded market square and townspeople strain for the best vantage point from which to see a queen and two duchesses with their skirts inches deep in mud.

Cecily watches as Marguerite straightens her back and raises her chin. Even windswept, she is queenly, thinks Cecily, while she herself feels only buffeted and is shivering now in earnest. The noise of the world falls away as they pass under the arch of the gatehouse into the abbey's precinct, and the animal smell of the market is overlain by incense, which catches in her throat hardly less. Once inside, she leans towards whatever feeble warmth the candles can offer and curls her toes to test they are still part of her. The stone flags are no less bitter than the mud of the road. She looks up the nave to the choir, where the brothers sing their adoration of the mother.

This shrine was raised by a woman, Richelde, whose son rode against the infidel in the Holy Land. It's hunkered ahead of them as they enter the Lady Chapel. It was once a dull grey shack, a peasant's cot standing alone in an open field, where the wind tested its seams and poor women paid pennies to cross its threshold. Now it is encased in gold at the stone heart of the abbey, its entrance guarded by a priest who demands of all comers the richest gift they can give.

Marguerite summons forward one of her guards. He takes from his pack a tablet of gold, upon which an enamelled angel upholds a cross of ruby and pearl; the blood of Christ and his mother's unquenchable tears. Her own offering is not so artful, but no less rich. A purse of money that will buy many prayers for baby Richard and, she hopes, a future for his father.

They enter the house on their knees; the door is closed behind them, and Cecily opens her eyes to light. A hundred candle flames reflect and dazzle against sheets of gold that line the inner walls. The scent of Heaven pours from incense burners hanging star-like from a spangled roof and there, ahead of her through the shimmer, sits the Virgin, her ivory gaze cast down to the Christ child, crowned and eternal in her lap. Cecily has never been immune to the Queen of Heaven's power and now it takes her again. She feels the lightness in her head that opens a door to prayer, and brings her hands together. But something is wrong. Her limbs tremble worse than ever and her breath burns hot in her lungs. Her whole body is a heartbeat and the golden light is fizzing, tinged with black.

'Cecily.' It seems a long time since she heard her name, whispered so close against her ear. And there is a hand laid on her brow, and cold hardness beneath her cheek. She opens her eyes to the gilded pool of the floor, and looks up to see Marguerite, her sharp face, her tilted eyes, curious.

'Lady, I think that you are sick,' says the Queen, then takes from within the folds of her dress a tiny silver flask and holds Cecily's head so she can drink the spirit from it.

They wait with her, the Queen and Jacquetta, till her strength returns and she can speak again. They make no account of her apologies and offer their arms to get her to her feet. 'I think you will not want the indignity of being carried from here,' says Marguerite as they turn towards the door.

She can only shake her head, and is surprised and grateful when her companions press close on either side and give her their arms to rest upon as they step out into the church. They guide her steps, necessarily slow, convincingly regal, to the door and then the gatehouse, where their women wait. Then Marguerite is speaking to them and asking where the Duchess of York's lodgings are and saying it's too far; that she must, instead, come to her own place across the market square, under the queenly banner of the Black Lion. A carriage is brought. She sits gratefully in it and is taken away, Marguerite's hand clasped in her own.

She has slept a little, in a warm bed under the Black Lion's eaves. She is warm at last, has eaten a little bread and drunk some wine. She has risen and been dressed and a maid has told her of the Queen's command that she wait upon her. So she has come downstairs to a wide low-ceilinged room, where Marguerite stands before a window watching the rain and Jacquetta sits in a ring of women before a comfortable fire. They rise when she enters and, once she has made her obeisance, guide her to a place closest to the warmth. Marguerite takes her own seat opposite and clasps her small white hands in her lap. Cecily begins to make her apologies, to offer her thanks. She stops when those hands are held, palm out, towards her.

The Queen says, 'No. You were kind to me once, when I was too ill to do what must be done. I have not forgotten. And I always pay my debts.' The hands are folded again. 'You told me you came to Walsingham to entreat God for your son.'

'Aye.'

'I think you came to entreat me for your husband.'

Cecily wonders how she knows. Then sees Jacquetta blush.

'I take the Virgin's example. Is it not a woman's duty to intercede for sinful men? I bring my plea, not to God's throne, but to your own.' She sees Marguerite smile. She is not immune to flattery.

'I will hear you.' Then, to the room. 'Ladies, leave us.'

Now they are alone and Cecily must humble herself. She

would rather be sick in her bed. But there we are. This is what she came for, after all.

'My husband grieves mightily the loss of the King's love. And your good opinion.'

'I suspect he grieves more the loss of his offices and favour.'

'Perhaps.' She shrugs. 'He is proud. But I believe . . . I believe his greatest sorrow is born of his present lack of usefulness. Whatever he has done since, he served the King well, in France and in Ireland—'

'At Dartford he did not serve his king.'

'Perhaps not.' That is a concession she will make. 'But he did not oppose him.'

'And he sent Jack Cade against us.'

This is a concession she will not. She holds up her hand. 'Your Grace, I believe you are with child. Am I right?' She wonders if Marguerite will tell her, share the secret still so little known. Then she sees that sharp chin rise and hears the confirmation in soft, sibilant French.

'Oui. Grâce à Dieu.'

'Then you will know the value of the oath I make to you now. On the souls of my children, living and dead, I swear to you, my husband had no part in Cade's business and knew nothing of the man. No mother would swear such an oath were it not true. You know that. My husband is no rebel. And he does not oppose the King, did not at Dartford, nor with Cade.'

'He opposes another who the King loves. And who is dear, also, to me.'

'You speak of Edmund Beaufort.' Cecily nods. 'I know not what to say, so will say nothing. Except that my husband has repented of it. Give him some role that will make him useful and keep him out of Beaufort's way. He will be content.'

'And, if I bear a son, will your lord bend his knee to him?'

'Most readily.'

'Yet men say York should be next for the throne?'

'If God is good, the child you carry will silence such voices.' She watches Marguerite lay her hands against her belly, turn her face to the fire. 'How far along are you?'

A whisper. 'A little more than three months, I believe.'

Cecily nods. She knows what it is to be barren; the pain that comes with hope. 'You will start to show soon. You will carry all before you. Your Grace, you have humbled my husband. Do not grind him into the dust.' A small white hand is thrust out. Cecily takes it and squeezes. 'I waited eight long years for my first child. Just as you have. And now look at me. I will pray for you every day, and for the great treasure you bear.'

Marguerite lets loose her hand, nods once, and the face she turns to Cecily is smooth again and still. 'I have heard your plea. The debt is paid in the listening. Let us see, when I have borne a son, what might be done for the Duke of York.'

32

June–October 1453
  Fotheringhay

Cecily had not known, when she fainted before the Virgin's face in Walsingham, that she too was with child. She and Richard had made love the night before she set out. It must have been then. Two months later, she knows it, bent double and bleeding on the stairs at Fotheringhay, carried to her bed in the middle of the day. The mess of it is bundled away with the linen, swabbed from the stone steps.

She begs absolution of her confessor. It is surely a sin to be thankful for the loss of God's gift. But she is too tired to carry – and besides, to what end?

By the time she's on her feet again, news has crossed the Channel of another death. Old soldier Talbot has fought his way through near seventy years of life. She supposes he would have wanted it to end on a battlefield. But he'd have preferred to be the toast at a victory feast, not salt in the wound of defeat.

He'd returned to France last year when Beaufort ordered him to win back Gascony.

'For God's sake why?' Cecily had asked Richard at the time.

'Because its people complain that French taxes are higher than English ones,' he told her. 'And because Beaufort wants to gainsay those who accuse him of giving up France without a fight.'

'As long as he doesn't have to do the fighting,' Cecily pointed out.

Quite so.

Talbot had gained Bordeaux and most of western Gascony by Christmas, but the French king himself came after him in spring. They tested each other's wits into the summer until, outnumbered but belligerent, the old man led his little army against a fury of French cannon to relieve Castillon. Those of his men still alive when he fell fled, so that his body was broken as much by their feet as by the French axe that brought his horse down on top of him. His herald found his body next morning, guided by the outstretched arm of the old soldier's dead son. He could only be certain of him by the gap in his teeth, got long ago in some other fight.

Jacquetta writes that the Queen is ripe as a cherry, and that the court can speak of nothing but the child to come. Still, it seems Marguerite has time to attend to the little things. In July, Richard's last office, that of steward of royal justice in the south, is granted to Beaufort. And Oldhall, still in sanctuary, is attainted. For treason at Dartford, though he was not there, and for plotting with Cade, who he did not know. His wife is put out of doors and his property, the lifetime's accumulation of a hardworking man, is a lick and a slurp for a hungry treasury. Impossible to help. Any favour from York would damn him further.

The building of Fotheringhay's church is almost done now. But it's full of her dead, and Cecily can't bear to go there. She looks down towards it from the castle walls, listens morning and evening for its bells and chants. They seem such thin things. The river carries them away, or the summer sun burns them up. If, in all this wide landscape, prayer cannot traverse a mile, or be heard above a swallow's song, there's little chance it will reach Heaven, or the ear of a God who has turned his attention elsewhere. She almost despairs, then remembers what her cardinal uncle used to say: 'We depend, all, from Fortune's wheel, and the wheel turns faster when pushed.'

So, she decides upon one more appeal to Marguerite. She will remind her of the promise given at Walsingham, to look mercifully on her husband. She will pretend, for the moment, that such a promise was made. She calls up her secretary, sets him to write, finds no words and sends him away again. The next day the same.

That evening, she visits her children. Anne is teaching Margaret and Elizabeth to pleat their dresses in the Burgundian style. She's a natural mother, watching on with pins between her teeth as her sisters court the mirror in their finery. Anne's own dress, pleated to precision, makes much of the swell of her breasts and the sharpness of bone at her neck. She's fourteen now, and must to Henry Holland soon. She asks, sometimes, when it will be and seems relieved when Cecily says, not yet. If the girl really can't abide him, I could have it annulled, she supposes. But, though a brute, he is a duke. She won't get another of those as things stand.

Edward and Edmund come home filthy from riding the riverbanks. When they're clean she plays chess with each in turn. They use the new set Edmund had last week for his tenth birthday. When it's Edward's turn he almost beats her.

'Watch,' she says, and shows him how he should have leapt his king from the threat of her queen.

'You're playing by the new rules,' he complains.

'French rules. The queen has more power there. They are the rules we all must play by now.'

He shrugs and laughs. 'I'll learn them, then.'

'I know them already,' says Edmund.

'You would,' says Edward, with a punch to his brother's shoulder that has Edmund laughing, shy, dipping his head.

'Don't worry. I'll teach you.'

Cecily smiles. Edmund, her studious son, and Edward, who

learns by throwing himself against every obstacle until it falls before him. Look at him, there's down on his cheek and muscle at his shoulder. None of Edmund's rangy thinness. They share a chamber still, of their own choice. Edmund runs faster, but when they wrestle, or practise swords, Edward can't help but win.

The little ones are asleep when she comes to them: George, her Irish dragon, and baby Richard, who everyone's taken to calling Dickon to mark a difference from his father. She watches them breathe. The evening is warm and there's sweat in the folds of the baby's neck, dampness in the curls at George's temple. She kisses their heads, gives an Ave for each, and goodnights their nurses. Sons and daughters. God-given for a purpose.

The next morning she calls her secretary again. This time, at her order, he writes.

In good black ink she has it set down that she is Marguerite's obedient servant and beadswoman; makes much of the honour of being received by her at Walsingham. She says she would rejoice to come to her again, but begs leave, for she suffers still under the same sickness that assailed her there. She doesn't mention the lost child. No mother-in-waiting wants to hear of that. She speaks instead of her great sorrow, and her lord's, at being estranged from their most Christian king, their merciful sovereign. A grief so deep, she calls it, that it is sure to shorten their days. She begs Marguerite to reconcile them to her husband's favour. Pretends to believe it's his opinion that matters.

On the subject of the royal pregnancy, she must be effusive. 'I pray daily for Your Grace's safe delivery,' she bids her secretary write. Though whether from childbed or this mortal life she doesn't specify.

The scratching of his quill ceases as she thinks and takes to pacing again. When she passes the window for the third time, she stops by it and looks down on to castle green, where Edward and Edmund stretch growing sinews to fire arrows into butts. She sighs. Alright.

'Set this down. I beseech God and his mother, to whom we lately prayed together, to prosper you and the child you carry . . .'

Window to fireplace and back again. The thunk of an arrow meeting its mark.

'. . . and to send the blessed fruit of your body into this world with speed and felicity, for the safety of England and the joy of its people . . .'

Thunk.

'. . . and for the longed-for solace of my simple heart.'

Dear God. Even her secretary looks askance at that one. She stares him down for a final flourish.

'Be assured, Your Grace, that though my body is wretched, I will not spare its pains to entreat God for the continuance and prosperity of your queenly estate in all honour, joy and . . . so on.'

She falls silent.

'Is that all, my lady?'

'That's all.'

It's been a labour. While she waits for the letter to be sanded and waxed for her signet, she allows herself to look ahead to the moment Marguerite's child will be born into the world; imagines taking its tiny feet in her hands, lifting them, and smashing the fragile shell of its skull against a wall.

Then, at last, all unexpected and as if by hand unseen, the wheel turns. Salisbury rides in on a warm September evening as Cecily walks with her girls across the courtyard to the keep. They've been inspecting the stillroom and dairies. Daughters must be trained in more than strategy. They turn their heads at the clatter of his coming and step forward to greet him.

'If anyone asks, I'm not here.' He greets his sister from the back of his blown horse, throws leg over pommel, slides down the beast's sweat-slick shoulder and grunts as his feet meet the ground.

'And I've not seen you, brother. But why don't you come inside and tell us where, in fact, you are?' She hears Richard's feet on the steps behind her.

Salisbury looks up to him, nods a greeting and steps forward to lay an urgent hand on his shoulder. 'I must speak urgently with you both,' he says. 'Alone.'

Richard looks from him to her, nods once, then turns to retrace his steps into the hall. Salisbury strides ahead of him, looking for all the world like a man who's made his mind up. Cecily signals to Anne to look to her sisters, then follows the men, relishing the remembered spring of anticipation in her step.

In the privacy of Richard's office Salisbury throws himself into a chair and wipes the sweat of a hard ride from his face. 'Well, Richard. You've been waiting for your chance. It's come at last.'

'A chance to what?' He's being cautious. Leaning against the window embrasure with his arms folded.

'To set down that bastard Beaufort once and for all.'

Richard cocks his head. 'I've tried that. Didn't get much support. You might remember.'

Ah, so there is resentment there. He's licked that wound alone.

'You will now. You'll have mine. And my boy's. Norfolk's, too. And we'll bring the council along.'

Cecily wants clarification, takes a seat across the table from her brother. 'You want to put my lord in the front line of your own battle?'

'I want him to be Lord Protector of England.'

She laughs, disbelieving. 'Why, is the King a child again?'

'Good as. Out of his mind.' He taps his temple. 'Senseless. Mad. Absent to the world. Can't wipe his arse. Can't rule his kingdom.'

'I've long doubted his capacity in each of those offices. What exactly leads you to do so now?'

And so the story comes out. Of how the King, arriving at his royal palace of Clarendon, fell senseless to the floor and did not rise. Not couldn't. Not wouldn't. Just didn't. Since then he's not spoken, knows no one, notices nothing. Only smiles sometimes at things he alone seems to see and weeps on occasion, silently and without cause.

'And you know this for fact, brother?'

'Seen it with my own eyes. The Queen's brought him back to Westminster. They're trying to keep it quiet. She is, I mean. And Beaufort, Chancellor Kemp. But it's been a month now and he's no better. You can't run a country without a king. Even a bad one. The council's paralysed. There has to be a protector, Richard. If it isn't you, it'll be Beaufort. Then we'll all be damned.'

Richard walks slow across the room to take a seat between them. His face is blank. 'There's been a choice to be made between Beaufort and me these three years past. I've heard precious few voices raised in my favour. Why now? Why yours?'

'Dear God, Richard. Do you know where the King was on his way to when he fell out of the world?' Richard shrugs. 'To join Edmund Beaufort, laying siege to my son at Cardiff Castle. Beaufort's scuttled back to the Queen's side now, of course, but his men are still there.'

Cecily smiles. This is what she's been waiting for and had almost given up hope of. 'So Beaufort's coming after the Warwick inheritance then?'

'Aye. And the King, before he lost his wits, said let him have it.'

'The Queen did, you mean.'

His turn to shrug. 'Aye. The Queen. And there'll be no curb on her will now.'

Cecily looks across the table to Richard. He's leaning back in his chair, eyes narrowed. The old ruby glints as his long index finger strokes across his lip. He sees her watching and raises a brow, then he pushes forward, nets his hands upon the table and looks hard at his brother-in-law. 'And then there's your own long dispute with the Percys,' he says.

There's been a balance of power in the North for decades. Neville and Percy. The East and West Marches. Opposing power bases held in tension by royal will. Now Beaufort's showing favour to the other side. It's made them bold. There've been incursions into Neville lands. Escalating threats from Northumberland and his hot-headed sons.

'I don't suppose King *or* Queen would help you there, either.'

Salisbury stretches his neck, grimaces. 'Sure they would not.'

'And you think I will?'

'In return for my support in this.'

Richard smiles, wolfish. 'Well. It's always good to know what the trade is.'

'So get yourself to London then.'

'Not yet. And not on your say-so. When the council calls. Then I'll come. When its members are ready to make their voices heard and stop cowering in corners.'

Salisbury is as irate as Richard is calm. 'And while you dither, Beaufort and the Queen—'

Cecily holds up a hand between them. 'Surely she must be due to go into her confinement?'

'Due to, yes, but showing little sign of it.'

'I can imagine.' She has held back from confinement herself, when policy demanded it. She taps a finger on the back of his hand. 'Then there's the task, brother. Confine the Queen and you isolate Beaufort. Without the King, or access to her, he's just one more voice on the council.'

Salisbury looks as if she's asked him to raise the dead. 'And how in God's name am I to do that?'

'Oh, brother, surely it cannot be beyond the wit of all you wise men in council to convince a solitary woman that her first duty is to protect her child?'

'She'd be a fool to leave the King's side now,' he blusters.

She laughs. 'You think like a man!' She takes his two hands in hers and speaks as to a slow child. 'What is a witless king, brother? What can he do for her now?' She tightens her grip, imperative. 'Unless he recovers, her only safety is in her belly. She needs this child to survive, and to be a son. Otherwise, she's finished.' Still he looks incredulous. 'Have council petition her for the sake of the country's safety. Remind her that she risks the royal succession and her child's life by resisting. Her own understanding will do the rest.'

'Alright.' He looks half convinced.

She lets go his hands, pushes them away. 'Be about it. Or, if you're squeamish, get your wife on to it.'

A grudging smile, a nod. 'If that's done, you'll come?' He looks to Richard, who leaves off turning his ruby to enumerate upon his fingers.

'The Queen confined. A summons from the council. Surety of its support.'

Salisbury nods.

'And one more thing. A voice other than mine to call for Beaufort's arrest. I'll second it, with enthusiasm. But I'll not demand it.' He spreads his fingers. 'Clean hands.'

You can say what you like about Richard. He takes hard lessons to heart.

A month later, the news comes.

Marguerite has a son.

Cecily is called to attend the Queen's churching; Richard, to a meeting of the Great Council.

Norfolk, Salisbury assures them, will make the call for Beaufort. Norfolk is Cecily's nephew, her sister Katherine's boy.

'Good,' she says. 'Family business.'

33

November 1453–January 1455
  London

Precedence and protocol dictate the churching of a queen. Marguerite is a stickler for both. Richard, too, in his way. Everything by the book, he says. The Queen will have her day and he will do his duty. The book says the Queen must be led from her seclusion to Westminster's chapel by the two highest-ranking men in England. She will lean on their arms. They will guide her steps. Well, it won't be the King, of course, so it must be Richard.

'And?' says Cecily.

They've been a week at Baynard's Castle, their town house on the Thames. The perfect place for making plans; the ears of the court can't hear them, and their allies can visit discreetly by the river gate.

'Well,' says brother Salisbury from his place by the fire. 'Edmund Beaufort will claim it, I suppose.'

'Oh, yes,' says Cecily. 'Let him step behind you, Richard. Perfect.'

Richard only shakes his head at her, amused. 'Then you will have to play your part alongside his ugly wife.'

But she's thought of that, too. 'Jacquetta is the widow of the King's uncle. I believe that takes precedence over Beaufort's wife.' She thinks again. 'Even over yours, in fact.'

'You'll come second to Jacquetta just to snub Beaufort's wife?'

'Just this once.'

They set it down.

Council approves it.

Three days later, she's on her knees beside the bed where Marguerite birthed her son and sits now in solemn state, straight-backed, sharp-faced. The Queen wears the colours of a fruitful harvest, russet cloth-of-gold layered with sable furs, sleek as a vixen's back. Marguerite has not spoken. She is not required to speak. But Cecily can see the tension in her, the thrum of a pulse at her neck, rosary beads biting the bones of her hands.

Beyond the wide expanse of bed kneels Jacquetta, in plump pigeon-grey, crop-full with pleasure. About the room, in places of lesser honour, a score or more noble ladies, wives of dukes and earls, bend the knee. Three of Cecily's sisters are among them, her brothers' wives, her own daughter Anne, for Henry Holland's sake. Cecily knows them all, their husbands, their children, their grievances and ambitions. She knows how close they are to the Queen, what binds them to the King, how deeply Beaufort has offended them, or if they're thick as thieves. More than ever, it's her business to know these things, now the wheel is turning so fast. Their names are on a list that is written only in her mind and in Richard's. Beside each name a note; how they might act, how they're to be dealt with, what must be done to keep them compliant. She has it by heart. She expects to be busy. But that's not for today. For now she folds her hands in her sleeves, and waits.

There's a noise at the door. She looks up as Richard steps through it, Beaufort at his shoulder. She hears Marguerite draw a long breath, turns in time to see her nostrils flare.

While Richard bows she fixes her gaze on Beaufort.

Now. What's he thinking? I wonder. Glad to have his queen back? Yes, well, make the most of it.

*

After the churching, back to the bed, and the sitting in state, and a feast that only women can attend and must be eaten in silence. The Queen can take food from no one but Cecily and Jacquetta, who must serve her in humility from the discomfort of their knees. It's painful enough, but Cecily bears it gladly for the sight of Marguerite eating from her hand.

After, Marguerite is required to present her son to her husband. It should be done before the court, but here precedent must be broken, for who would expose such a king to so many eyes? Just the council then; men whose job it is to see things done properly. A king must acknowledge his heir; must be seen to own his son. Cecily and Jacquetta escort her to his chambers, where the men wait in rows with bland, empty faces, like clean-licked plates ready to be filled again.

Henry is a thin wash of colour poured into a chair. His people have done what they can to make him kingly, but his rich clothes swamp him and they've left off the crown, for it seems his neck, were it not propped upon cushions, would scarce support even the weight of his head. Marguerite kneels before him and holds the swaddled child before his face. Cecily and Jacquetta settle her skirts, smooth her furs and come to their knees at her back. When Jacquetta bows her head in deference, Cecily raises hers to watch.

'Lord husband,' Marguerite says, that soft French voice, so appealing. 'Here is your son.'

'Your son, Your Grace,' the King's attendants repeat softly in his ear. 'Your son.'

Henry's eyes, watering and rheumy, barely blink, and when the child sets up a cry, he closes them, as if pained. Cecily sees Marguerite falter then, just a little. Her shoulders slump and a shiver runs through her. She turns to Beaufort, who looks pointedly away, and it's left to Richard to step forward, to reach out a hand to raise her.

'Lady, be comforted. He will know his son when he is well again. Just as we know him today.'

But she turns from him to Beaufort, a hand held out and shaking. 'This lord,' she tells the room, 'is godfather to my child, and has sworn to protect him.' She looks about her, at the grave faces, staring. 'You, too, must swear. All of you. Loyalty and protection.' And her voice almost breaks on the appeal.

Then Beaufort, at last, does take her hand because, really, someone must, though it looks, to Cecily, as if it burns him. Marguerite seems to leech strength from his touch, grips his fingers till her knuckles whiten. Jacquetta, ever sentimental, lets out a hiccuping sob, and Beaufort turns on her a face like thunder, till she blushes and looks away.

Now, what's all that about? thinks Cecily.

The council meets three days later. Cecily, hands schooled to patience, waits in her window seat at Baynard's Castle, watching the river traffic ply its way between Westminster and the Tower. In the third hour after noon a dark barge comes down, dull and heavy in the grey drizzle. Between the broad backs of a dozen guards is a bowed head.

Cecily leans closer to the window. Is it?

As the boat passes the head rises, the face looks up. It's Edmund Beaufort, and his hands are bound. So, Norfolk has spoken and the council's task is done.

Beaufort can't possibly see her, but perhaps he guesses. His long jaw juts forward, his shoulders push back. She can't see his eyes but imagines them, flashing. Still defiant, then. He is the King's favourite. The Queen's lover, some say. Today he is her husband's prisoner. But his face says he isn't beaten. He won't be beaten till he's dead.

Nor will Marguerite, she supposes. But it will be a blow to her, the loss of Beaufort. She wonders who will tell her.

Richard, surely. He will call it his duty. It will be interesting to hear how she weathers it.

He'll come soon, and she'll ask him.

An hour later, men's laughter on the stairs. Salisbury is first through the door with his son, the wide-smiling Warwick. They pull Richard after them, slapping him on the back and calling for wine. Richard is a lull in the wind of their arrival. His the voice of calm. He takes her hand, kisses it and winks.

'There must be caution now,' he tells them. 'Due care. I'm not Protector yet.'

'As good as, as good as!' Warwick, crowing, pours drinks and passes them around.

'And speaking of the need for caution, what of the Queen?' Cecily asks, taking hers.

Warwick looks like he doesn't understand the question. 'What of her?'

Richard steps in. 'She's for Windsor. She has a husband and son to nurse. The King's doctors advise seclusion if he's to recover.'

'He could be as well secluded here. Besides, it's hardly in our interests that he recover. But I asked about the Queen, not the King. I'd rather she were here, under our eye.'

'I'd rather she were in Hell,' says Warwick. 'But Windsor will do. As long as she's a distance from me.'

There's no point arguing it now, while Warwick is swaggering and her brother laughing at his jokes. But she reminds Richard, later, when they're alone, that Marguerite is a woman who can do very great harm, even from a distance.

'I know,' he says. 'You're right. I'll tend to it.'

Easier said than done. Though the council make him Protector in practice, they're leery of putting their names to any paper that confirms it. They fear the King may come to his senses and want to know why his favourite is in prison and his enemy at the head of his Government. They certainly don't want to make any move that would appear to confine him. So, when the Queen says she would rather remain where she is, and the King with her, they hold up their hands, shrug their shoulders, shuffle and nod.

Richard is obliged to exercise power without authority. It's a tiresome way to live, for no man will make a decision unless backed by his peers, and no writ passes without a score of signatures. The Queen stays put and Somerset, though imprisoned, is not brought to trial, no matter that, every day, Cecily asks Richard why his head has not yet met with the block. And every man looking over his shoulder and asking, what news of the King today? How does the King?

Just when Cecily thinks her nerves will be worn away by it, Marguerite herself steps in to help. She has, indeed, not been idle in Windsor. Between nursing her son and tending her husband she's found time to formulate a case. In the days after Christmas she sends John Kemp to present it to the council. Kemp is Chancellor and cardinal too. A politician with God on his side, who loves his king, owes his high office to Beaufort's influence and, at eighty, is too stubborn or too old to trim the sails of his allegiance. The Queen, he tells them in a voice that's used to being listened to, claims her right to rule as regent: for her husband, until he is recovered, or for her son, till he comes of age.

'Tell them,' says Cecily, when Richard reports to her the council's shock and fluster, 'that if they want to be ruled by a Frenchwoman with Beaufort at her side, then by all means . . .'

By no means, obviously. A Parliament is called and Richard put at its head with authority, and the council's backing, to refute the Queen's claim. A month later, when Kemp is found dead in his bed and the way is clear, he is offered the role of Protector.

'Tell them you can't accept,' says Cecily.

So he explains to them, humbly and in writing, that he fears himself unworthy, and will take up the role only at their insistence. He looks to the peerage of England to exercise the King's authority in this matter.

They insist.

'Ask them to clarify their terms.'

They do. He is to be head of the King's Council. More even than Regent, he is to assume personal authority for the rule and defence of England, against enemies overseas and rebels at home.

'Rebels at home. Good,' says Cecily. 'Now no one can move against us. And, if the King ever wakes up and asks, "Who made you Protector?" you need only point the finger and say, "They did."'

Richard rules the kingdom as he ruled France and Ireland; by putting men into roles who are fit for the job and by giving good men reason to be loyal. And by paying his debts. Warwick's land dispute is made to disappear. Salisbury is given dead Kemp's chancellorship, and Richard summons the Percys down from the North to account for themselves. When news comes that they're gathering men and have made common cause against him with Henry Holland, he rides north himself to knock heads together. It's quickly done. Holland has no more sense than his dogs, all bark and no bite. Richard locks him up and leaves him to stew. Henry Percy, though, could raise an army if he put his mind to it. Richard slaps his wrists and placates him with a seat on the council.

Thank God, people say. Here's a man who knows how the world works.

England gets used to good government. Cecily gets used to being something very like a queen and, at Baynard's Castle, holds something very like a court, where men seek her influence and women promote their daughters to her attention.

Some she keeps about her for policy's sake. Others because she likes them, familiar faces from the old days in France. Alice de la Pole, it seems, has left the loss of William long behind her and has the interests of a twelve-year-old son to promote. Margaret Talbot, who has found little to mourn in her old soldier's death, brings the dark-eyed Eleanor, who lost soldier-father and soldier-husband on the same field and has never looked so well. The gilt-haired Elizabeth will make Jacquetta a grandmother soon. She has every man at court writing verses to her beauty and a young husband who, Cecily confides to Richard, would be the envy of all, if anyone could remember his name or where he comes from.

Cecily brings her own daughters to court and watches them shine in this new fellowship. Jacquetta is everywhere among them, and seems to have forgotten the Queen.

Cecily has not. Richard says her teeth have been drawn, let her stay where she is and not bother him. But Cecily rides to Windsor from time to time to be sure she hasn't learned new ways to bite. She goes to be certain the King still slumbers; tells the world she goes to see the prince still thrives. He does. She looks for signs of Henry's weakness in the infant's sleeping face. Finds none. He wakes, sudden, with a piercing cry and a look, scowling and defiant, that she's sure she's seen before, on another man. Not the King.

She leans forward to peer closer, but recalls herself, pulls back into a curtsey. She looks up to find Marguerite's white face fixed on her and senses, beyond the tight line of her lips, teeth still there and ready to bite.

She smiles over the sharpness in her own mouth. 'You have your prayer, Marguerite. A healthy son.'

'A prince, lady. Your sons will bend the knee to him.'

'As willingly as I do now. All four of them.'

The Queen says she will walk with her, to her carriage.

That's right, she thinks. See me off.

'I read your letter,' Marguerite tells her as they step out into cold brightness. 'I read it with pleasure, even now, and cherish the pains you must have taken to write it.'

She looks into Marguerite's face. The sun shines upon it, and the hand raised to shield her eyes cannot hide the venom in them.

She smiles. 'You never replied, though. Did you?'

When a second Christmas comes, she is pleased to tell Richard she's with child again. He wraps her throat in emeralds and gives her a Flemish tapestry, upon which a dark-eyed Salome dances. 'For,' he swears, 'I would give all the world just to see you dance.'

'If I asked for a head, then, would you give me Edmund Beaufort's?'

His smile tells her he believes she speaks in jest.

Then, at Epiphany, comes word from Windsor. Just as once kings visited a God, now God has visited a king and healed him. Henry is awake.

The dancing is done.

34

The recovering king remains in Windsor with his queen. He's not strong enough, yet, they are told, to see his Councillors, but letters come in his name, asking questions, issuing orders. Richard gives them to Cecily to read. She hears Marguerite's voice in every line. She chides Richard for the diligence of his replies: careful reports of his government's progress; the security of England's borders; disputes settled; steps he's taken to stabilize royal finances.

'Do you think he sees them?' she snarls. 'No doubt the Queen uses them for tapers.'

But Richard keeps doggedly on.

'You should go to him. Tell him to his face how things are.'

Richard only shrugs.

'Right,' she says, impatient after two weeks of this. 'I'm not a Councillor. If you won't go, I will.'

She speaks first to Henry's doctors, who say he improves daily. They show her a king who sits a little straighter in his chair, knows her when she kneels to him and simpers like a child when she kisses his blue-veined hand.

'Lady Cecily,' he says. Then nothing, for a minute or more.

'I'm come to wish you well, Your Grace,' she tells him, slowly. 'To assure you of our prayers; mine and my lord's.'

He looks puzzled, as though he struggles to recall the name of a face he cannot see.

'The Duke of York, Your Grace,' she explains. 'Your cousin and good friend.'

There is distress, and his eyes drift right, to where his queen stands, frowning.

'York,' Marguerite tells him, sharp, a grasping hand on the thin slope of his shoulder. 'Who, as I have told you, rules in your place.'

A breathy sigh, his mouth spittle-stringed. 'Oh. Yes, yes. He has stolen my crown, you say.'

'No, Your Grace,' Cecily reassures. 'He keeps it for you. Until you are ready to take it up again.'

He knits his brow, as if it is a bother to think of it. 'Ah, well then let him wear it a little longer.' Then a grin, naughty, a child playing truant. 'It is irksome.'

'My lord,' Marguerite leans to him, bristling. 'We pray you will soon take back your power.'

The white hand is raised. He has not forgotten how to be peremptory. 'Soon enough. I cannot bear the business of it. And cousin York serves well enough for now. We will write him, Lady Cecily. The Queen will write . . .'

'I am very sure she will,' Cecily assures him.

'As the King makes known his wishes,' says Marguerite.

Cecily nods, feigning belief. From her place at his feet, she leans forward to the King. 'I bring my lord's congratulations, too. He speaks ever of his joy that my dear friend, your queen, has blessed you with a son.'

At this, his face lights. 'Ah, yes! You must see him. Send for the boy, Marguerite.' When the Queen turns to speak an order, his uncertain hand seeks Cecily's again. 'You prayed with her at Walsingham and your prayers were answered. He is God's gift. Our holy Edward. We have named him for the Confessor, both king and saint.' He leans in, confiding. 'I think the Holy Ghost begot him.'

She looks into his face for the jest and finds none. Only eyes overly bright, fervent but unfocused. She smiles up into Marguerite's taut white face, squeezes the King's pliant hand. 'I am sure you're right, Your Grace.'

On the long road home she lets the sway of the carriage take her back ten years, to the river at Rouen, when Marguerite was a green, sick girl, determined but unable to do what a queen must. She remembers the lesson she gave her out of pity. 'When a thing is impossible to do, Marguerite, you must find a way to make it appear to be done.' And by sleight of hand and costume, Alice de la Pole carried a crowd. Cecily's hands fist in her sleeves now, and the remembered smell of sickness sears her throat.

You have put a bastard in your cradle, Marguerite. And shown the world a prince.

Richard, when she tells him, runs long hands down a weary face and shakes his head. 'You cannot know for certain.'

'I know Marguerite. And what she might do. I need no proof.'

They are alone in his office, business all about him, the endless ink of governance on the vellumed backs of beasts. She sits across the desk from him, reaches out, pulls his hands into hers.

'Richard, that boy is Edmund Beaufort's son. You manage a kingdom for a madman and a bastard. Soon that madman will ask for it back. Will you give it?'

He pulls back from her, his face closed, his arms folded tight to his body. 'It's not mine to keep.'

A hiss of disdain and frustration escapes her bared teeth as she rises to her feet and starts to pace.

'Cecily, whatever the boy is, Henry is an anointed king. To put him aside is . . .'

'Something you have not the nerve to do.'

'. . . is treason.'

She turns, leans to him, throws her hands in his face. 'Is justice. When a king is too weak, or too mad to rule . . . It is your duty. And you shirk it.'

He's on his feet now, his strong fingers biting her wrists. She's pushed back into her chair and feels the pent-up fury in his leaning frame.

'Alright. Alright. In terms you will understand. I don't have the support to depose a king. The council won't back it. The nobles don't want it. Too many of them have grown fat on Henry's negligence. You think they want good government? They don't. They baulk at every reform that will cost them money. Block anything that threatens their interests. I am not the king for them.'

'Salisbury and Warwick—'

'Are no better than the rest. Do you think they support us out of love? Family sentiment? You know better than that. They wanted me to kick Percy arses for them. Good. I've done it. They wanted Beaufort put down. I've done that.'

'They want him dead!'

'I'm very sure they do.'

She pushes back against the weight of him. 'So do I! So why in God's name does he still live?'

He steps back at that, turns from her. 'Because I didn't think I needed to kill him. Because I didn't want his blood on my hands.' His shoulders slump. 'Because it has been easier not to.'

'At least you own your weakness. And now, because of it, we will very soon see him back at the King's side.'

She's right. In February, Henry writes to order Beaufort's release from the Tower. The council concedes and Richard gives way. What choice, really? At least the charge of treason still hangs over him, and council denies him the King's presence until that charge is answered. But there are few, now, ready to press for a trial, and men who clamoured for Richard's attention yesterday give him a wide berth today. At Baynard's the women who kept Cecily such good company are suddenly busy about their own affairs. Beating a path to Marguerite's door, no doubt, thinks Cecily. She imagines the road to Windsor, bustling.

Walking the narrow garden beside a sullen Thames, Jacquetta tells Cecily she will go with her daughter to Leicestershire. Gilt-haired Elizabeth must begin her lying-in, and wishes to do so at home.

'You will send me news, Cecily?'

'As you will die without it. Does the Queen know you're going?'

'I've written.'

'You do not visit?'

'Travel west to go east?' She shakes her head. 'I've no wish to tire Elizabeth.'

Wily Jacquetta. 'Yet you've been so close these last years. And spent much time with her.' She cannot help but ask. 'In all that time, was she much alone with Edmund Beaufort?'

'I never saw them so. But then, if I had, they wouldn't have been, would they?' That guileless laugh, that artless smile. 'I cannot say it didn't happen.'

Cecily is not fooled. Jacquetta is no stranger to the secret ways of adultery; doors that close on a whisper, soft shoes in quiet corridors. On a long-ago winter morning she was, herself, discovered alone with the Duke of Bedford, in the almost-dark of a French stable, his hand on her thigh, while his wife slept, warm and oblivious in her bed.

Things unravel fast now. The King returns to Westminster with his queen. He looks thin, speaks slow and begs others to do likewise. But he has his wits about him, as much as he ever did, and has no need, he says, of a protector. Richard surrenders his post. Edmund Beaufort is welcomed back to the council. There's barely a shuffle as he takes his place. Henry Percy is first to reach across the table and shake his hand.

'No trial, then,' says Cecily, when Richard tells her of it.

'The King himself has sat in judgement over him. And found him innocent.' Richard paces the hall of Baynard's, while Cecily sits at table, rubbing a hand across the swell of her belly in a semblance of calm. 'He is restored utterly, Constable of England, Captain of Calais . . .'

'And you are plain old Duke of York again?' She looks for anger in Richard's grimace, and finds only shame.

'And I suppose we must be thankful I am still that.'

'Not for long. Beaufort won't forgive you now. You'll be lucky to keep your head on your shoulders.'

He sits beside her, takes her hand. 'I'm sorry. I should have killed him when I could.'

She says nothing. What could she say except, yes, why didn't you?

There's more.

'Henry Holland, too, is free,' he tells her. 'The King orders me to keep him in check. And to send our daughter to him, now she's of age. He thinks she may settle him.'

She nods.

'And your brother is no longer Chancellor. He is, as you will imagine, very angry.'

She massages the ache at her temples. 'Then we must be thankful for small mercies.' When she opens her eyes he is looking at her, puzzled. 'It will keep him and his son on our side. Without them we'd be completely alone.'

When Richard is not invited to the next council meeting, nor Salisbury or his son, and their way to the King is barred, they know it's time to leave the city; to get into country where they can call up men to fight, if they have to. And to stay together. They head north, to Neville strongholds.

On the day of departure, Cecily sends her children to Fotheringhay. All but Anne, who must go with Henry Holland.

The girl had not wept when Cecily told her, but her face had paled, and she'd sat very still beside her.

'You're lucky,' Cecily told her. 'You have a husband still in favour with his king.'

'And I am, at least, taller than his dogs now. And more able to command them.' She smiled then, and held her mother's hand very tight.

'I am proud of you.' But there was shame as well as pride, which must be faced down.

She had sworn, when this child was in the womb, to break the bones of any who sought to harm her. Now she gives her into the hands of a man with a stick.

Two months in the North and they must move again.

The King has called Richard, Salisbury and Warwick, all three, to a Great Council in Leicester. It isn't where they're going. The meeting, they are told, will discuss the preservation of the King's person. It seems more likely to bring about their own destruction.

Eyes and ears left behind in London warn of a royal army in preparation, of Edmund Beaufort calling up West Country men. They remember Gloucester, who came to the King when called for, and did not live to leave.

The summons found them at Middleham Castle, where granite walls amid the green folds of Wensleydale keep their strategies secret.

'So, we move to intercept the King between London and Leicester, bring the battle to him.' Warwick digests news hungrily, thinks fast.

Cecily watches him. He's become quite the captain, with all the decisive swagger of youth.

Her brother Salisbury has a cannier head. 'Careful, son. We've no quarrel with the King. Only with his counsellors.'

'We put an end to Beaufort.' Richard is emphatic. 'That's all. And by negotiation, if we can. We fight only if we must.'

'Oh, for God's sake, let's not have another Dartford,' says Cecily. 'If we threaten a fight we must be willing to have it.'

That night, she seeks her brother out alone, takes his arm and urges him. 'Let him not be made a fool of again. They will kill him this time.'

'Never fear,' he tells her. 'We go to take possession of a king. And there are more scores to settle than Beaufort's.'

Now they're heading south with an army at their back. Salisbury's wife and Warwick's have stayed north. Cecily would not, though at seven months gone, the journey wracks her. They'll gather men from Fotheringhay on the way. Cecily will stay there, with her children. Closer to wherever the confrontation will be.

And to London, where they hope to go after.

They go to the church when they arrive, hear mass, then walk together from tomb to tomb, touching their dead. Cecily looks about and wonders where, among these reaching arches, she would lay Richard. Close to the altar in God's sanctuary, she supposes, beside their firstborn son. But she shakes her head. That day is far off, and she will not court it with thoughts.

Her living children are in hall to meet her when they come to the castle. Elizabeth and Margaret, who seem lost without their older sister's shepherding. Five-year-old George, who earns a cuff for pulling on his mother's skirts. Little Dickon, who toddles smilingly to his father, and is pulled up into his arms. She can't help but look about for Edward, though she knows he isn't there. He's with his own household in Ludlow. She hasn't seen him, or Edmund who is with him, for more than a year. They should all be together now. She lies awake that night, thinking how best to protect them if the worst comes, kicked and bothered by the child still to come.

In the end, she does sleep. When she wakes Richard is gone, the bed beside her cold.

She pulls on a robe and goes to his chamber, where his squires are dressing him, the window's chilly dawn sunlight helped by candles about the room. His hair is damp at the temples and his face freshly shaved. She sends them away and finishes the job herself, tying his points, shouldering him into his doublet, smoothing the leather of his boots from ankle to knee. He goes armed, but not armoured. That's packed with the baggage and strapped in a cart. She knows exactly which cart, which chest. She has tested its straps, signed the cross on its breastplate, reminded the squires who travel with him of the details of its care; they, nodding all the while and attentive, though they know every inch of it.

She steps back to look at him. No one can pretend he is young any more. He will be four and forty come summer's end. There's grey in his hair and lines about his eyes. And the bones of his cheeks are sharp and shadowed. He is but flesh and blood, and will likely fight a battle before she sees him again.

'Marguerite has made a very grave mistake, you know,' she tells him, taking his hand to tie the laces at his cuff. 'She should not have made an enemy of my brother. There was no need, and we've gained by it. We're cleverer than she, you and I. We do what we must.' She lays a hand on his breast and looks into his face. 'We're not vicious.' She takes up the strings at the other wrist. 'Beaufort must die to make us safe. That's all. My brother, too, wants him dead. Even more, he wants to kill Henry Percy. Let him. It's to our advantage. We can control the King with Beaufort gone. But, were the King to die,' the last knot is tied and tucked beneath velvet, 'it would be no great cause for grief.'

35

With Richard gone, only the weary hours of waiting remain; their passage marked by the tolling of church bells and the discipline of prayer.

At noon on the fifth day, as she comes from mass, her steward brings word of a messenger spotted from the walls, riding hard and in York's colours. By the time he comes in under the barbican she's down the steps to meet him. He slides from the saddle and comes at a run. He must catch his breath, but his face is a blaze of confidence and his hand holds a letter closed with Richard's seal.

'My lord lives?' she asks him.

He pulls in a breath and gains power to speak. 'Aye, lady. All of yours are safe. A battle was fought yesterday through the streets of St Albans. The Duke of Somerset and Earl of Northumberland, both Beaufort and Percy, are dead. The King was injured but will be well. Your lord duke is with him. I left them yesterday evening. They ride for London this morning—'

'And the Queen?'

'In Greenwich, with the prince.' He signals the paper, now in her hand. 'There is more, I am sure, in the letter.'

'I will read it. Wait here for my reply.' She's off now, remounting the steps, calling for pen and ink.

'The duke begs you remain here at Fotheringhay,' the messenger calls to her. 'Till he's sure of the city's safety.'

'Does he now?' Thrown back at him, over her shoulder.

She closes the door of her chamber. Walks slow to the window, rests her hands against its sill and her brow against its glass. Her heart pounds. It had soared with exaltation at word of Beaufort's death. She should make confession of that, she supposes, but to what end? She's not sorry. She opens her mouth and a gasp of laughter escapes it. The back of her trembling hand bars more. She breathes deep, steadies herself, sits, and breaks the seal.

He tells her first what she most needs to know; the numbers and names of the dead. The one that matters most to her is Somerset, damn him to hell. The rest are her brother's northern rivals. Henry Percy. His nephew, Thomas Lord Clifford. Others who have given Salisbury and Warwick reasons to grudge them. The cobbles of St Albans are slick with her enemies' blood.

Then, because, as ever, it is foremost in his mind, he assures her he kept his loyalty.

'When we came to the town in the morning,' he writes, 'the King's banners already flew above it, his soldiers arrayed on its walls. I had my heralds call out that I wanted no battle here. Only the surrender of the traitor Beaufort. That given, I would tender my allegiance to the King.'

She imagines her brother shrugging and letting him get on with it. Always useful to be able to say we tried.

'But the messenger that rode out to say I must quit the field or die a traitor's death, with every man in my company, wore Beaufort's colours. And when I pressed him, before God, whether his words were the King's or his master's, he hung his head for shame. And so, we set ourselves for a fight.'

Thank heavens for that. Her rapid hand turns the page.

'Warwick took Beaufort down,' she reads. 'He was first into the fighting within the town. While I led an assault on the barricades to the south, he broke in with his father through the north wall. Our ruse. It worked.'

He doesn't mention that his was the most dangerous part; facing the enemy where its defence was strongest, drawing their fire. She feels her breath come shallow, and needs no words from him to conjure the bubbling terror of battling forward, hand over bloody hand. She's imagined it every night he's been gone, and feels now the wind of arrows pouring from the walls, feels in her sinews the desperate clamour to cut through any barrier, wood or flesh, to come out of bowshot and into the town. Once through, she's with him in close-quarter fighting all the way up narrow St Peter's Street in a press so thick she can hear the breath of each man that tries to kill him, hemmed in by walls and doorways, by carts and horse troughs and anything moveable, piled high to hinder them.

'Then suddenly we came to the market square and it was mostly over,' he writes. 'And there were your brother and nephew, most cheerful, with what was left of the royal forces already running and the first of the townspeople creeping out from their hiding places.'

Folk came, no doubt, to gawp at the redness of noble blood in their streets. Most of it was Edmund Beaufort's. He lay splayed on his back in a pool of it, arms thrown wide and smashed to angles by hammer blows. She relishes the detail of his torn-off helm, his blood-sodden hair, the slash across his face that had taken an eye, split his nose, smashed his lying teeth and severed half his jaw. She imagines the sword blow that wrought such damage, the swing of it from Warwick's swaggering shoulder, the crash of blade on bone. Richard's words paint a bald picture, her imagination gives it colour.

The King, he tells her, had put on armour, though he bore no sword and made no move to fight. 'By then they'd taken him in at a tanner's shop where some frightened-half-to-death field surgeon was fussing over a wound in his neck. Stray arrow. Not serious. I've brought him to the abbey for proper attention. I told him Beaufort was dead and that's ended my quarrel. I gave him my loyalty, as I always have, your brother and Warwick the same. He threw his arms about our necks, sobbing, and crying a pardon for all. Dear God, Cecily, what to make of him? So, I will take him to London and put the crown back on his head, but we must have the rule of him now.'

Cecily raises her head and lets air flood her lungs. It's done, but doesn't feel like an ending, and the elation of Beaufort's death quickly ebbs. The dead of St Albans – Beaufort, Percy and Clifford – have sons who saw their fathers die, and by whose hand. It would be better were they dead, too. But they're free, she has read, Percy and Clifford retreating north, and Henry Holland with them. Henry Beaufort, Somerset's son, taken from the town on a cart, clutching a leg wound and cursing. She folds the paper. Well, let it rest for now.

Her greatest regret is that Richard didn't think to open the wound in the King's neck a little wider, and let the mad blood flow from it.

36

Cecily sends Richard's messenger ahead with love and thanks-giving, but ignores her lord's wish that she stay where she is. She arrives in London in time to see Henry brought to St Paul's.

He comes in, flanked by Richard and her brother. Warwick, walking ahead, bears the royal sword of state, sharp, unsheathed and pointing skyward to signal the coming of the King. Under the eyes of Archbishop Bourchier, Richard returns the crown to Henry's head and reaffirms his oath. Then Salisbury and Warwick, the same. Their stern faces subdue the crowd. Henry is king. But there can be little doubt in anyone's mind who's in charge.

There's no pretence at celebration, no feasting or games, and the crowd in the street hardly knows who to cheer. After the ceremony the lords escort a dazed-looking Henry across the river to Lambeth Palace, to rest and recover as a guest of the archbishop. He declares himself happy to be in a house of prayer.

Good, thinks Cecily. Let him stay there.

Then to Baynard's Castle, which buzzes like a hive.

They close the doors on everyone and wear away the night in planning. Richard and Cecily, Salisbury and Warwick, deciding how things will be.

By the time Londoners wake up, they have news to digest with their breakfast; Richard of York is Constable of England once more, Edmund Beaufort died a traitor's death, and the loyal council will guide the land until the King is well.

Is he ill again then? people ask each other around full mouths.

The only answer is a shrug.

★

When June comes, and the city seems settled, Cecily gives in to Richard's urging and returns to Fotheringhay. In truth, she's weary, short of breath and sleepless, and the thought of lying-in through the city's heat and stink sickens her.

She begins her confinement at midsummer and is delivered of a daughter on St Margaret's Day, which should be propitious, but is not. The babe gasps and struggles a fortnight before dying. Cecily is surprised that grief's blade still cuts so deep. You'd have thought, by the fifth loss, its edge might be dulled. She had named this one Ursula, for the virgin saint, and intended her for the cloister. But when you offer a gift to God, you must be prepared for Him to take it early.

Richard writes and says he will come to her. She tells him to stay where he is, where there is business to be done that might have better profit than her own.

So, while she recovers and seeks solace in her living children, Richard studies to manage a king who is little more than one.

'I am learning, I suppose, what Edmund Beaufort knew well enough before me,' he writes. 'That the King will let you do most anything if only you spare him the work and give him the credit.' And yet he speaks of days when the King is capricious, querulous and changeable; when it is necessary to walk as if on knife blades and make few demands. And there are days, too, when he sickens, and wants only his priests and doctors about him.

'And the Queen?' Cecily asks.

'I never see her. And the King sees her little enough, I think. She's always with the prince.'

'Don't imagine she is idle.'

In July, Parliament meets. It does what they need it to do; makes Beaufort's guilt explicit, exonerates York and his allies, sets the wheels of business moving forward again.

The King, Richard writes, starts pliable, happy to please, but within days grows weary, impatient, complains of pains in his head. 'So I encouraged him to retire a while and leave business to me. I've sent him to Hertford. The Queen with him.'

Cecily sighs. 'I'd have kept them apart.'

'What, should I lock her up? Let be, Cecily. He cannot govern his kingdom. Let him at least govern his wife.'

Isn't it rather the other way around? Idiot.

Come November, when Cecily is back in London and Parliament is to meet again, Henry sends word that he's too ill to attend and names Richard his lieutenant. The Commons want better than that and say, for God's sake, make him Protector again and be done with it. The Lords agree, but don't much like it.

Richard was right about one thing; they don't welcome his reforms. He's been lifting up rocks and looking under them, opening cupboards and setting skeletons rattling, holding men to account who've been used to doing what they like. For years the King has impoverished the treasury, with imprudent gifts to men who've done little more than flatter to earn them. The Commons say they've been taxed too high to pay for the King's generosity to men already wealthy. Richard thinks they're right, and wants it back.

All of this means that, though it should be easier to rule as Protector, actually it's harder. And if the King is quiescent, his queen isn't. She makes known her opposition to Richard's reforms which, she says, slight men her husband has favoured. Suddenly such men speak warmly of her. Nor is she appeased when Richard settles on her son the duchy of Cornwall and earldom of Chester, and enshrines in law his princedom of Wales. 'It's his due,' she says.

'It's more than I would give to Beaufort's bastard,' Cecily complains, when she hears of it.

'We've no proof he's anything but the King's son,' says Richard. 'Would you have me go to war because a man who is dead may have cuckolded the King?'

'Would you let a bastard sit on the throne of England?'

'Had I proof of it . . .'

There is no proof, of course. And the risk of war too great.

She consoles herself; the bastard is a child yet, and may die. Or a time may come when men will be ready to believe it without proof.

Come February, the King returns to Westminster, walking and talking and looking like himself again, the Queen on his arm and smiling. He tells Richard he no longer needs a protector, though he loves his cousin still, his trusted counsellor, his old friend. He wants peace, he says, between all the lords of England; between all the lords of England and his queen.

'I've no quarrel with anyone,' Richard tells him, 'while I've surety of your good faith.' It's the best he can do.

Parliament is dismissed and Henry declares a royal progress.

York and his duchess are not invited to attend, though young Henry Beaufort travels with them, and Henry Holland whips up his dogs to run slobbering beside him in the royal train. The Queen has the ordering of it all, and though the proclaimed intention is to bring the King's justice to the whole realm, they progress no further than Kenilworth, where, far from court and Commons, they settle.

'The Queen will have the rule of him now,' Cecily tells Richard. 'And she is our utter enemy.'

37

It's a sad lying-in. No one awaits the birth of Henry Holland's child with enthusiasm. Least of all its mother. 'I want only to be done with it,' Anne complains.

Cecily has travelled hard to be there for its coming, riding into Exeter on the skirts of winter's first snow storm. Her daughter, who has sickened every day of her pregnancy, is pale and, Cecily quickly decides, ill attended. No family to hand, either her own or her husband's. The sisters Anne loves, being maids still and young, cannot join her in this place of women, nor childless Eleanor Talbot, who has become a friend. Only mothers here. Cecily would have asked Jacquetta to send the gilt-haired Elizabeth, but the girl is heavy with her second child and would be foolish to travel so far in winter. So there are only the household women, who are so far from youth they could lend years to Cecily. They go about their business efficiently enough, but the room's only warmth comes from its well-stoked fire. Cecily thinks of her own first lying-in, of her sister's comfortable company and the Virgin's girdle, gift of Richard's heart, daily in her sight.

'What of your husband's sister? Has she not given her house an heir yet?'

Anne shudders. 'No. But I wouldn't have her here even if I could. She's as sour as her brother and, I hear, so disliked of her husband he will not bed her.'

'What a family.'

'You gave me into it.'

That stings. 'Then I hope you will redeem it. Where is your husband?'

'Where do you imagine? With the Queen in Kenilworth.'

'Do you not mean with the King?'

'If you choose to imagine there's more profit in his company than hers. My husband is among the men whose support she buys. It doesn't cost much to buy Henry. A manor here, a small estate. A little patronage. Pat his dog and he's all yours. Henry Beaufort, now, Henry Percy, his brother Egremont or John Clifford, they're more expensive.'

'And with what does she buy them?'

'With promises, what do you imagine?'

'Promises of what?'

'Of revenge against my father.'

Cecily nods. It's no more than she's imagined. 'And your husband tells you this?'

'He's not very clever. And his mouth is the biggest thing about him. That's to my advantage. Yours, too, I suppose.'

'Yes. I suppose so.' Anne reminds her of her own mother. If she'd hoped for an affirmation of love between them, here it is. Information she can make use of. Loyalty to her house.

Now she hears her own gift of love knocking at the chamber door. She's brought Annette with her. Annette, whose powerful prayers brought her safe through so many childbeds, who has been a constant presence in her children's lives.

She watches Anne's face light with a smile as Annette crosses the room, sees her wrap thin arms about the nurse's neck and press a kiss of welcome to her cheek. She hears the sigh like a homecoming, 'Annette.'

'Ma puce.'

*

The days of waiting pass peacefully enough. They read much. Cecily has brought a book of saintly women, written at her commission by the poet friar, Osbern Bokenham. As a young man Osbern travelled through all the holy cities of Italy, before giving himself to God at the holy priory of Clare. Cecily has long been his patron and for her he writes, while his brothers in Christ watch over the graves of Richard's royal ancestors, men and women long gone, whose blood binds him to England's kings.

'I visited Father Bokenham this summer,' Cecily tells Anne. 'I had business in Suffolk.'

Her daughter raises a brow to ask what that business was.

'Oh, nothing so much. Some property we might buy.' Cecily likes the flat fens of East Anglia, its bright skies and long views. She has Clare Castle, of course, but dreams of somewhere finer, where she can lay out gardens in the Italian style. A house for living, not a castle for defence. Though perhaps now is not the time to indulge such peaceful fancies. She's laid out no money yet. But here's the real news. 'And a husband for your sister, Elizabeth.'

'Tell me he is a good man,' says Anne.

'He is a duke. And the good son of a good mother. Though the less we say of his father the better.'

'Oh. John de la Pole,' says Anne, soft and knowing.

'How clever you are.'

'Does it not pain you, to give a daughter to William de la Pole's son?'

Cecily shrugs. 'I give her to Alice de la Pole's son. She's had the raising of him since William died. And wit enough to hold on to her lands as well as her son's title.'

'He has not much money.'

'No, but he has a dukedom. And something we need perhaps more than that; the friendship of both king and queen. Or at least his mother has. Women, too, can forge alliances, you know.'

'Ah, that's well then.' Anne folds her hands over her belly. 'When?'

'In the spring.' Cecily lays her hand on Anne's. 'Elizabeth will do well enough. The boy is but fourteen. She'll go to Alice's household for now, a place of learning with a woman at its head.'

'Fortunate girl.'

Cecily's final business in Suffolk was with Father Bokenham himself. A gift for Richard that will mark both Christmas and the coming of his first grandchild. It's even more poignant now, since the child is a girl.

As he rolls the fine vellum across a width of table in Fotheringhay's hall, Richard smiles. On it, in the poet priest's elegant hand, is Richard's lineage in verse, back to the third Edward, from whom he and his king claim common descent. It is illustrated with images of every generation, and above each gold-traced figure flies the heraldry that proclaims their power. Such genealogies are common enough, but this one is rare for its beauty and for the precedence it gives to the women of Richard's line, ending in the greatest of them all, Cecily herself, and the children she has borne him. He's reading their names, from grace-given Anne to God-called Ursula, when she draws his attention to the head of the roll, where the sons of the third Edward stand side by side.

'Here,' she tells him, and points.

Richard's descent is shown, not from the fourth son through the male line, but from the second through the female. For Edward's second son had a daughter, who is Richard's great-grandmother. And that lady's granddaughter is Richard's mother.

'Henry, our present king, is descended only from the third son. Seen this way, you have the advantage.'

'This is a dangerous game, Cecily.'

'Oh, it's nothing,' she says, smiling into her sleeve. 'Just a jest, for our own amusement.' She walks around the table to stand beside him, leans her body in to his.

He moves away a step, and his voice comes low. 'Yet you know this claim brought my father to the scaffold, running to put a crown on his wife's brother's head.'

She shrugs. 'That brother had a right, and you're the inheritor of it. There's nothing in English law that says a man can't claim a crown through the blood of his mothers.'

'Nothing in law, but much in custom.'

'The Queen thinks much of female power. A woman herself, yet she daily usurps her husband's authority.' Her finger traces the line again. 'I only say that, one day, you might do the same with better cause.'

'Leave it, Cecily. I'm still in favour with the King and, if I keep my wits about me, might remain so. I challenge nothing and no one. The King is the king, and the King has a son.'

'Pah!'

He raises a hand. 'So far as we know it, he has. And, before you speak again, I wish to know no more.'

'And are you in favour with the Queen? Or with the men she keeps about her? My daughter tells they came at you with swords last month when you attended the King at Kenilworth.'

'God's blood, how does she know that?'

'Because she has a husband who keeps company with the Queen and doesn't know when to shut up.'

And so he confesses to her of the fracas in the streets when he came from the King to his lodgings. They were young men, foolish and perhaps a little drunk, and Richard had armed guards about him and the city watch had been on hand, so no harm done. But they were foolish enough and drunk enough that they still wore Beaufort badges on their sleeves.

'You didn't press this with the King?'

'And give Marguerite the confrontation she wants? No. This was done to goad me, not to kill me. I'll not be goaded.'

She sees that. Acknowledges it with a nod. A serious attempt would have been a knife in the dark, not boys waving blades in the street. She looks again at King Edward's sons on vellum and the line of women that could make Richard a king. 'I wish we could make this real.'

'Would you have me end as my father did?'

She looks him full in the face, sees only sadness. She shrugs and begins to roll Bokenham's gold-spun images away. 'Oddly, I begin to believe this might be the only way to prevent that.'

He turns from her towards the door.

She watches him go, and sighs. 'Double your escort. Keep from the court.'

For a year Richard heeds that advice. Head down, nose clean. He works for the King when called to, but keeps from his company, which all men know is entirely taken up by the Queen, with Edmund Beaufort's son, Henry, at her side. At every step Marguerite challenges Richard, puts stones in his shoes and rocks in his path, speaks against his recommendations, meddles in his affairs.

He bears it quietly. He is, as he says, not goaded.

Then, with the passing of another Christmas, comes a summons from the King. It complains there has been little peace among England's lords since St Albans. That the sons of those killed there bitterly bewail their fathers, and their cries pain his ears. He says he wants an end to discord.

'To his wife's nagging, he means,' says Cecily.

The summons calls Richard, Salisbury and Warwick to a Great Council in London, to see how such an end might be achieved.

Richard reads it aloud to Cecily, rubs his chin, turns the ruby upon his finger and shrugs. 'I've no choice but to go.'

'Then go well armed. And I come with you.'

Baynard's Castle rattles with the sound of men in harness, the scraping of steel on stone. They guard every doorway, crowd the courtyard, stand sentinel at the river gate. And, when Richard rides out to Westminster to meet with his king, a hundred ride in close formation about him, blades naked, eyes cold. Her brother Salisbury travels likewise. Salisbury's son Warwick, made Captain of Calais after St Albans and still tenuously in post, has brought six hundred of its garrison with him; men well versed in keeping the peace by looking ready for war. They are seasoned men all, picked for their sobriety and steadiness of hand.

'We're not here for a fight,' Richard assured London's mayor on their arrival. 'Just ready to handle ourselves if one is offered. You've my word on it.'

'I wish I could say the same of other lords,' says the mayor.

At dusk, the day before the council begins in earnest, a clatter in the courtyard sends Cecily running. There's a melee, with men circling high-tailed horses, Richard shouting orders and her brother cursing. Torchlight captures the shine of blood as two men are helped from their saddles and another is lifted down from behind his fellow, limp and heavy and dead.

'Richard!' she calls.

He comes to her through the crowd. 'Nothing, Cecily. It's nothing.'

She runs her eyes the length of him; there's only the dark sheen of fur and velvet, his face pale but steady.

Next morning, the mayor petitions the King. The lords Percy, Egremont and Clifford are required to remove their lodgings and their men beyond the city's walls. The lords Somerset and Exeter are bound to keep the peace, for they are a terror to the streets and a threat to the lives of Salisbury and York.

'Just high spirits,' Richard tells his king.

Salisbury curses and spits.

'I'll not be goaded,' Richard reminds Cecily.

He will be goaded neither in the street nor the council chamber, it seems. For the next three days, at the end of each wrangling meeting, Richard, Salisbury and Warwick return grim-faced to Baynard's. Salisbury rants and Warwick paces, but Richard only sits frowning, twisting the bull's blood ruby about his finger while he waits for them to calm.

Cecily waits, too. They've agreed their strategy and, though it's gall to her, she'll follow it. They will swallow their pride, they will make a peace. They will not be goaded into a war they cannot win.

They are told they must make reparation for their aggression at St Albans. That Somerset, Percy and Clifford must be compensated for their dead fathers. Money must be counted into their grasping hands, prayers bought at St Albans Abbey for the souls of their dead. Marguerite with her tally stick has decided how much.

'I would cheerfully pay twice the sum for curses,' says Cecily over the dregs of her wine, in the small hours, when Salisbury and Warwick have stomped home to their beds.

Richard turns the glass in his hand and sighs. 'I am very sure of it.' He stretches his arms above his head, cricks his neck. 'I'm rarely troubled by money given to God's house, but lining Beaufort's coffers, Percy's and Clifford's. That's . . . irksome.'

'There is a way around it, of course,' says Cecily. 'Tell the King we are content. But that he should take the payment from the debt the treasury owes us for Ireland. We'll never see that money anyway.'

She watches Richard's smile widen. 'I'm so very glad to be married to you.'

'Quite right. How seems the King?'

His smile disappears. 'As if his head were a beehive. He startles and stumbles. His anger is vicious and his plaints maudlin. The Queen drives him. But, I hope, with every concession I make he sees that I give him the peace he craves.'

'It's a poor game.'

'I hope to teach him to love me again.'

'Richard, his mind holds on to love as weakly as to purpose. He'll forget by tomorrow. Anyway, the Queen is our enemy, not the King.'

'Yes. We must hope she is not as clever as you are.'

'Clever enough to convince the King he got a son by praying for one.'

'Cecily.' He puts down his glass, stands. 'And now I'm going to bed. You can come with me if you promise not to speak of the Queen or her son.'

'Her bastard.'

'Goodnight.'

The final concession is, perhaps, the worst. Though Cecily comforts herself it is at least as painful for the Queen as for her. On this cold March morning, they must endure together the gawping of the crowd as they process through London's streets, from Westminster to St Paul's. They go to mass, at the King's request, to give thanks for the new accord between the lords of St Albans. A celebration of love, he calls it, an act of reconciliation. They will walk there together to share their joy with the people.

'We are at peace under God!' The King is gracious, laughing, shrill, kissing cheeks and joining hands. His face flames with excitement.

The Queen's burns with humiliation. For she must walk

behind her husband, hand fast in love with Richard Duke of York. Behind them Salisbury must link arms with a frowning Henry Beaufort, Warwick with Henry Percy. Cecily takes the arm of Henry Holland. She gives her son-in-law the best of her smiles and asks after his dogs. She'd like to see them eat him, but there we are.

Before God they will pledge their good will, each to the other. And their loyalty to the King. Music strikes up. She lifts her chin. Off they go.

Behind the loving procession, in close array, follow the escorts of each lord, swords loose in their scabbards, fingers itching.

When the mass is done, and they step from the church, Cecily offers the Queen a deep obeisance. 'How my lord and I rejoice in our return to the comfort of Your Grace's love.'

The King beams, bouncing on his heels, while the Queen inclines a glance, blank and white.

Lifting her eyes, Cecily sees Richard's smile. It looks courteous enough. She alone sees the mockery in it. Marguerite had hoped to end this week with his head on a block, not her hand on his sleeve.

It's a small triumph, and expensively bought. But Cecily will take what pleasure she can from it. She has little choice, for it must sustain her. She reads Marguerite's heart in the book of her own. She knows vehemence grows fat on the pap of frustration, and humiliation is surely the father of hate.

'It's not over,' she whispers to Richard as they take their accustomed place at each other's side in the carriage that will take them home to Baynard's.

'No,' says Richard, in a voice that sounds suddenly tired. 'It never is.'

38

June 1459
Fotheringhay

A tiny thing, a swan in silver, its wings an outstretched challenge, its strong-sinewed neck encircled with a crown. It nests in the palm of Cecily's hand, glints in the light from the window. She runs a fingertip across its etched feathers, tests the sharpness of its covetous beak, then closes her hand upon it and sighs. Henry Holland, her daughter writes, wears one on his breast. They are embossed on the collars of his dogs. He has, she says, many hundreds of them. They are the badges of fealty he gives to soldiers who swear their oath to the Queen, to be her men and fight for her. And my husband is not alone, Anne writes. The sons of St Albans, too, have grown wings.

It comes as no surprise. Since she parted from the Queen on the steps of St Paul's and came to Fotheringhay, they've been drawn relentlessly towards war. There've been signs enough, for those of a mind to see them. Armaments pouring into London and the ports. New serpentine cannon peering from royal battlements. Men whisper behind their hands that the Queen rules from Kenilworth while the King sickens. That she beggars the treasury to buy the favour of all men, save York, Salisbury and Warwick. For them she intends utter destruction.

Through it all Richard has gone about his business. Quieter than is his wont. Sterner. When at home he has called often on his arms master, come back sweat-drenched and sullen from the practice field. There's more muscle about him now than at any time she can remember, and the sinews that bind it to bone run taut. 'It's harder to keep,' he joked when she admired it, 'now I'm such an old man.' She remembers something her father used to say. That a bright sword has no edge in a dull hand. That the body is the first weapon.

Her brother, she knows, broods in the North. She's never seen him anything but battle fit. The Scots keep him in training. His son Warwick hasn't left Calais since last autumn. Says he will not, though the Crown hasn't paid his wages. He's a thorn in Marguerite's side there, for sure, loved by London's money men for keeping the shipping lanes free of pirates. Not averse to a little piracy himself.

So they've been putting themselves in readiness, all three, with never a word spoken. Now a swan flies in through their window and calls them to arms.

Cecily lays it in Richard's hand, the swan and the parchment it came wrapped in. Anne's gift of warning.

'It's not the King's cognizance,' he reflects, turning it slowly in the light of his eye. 'The swan was given to the prince. Does she recruit in the name of a five-year-old boy?'

'She's building an army, Richard. And its oath is given to her son. The King need only die and she will rule through the boy entirely.'

He turns it once more, its flared wings glinting, then closes his fist on it and sighs. 'Perhaps he need not even die.'

'What do you mean?'

He opens his fist on the table and lets the swan lie there. He makes a steeple of fingers, pressed thoughtful to his lips. 'She need only convince him to give up his throne in his son's favour.' His smile is tight and sickly. 'Catch Henry on one of his mad fool days and he'll give you the coat off his back.'

'But the next day he'll wake up sensible and want it again.'

She sits opposite him, turns the swan to face her, looks hard at it, so she need not look at him. 'She'd do better to put a pillow over his head and be done with it.'

'Cecily . . .'

A shrug. 'She'd need to, eventually. A deposed king is too dangerous to leave alive. You never know when some idiot might decide he's worth fighting for.'

'What? Some idiot like me?'

'Don't provoke.'

The swan lies between them and the bull's blood ruby on Richard's finger is turning again. 'You think she'd do that? Kill her husband? Whatever else he is, he's an anointed king.'

'Oh, Richard.' She shakes her head in exasperation. 'I think Marguerite's fought with her back to the wall so long, there's nothing she wouldn't do to reach safe ground. She has a husband worse than useless to her, and a son who just might be her salvation. Think what you would do in her place. No, better, think what *I* would do.'

The smile he gives her is a thin ghost of his old teasing one. 'I see I must strive ever to be useful to you.'

'Do.' The jest is a poor one and quickly dies. Perhaps she should tell him there's a difference. That Marguerite never had the chance to study Henry, to know his heart and say of him, as I did of you: yes, I choose him.

But that's not what matters most now, and there are more important things for him to hear. So, instead, she takes his hands in hers, kisses their knuckles and whispers that, in a world ruled by Marguerite, he would never be allowed to live.

He leans, in turn, to set his lips to her bowed head. 'Oh, I think she has me marked already.'

He frees one hand to reach into his breast for another missive. 'This came today.' He pushes it towards her across the polished wood. 'I am called to a Parliament at Leicester in

November. Your brother and Warwick, too. I think, if we were to go, we would not leave it alive.'

'Then we must act.'

She counts her heartbeat.

. . . seven . . . eight . . . nine . . .

Before he answers.

'Yes.'

And so to Ludlow and a summer of preparation.

Salisbury and Warwick swear allegiance to Richard, second only to the King. They will muster men; Salisbury in the North, Richard in the West.

Warwick will come back from Calais. He will bring his garrison and draw up the men of Kent as he comes.

They will meet at Ludlow in the autumn and march upon the King's party as it travels to Leicester for the Parliament. They will do as they did at St Albans. They will separate the King from those who control him. They will take control themselves.

And, this time, not let it go.

39

July–October 1459
Ludlow

A long July day is coming to its close when Ludlow finally comes into view. First, the high, square tower of St Laurence's, then the castle, safely hemmed by the Teme's reaching arm. For want of a wind to set them flying, the pennants of York hang heavy from its walls, and though the sun is lowering, the day holds hard to its sultry heat. As they begin the steady descent to cross the river at Ludford Bridge, Cecily grimaces at the shift of her weight in the saddle and the taste of dust in her mouth. Dickon rides astride Richard's saddle, just as Edward did so many years ago. The boy has long since fallen asleep, his head against Richard's chest, anchored by a weight of arm. His face is flushed and his dark hair sweat-flattened at neck and brow.

'Doesn't he make you hot? We should have put him in the carriage with the others,' says Cecily. Margaret and George have long since tired of riding, and trundle with their nurses further down the line.

Richard only smiles down at the boy. 'Let him be. I see little enough of him.'

He seems precious to Richard, this little boy. Cecily wonders why. He's slighter than the others, dark where they are fair. He hasn't George's boldness or Edmund's grace and, of course, no one can hold a candle to Edward. Perhaps it's because Richard senses, as she does herself, that he's the last. In the four years since Ursula, her womb has never quickened. She is forty-four this summer. Her blood comes rarely now and she marvels, when it does, that she endured it so long, the mess and the ache. It's a relief to lie with her husband and not wonder, for days after, whether this time she has caught; not to shield her heart, as her belly grows, lest this child finds better rest in a tomb than a cradle. She has borne twelve children. Seven of them live. She's thankful for each of them, and glad to be done with it.

She told this to her confessor last winter, expecting a penance.

He only smiled, patted her hand and said, 'God is merciful.'

She's called from her thoughts by the boom of Ludlow's castle gates being drawn open, and Edward's voice calling down from its walls.

'Mother! Father!' His arm about his brother Edmund's shoulder, and pointing. A wide-armed wave, then he's gone, and Edmund following a moment later.

By the time they're through the gate Edward's there before them, reaching for her reins and talking across her to his father of men arriving, of the muster already begun. He pulls her horse to the mounting block, then she's down and he's on his knee before her, kissing her hand.

'Get up, Edward, let me look at you.'

And, dear God, there rises a golden wall of him. She's tall enough, but she must raise her eyes to see his face and reach her arms to draw his head down for a kiss. It's close on two years since last she saw him, and the boy she remembers will never be seen again. He's a man now, or nearly, seventeen this spring. She should have expected it. The head of Ludlow's household sends monthly reports of her boys' progress – their learning, their growth, their prowess at arms – but nothing could have prepared her for the hammer blow of his presence, the theft of breath from her lungs.

And behind him comes Edmund on springing steps, only an inch or two shorter than his brother, but seeming half the breadth.

Edmund, made for speed. Edward, built to stop armies.

'Dear God, Richard,' she says, as they step ahead of their children into hall, 'he'll win battles for you.'

Through summer and the low-sunned days of September the muster continues. Beyond Ludford Bridge, an encampment grows. Richard continues to train alone, though his sons take on all comers. Few are fool enough to come for Edward, unless he agrees to fight them two at a time. Most afternoons Cecily comes out to watch, and, when he sees her, Edward draws up his height and fights harder. She lets him kiss her hand when he wins. He always wins, though Edmund gets a blade past him once in a while, pitching light-footed speed against superior strength. They've trained together long enough for him to predict his brother's strategy and outstep him. It delights Cecily to see it. Edmund's always had a tactician's mind, her chess player. 'Good lad,' she shouts. When he turns to accept her salute, Edward grabs his ankle and they're down on the ground, rolling like pups.

Richard names Edward and Edmund among his captains and draws them into his counsels. Now, when she and Richard talk strategy, more often than not they're there; Edmund, saying little but noting everything, Edward talking too much, bold where his father is thoughtful, subsiding with a grin when his mother slaps his arm and tells him to shut up and let her think.

'Speed up, Captain Mother,' he chides her, and laughs when she slaps him again. But when she speaks, he listens. He's learned that much from his father.

Salisbury and Warwick are expected by September's end.

Her brother is first to arrive. Cecily is in hall when a scout comes an hour ahead of his master with news of ambush and battle and casualties coming in. She sends him back with orders for the able men to join the encampment at Ludford, for the injured to be brought within the castle walls. By the time they're stretchered in, she has surgeons and apprentices standing ready with their medicines and knives.

'These your boys, are they?' her brother asks Cecily as she hurries beside him up the steps to the keep. He's stiff from the fight and the hard riding that followed it, but otherwise hale.

'They are. Edward and Edmund.'

'Hope you're ready for a fight, lads.'

'They're ready,' says Richard.

'Seems we've missed the first one already,' Edward complains.

In the chamber above the hall Cecily pours wine for her brother, sits him down. She notices that her hands shake and realizes she's never seen the aftermath of battle before. So many injured men. She'd thought they might be screaming, but they were silent for the most part, grey-faced and still after a three-day push across country to the security of Ludlow's walls. Their blood was clotted black on bandages and blankets, the stench of rot already rising from the worst of them. They lie now in cots and on pallets in the great hall below, in ordered rows. Her brother has instructed that those most likely to die should be laid nearest the door, where they are tended by priests instead of physicians. Even here, Cecily observes, there is order. Economy and provision. She looks at Richard where he leans by the window. His face is pale. She's never seen him injured, and her sons are not yet blooded. She swallows the thought of it, clenches a fist.

'How many dead?' she asks. It's the most important question.

'Less than five hundred of mine. So far. Near four times that of hers.'

'Hers?' says Richard.

'Well, hers and her boy's.' Salisbury digs into his sleeve,

draws out a silver something and throws it across the table, wings clattering. A swan. 'I've more of them if you want them. I faced down eight thousand. They seemed keen I not reach Ludlow.'

'They knew where you were headed then?'

'You surely don't imagine we're not watched?'

Richard's nod concedes the point.

It was a bad moment, her brother confesses, for he'd only half that number. But he hasn't lived so long without learning a few tricks. He pulled a feint, he tells them, drew the enemy on to poor ground about a brook and turned on them. 'They gave up then and ran.' He rubs a fist across his grizzled chin. 'I had to leave the dead unburied. Had to push on here before the bastards could bring up reinforcements.' He shakes his head. 'Never good.'

Cecily imagines it. The litter of bodies across Blore Heath, and the stream running red.

You can only talk for so long and at last you have to rest. Her brother is asleep on his feet when she bids him goodnight at his chamber door. She kisses his grizzled cheek and urges him to sleep well. 'I wouldn't want to lose you, you know.' It's shaken her, a little, to think she had come close to it.

'Oh, I'm tough to kill. A wily old badger.' But he smiles a little, as if pleased to think she'd miss him.

She's halfway down the corridor when she senses him watching her. She turns and sees he's leaning against the door jamb, candle in hand. He looks pensive. And old.

'How did our father have it so easy, hmm?' he asks. 'Never saw him tearing up and down the country like this. Died in his bed.'

'He put a strong man on the throne early, and left him to it. We might all take a lesson from that.'

He grunts and disappears, leaving her alone in the dim-lit corridor. She puts up a hand to shield her candle from the draught of walking and suddenly, in its flame, sees the brilliance of Raby in the old days. The flash of her father's broad smile as he strode among men who lived by his word. Her mother, queen-like, taking his hand for the dance. Cecily, too, had thought to live as they did. Knows it to be all Richard ever wanted. She'd seen him bewitched by it, that first night in Raby's hall, looking shy at her over the rim of a spiced cup nursed in chilblained fingers. Her heart shivers at the memory. She holds the candle aloft and walks on.

She finds Richard in his shirt sleeves, looking out from the high window of her chamber to where the campfires of their army burn. More now, since Salisbury is come. Taking her place by his side, she strains her eyes to penetrate the darkness beyond the flames. She wonders where Warwick is. If he, too, faces an assault of swans.

It's been agreed. They'll wait a week, then march out – with or without him. Letters will be written to the King. They will appeal for peace, demand only the suppression of the Queen's men, the restoration of York at the King's right hand. Cecily thinks it a waste of ink. But Richard insisted and Salisbury concurred.

'Who will read them?' she asks now.

'I have to try, Cecily. Before man and God I must be able to say I did not make war upon my king.'

In the end he hasn't much choice.

Three days behind Salisbury, Warwick arrives. Three days after that, they ride out. Fifteen thousand men. It's quiet when they're gone.

Looking out from the walls, Cecily hears the sound of birdsong for the first time in weeks and, instead of the banners of fighting men, the hills fly the colours of autumn, russet and yellow pouring down the hillsides to the river.

*

On the seventh day of listening she hears hoof beats, sharp and fast, and shields her eyes to see a horse in full gallop, its rider stretched along its neck. She meets him at the mounting block, horse and man a-shiver with news.

'Your lord brings his army back to Ludlow apace,' he tells her. 'The King and twenty thousand in pursuit.'

'The King?'

'Aye, lady.'

'What fool put him on a horse?'

They'd said a mass at Worcester, Richard writes her. They sent again their assurances to the King; to Windsor, to Westminster and Kenilworth, unsure of where he'd be found.

Then, not a day out of Worcester, came word of an army led by Marguerite with Henry beside her, flying the royal leopards of England, not a day's ride away.

They pulled back to Worcester. Richard wrote the King again. An answer came back.

Surrender, or face your king on the battlefield.

The signature was Henry's, a shivering scrawl and blotched, the words all Marguerite's; the threat of attainder, the promise of death.

Ludlow's castle is defended by the river, west and south. Now the meadows to its east become an earthwork, with ditches and mounds and sharp impaling stakes, and men digging, blades on whetstones, prayers and masses, and priests peddling absolution at campfires. Men muttering and asking, will we fight? For we came to free the king, not to battle him. And Richard saying he will parley, and Cecily shouting, God's blood, man!

And then the King's army comes, lining the horizon. And its herald cries out the Queen's words; that there will be no parley, but a pardon for any man who will desert York's cause. For York himself, for Salisbury and Warwick, no mercy.

So those lords go down to spend the night in the meadows with their men, to be ready for whatever tomorrow will bring. Richard takes Edward and Edmund with him.

Cecily brings her other children together, their nurses and maids.

And the castle, at last, is quiet.

She's woken by shouts and boots on the stairs.

They're back.

Even Edward's face is pale now, eyes wide and staring, for the worst they can imagine has happened. Between watches, under a moonless sky, a third of their army has deserted, scaling the earthworks to claim the King's pardon.

'We fight with what we have left,' says Warwick.

And Edward shouts, 'Damn them, yes!'

'Shut up,' Cecily tells him. 'Sit down!'

Steady Edmund, who has had the sense to say nothing, pulls his brother down into a chair, leaves a hand on his arm.

She takes Richard's face in her hands; its skin is cold and clammy, his lips drawn back from his teeth. 'Can we win?' she asks him. She sees the shame in his eyes.

But his answers are always honest. 'No.'

'Then you must run.'

'No!' Edward is on his feet again.

'Sit down!' She reaches for Warwick, pulls his arm. 'You, to Calais. And your father with you. You can hold out there, can't you? You've ships and a garrison, haven't you?'

Her brother catches her drift. 'No more defensible place in all the world,' he assures her.

She turns to Richard again. 'You, to Ireland. We've friends there still, haven't we? Get yourself an Irish army.'

He hesitates.

'God's blood, Richard, if you run today you can fight tomorrow. But by all means stay, if you want to follow your father.'

That puts metal in him. 'What about you?'

They'll be heading across country with nothing that can't be stuffed in a saddle bag. Impossible to take a woman and three children. 'I'll stay safe enough.' She looks towards the fire, where Margaret has her thin arms about George and Dickon. 'Do you think I'll let Marguerite murder my children?'

'I know who I'd back in a fight,' says Edward.

'Alright.' Richard is moving again. 'Edward, Edmund, you're with me.'

They nod, stand straighter.

Then, 'No,' says Cecily. 'Not both of York's heirs together.'

They cast about, see the logic but don't want to part.

'We must go now if we're going,' her brother hisses.

The choice must be hers, but how can she make it? She can't believe her sons might die, not now with her hands on their breasts and their living hearts beneath. But flesh is soft and swords sharp and all look to her for an answer and there's no time. Dear God, nowhere is safe.

She thinks of her brother outwitting the Queen's army not a month ago at Blore Heath, first to enter the streets at St Albans, holding the North and always winning. She looks from him to Richard, and knows.

She clenches her fists against her sons' leather gambesons and pushes them both away. 'Edward, go with your uncle.'

40

She's pushed them away and they're gone. Horses' hooves muffled by sacking, skirting the walls to the postern gate, down to the wooden bridge that crosses the Teme at Dinham. Then to saddle, and a mad gallop into the shadowed hills of Wales. She knows the routes they'll take, has hunted them often enough. They'll part before morning, if they live that long. Richard and Edmund for the Welsh coast, Edward and the others south into Devon to find a ship for France. They're good riders, her sons. Edward on that big bay mare of his, deep-winded and fast.

She looks to her young ones, mute by the fire. She's promised her husband she'll keep them alive. So that's to be her business now. Salvage. Annette's arm is about Margaret, who holds George's hand firmly in her own. White-faced Dickon presses close to the side of his young nurse, little Jane Malpas, not much more than a child herself, not crying but on the verge of it. She kneels before them, aches to hold, but a single touch will set her howling and leave her useless, so she clasps her hands and speaks.

'Now then.' Her lips crack, she licks them uselessly, her tongue tinder dry. 'Nothing to be afraid of. You will stay by me, at all times. Do anything other and I'll whip you. And of anything you've heard in this room tonight, say nothing. Do you understand?' She waits for them to nod, then regains her feet. 'Annette, find Marshal Reynold and Steward Stamford. Bring them here.'

When they come, even her peaceful steward has a sword strapped at his hip.

'You won't be needing that,' she tells him. She says how it will be. 'Tomorrow morning, shortly after dawn I imagine, our army will surrender. They're promised pardon and will be allowed, I hope, to disperse. The King's forces will then come here. They're not to be resisted or opposed.'

Marshal Reynold can imagine no world in which Ludlow is given up. 'Lady, we have enough men within the walls to withstand a siege—'

She holds up a hand, her thin white fingers cold beyond feeling, likely to snap. 'Barely. Our fighting men are out in the field. And besides, there will be no siege because we have no hope that anyone will come to relieve it. There will be no fighting. We will surrender Ludlow into the King's hands. Steward Stamford, bring all the castle's women and as many of the men as you can into the great hall. Bar the door and keep them there.'

He nods, then swallows, clearly afraid. 'Lady, where is your husband, our duke?'

Where?

Away and riding hard, she hopes, her sons flanking him. She feels the speed of their flight against her face, the rush of their breath in her own lungs, heads low over their horses' necks, backs tense against the threat of pursuit. They scout the ground for ruts or fissures that might catch a hoof, snap a leg and send a rider flying. Even the earth they move across is an enemy now, and the cloud-shrouded moon a poor ally. She closes her mind to it. They are beyond her help. She can do nothing but keep their way secret. She holds a brittle finger, hard against her lip. 'If you don't know, they can't make you tell.'

When he turns to go she tells him to take Annette with her, and Jane. 'All of my servants. And the children's, too.'

'But who will wait on you?'

'I will wait on myself.'

Dickon clings to Jane when she turns from him.

'Let us take the children,' Annette pleads.

Cecily steps forward to prise Dickon's fingers from the girl's skirt. 'No. I have need of them.'

Margaret reaches for Dickon's arm and draws him to her.

'Understand, I am in the business of buying mercy, Annette. I must play the defenceless mother and trust that even Marguerite's men will scruple to murder children.'

'And if they do not?'

'Then their deaths will be before my eyes and I will know who to curse.'

By the time the sky begins to lighten she's been standing at the foot of the castle's steps an hour, straining her ears to hear. No clash of arms from Ludford way. That's good. No sound of the town's stirring. Its people are not fools, she knows. When the King's army appeared yesterday, most packed their bags and sought sanctuary in the town's churches or security within the castle walls. Steward Stamford has done his work and, at her back, the hall is crowded to the rafters.

She's looking east now but there's no sun to shield her eyes against, only louring clouds and the threat of rain. Dickon's hand is cold in hers and she can feel his trembling through it. She holds Margaret close against her, George tucked firm between them. He started to grizzle a while ago, complained of hunger, but stopped when Cecily slapped him hard. Waiting is dreadful, so it's a relief, almost, when she hears the sound of horses, the jangle of harness, and a tramp of men marching through the town.

As the castle's gates swing open, she brings her children closer still, slightly behind her but well in view. At the head of the column fly the lions of England, the rose of Lancaster, the prince's preening swan; and beneath them a young man's face, a jutting chin beneath a raised visor. Henry, Edmund Beaufort's son; Duke of Somerset since Warwick swung a blade at his father. He raises a hand and the column stops. Left of him another knight, younger still. His brother, she guesses, another Edmund. And on his right, thank Christ, Buckingham, her sister's husband. But it's Henry Beaufort who rides forward till she can smell his horse's grassy breath, the polish of its harness.

She falls into a deep obeisance, drawing her children into the pool of her skirts.

'My lord,' she calls him, from her knees, 'I commend me to you and to our king.'

She hears the shift of hooves on the cobbles, discomfort passing from rider to horse. Few men have seen Cecily bend.

'Madam. Where is your husband?'

She looks up, widens her eyes. 'Not with his men?'

The horse prances and he's forced to rein in. 'Neither your husband, sons or brother. You are deserted, madam.'

'Then God help me.'

He orders her to stand and she does, bringing her children, too, to their feet. She watches him dismount, step towards her. He favours the leg that was wounded at St Albans. She can't help but notice, to hope it hurts. He's not so tall as his father and she looks at him, level. He draws his sword, long and ringing.

She steps back a half-pace, but does not cower. 'I am the King's loyal beadswoman. I've opened my gates to you. Ludlow is yours and I surrender to your mercy.' She speaks loud so all can hear. 'I am sure you will not threaten the lives of my innocent children, or those of my people who have sought safety here.'

He leans towards her, his bare blade between them, his face sneering. 'I am not fooled by you, madam.'

'Henry.' Buckingham's voice comes from behind, full of warning. 'This is a noblewoman of my family. Remember it.' He dismounts, comes to her, puts himself between her and

Henry Beaufort. 'Sister.' His voice is clipped and he cannot look at her. 'You are the King's prisoner.'

'I most readily submit to him.'

'Your husband has caused us much trouble.'

Henry Beaufort is striding back to his horse. 'Never fear. Ludlow will pay the price of it.'

They put her in the Mortimer Tower, its topmost room.

'Stay put,' Buckingham tells her at its door. 'You're in my custody now, a prisoner of the King.' He shifts his feet, can't look her in the eye. 'I can't stop what will happen here today, but you'll be safe enough. I'll set a guard below.'

Then, for the first time in her life, a key is turned upon her and she is constrained.

She looks about. The room is small, its fireplace is bare, there's a bed, narrow and low. Above it, Christ in agony. A priest's room then. There's a window that looks down on to the bailey and the town beyond the walls. She steps to it in time to see Buckingham turn his horse about and ride out through the gates back into the town, his raised arm drawing men behind him. Into the quiet he leaves behind comes a low muttering and a chink of steel. She looks down and there's his promise kept; a guard of twelve, metalled and stout at the tower door.

She sets herself on the bed, far from the window, and pulls her children to her. Dear God, it's cold! The wall is ice at her back, George's teeth chatter and Dickon's eyes are wide and blank. Margaret has one of each boy's hands clasped tight in her own, drawn deep into her lap. Cecily suddenly remembers Raby; that in her mother's care she never once had cause to fear. Now her own children are deep in terror. Marguerite, she thinks, if you were here, I would tear out your heart.

'We are perfectly safe,' she tells them, her voice surprisingly steady. 'And God himself watches over us.'

Margaret looks at her, chin up, mouth pursed, and nods, but her face is chalk-white and a blue-veined pulse leaps at her throat.

'Brave girl,' she tells her.

Already, beyond the window, the noise is rising. She pulls the thin blanket about them all and draws the bundle of hands from Margaret's lap into her own.

Henry Beaufort's soldiers are loosed now. They've been promised a looting and she can hear their roaring avarice above the smashing of glass, the cracking of wood and the roaring of beasts chased through the streets. Already the corner of sky she can see through the window is blackening with smoke.

She knows what happens when a town is sacked, she's heard the stories. They're taking everything that can be carried, breaking everything that can't. They're slaughtering the livestock and burning the stores. Men fool enough to defend their homes are falling to sword and cudgel and flying hooves. And any women left in the town, dear God.

I've done what I can, she tells herself.

But the castle gates stand open, and before long the soldiers come pouring in. The noise of them is so loud it seems they're in the room with her, and the smell of burning seeps through the walls. She pulls her children closer, Dickon's head against her breast, but when a deep pounding sounds below George breaks from her hold and rushes to the window.

'They're breaking into the hall,' he tells her, leaning out to see.

'Get down, George.' She imagines a stray arrow, tearing the air.

'They're chasing . . . everybody . . .' He falls quiet but continues to stare.

She leaps from the bed, pulls him down, but he strains to look again. And now she sees it herself she can't turn away. In every direction her people are scattering, struck down as they run. A priest throws open the doors of the chapel, some reach it, others push on to the gates, disappearing into the chaos of the town.

Across the green an anvil is being dragged from the burning smithy and soldiers are driving men, men of her household she'd ordered disarmed and stood down, towards it. They take the first of them and push his head to the metal. She watches the hammer swing once and turns aside. And there, running for the gate, is little Jane Malpas. Her coif is gone and her dark hair streams behind her, until a fist reaches for it and pulls her down. Then she's on the ground and a soldier astride her, flipping her on to her belly and pulling at her skirts with one hand, the other still fisted in her hair, while others grab her arms and legs, jeering and fumbling at their crotches, eager for their turn.

She reaches again for George, lays a hand over his eyes, but he pulls away, his gaze fixed in fascinated horror.

'Get away!' she hisses, repulsed, and pushes him towards the bed.

When she looks to the window again, there's Henry Beaufort, riding calm through the melee, his visor up, teeth bared. Beneath her window, he stops. She pulls aside so he can't see her.

'Are you watching?' he yells up. 'York's bitch? Tell your husband.' He raises an arm to signal all behind him. 'Payment for my father.'

She staggers back to the bed, Margaret reaches for her hand. She takes it, gathers her children to her again, and hides her face from their sight.

She has no idea how long it goes on but, at last, night falls. The boys are asleep and Margaret's lips move in silent prayer. Her heart is quiet and cold. The only sounds now are of drunkenness, and somewhere, far off in the night, a woman keening.

41

Her sister Anne is a gentle enough gaoler. Cecily is given rooms for herself and her children; a maid to wait on them. They have food, clean clothes. There is wood for the fires. She's warm as she feared she never would be again after three days in that bitter room, watching from the window as Ludlow's castle was emptied. Its hangings and tapestries, its plate, linens and furniture. Richard's things and hers, her sons', all inventoried, packed on to carts and rolled away. The rampage was over the first night, the bodies cleared next morning. The rest was stocktaking. The parcelling up of all York has and is, so that it can be given to others.

When Buckingham came for her, she had nothing but the clothes she stood in. They were filthy and stank, and in them she travelled four days in a lurching coach at the rear of his army to Maxstoke, her sister's home in the Midlands. There is one mercy. As they were brought from the tower to the castle ward, Annette appeared from somewhere, bruised and battered, but otherwise hale, and begged leave of the duke to travel with her mistress.

In the quiet of the carriage Cecily grasped for her hand. 'Are you much hurt?'

'No more than you see.'

'And Jane. Did you . . .?'

Only a shake of her head, a fluttering hand that says, ask no more. 'I have bought prayers.'

Annette cares for the children now, beds down each night beside Dickon who, she tells his mother, cries bitterly in his sleep. Cecily can't think of that. She weeps at night herself. By day she must be calm and think straight. Parliament has opened at Coventry and she is called before it.

When the time comes, she travels with her sister, leaving her children with Annette, safe, she hopes, behind Maxstoke's red stone walls, its broad moat. She's not allowed a horse and Buckingham's men ride close about the carriage.

'What do they think I'll do,' she asks, 'run?'

'Well, your husband did,' Anne reminds her.

And because it is so ludicrous, they laugh, gulping. Cecily reaches out and takes Anne's hand, squeezes it. She knows her sister has prevailed upon her husband to speak to the King on her behalf. To counsel him towards mercy. He's a fair man, Buckingham, able to see both sides of an argument, tired of being pulled in two directions.

That night, in their Coventry lodgings, he tells her, in plain language but avoiding her eye, of the ruin that is upon her. The attainder that Parliament has passed against Richard and her sons, against Salisbury and Warwick, strips her of everything. Land and titles, property and rights.

She nods. It's as she expected and what she has steeled herself against.

'I could do nothing for your brother's wife,' he tells her. 'She's declared traitor, too. Men have been sent north to arrest her.'

That's ice in her belly. 'How so?'

'Some trumped-up nonsense that she drove your brother to rebel.'

303

This is a new kind of fear. She feels for a moment the thinness of her neck, the horror of laying it down. 'Am I also in such danger?'

'Do you think you'd be here with us if you were?'

'Then why Alice and not Cecily?' her sister asks.

A moment's thought and she doesn't need Buckingham to give her the answer. 'Because our brother holds the earldom of Salisbury in right of his wife.'

'Aye, and rich lands along with it.' Buckingham nods.

'And Marguerite wants them.'

'The Crown wants them.'

'Same thing.'

'Don't, Cecily. I'm with you only so far. The point is you don't have a conspicuous earldom in your jointure, so there's an opportunity for mercy. But whatever you do have, assume it gone. You'll lose your life trying to keep it.'

'Good advice.' She nods.

So, she comes to her king on her knees, is abject and asks for nothing. She looks about the chapter house at the lords gathered. She sees no friends there, they've not been called. This is a Parliament peopled by her enemies, Queen's men, swan badges prominent on every breast. It's hard to imagine that the king before her put on armour and led an army to Ludlow. She wonders how it was done, whether they propped him in the saddle or left him with the baggage, for he looks as though a strong wind would take him. His fingers tap listless on the arms of his chair, his eyes flicker and he asks constantly for things to be repeated.

Henry Beaufort, standing beside him, reads out the charges against her husband. That he is a traitor of ten years' standing, the power behind Jack Cade, the aggressor at St Albans, a rebel at Ludlow and his king's would-be assassin. He reads slow, for the King's sake. With relish.

'Do you acknowledge your husband a traitor?' Beaufort demands of her.

She looks up and sees the King's eyes flicker towards her, blinking and troubled. 'I think you do not need my word to make him so.'

'The King's word makes him so.'

'Why, then, so he is.'

'And did you incite him, madam, into treachery?'

'Do you think him a man so easily led?'

'And yet –' the King now, rousing himself in his chair, querulous and pointing – 'is sin not seeded in a woman's tongue?'

She sees the men about him shuffle their feet, Henry Beaufort jut his chin. Poor dogs, she thinks, to fawn on such a master.

She ignores them, fixes her eyes on Henry and softens her voice. 'And was not salvation born of a woman's womb?'

'And of Christ's wounds.'

'And his mother's tears.'

He smiles at her now, reminiscent and soft. 'Your husband once told me so.'

'He is a speaker of truth.'

Henry Beaufort grows impatient. 'Are we here to argue the divine or to deliver justice?'

She keeps her eyes on the King's face, dares to raise her voice a little. 'Is there a difference?' She leans closer, quieter. 'Is there a difference, Your Grace?'

He shakes his head. 'No. We seek God's justice, do we not, Lord Beaufort? Upon this sinful woman.'

She lowers her head. 'Redeemed through suffering.'

'Your Grace . . .' Henry Beaufort blustering, wishing, no doubt, that his queen was here to manage her husband.

The King waves a hand at him, scowling, turns back to her, reaches a finger, curls it to beckon her close. All around men are whispering behind their beards, their hands open. She edges forward on her knees, intent.

He leans to her. 'Lady Cecily. I ask you before God. Does your husband seek my crown?'

It's almost laughable, to tell the truth here. 'Your Grace,' she speaks clear, lets her voice be heard. 'I swear upon my soul, there is nothing on God's earth he covets less.'

Now here's the dangerous question. 'And you? Do you wish it for him?'

The lie comes easy. It's no heresy to placate the mad. 'On my children's lives. No, indeed.'

He smiles and leans back in his seat, eyes fixed on air. 'We are content.'

'Your Grace. The Queen expects . . .' Henry Beaufort, harrying.

'We are content!' A shout, vehement, vicious, that turns heads and quells the room. 'Do not vex us!'

She thought her head could get no lower. She brings its brow to the cold floor. Waits for his voice . . .

'Lady.'

. . . and looks up. 'Your Grace.'

'Ask of us what you will. Are we not merciful? Is God not just?'

Careful now. 'Nothing, Your Grace. I understand my lands and goods are answerable to my husband's fate. Only, I have three young children with me and lack means to care for them.'

'You shall have it. A thousand marks, annual.' It's an outrageous sum, more than she'd ever have dared ask. The muttering begins again, till the King's voice cuts it off. 'Annual, for life! Set it down.'

Her heart slaps against her ribs; she had not thought hope so painful a thing. Her mouth is dry and her bladder presses, but she speaks again. 'Your Grace. You offered pardon to all who opposed your armies at Ludlow and Blore Heath. Men who did no more than follow their liege lord, as God and honour demanded.'

'Most surely.'

'Yet many still go in fear of their lives. Their pardons not writ.'

He looks puzzled.

'A man needs something,' she urges. 'A paper to show to the officer or bailiff who comes for his life or his goods. He may not say, it was promised. He must say, look, here it is.' She does not say, a man may not fight for Richard returned, if he is dead.

'They shall be writ. Beaufort, Buckingham, see it done.' To her, 'Is there more, madam?'

She shakes her head. 'No more. I thank you. Am I a prisoner still?'

'Your sister's honoured guest, is she not, Buckingham?'

'Aye, Your Grace.'

The mad king smiles at her, benign and foolish. 'Stay within her loving bosom, until your lord is dead.'

The business is over. Buckingham leads her from the hall, into the air, which her lungs gasp for. She leans against the bare wall, chest heaving. Beneath her skirts her legs are wet and the stink of it acrid in her nose.

'God's bones, Cecily, you could talk your way out of Hell's mouth.'

She judders and relief cracks a laugh in her throat. 'Yes. Send me there. Let me try that.'

A week later, as Parliament ends and they make ready to return to Maxstoke, the writ comes. A thousand marks, payable on the quarter days, the first at Christmas. Her young ones have their lives, though they can be earls of nothing and dukes of nowhere.

If Richard doesn't come back, what can she make them with a thousand marks? Something, surely. Not much.

'I am your debtor till December,' she tells her sister, who only nods and squeezes her hand.

'I will keep an account.'

42

June–July 1460
  Maxstoke

Buckingham's letters to his wife end always with the same injunction: of this, say nothing to your sister. From them, Cecily has learned that Richard rules like a king in Ireland, men flock to him in defiance of England's rule. That Calais opened its arms to her family, then closed its gates to Henry Beaufort, when he came with ships to wrest them from it. That Warwick and Edward run the Channel like pirates. They've raided the royal fleet at Sandwich; the golden Woodville, who had command of it, was torn from Jacquetta's bed, humiliated and mocked. Well, that's worth a smile. Poor Jacquetta.

She hears that her brother's wife has evaded capture and is with him now in Calais. That Warwick met with Richard in Ireland, and evaded Henry Holland's fleet on both the outward and return journeys.

'Your son-in-law, it seems, had not paid his sailors,' Anne tells her, 'so they refused to engage.'

Cecily can't hide the grin that splits her face at that. She allows herself a vision of her swaggering nephew, salt-sprayed and laughing at his ship's prow, while foul-faced Henry Holland snaps and snarls like a dog on a leash.

'I shouldn't tell you these things.' Anne folds the paper in cross fingers. 'It's not for your pleasure.'

Disobedience to her husband makes her sister's temper

short, so Cecily reaches a hand to her, placating. 'I know. You tell me out of pity and because you have a good heart. And why not? I can do nothing with such news but smile at it.' She takes both her sister's hands in hers, squeezes. 'You could get word to them for me, if you would.' She's asked a hundred times, and the answer is always the same. No words, just her hands pushed away and the swish of Anne's skirts as she leaves, moving fast as if she flees temptation.

Today, Cecily can see, the news is serious. She hears rapid footsteps and looks up to see her sister coming down the garden's gravel path, head down, stiff-armed, parchment in hand. She gets up from the warm grass where she and Margaret have been wasting their time with sewing, while Annette tries to interest George and Dickon in a game. The boys are tetchy, too old for such things, but Buckingham forbids weapons training. Says he will school no fighters for York in his house. She lifts her chin, puts her needle aside and goes to meet her sister. Richard has written to his king, she hears. Salisbury and Warwick's names, too, are upon the writ. They declare themselves loyal. They sue for peace and offer it in return. They vow allegiance and good service. They ask only for the King's corrupt counsellors to be removed. The usual names, the usual complaint.

'They cannot expect to be heeded,' Anne complains.

'I should think not. How was the message sent?'

'By proclamation to the Archbishop of Canterbury, and to the Commons.'

'And does your husband say how the King has responded?'

'He has affirmed them traitors, courting death. I'm sorry.'

Cecily is not, though she makes a sad face and turns away. Reconciliation has been offered openly, so that the lords of England will understand Richard to be an unwilling aggressor. Its rebuttal has been heard, so they will know he has no choice.

It can only mean one thing. She lets her eyes travel the

garden, where the hum of bees among roses tells her the fighting season has arrived.

They're coming home.

Because Buckingham is with the King and Queen at Kenilworth, news of their arrival doesn't reach Cecily until they've already taken the capital. Not Richard or Edmund yet, but Salisbury, Warwick and Edward.

'They landed on the Kent coast with two thousand,' writes Buckingham. 'They'd gathered five thousand more by the time London's damn mayor opened its gates to them. The Tower holds out but the city's lost. I'm to march south,' he tells his wife, 'and engage their army.'

By the time more news comes, Buckingham is three days dead.

She hears her sister's screams and comes running; finds her in the hall, floored at the feet of a messenger. He wears the King's colours, but opens his jerkin that Cecily might see he bears in secret the blue and murrey of York.

'I come from your son Edward,' he whispers.

'Into his enemy's house,' she answers. 'Brave man.'

He shrugs, but looks as if courage might fail him, for men of Buckingham's household have gathered and knives glint at their belts.

She kneels and takes her sister in her arms. 'Anne,' she calls to her. 'Listen now. Let's send these people away that we might make sense of this.'

Anne nods, distracted.

Cecily orders, and the room empties. The paper she takes from her sister's hand is addressed to herself, and Edward's signature is scrawled at its foot, rushed and blotched. She reads fast, of a battle won at Northampton. Of Buckingham dead, the King taken.

'We're for London again, mother,' it tells her. 'Stay where

you are for now, if you can do so safely. The city's not secure yet. I'll send for you.' She casts the missive on the table, draws her sister's head to her shoulder, holds her till the crying gives way to shuddering breaths. The messenger tells them all that Edward would not trust to paper; that those she loves still live, that Salisbury holds London, that her son and Warwick are the victors of Northampton. He says Edward was first across the barricades; that his enemies fled from the sight of him. The Duke of York is still in Ireland, but will surely come soon, now the tide has turned. Her heart would soar, did not her sister's sobs draw it down.

'You return to my son?' she asks the messenger. He says aye and she instructs him, 'Tell him that, when I come, I will bring my sister. He will take her under his protection. She will not be harmed, nor arraigned. She will keep her jointure. And her children, provided they do not rise in arms against us, will be free to inherit their father's lands and titles. Tell him I must have this in writing before I come, for she has given me shelter, and her lord preserved my life at Ludlow. Repeat the message, so I know you have it.'

He does, and is gone, and, if he wonders how a woman dare order so great a young lord, he has sense not to say so.

Three weeks pass. Cecily spends them at her sister's side, who has taken to her bed and will not rise. It is torture to be still, but she must wait for Edward's word. And it is well enough, she thinks, that she should suffer a little, that she should give this time in recompense to her sister for the husband her cause has killed. Sometimes Anne weeps in her arms. At others she turns her face to the wall and will not speak. She calls Cecily a bitch and a whore. She slaps and punches her, calls down curses on her head. Then she grasps her hands and begs forgiveness, thanks her over and over for the preservation of her sons.

One day, at last, Anne wakes clear-eyed. She takes a little breakfast and says she will walk in the garden. Cecily paces beside her, feeling the tremble in her frame.

'You know, it could have been the other way about,' Anne says. 'My husband might have killed yours. He might have killed your sons.'

'I know,' Cecily says. 'It is bloody.'

'Could you have forgiven it?'

Never, Cecily thinks. 'I don't know. I hope so. Perhaps it is a thing beyond forgiveness.'

Beside her Anne nods. 'Yes, I think so.' Then she reaches out a hand and Cecily takes it, wraps it tight under her arm as they walk back to the house.

At the end of July, an escort arrives with its paper for Anne.

And Cecily, at last, is free.

43

It's a fine house, Fastolf Place. South of the Thames with gardens down to the water, but today its view is marred by the damage done to London's Tower on the opposite bank, its walls greyed with smoke and tar, pockmarked with cannon.

'It held out against us eighteen days,' Edward tells her, looking out from Fastolf's lawns. 'Have you ever seen wildfire?'

She shakes her head.

'No, of course not. Burns like the very devil and water makes it worse. They poured it from the walls. The whole river was alight from men on fire leaping into it. We're still pulling out bodies, burned black.'

She lets her eyes cross the water, and sees him among the smoke and fury, burning brighter than any fire. It makes her heart race. She wonders if he's spoken of it to others, or waited to confide the horror of it to her. There's a scorch across his knuckles, a fast-whitening scar.

'Is this all?' she asks, tapping it.

He shrugs. 'Nothing touches me, mother.'

'Invincible, are you?'

He grins and looks, for all he's seen and done, a boy again, so she draws down his head and kisses it.

'Will you be comfortable here, do you think?' he asks her. 'Till father comes?'

'Why isn't he here already?'

'You should know that better than anyone. Not all your men together, remember? Not all at once?'

'Ah. Yes.' He's wise to her, this one. 'I parted you from your brother with good cause.'

He shrugs as if it doesn't matter. 'Anyway, the house? I've the let of it as long as we need. Salisbury, Warwick and I are at Baynard's. But it's chaos most of the time, men coming and going at all hours.'

She can imagine. Power base, centre of operations, the place of decisions and action. 'And when have I not wanted to be in the thick of things?'

'Well, you, of course. But I thought somewhere quieter for Margaret, for the boys.'

'Yes, certainly. For them.' He's tall, but she can still stare him down.

'I'll send a river boat for you. Every morning.'

And so each day she's part of it, the marshalling of men and arms, the reordering of government, the isolation of the King. The terrible attainders are overturned, so that Salisbury, Warwick and Edward Earl of March, remade, can pick up the threads of government. They make it clear they do so only till York comes from Ireland, to take up his role as . . .

'As what?' says Cecily at last.

It's late in the evening, the passage of feet has ended, the last messengers gone. Alone, finally, among the debris of business, they've drawn up chairs, poured wine, caught their breath.

Salisbury rubs his hand across his chin. He looks tired but leans forward in his chair, squares his shoulders as if for a fight. 'As first Lord of England, and Protector of the Realm.'

'Not king?'

'We have a king.'

She scorns. 'We have Henry, you mean.'

'Until one of us sees fit to slip a knife between his ribs.'

Warwick makes it sound like nothing, but her brother takes to his feet, squares up to his swaggering son.

'We don't kill kings, boy.'

Warwick only shrugs and turns his back. Cecily notes it. He wouldn't have done it a year ago. In exile and adversity, power has shifted, father to son, age to youth. Warwick is a man in his prime now, gone thirty and battle proven. There's one, thinks Cecily, who won't bow easily to any authority.

'We've been here before, father,' he says. 'The only way to secure England is by ruling it.'

'Aye, right enough. We rule through the king.'

'We've tried that, twice,' says Cecily, 'it didn't end well. We need something more conclusive.' She sighs. 'But I agree, we can't kill a king. Not because I wouldn't like to—'

'Then why?' asks Warwick.

Edward has the answer. 'Because it would make a martyr of him and murderers of us. And because we have too many enemies still at liberty who'd make much of it.'

'Well done,' Cecily tells him. 'There's more to you than muscle, then.' She turns to Warwick. 'Today Beaufort, Northumberland, Clifford and Exeter have no better cause to fight for than a foreign queen everyone hates. Do this and they'll have God's cause. They'll raise the country against us.'

'And also because the King has a son,' reminds Salisbury. 'And he's in the Queen's hands, not ours.'

It's true enough. Marguerite fled when she heard Henry was taken, and, if any know where she is, they're not saying.

'Killing the King doesn't make Richard his heir.'

'Ah, well. Perhaps I can help with that . . .' Cecily takes a moment to smooth her sleeves. 'The Queen's son is a bastard.' She speaks the word with certainty, relishing the feel of it in her mouth.

'Yes, yes, Beaufort's boy, we've heard the rumour.' Salisbury is dismissive, pushing back into his chair.

'We don't know where it comes from, mother,' says Edward. 'Or whether it's true.'

'Foolish boy, where do you think it comes from?'

They stare at her.

'From you?' Salisbury, incredulous.

'Women have no swords, brother. We do our work by talking.'

'But, is it true?'

'That's a foolish question. Personally, I'd stake my life on it. But, in fact, it hardly matters. It's true if men believe it. If they want it to be. If it's in their best interests. They can have Richard's good rule or the mad king and his bastard. We should tell them so.'

Salisbury is first to speak, spreading his hands flat upon the table, not catching his son's eye. 'We bide our time, then,' he says. 'Protector first. Let words do their work, the King's incompetence, the boy's bastardy. We wait till the time is right, then we depose the King, not kill him.'

'All very well,' says Cecily. 'But when is the time right? Do you imagine the Queen is idle? We'll have to fight her, sooner or later. Sooner, probably. Better to do so under a royal standard, with men fighting for an anointed king, rather than against the wife of one.'

'I agree,' says Warwick. 'We force the deposition. Let York take the throne immediately.'

It's what she wants, but still, Cecily feels her heart constrict. It will only work if the lords support it. Her brother's caution, her nephew's bravado, both feel wrong. If only she were certain. She's been sequestered a year, lost to the shifting moods of men. 'A bid for the throne is a dice we can throw only once,' she urges them. 'Will we get the support?'

'Yes, of course,' says Warwick.

Salisbury pulls his hands down his face, rubs tired eyes. 'It's possible.'

She looks to Edward.

'Well,' he says. 'We'd have some talking to do.'

By night's end they're agreed. Richard's not here yet. Before he comes they'll fight a woman's war, with words. They'll remind men of his record as Lord Protector, of the chaos of Henry's rule, the risk of the throne passing to a French woman's bastard. Protector first or king now? There'll be time to make a judgement when he gets here.

It's past midnight when Edward walks with her down to the river, to the boat that waits to take her back to Fastolf's. 'Is it true, mother,' he asks, as they tread the path to the jetty, 'did Edmund Beaufort really get a child on the Queen?'

She sighs. 'I think, rather, she got one on him. She needed an heir, Edward. You've seen the King.'

'Aye.' Who can see the King and not wonder? 'But such a terrible risk.'

'Did you think that, when you broke the barricades at Northampton or threw your strength against the Tower? Did you shiver in your boots and say, "Oh, but it's a terrible risk"?'

He smiles, rueful. 'It was much on my mind.'

'It didn't stop you, though, did it? Don't imagine Marguerite to be less brave than you are.'

'Would you have done it?'

'In a moment.'

He laughs. 'Well, you're braver than us all.'

She laughs with him, takes his arm. 'Is Warwick right? Can we get the support?'

'If anyone can, he can.'

'He's very bold.'

'Wait and see. He makes impossible things happen every day. He's not afraid of anything. He says a thing will be so, and it is.'

'What of your father? You went with Warwick to Ireland. You've seen him. Does he want it?'

He grimaces. 'I think he wishes he could stay in Ireland.' He smiles when she frowns, chucks her under the chin. 'Only if he could get you there.' Then, serious again. 'No. He comes for the Crown, I think.'

It seems he does. He writes in mid-September and bids her come towards Hereford to meet him. As she looks down the Wye's steep valley slopes to his encampment she sees, flying above it, the royal standard alongside York's. It sets her pulse racing. When he comes from his tent to greet her he doesn't speak. Just wraps his arms about her, breathes deep, then pulls back, a little shamefaced but smiling, and hands her to her son.

She holds Edmund at arm's length and takes the time to look. His face hasn't lost its summer burnish, his shoulders are broader than she remembers. She feels the muscle of his arms. 'You've been working,' she says. 'Irish sword play, I suppose.'

And there's that slow, lovely grin, the dip of his head, a glance to his father. Still a boy, after all. Easily flattered. There's more than just a year of age between him and Edward now. There's blood and battle and the making of a man. Tears threaten and she blinks them back. She gambled this one's life and still bears the shame of it. She'll do penance.

Richard, too, has aged. She realizes it painfully that night, when she watches him sleep. His hair is almost full grey. She mourns its dark lustre, but this suits him, too. He's silver in the light of the night candle and has kept his lean fitness. Beyond the tent's walls she can hear the low sounds of the camp, the clink of steel as guards pass, the whickering of horses at picket. He's brought men from Ireland and recruited more from Wales. They're a comfort. He's come back to make his claim. He confirmed it that evening as they dined. Rightful King of England, through mothers and from King Edward's second son. Just as Father Bokenham drew it out, his gilded figures handing down the right.

He's met with Warwick already. Salisbury's son was in the Midlands when Richard landed, talking up their cause, scouting for news of the Queen's party. He rode west, met Richard at Shrewsbury, and hurries ahead now to London, to prepare the way. 'He urged me to be bold,' he told her. 'He's right. I've been a loyal fool long enough.'

In the morning, barely dawn and the light grey through the tent's walls, he wakes her to love. But when he's in her, suddenly fails and falls back.

She makes light of it. 'Have you forgotten how?'

'I've been too long away from you. It has unmanned me.'

She curls on her side and lets him spoon his body about her back, his lips against her hair, his hand between her breasts.

After a little while he speaks again. 'It was hard to leave you, in Ludlow. If you'd been harmed, or our children, I know it would have been all my doing.'

'Make us safe now then,' she tells him.

And he says, 'I will.'

44

From Hereford to Gloucester, to Abingdon and Oxford, a steady progress towards London, a coming in state. And in every town and village men welcome Richard back, ask if he's to be their king now. We want change, they say. They're tired of idiot kings and French queens and rich men doing what they like, and no justice unless you can pay for it. Which is a joke, because there's no money left once the taxman's been. And that's another thing, paying through the nose to keep a soft-headed king in comfort. And what about France, eh, wasn't that meant to make us all rich? And is it true the King's a cuckold? Laughing snide at that last and nudging, spitting in the street.

'They'd make you king tomorrow, father,' laughs Edmund, as the crowds jostle their horses.

'Aye,' says Cecily. 'But they don't sit in Parliament and they don't have a vote.'

Tomorrow will be their last day on the road. Warwick's sent word that their way lies open. Parliament is in session and waits upon Richard's arrival. Be bold, Warwick says. Seize the day. Richard seems to take little joy in the news, no more than he has in the journey. Today, as every day, he's listened to men's complaints, smiled at their jests and told them to expect better times ahead. But he's made no promises, and between the towns, in quiet open country, his face has been stern, sometimes sad, and there's been little talk in him. She's ridden beside him all the way, but tomorrow she'll take to the carriage with its eight coursers in summer blue. She'll arrive in London like a duchess. Better still, a queen.

There's a chill in the air now darkness has fallen. He's wrapped a cloak about himself, brought another for her where she sits in the tent's doorway, watching the camp settle. He puts the rising moon at his back, looks west, the way they've come, towards the wild country of Wales and the sea beyond it.

'Wishing you were still in Ireland?' she asks him.

He smiles, rueful. 'They were good days.' He pulls up a chair and sits beside her. 'Not just now, I mean. When we were there together.'

She moves to rest her shoulder against his. 'When we danced in the hall at Trim and Ormond called you King of Ireland?'

'Ah, but the stone said not.' He's remembering that last day of pleasure, when they rode to Tara in the heat of summer and summoned the pagan gods. 'I laid my hand upon it and there was only silence.'

'There is a better kingship waiting for you.'

'Aye,' he says. 'Perhaps.' He empties his cup into the grass.

On the edge of camp, the sergeant calls the hour.

'Let's to bed.'

They draw quite a crowd, riding up to Westminster Hall with eight hundred men at their back, and the colours of York and England snapping above their heads. There's ragged cheering, men nodding to their wives, nudging their neighbours and guessing what's afoot. When Richard hands her from the carriage, Cecily spies Edward, waiting on the steps. He's leaning down and pointing their way. He has the boys with him. His reaching arm rests on George's shoulder, a restraining hand holds Dickon's thin wrist. Margaret hovers just behind with Annette.

Richard doesn't wait but walks straight to them, kisses Margaret's head, kneels to the boys and pulls them close. When

Dickon locks his arms about his neck, he laughs and jiggles him. 'You haven't forgotten me then?'

The boy pushes his head into the crook beneath his father's chin and shakes it, vehemently. 'Never,' Cecily hears him whisper, as she comes up behind.

'Boys, you must go with Annette and your sister now, your father has work to do.' As she prises them away and hands them to the nurse, Richard straightens, turns to Edward, pulls off his gloves.

'They're all inside?'

Edward nods. 'Expecting you.'

'Warwick and Salisbury?'

Edward nods again.

'And the King?'

'In his chambers, out of the way.'

'Good. Let's get this done then.'

Cecily walks with them as far as the door to the Painted Chamber. Beyond it she cannot go, for here the lords of England meet in Parliament. She hears rising voices as the doors are drawn open, then a hush of expectation. Richard looks at her, nods once, sharp, and is gone, Edward and Edmund tall at his back. The guards, who have the keeping of the doors, look nervous; as if they don't know what to do with her, as if she shouldn't be here. Certainly she's a spectacle in this place of business, where only clerks sit scribbling, and couriers hover with their satchels, waiting for dispatches and orders to ride. She walks the length of the corridor to the open door that gives on to the world, then back again to the place where a new world is being ordered; where the dice is to be thrown. Blood pulses at her temple, her heart beats high in her chest.

She remembers the Parliament at Coventry, where she humbled herself but spoke with her own voice, and won. This time she must trust the words of others to do her work; swaggering Warwick who wins men with smiles and Salisbury, whose doubts she knows. Richard, who she knows in her heart would be content to rule only Ireland. 'The throne is the only place of safety for us now,' she told him last night. 'And you have sworn to keep us safe.' He'd lain sleepless, holding her hand over his heart, while she counted the hours by its rapid beat.

The guards shuffle. She turns from them, imperious, takes a place on one of the benches that line the walls, smooths her sleeves, folds her hands in her lap and frames her mind to patience. And then, before she can fathom it, the smack of a door slammed open, and Richard striding out, his face pale with anger and humiliation. Edward and Edmund come behind, hands on sword hilts.

'To Baynard's. Now!' Richard shouts.

Sweet Christ. She picks up her skirts and follows.

They take to the river for the journey. Richard will not speak, so she draws the tale from Edward.

'We came into the chamber, father laid his hand upon the throne, claimed his right to kingship, just as Warwick had counselled he should.' His voice veers from bewildered to bitter. 'He said the way had been paved for us, that there would be cheers of acclamation . . .'

'Nothing?'

'Ours were the only voices raised.'

She watches Richard's face, stone-white beside her, and feels the blow to his heart. For a second time, and when it mattered, he has asked for kingship and been answered with silence.

'They did not say no.' Salisbury's voice is low, placatory.

It's night now. He and Warwick have come at last to Baynard's from the Parliament, and George Neville with them, Warwick's brother, the worldly Bishop of Exeter and, since yesterday, Chancellor of England. Cecily met them at the river gate and brought them to Richard as he'd commanded her to do, before he closed the door of his chamber upon her and refused to heed her calls.

Now they're gathered, and whatever Richard has done in these hours alone, he's steady enough now to speak.

'They did not say yes.' He sits opposite her, flanked by his sons.

Edmund's eyes are fixed on the table before him. Edward's are upon Warwick, who leans against the fireplace, arms folded.

'You said all was ready,' Edward challenges him, 'that we would carry the day. We would have their voices, you said.'

Warwick pushes off from the wall, walks to the window and turns. 'We will yet.' He throws out an arm, chances a smile. 'This is a first move. Parliament's a woman, you have to talk your way into her favours.'

Cecily feels her nostrils flare. 'Brother, I think your son should sit down before I knock him down.'

Warwick doesn't come to table, but lowers himself into the window embrasure, noisily spreading his legs, the swagger not quite gone from him.

Cecily ignores him, looks to Salisbury. 'Now, tell us what went wrong today. And what we must do to put it right.'

'They fear the Queen.'

'With good cause, probably.' Richard's voice is a blade on a whetstone. 'Where is she? What's our intelligence?'

Salisbury heaves a breath. 'We don't know exactly. She's been in Wales, with Jasper Tudor, but she's not there now. Word is she's heading north. She's ordered Henry Beaufort to bring men to Hull. Exeter's there already, gathering an army.'

'I imagine Jasper Tudor, too, will be drawing up forces.'

Salisbury shrugs. 'I imagine. There's no turning Jasper. He's a bastard and a Welshman, but he's loyal to his brother the king.'

'Northumberland? Clifford?'

'The same, further north.'

Richard scoffs. 'I can see that certain knowledge of three gathering armies might give our friends in Parliament pause.' His hands are netted before him, the ruby glinting as it turns. 'Your son did not tell us this. Either when I met him in Shrewsbury or in his message two days ago.'

'I did not think Parliament so lily-livered,' Warwick grumbles.

Salisbury rubs a hand across his chin. 'Look. The point is they haven't said no.'

'What have they said, exactly?' Cecily asks.

'That we should put your claim before them, in writing.' It's the first time George has spoken. 'They want time to consider it. You know how this works, Richard. No man alone will say aye and make himself the Queen's enemy. They must all be able to point to the man next to him and say, it was his idea.'

Richard nods and sighs. 'Yes, I know. Then we will put our claim in writing, as they say.'

And so they set it down. That Richard is the rightful king, just as Bokenham has shown it, from the third Edward's second son, through the women of his house. That the royal line was usurped by the current king's grandfather, and rule of England has been out of joint since. That Richard is come to set it right.

Chancellor George takes the declaration to the lords in Parliament, who talk and talk, but can't decide, and so put it to the King, who looks at them with his rheumy eyes and says he loves his cousin of York, but God gave him his crown and he's not sure what man can take it from him. So they go from him to the justices, who suck their teeth and fold their arms, and say they cannot judge so high a matter that touches on the king's estate. Last of all they call the royal attorney, who shrugs and says, 'Well, if the justices can't help you, I'm sure I cannot.'

So Parliament sends back questions to Richard. They complain of troubled consciences. 'How can we make you king,' they say, 'when we have, to a man, sworn oaths of allegiance to Henry?'

'Are they serious?' asks Cecily. 'Go back, George. Tell them their first allegiance is to God, and that God's law makes Richard king.'

Still they prevaricate. They say, 'But we've passed many acts confirming Henry's right to the throne, and our fathers swore them to his father before him, and his. How can they be overturned?'

'Easily,' Cecily says. 'Remind them the King's grandfather was a usurper. If he was a true king he would have needed no Act of Parliament to make him so. And since he was not, no act can.'

'Then why,' and by now they're desperate, 'has the Duke of York not claimed his right before?'

'God's blood!' says Cecily. 'All these long years my lord has put off his claim for the sake of peace. Now the king's weakness lays waste to the country. Should we not prevent that? Ask them, do they want to be ruled by a French queen?'

George nods, makes for the door and the long tread back to the chamber.

'Wait,' says Richard. 'Tell them that the right, beyond any doubt, is mine. Tell them that right may rest a time and be silent, but it does not perish.'

When George is gone, Cecily sits by his side, takes his hand, nets his fingers with hers and kisses his knuckles.

'Well said,' she tells him.

He leans back in his chair.

She follows his gaze to the view from the window, of the

river's tide falling from Westminster and George walking against it.

In the end, after days of wrangling, a compromise. They are met again, Cecily and her menfolk, and Chancellor George brings the news. 'Parliament will make Richard the King's heir,' he tells them. 'Next in line when Henry dies. Protector, meantime, with full governance of the kingdom.'

Cecily looks up from perusing the paper he has brought. 'They will disinherit a prince then, but not a king?'

George shrugs. 'They think the prince a bastard.'

'And so he is.' She scans the page, turns it back and forth, points. 'But they have not set that down.'

The room falls silent, just the grumbling of the fire, troubled in its grate. She looks from Warwick to Salisbury and her sons. Their eyes are fixed on Richard, who at last stills the ruby on his finger, stretches his arms before him, flexes his neck and says, 'Alright.'

'It's not enough,' says Cecily, so sharp that Richard winces. 'They must say why Marguerite's son cannot inherit. Make it clear.'

'Oh, I don't think they can prove that case, any more than you can, Cecily.'

'She will fight to restore him then, and never give up.'

'Then I will have to destroy her.'

'Even if you do, you have ten years on the King, you may die before him.'

'Then our son will inherit.' He smiles, soft, looks at Edward. 'What a king he will make.' As Edward squares his shoulders, lowers his head, Richard speaks to the room. 'Are we agreed, gentlemen?'

And they nod, still silent.

Richard looks again to George. 'I suppose, with all those grand titles and privileges, I also acquire the right to defend myself?'

'Expressly so.' George retrieves the paper from Cecily and reads, 'You are given full authority to suppress trouble in England, with power to command, in the King's name, the support of all his subjects. Any who move against you, or against your kin, are guilty of treason.'

'Including the Queen?' Cecily wants clarification of every point.

'It is clearly implied.'

'Then enough of this talking.' Richard rises to his feet. 'While we dither our enemies gather. Salisbury, you and I will go north to deal with Northumberland, prevent him meeting up with Exeter and Henry bloody Beaufort. Edward, I want you to go first into Wales, raise men and follow us north. But watch your back, Jasper Tudor will be at it.'

'Am I for Wales too, father?' Edmund, still so young, eager not to be left out.

'I've grown rather used to your company, son. You're with me. Warwick, gather a force about you and keep close to London. Be ready to come to us at need, but your first priority is to defend the capital. And the King.'

He comes late to her chamber that night, leans against the door jamb, looking in. She's dressed for sleep and her hair is down, braided on her back. 'I'll understand if you don't want me here.'

She doesn't, but can't clearly say why. 'I wanted a crown for you.'

'Perhaps I'll get one yet. When I fight the Queen and win.'

'They should have let you fight as king. Men fight harder for a king.'

'Yet a king may die, just as easily as any other man.'

'You must not die.'

He looks past her, and away. 'Do you remember what Ormond said, that day at Tara? He said you have to do more than lay your hand on the stone to be a king. First you have to bed the Queen of the World. Well, I've done that. Then ride your horse full gallop at a wall. I suppose Marguerite is my wall. If I'm meant to be king, she will fall before me.'

'A test then?'

His eyes return to her face. 'I suppose.'

She puts out a hand. 'Come here.'

45

Thanks to Parliament's long disputation it's deep winter by the time Richard rides out. A poor time for campaigning, but they'd be fools to rely on Marguerite to idle away the cold months. Edward left for Wales yesterday, a wall of fur-wrapped muscle, his bright head shining in the frost. On the brink of departure he pulled George and Dickon on to his saddle, as if he meant to take them with him, and rode the courtyard in trotting circles till they squealed. When he handed them down they hung on his stirrup, laughing.

Cecily steeled her heart to scold him. 'That horse is a danger and you are a fool.'

He leaned down, smiling, to kiss first Margaret's cheek then hers. 'Hold the city, Captain Mother,' he ordered, and winked. 'You're in charge.' Then he grasped his father's arm, clapped his shoulder and was gone.

This morning it's raining and Dickon is snivelling, and his father is on his knees to him saying all will be well. She's watching him from the corner of her eye as she farewells her brother, and sees Richard press something into the boy's hand. Then Edmund steps up and tries just to kiss her cheek, as Edward did, but she wraps him in her arms and presses her lips to his forehead, for she's not forgotten the last time she sent him with his father, and has had no time yet to make penance for it. He pulls away and mounts, and only Richard is waiting. She rests her hands on his shoulders. He's drenched already, and has so far to go. Her hands smooth raindrops from fox fur and pull his cloak tighter about him. This is all she can do to protect him now, and is little enough. She lifts her head, and he's looking at her, half smiling, wholly sad. And she thinks, as she so often does, that none living knows her heart as he does.

'My Queen of the World,' he calls her now.

'Come back a king then, and bed me.'

When he's gone, and the sound of marching men has fallen to silence, she turns and leads her boys inside. George runs ahead, but Dickon stays close.

'What did he give you?' she asks.

He holds up a tight closed fist. 'He said to keep it safe for him.'

She unfurls his cold wet fingers and there, dry in his palm, lies the bull's blood ruby on its golden ring.

It's a quiet Christmas. The King wants no festival, but he comes to table on feast days, as Chancellor George says he must, and Cecily sits beside him, reminding the court of who her husband is. Otherwise, he's for prayer and the company of priests, which is a relief to her and everyone, though who can imagine what he prays for? Her sister keeps her company at Baynard's. She comes, she tells Cecily, when she can bear the emptiness of her own house no longer.

'I expect to meet my husband at every turn. Last night I ordered the maid to let down my hair. I was sure he was out drinking and would come home wanting my bed. She thought me bewitched or senseless, I'm sure.'

'It's natural to miss him,' Cecily tells her. 'It will get easier.' She wonders if it will, or if it should. She misses Richard. She missed him all those months he was in Ireland and she was her sister's prisoner. But, at least then she'd had the comfort of knowing him still living; busy elsewhere, of course, doing things without her. In danger, yes, but breathing still, holding her first in his thoughts as he always has. She tries to imagine being beyond hope of that comfort, but draws her mind back from it as she would her hand from a fire. She's never been first in anyone's thoughts but his.

Across the room Anne has laid down her sewing and is crying again, quiet and unobtrusive, pointless. She wants to shake her, but it was this tearful sister who kept her sane through those desperate days, sharing Buckingham's letters, his snippets of news. So instead she sits beside her, holds her hand while she weeps, and doesn't call her foolish.

She bites her tongue and does not say, I myself cannot sleep for worry, for I have husband and sons beyond my reach.

Anne is with her the evening Warwick comes with his mother, Alice, who braved the sea to escape the block, but trembles now as she takes Cecily's hand and stares at her with red, pain-shot eyes.

'Cecily, you must listen to my son,' she says. 'He has news. I've come that we might bear it together.'

Cecily stares at her, pushes away her hands as if they carry contagion. 'Sit down, Alice. I will hear him.' She turns to Warwick, and it takes all she has to raise her chin and bid him speak.

There's no swagger in him now. He speaks of an army led by Beaufort, Clifford and that dog, Henry Holland. Of a battle in thick snow outside Wakefield. 'My father,' he tells her, 'my father, your brother, is dead . . .' And here he hesitates.

She feels Alice clawing at her sleeve, hears her sobbing and resists the itch to slap her. And there's Anne, her sister, standing too close, with her hands before her mouth, eyes wide, because she knows what's coming; knows as well as Cecily does herself.

'Richard?'

Warwick gulps, looks away.

'Say it.' She clenches her fists, feels nails stinging palms. 'Richard. Edmund. Say it. Dead.'

He nods. 'Yes.'

She feels the women's hands at her elbows, the air pulled from her lungs. She struggles to stay upright, pushes help away. There is a rage rising in her that is terrible, that could tear walls and rip throats. The faces that spin across her vision, wide-eyed and horror-struck, tell her she is monstrous, thought-blown and mad. Who are they to think so? 'I am betrayed.' She growls, an animal, cornered and backed. She must move. Her legs stagger, tilt her about the room. 'Betrayed. After all and everything, he has betrayed me.' The floor is a beast that bucks beneath her and must be fought down.

Arms reach out for her, but she cannot be held. She reels from them and hears her sister's voice a world away, making a thin shiver, a useless nothing of her name. 'Cecily . . .'

She turns on her. 'He swore to me he would not die! He swore it!'

But, of course, he had not. He had said he would put himself to the test. He would ride at the wall. For his Queen of the World, he would do that.

And he has taken Edmund. But no, she had given him, sent him with his father. The son she did not choose.

There is searing pain as her knees meet the floor and her hands fist in her hair. She twists to deepen the agony, rips at her scalp and wishes her fingers blades, for pain opens at last a safe place within her, where she is not mad and can still her breath. The stone floor is cold on her cheek. It's quiet now. There's only her stuttering heartbeat and her sister's useless sobbing. 'Shut up! What have you to cry about?' Not fair. Not fair. She has lost as I have. No, no, for she has not lost Richard. What is Buckingham beside Richard? And what am I without him? She feels the horror rise again, the rushing blackness, not rage now but terror. She shakes her head at it, bares her teeth and snarls. She is York. Yes. Still that. Husband gone. Son gone. Brother. What next? What to do? Upstairs, sleeping. Please God asleep. Daughters, sons. Richard's children, the rich coin he has minted in her. Hers to keep. And somewhere, somewhere, dear God . . .

She throws out her arms, stiff and shaking. 'Get me up.' Hands grab at her, haul her into a chair. She hears a voice, almost her own. 'Where is Edward?'

'West, lady, mustering men.' That's Warwick, telling her what she knows. Idiot.

She had meant which field, which hillside? Is he safe or harried, hungry or fed?

She means, has he men? She means, is he ready? She means, will he come?

'Call up my secretaries. Get paper. Get ink.'

She speaks, they write and, in the dark before dawn, men are pulled from their beds and put into saddle. A dozen riders by a dozen routes. They carry both summons and warning. 'Edward, your father and brother are dead. Come south and avenge them. But guard your life. You are the King's heir now.'

The last footfall is gone from the stair. She has done all she can tonight. But for one thing. She sends everyone away and calls for Annette. 'You must pray for him, Annette,' she urges, drawing her into the room. 'From the day of his birth your prayers have bound him to life.'

'What shall I pray?'

'That he will live. That he will come to me. That wrath will conquer his grief but not his reason.' He's eighteen, still green, and all that stands, now, between her and destruction.

Annette nods. Her eyes are clear, her voice calm, her hand steady and cool against her mistress's cheek. 'I will pray if you will rest.'

So she lets the good nurse take the clothes from her body and lay her in her bed. When she is given a cup, she drinks it. Then she lies quiet and follows the words of the Ave, as certain as rosary beads, as familiar as her name, a path through the cold and the darkness to the hope of her fire-born son.

46

In the days that follow, while prayers travel west, news leaks south of Wakefield and its bloody aftermath. She'll not shrink from it, nor consent to hear it second-hand or sifted. She calls each witness to recount his tale in person, to give details that feed her resolve.

They tell of a hard march. Of weather that turned so hard and so vicious that even the North men among them said they'd never seen its match. Of a scourge of snow storms that filled the valleys and made the high moors nigh impassable, while ice-laden winds froze their water in its skins and cracked the leather of their harness. They lament a belly-gripping scarcity of provision in a country laid waste by an enemy greater in number and better prepared; that harried and nipped at their heels, pushing for a fight they seemed certain to win. With Christmas coming on Richard holed them up in his castle at Sandal. Lean pickings, but a safe enough place to sit out the weather and wait for Edward to square the odds with his reinforcements from Wales. She hears how the waiting chafed on him. How they kept a cold Christmas, with little cheer and poor fires and men sleeping in draughty corridors or out under canvas for want of room, but every day her lord and her son coming among them, telling them to take heart and hold on.

Then, just before the year's turn, here comes a bevy of northern lords with eight thousand men. They swear they'll fight for York. Then turn their coats for Lancaster.

'Your lord felt with them we'd enough to get the job done,' one old soldier tells her through new gaps in his teeth. 'They marched out with us, shoulder to shoulder. Then fell on us like dogs.'

She takes those lords' names, crafts a curse for each. And one for Richard, who was fool enough to trust them.

At last a man comes who can tell her how Richard died in the first hour of the battle, his horse cut from under him in the charge, a poleaxe blow that caught him as he fell, buckled his armour and made a cave of his chest. Another saw, much later and at Marguerite's order, the despoiling of his body, the severing of his head, the mockery of a paper crown and the hammering nail that fixed it to his skull. He tells her how Marguerite laughed, and let Henry Beaufort kiss her hand. And how the Queen's infant son dabbled his fingers in her husband's blood.

The man who speaks of Edmund shakes so hard he rattles, and weeps when he's done. Edmund, who always ran so fast, couldn't outrun the horsemen who pursued him in the rout. They brought him, bloodied but breathing and still in charge of himself, to Clifford, who stood him on Wakefield Bridge, called him York's cub and cut his throat with a bodkin.

'Was he afraid?' she asks the trembling squire.

He looks at her as if he doubts her sanity, and lacks the forethought to lie. 'He was a green boy, lady. He was scared witless.'

She welcomes the blow, gives him money for his pains. It is part of her penance, to hear the worst and bear it. That night, at her prayers, she makes his words her Ave. A green boy, a cut throat, York's cub. Edmund. Grey-eyed, loose-limbed Edmund. The son she did not choose. She lights candles for his soul, holds her fingers to their flames and begs forgiveness. What use? She could sear the flesh from her bones, she thinks, set all the world a-fire, it would never be enough.

*

There's news that feeds her anger and news that feeds her intelligence. With Warwick she questions every man for the names and numbers of their enemies, for signs of their intentions, hints of where they'll strike. Piece by piece they have it. While Beaufort slaughtered Cecily's menfolk at Wakefield, Marguerite sold England to the Scots. In return for a mercenary army she has given the border town of Berwick, and a marriage with her son that will make Scotland's daughter England's future queen.

'Our first piece of good news,' Cecily tells Warwick, who looks, for a moment, bewildered. 'Think, man. There's only one thing the English hate more than the French and that's the Scots. Now our French queen brings a Scottish army against us. Surely we can make something of that.'

They can. They spread the word, and the numbers in Warwick's small army, Richard's planned shield wall for London, begin to swell.

Still no word of Edward but, daily now, rumours come of Marguerite's bloody progress south. Those who flee her path say she rides armoured at the head of her army, her son saddled before her, flanked by Beaufort and Percy, Henry Holland and the butcher Clifford. They cut a swathe of destruction the length of England; houses raided, churches robbed, women raped. Men are tortured to reveal their wealth; killed if they won't give it up, killed anyway when they do. As Peterborough, Huntingdon and Royston fall, London's citizens start to whisper in the street that, when Marguerite comes, they must throw open the gates to her and beg mercy. The mayor sends to Warwick to say, 'What will you do?' And still, still, no word of Edward.

They can wait no longer. Warwick has nine thousand men and leads them north.

'It's less than the Queen has,' Cecily points out to him.

'They're fresh, though,' he says, reaching for his swagger, his bravado. 'They haven't marched three hundred miles in winter.' He plucks the King from his prayers and takes him with them. 'For morale,' he says. 'Let our men see that they fight for God's anointed under a royal standard, against a foreign queen and a disinherited bastard.'

For God's sake, don't lose him, she thinks.

She would have sent for William Oldhall, but his heart gave out as this winter came in, still attainted, still in sanctuary, pared from the world by his loyalty to York. So it's one of his men who answers her desperate call at dead of night. John Skelton, who Oldhall had the raising of and loved like a son. He stands now in her little boys' chamber, cloaked for travel, bags across his shoulder laden with her coin.

'Can I trust you?' she demands, as she hurries Dickon, still half asleep, into a thick woollen surcoat, and Annette does the same for George. The bull's blood ruby is on a cord about Dickon's neck. She tucks it deep, pats it down.

'More than most men,' he tells her.

And that must be good enough. There's no one else. He's a man of business, Skelton, not a soldier, but as handy with a knife as any merchant who carries a full purse around London's streets. Anyway, it's not a soldier she needs now, it's a man who can keep his wits about him and knows his way in the Low Countries. Skelton's traded wool through the ports of Bruges and Antwerp ten years or more and has command of a ship. That's all she needs. All she can hope for. A man who can get George and Dickon out of England.

London's shield wall is lost. A hard-ridden messenger brought the news to her door at midnight; a Lancastrian night march, a flank attack, a swift and dark defeat. Warwick's army lies in its gore and the King, who was his standard, is in Marguerite's hands again.

'Does my lord of Warwick live?' She hopes he does; that he will cling to life long enough for her to beat him senseless.

'Yes, my lady. He says to tell you he's leading what men he has left west to find the lord Edward. He bids you buy time. Do anything you can to keep the gates of London closed to Marguerite.'

Tomorrow she will rail at Warwick's failure. Tonight there is no time. The armies clashed north of St Albans, which means Marguerite is just one day's hard march away. After Wakefield, after the cutting of Edmund's throat, she can't imagine even the youngest of York's sons will be allowed to live.

So now, in the cold hour before dawn, she's bundling them down ice-slick steps to Baynard's river gate. George is snivelling and Dickon wide-eyed, stiff with shock. Skelton is in the boat already. For secrecy's sake he'll row it himself to the wharves beyond the Tower, where his ship stands waiting for the morning tide. His legs spread for balance, he holds up his arms and she hands them down, like packages, like cargo, like the nothing they'll become if Isabella doesn't agree to shelter them in Burgundy.

'Do you think she will?' Annette had asked in the frantic hour when they pulled the children from their beds.

Cecily wasn't sure, isn't still. It's a demand made of friendship, no gain in it. Just one woman saying to another, keep my children alive. Such things are rare. 'I would do it for her.' She wonders if that's true. 'Beg her, if you must.'

'Bah,' she says. 'You're their mother. You should be going with them, not I. Isabella would not tell you no to your face.'

It shames her more than a little. Annette's probably right. 'I'm sending you. I must hold the city for Edward.' She cannot let him fight alone, or bear again to have a sea divide her from him.

'Always Edward.'

Now, as Skelton's first pull on the oar draws the boat from the dock, she remembers she did not kiss her boys, or sign the cross upon their brows. She watches Annette tuck them, one beneath each arm, then look up. She holds the nurse's accusing stare until it disappears, with the sound of the oars and the boat's tiny bobbing light, into the river's dark flow. Then she sits down on the cold steps, wraps empty arms about her knees and scalds her face with tears.

47

When she returns to the house, her daughters are waiting. They pull her river-damp cloak from her, sit her by a hasty fire, wrap her hands around a cup of warmed wine, and when she's ignored it a good while for staring into the flames, remind her to drink. She does so, to please them, though the wine is grown cold and cloying. They settle on cushions at her feet, leaning against her. When the cup is empty, Margaret takes it from her, sets it down, and puts her own hand in its place. The comfort she finds in the weight of their bodies, the squeeze of Margaret's fingers, the feel of Elizabeth's hair under her hand, is a sin she must take to confession tomorrow. She should have made them go. She'd woken them at dead of night and asked if they would flee with their brothers. 'I can't be certain Marguerite will not stoop to killing women.'

Both said no. Elizabeth's husband, the young Duke of Suffolk, is wherever Warwick is. Not dead, the messenger has said. So she'll wait for him. Margaret simply thought a moment, cocked her head in that way she does when she's decided something, and said, 'I think I'll stay with you, mother.' She has a loyal heart, this Margaret, youngest of her daughters. She feels unworthy of it, but thankful beyond words, in this moment.

Now they wait together for the morning, for the traffic to grow on the river and the streets to begin their teeming business. But the light comes slow and the sky stays leaden, the river is slack and the streets quiet. The news has come to more doors than hers, then. London has heard of St Albans and is holding its breath.

She sends a note to the mayor, in the name of her son, the King's heir. He is coming, she writes. And it would be his order that the city's gates remain closed to his enemies. She commands his obedience in Edward's name. She waits a frantic hour until word comes back.

The gates remain closed. For now.

She calls her confessor and, through the day, with her daughters beside her, keeps the offices of prayer. She finds their voices must speak for her, for no words will form on her own lips. Her heart cries out for mercy, for forgiveness and salvation, not to God, but to Edward, though his power to save is no more certain. And while her daughters pray, she pummels her mind for anything she might do to prevent the city opening its gates and giving her to her enemies.

Dusk comes early and brings a soft fall of snow. When vespers is done, and she's wet her lips with a little wine, she leans her head against the cold glass of the solar window and cranes her eyes west, to where she last knew Edward to be, until the winter sky turns black. Below her, the lighter man with his flaming brand carries fire from sconce to sconce along the riverbank. Then, in the glare of his torch, she sees a small boat slide up to the dock. A hooded figure gets out, shakes snow from his cloak, hands over coin and hurries up the steps. Her house guard challenges him, and he answers in a voice she recognizes. William Hastings, a knight lately sworn to Edward's service, whose father served with Richard in France. She hurries to meet him, draws him inside with her own hands.

'I bring news to cheer you, lady,' he tells her when the servants are gone, the doors shut and only she and her daughters remain.

'Edward lives?' The words leap from her mouth, desperate for confirmation.

He barks a laugh. 'And strides the world.' Serious now. 'He sends me to you. Bids you take heart. He's a week from London with twenty thousand at his back. He ordered me to tell his Captain Mother that he's coming for his crown.'

The relief of it almost takes the power of speech from her, but a week is an impossible distance when the enemy is at the door. 'Well and good,' she tells him, 'but Marguerite is a day away at most.'

'Aye,' he says, swiping a hand across his face. 'I've spied that as I've travelled. Listen. London must hold, or all is lost. I urge you, go to the mayor in the morning, tell him Edward is coming. Tell him Marguerite's army is ill provisioned, almost dead on its feet. Scotland gave her men, but not the money to pay them, or the supply lines to keep them fed. That's why the plunder's been so bad. But they're on their knees now. If London doesn't let them in, or provision them, she can't hold.' He's earnest. 'London need only keep its gates closed. She's waiting for reinforcements, but they won't come. She'll know that by now. The fear of God must be upon her.'

'What do you mean, they won't come? Why?'

And now he indulges his face with a smile. 'Because your son has destroyed them.'

She hears Elizabeth and Margaret exclaim beside her and feels behind her for a chair. 'For God's sake, man, tell me of that.' She can barely breathe as he recounts the tale.

How Jasper Tudor was marching men to join the Queen before Edward intercepted him on the Welsh border, on their own lands, south of Ludlow, on the broad moor that runs down to the river at Mortimer's Cross. 'None would have believed it,' he told her. 'Not nineteen yet, but more full of courage than any veteran of the wars. And nerves of steel. It was cold enough that morning to freeze sword to scabbard, the land about us all ice and bog. And the army we faced, well, twice the size of our own. Then, the strangest thing,' he shakes his head, 'I can't explain it, even now. You'll think I tell you tales. A trick of the light perhaps? The mist? But I swear on my faith I saw three suns rise behind us, not one.'

She hears the girls gasp and feels her heart trip.

'You are incredulous,' he says. 'I don't blame you. I only believe it because I saw it with my own eyes. Men trembled like the end of the world was coming. I thought they'd break and run and we'd be finished, but there goes Edward, gallop- ing along the lines. "See how God favours us!" he shouts. He declared it a sign of providence; that the three suns were for the Trinity and the living sons of York.'

Her heart regains its beat, faster now and strong. 'He was born under the sun,' she says with certainty. 'Yes. It would rise for him.' She imagines its three-fold light blazing on his armour, his blinded enemies staggering.

'Well, right enough, it did,' Hastings grants her. 'Men would have followed him into Hell's mouth then. We had victory within the hour.'

She closes her eyes and lets exaltation flood her veins. The mad boldness of him, to summon even the sun and make it his.

But Hastings is still speaking. 'Edward will smash Marguer- ite to pieces,' he says.

She nods, yes, of course he will.

'But you must keep her from the capital. If she takes it, she wins. We can't besiege London in winter.' He's staring at her now, and she must gather her wits. 'Will you do it? Will you go to the mayor?' That smile again. 'Edward says you've a mighty power of persuasion.'

She reaches for his hand, grasps and brings her brow to it. 'While I have breath London will open its gates to none but him. I swear it.'

He sets his lips to her fingers. 'Good. He said it would be so. Now I must be gone.'

'Where?'

He's on his feet and heading to the door. 'To spread rumour and hope among the people of London. If I've anything to do with it, every man in the street will be your ally.'

48

London's mayor, Richard Lee, is a merchant. He doesn't much care who's king, as long as it doesn't interfere with trade. He's also a southerner, who's never ventured north of the Wash and believes the Scots to be savages. That's an advantage. Cecily dresses finely for her meeting with him, puts on her highest hennin and the ruby-clawed dragon Richard gave her when George was born. She has need to appear dauntless. The mayor and his aldermen are packed so tight into Guild Hall's chamber that she can smell the sweat of their fear and see their tremulous blinking. They've taken York's side these months past, financed his campaign. That will take some explaining when Marguerite comes. She draws herself up to speak.

'Before we hear you, Lady Cecily,' says Mayor Lee, 'you should know that the King has written to demand entry to his city, and we are of a mind to grant it.'

She smooths her sleeves and breathes deep. 'The Queen has demanded, you mean?'

'In the King's name.'

'The Queen does not speak for the King. She has captured him. He is in her power. But let that go, for now. You hope, by opening to her, to stay safe?'

'She would hardly sack her own city.' He sounds certain, but his lips are thinned to blue, and sweat beads on his brow.

'The Queen leads a foreign army against us and pays them with plunder. She's promised them London as their greatest prize and has no cause to love you. You've harboured her enemies. Did Warwick not march against her from these very streets, victualled at your cost and with your blessing? Did my lord not buy arms at your credit?' There is muttering in the chamber, and she raises her voice to speak above it. 'You think to exchange surrender for mercy? There will be none. I gave up Ludlow without a fight and was made to stand by while the town was taken apart.'

'But Warwick is defeated already, what hope for us?' A voice from the back of the room, strangled and afraid.

'Warwick lost a battle, but is not defeated. He has joined forces with my son, the King's heir. They ride for London with twenty thousand men. How many has the Queen?'

'And yet,' says Mayor Lee, 'the Queen is on our doorstep. Where is your son? We have only your word that he comes at all.'

'A week away at most. I've certain knowledge of it.' She tells them of his victory and God's sign of the sun. 'If you open the gates to Marguerite, you close them to God's chosen. We need only hold fast. The Queen waits for reinforcements that will not come. Send out scouts to see. You will find, north of London, an army on its knees.'

They agree to wait. They will send scouts. They will send, too, provisions with promises of good will, but not open the gates.

'Provision them and you lengthen the time they can stay in the field,' she tells them as she leaves. But accepts she's done enough for now. She has bought a day.

That night, she learns that the provisions meant for the Queen have been carried away by Londoners, who cried out for York and damned the house of Lancaster. 'That's Hastings,' she tells her daughters. 'He does his work well.'

Next day, she returns to the Guild Hall.

'Our scouts say five thousand,' Mayor Lee tells her.

She shrugs. 'A quarter of my son's force. Less. Keep the gates closed.'

'The King swears no harm to the city.'

'The Queen, sir. You'd be a fool to trust her. Her army murdered my seventeen-year-old son, after battle was done and he a prisoner disarmed. She is murderer and traitor, both.'

'Traitor?'

'Aye. You owe her no allegiance.'

Each man turns, one to the other, perplexed.

'The Act of Accord that made my husband the King's heir makes a traitor of any who rise against him. And yet, and at her command, his head, my son's and my brother's look sightless out from the walls of York. Would you betray your city to such a one?'

And another day is won.

When she returns to Baynard's, she finds three daughters, where she had left two. Her eldest, Anne, turns a tear-streaked face upon her from the circle of Margaret's arms. It's a shock to see her. She's been at her husband's London house this while and keeping her distance.

'He's with the Queen's army,' Anne says, 'that bastard Henry Holland. Well, I'll not be at home when he comes. I'll not have his murdering hands upon me.'

'You will stay here,' Margaret comforts her, 'here with us.'

Cecily takes her from Margaret's arms, sits her down, kneels before her, folds her hands in hers. Why must she always be cruel to this child? 'Anne, where is your daughter?'

She snivels. 'At home.'

'You must go back to her.'

Now she cries in earnest. 'I will not.'

'No, indeed,' says Margaret, eyes darting from sister to mother. 'We will send for her in the morning. We will bring her here and you will both stay safe with us.'

She watches Anne nodding and weeping, Margaret's pleading eyes. She sits back on her heels and relinquishes Anne's hands. 'Stay tonight,' she says.

*

Next morning, she goes early to her daughter's chamber and finds her already dressed, sitting by the window, which has barely begun to lighten. Anne looks so small, never grew to her mother's height, but her back is a plumb line and her chin steady. 'You've come to tell me I must go back,' she says, not turning from the view.

Cecily comes to stand beside her, keeps her own eyes on the water, too. 'Anne, Marguerite may yet win. If she does, you alone, of all of us, have a husband who can keep you safe.'

'He despises me.'

'He will despise you more if he finds you in the house of his enemy. Think, Anne.' She lays a hand on her daughter's shoulder and feels it shrink from her touch. 'In Marguerite's England, you will be the only one in a position to plead for your sisters.'

'Or for my mother, I suppose.'

'Oh,' she takes back the hand, folds it in her sleeve, 'I can shift for myself, you know.'

'Yes.' And now she turns with narrowed eyes. 'You always could. I doubt you will miss my father at all.'

'Oh, Anne . . .' The bitterness of loss threatens the beating of her heart; the missing of Richard that will never be done. She grasps the back of Anne's chair, grips it till she can speak again. 'You are more my daughter than you imagine. Had you put a knife in my breast you could not have cut deeper.'

Anne's head falls. 'I'm sorry . . .'

'Don't be. There's no need. I've wounded you, I know. Many times and grievously. It's good for my soul to be reminded. And fair that I be punished. There is much that I regret. Little I can remedy.'

They are quiet for a time while the winter sun, thin as a corpse, creeps into the room.

At last Anne stands. 'I must go home and wait for my husband.'

'I hope he will not come.'

'I hope Edward kills him. Where is he, anyway, Edward? Why does he not come?'

'I cannot tell you. But I have cause yet for hope.' Still she cannot look at her. 'One thing I swear to you, Anne, for all I've done. If we win through this, you will never again go back to Henry Holland.'

Later that morning, the mayor waves a paper in her face. 'This comes expressly in the King's name. His wife may be a traitor, but can we deny the King his city?'

'The city doesn't want him. Have you not heard in the streets the cries for York?' She takes the paper from him, reads, hands it back in disdain. 'It bears the King's name but has the Queen's French stink upon it.'

Next day, when she comes again, the council is resolved to send a delegation to the King, to satisfy themselves whether it is his will they defy, or the Queen's.

'Then send women, not men,' says Cecily. 'For they will be dealing with Marguerite.'

They send her sister Anne, Buckingham's widow, and Jacquetta, who have both called the Queen friend.

'Perhaps you will see your husband,' Cecily snarls at Jacquetta as she passes by her. For the golden Woodville wears the Queen's silver swan and stands in her army. 'Tell the Queen my son is coming,' she calls after them. 'Warlike Edward. She will remember him.' Let them go, she thinks. It buys me a day.

Jacquetta and Anne return, next morning, with a letter of assurance they swear was dictated in their presence. 'By the King or the Queen?' Cecily demands.

'By the King,' says Jacquetta, chin raised, 'who demands the return of his city, the reinstatement of his son and the punishment of the house of York, which opposes his royal will.'

The mayor looks to Cecily, hands spread and desperate.

Her smile is savage. 'Then he is condemned out of his own mouth, an oath breaker, aligned with traitors. His signature is on the Act that made my husband, now my son, his heir. Write back and tell him he betrays himself and us.'

Cecily watches Anne and Jacquetta led from the chamber.

Her sister, who did not look at her as she gave her testimony, hesitates at the door and turns. 'Gentlemen . . .' Her eyes are on the ground, her voice quiet, but she clears her throat and speaks louder. 'Gentlemen, it looked to me as if the Queen's army was in disarray. They seem fewer, now, than five thousand, and disheartened. Even the Queen looks thin and hungry.' She looks up, to Cecily, speaks clearly, and is heard. 'I think they cannot stand against you long.'

Cecily crosses the floor to kiss her. 'Thank you, sister.'

Anne lifts her hands from her shoulders as if they burn her.

The council takes heart. The gates remain closed.

That night, it snows, quiet as a dagger and more deadly. Then comes such a dawn that hungry men, who sleep on open ground, don't live to see.

When she comes at noon to the council chamber, Cecily finds men laughing. Mayor Lee greets her at the door. The scouts, he tells her, have brought word. The Queen has decamped her ragged army, and trailed it and her husband north into the still-falling snow. The only sign she was ever there is an army's filth left on St John's Fields and a trudge of tired footprints that wind and weather will cover soon enough.

'The city is York's,' he tells her. 'We pray you will stay to help us prepare your son's welcome.'

She accepts the cup of warmed wine he hands her and drinks it down, welcoming the heat it brings to her cold blood, the scent of spice and citrus that floods her head like relief.

49

So little time to make ready. Two days and two nights since Marguerite drifted with the snow. Scant hours to draw out Edward's claim, to expound upon the arguments she rehearsed before mayor and council: that the Queen is a traitor, the prince a bastard. The King a usurper and breaker of oaths, forsworn, unfit to rule.

She has made it the subject of sermons in every London church. Had it proclaimed from street corners for the common crowd to hear. It has been presented to the guilds, announced in the law courts and the merchant halls. She has spoken herself to Europe's ambassadors, who learn quickly that, if you want to know what's happening in England, best come to her door. There can be no one left in London ignorant of Edward's right to rule, of his descent, through Cecily and Richard and through his long mothers, from the third Edward.

It's an hour before midnight and she's been at it since dawn, and the dawn before that. Though her daughters urge her to rest, she says, not yet. All must be ready and she must be sure of it. So they trail behind her to at least make sure she eats a little, to push a cup of wine into her hand between the close of one meeting and the opening of the next. And now, as the city sleeps, they walk with her the shadowed length of Westminster's great hall. Five hundred echoing steps from its great north door to the black marble table, high on its dais where, for as long as men remember, England's kings have taken up their dignity and conducted their business. Despite the hour, and a cold so deep it stiffens paint and makes fingers clumsy, the work goes on. Around braziers and in clusters of candle-light, London's craftsmen work through the night to draw out Edward's story for all the world to see.

She has briefed them herself, of course, and now the royal lineage Father Bokenham so artfully described for her husband is being brought to life for her son. On boards and banners the length of the hall England's bright future is spelled out; its long wait for a worthy king is over, the wasted years and false dawns forgot. The will of God, so long frustrated, is reaffirmed, and the hopeful prayer of every heart is gloriously answered in Edward.

It's all much cruder than she'd like; its colours garish, its figures sketched and brief. Never mind, time is short now. The message is clear enough and can be perfected later; gilded and glorified, set to verse and song.

She turns to the master of works who paces at her side. 'It will be finished by morning.' It's not a question.

'It will, it will,' he tells her, wringing his hat. He wouldn't dare say otherwise.

She comes, at last, to the steps that lead in shallow risers to the dais and the high seat upon it. 'Well?'

And the master hurries forward to order the lighting of more candles as her daughters catch up and gather round.

'Watch.' She tells them, and signals to the darkness of the vaulted roof.

The candles lit, men lay down tapers and take up ropes to send two great chandeliers high into the air above her. She follows their light up and up until, beside her, she hears her daughters gasp.

'Well, mother,' says Anne, laying a hand on her arm, 'I am, as ever, amazed by your industry and imagination.'

There, in the flickering space above the king's high seat, hangs the culmination of all; three golden suns enmeshed in York's white roses and, striding among them, a gilded Edward, sword aloft, flanked by angels. As they watch, more workmen scrabble with ropes among the rafters and a golden crown descends, as if from Heaven, to hover above his head. Cecily lets her smile widen. Yes. Tonight, in candlelight, he shimmers. In the brightness of day, he will dazzle.

'Oh, I don't know,' Cecily says, lowering her eyes at last and smoothing her sleeves. 'There's nothing imagined here. Only now you see him as he is.'

It's an hour past noon when her nephew George, bishop and Chancellor, comes to fetch her from Baynard's to St Paul's. As he hands her into the carriage, and her daughters after, she realizes that her hands tremble and folds them, one within the other, to keep them still. 'What word this morning?'

'When the bells rang for terce Edward was five miles from the city. He's expected at its gates within the hour.'

She sits back among the cushions and closes her eyes, clenches her jaw against the spinning of her head. She didn't make it to her bed last night. Indeed, she's barely slept since that desperate night when Warwick came to say her lord and son were dead. Too much to do, she has told her daughters when they fretted. Too much to think on. But in truth, the sights that come too readily when her mind is unguarded make sleep unwelcome: a paper crown, a broken breast, Edmund's grey eyes, full of light, as she imagines they were that morning, five days after Christmas, when he rode out behind his father into the winter of his first battle. How might those eyes have looked to Clifford as they fell upon his bloody knife, watched its thin blade arc and fall?

She pulls herself from the thought of it and catches George's eyes watching her from beneath his heavy brow.

'Are you well, lady?' he asks. A question not worth answering.

'Is all in place?' They've been through it a thousand times, but she needs to hear it again. A thanksgiving at St Paul's, then to Westminster Hall where Edward will take his seat beneath her gilded suns and swear his royal oath. 'The Lords stand by to confirm it?'

'In all their fine array. And the streets between lined with men who will shout their lungs out for him.'

'Good.'

It must be done quickly for, as soon as might be, Edward must ride north on the Queen's tail. He must make speed to do the one thing that, in all these years, and at the last, Richard failed to do; to grasp the neck of Lancaster and break it in his hands. Today he will be proclaimed, but not crowned. He will take his oath, but not his ease. He will be offered a kingdom, and he will smile, all graciousness and humility, and say, I thank you, but let me earn it first. And every heart that hears it will be his.

Last night, from Westminster, she sent a messenger, so that Edward might know of their plans before entering the city. A note came back at dawn, scrawled in her son's own hand. 'All well, Captain Mother,' it said. 'God keep you till I see you.'

She jolts as the carriage comes to a halt. To be seen by him. To see him living. How her eyes hunger for it.

As she steps from the carriage to climb the wooden steps of the platform set up for her at the cathedral's north door, she hears a roar in the distance and knows he's close; that even now he's passing through Newgate. She need only watch for him now, over the heads of her retainers dressed in the blue and murrey of York, over the cheering crowd, through the smoke of the bonfires burning in the street and the air hung with cries of *Edward! Edward! York! York!*

At last she sees him, shining in the distance, his helmet held in the crook of his arm. He's laughing, waving at the crowds, leaning down from his deep-chested horse to receive laurel boughs and kisses from women his guards can neither hold back nor restrain.

Edward. A feast for the starving.

She lets her heart ride to him on the crowd's roar.

And now he's here, dismounting, setting his foot to the step; her vision is full of him, hampered only by the mist of her breath on the cold bright air. She holds out a hand. He takes it and kneels. She thrills to the warm hardness of his lips on her fingers, then she's in his embrace, his head lowered to her brow, his cheek burning against hers.

'Give them to me, Edward,' she whispers in his ear. 'The butcher Clifford. That bitch the Queen.'

'In good time, Captain Mother,' he promises.

She looks out across his shoulder through a sudden sting of tears and it seems, for a moment, that three suns shine again in the sky, that fickle trick of Heaven's light that Edward seized upon in battle and harnessed to his will. She will make it his blazon.

'You are the sun in splendour,' she tells him, and gives him over to the glory of the crowd.

Epilogue

On 29 March 1461, Palm Sunday, between the Yorkshire towns of Towton and Saxton, Edward defeated his enemies in England's bloodiest ever battle. Around a tenth of the fighting-age population took to the field. Almost half of them died.

He fought under his banner of the sun in splendour, and was crowned beneath it as King Edward IV on his return to London, on 28 June 1461. As Cecily promised, the sun became his blazon and the symbol of his reign.

Before leaving London to secure his victory, Edward had given Cecily sole command of his household, effectively making her England's regent during his absence. From the day of his coronation, she no longer styled herself Duchess of York or Dowager, but as Cecily, the King's Mother.

Acknowledgements

In the years I have spent thinking about and writing this book I have received encouragement from so many people. There are some to whom I owe special thanks.

First, to my partner, Caroline, who has listened to me witter on about Cecily Neville for thirty years and more, and patiently accompanied me on more fact-finding trips than even I can remember. Only I know the depth of the debt I owe her. Also to Caroline's family, who have become my own.

My brother, John Garthwaite, deserves top billing. He and his wife, Shirley, have been my lifelong supporters, not just in writing, but in every endeavour. Thank you.

Next come my patient and enduring friends Susan Aslan, Amanda Barry, Lisa Betteridge and Suzanne Howe. A more supportive group of women you could never hope to meet. They have shared in every triumph and (near) disaster. Most particular thanks to friend-of-my-heart Pamela Petro, a writer of extraordinary talent and unsurpassed generosity of spirit. Her patient and insightful readings of numerous drafts have been invaluable.

A special mention to Sarah Moss whose close reading and considered, equitable advice kept my keel even. Also thanks to Elanor Dymott and Tim Leach, colleagues at the University of Warwick, for their enthusiastic engagement with *Cecily* and generous congratulations when all came good. Among my fellow students, a special mention for Ellen Lavelle and Steve Gay, who read the entire book in instalments over the two-year writing period. They are more insightful readers than I can ever hope to be. Also Katie Hall, Costanza Casati, Anna Maria Colivicchi, Anna Lodwick and Penny Sandle-Keynes.

My gratitude always to Chris Cleave for his invaluable advice on the application of WD40 to my writing engine, and to Maggie Gee. Between the two of them, they got the words to flow at a critical time. A mention, too, for colleagues at Arvon: Barry Walsh, Anna Jefferson, Janette Keene Taylor, Kate Tindle and all. What a week that was.

To Joanna Laynesmith, Cecily's biographer, and to Mathew Lewis, Richard Duke of York's, I owe a profound debt. They have answered my questions patiently and shared their extensive knowledge as generously as only truly good people could. Thank you. I hope you'll feel I've done justice to 'your' people.

Peter Diamond has lived up to his name in every respect. Since I met him in a creative writing class more than twenty years ago he has encouraged me to write and made me believe I could. Nothing I can say will ever be enough. And thanks to Rosemary, his outstanding wife. Together they provide a masterclass in living well.

Thanks to Joan Wasylik for being my enthusiastic tour guide in Paris and Rouen. She knows – and took me to – all the best restaurants. Also to Marilyn Miller, whose professional insight into the state of mind of several of my characters has, I hope, added depth. And to Martin White, simply for reading and having a generous heart.

It is customary at such times to thank one's editor and agent. And I do so here, but with nothing customary about it. Their work has been in every way exemplary but, better yet, their passion for this book and the care they have taken with it have been a source of elation. Imogen Pelham of Marjacq Scripts; Katy Loftus and Vikki Moynes of Penguin Random House – thank you. Appreciative applause also to Penguin's Olivia Mead and Georgia Taylor for inspired and inspirational work in publicity and marketing, to Julia Connolly for show-stealing cover design and to Emma Brown and Shân Morley Jones for thoughtful copy-editing.

And a final, long-overdue thank you to Keith Hill and Bob Martin, teachers of history and English respectively at the Manor School in Hartlepool way back in the 1970s. They sparked in me a love of history and language that has enriched my life immeasurably. Without them this book would never have come to life. And so, to all good teachers everywhere, keep the flame alive and please, pass it on.

Table 1: The Descendants of Edward III

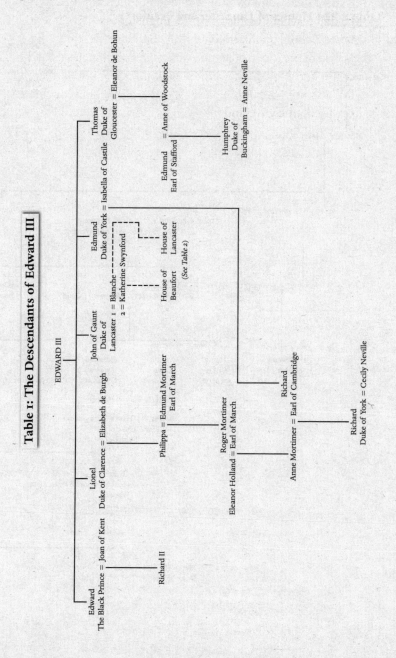

Table 2: The Houses of Lancaster and Beaufort

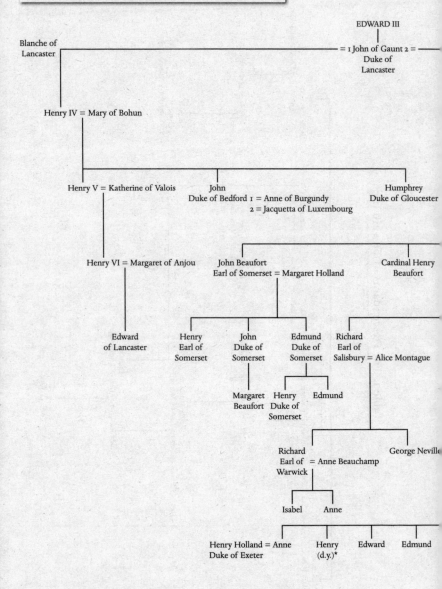

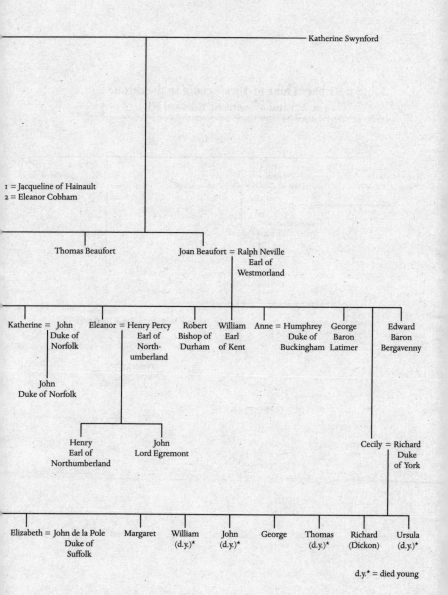

Katherine Swynford

1 = Jacqueline of Hainault
2 = Eleanor Cobham

Thomas Beaufort

Joan Beaufort = Ralph Neville
Earl of
Westmorland

Katherine = John
Duke of
Norfolk

Eleanor = Henry Percy
Earl of
North-
umberland

Robert
Bishop of
Durham

William
Earl
of Kent

Anne = Humphrey
Duke of
Buckingham

George
Baron
Latimer

Edward
Baron
Bergavenny

John
Duke of Norfolk

Henry
Earl of
Northumberland

John
Lord Egremont

Cecily = Richard
Duke
of York

Elizabeth = John de la Pole
Duke of
Suffolk

Margaret

William
(d.y.)*

John
(d.y.)*

George

Thomas
(d.y.)*

Richard
(Dickon)

Ursula
(d.y.)*

d.y.* = died young

Table 3: Richard Duke of York's claim to the throne via the 2nd and 4th sons of Edward III

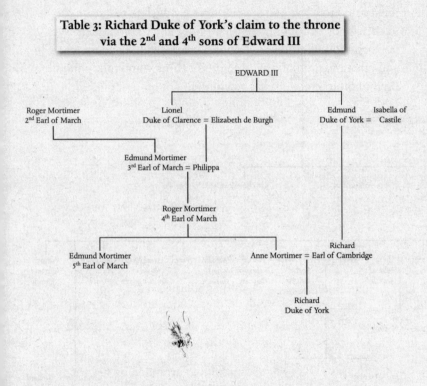

Reading Group Questions

It occurred to us that many readers may wish to discuss *Cecily* in their book groups – there's certainly lots to talk about! We hope the following questions will spark lively conversations and offer a variety of ways you might think – and talk – about *Cecily*, both the novel and the woman.

1. Cecily lived more than 500 years ago in a very different society. How well did you feel you could relate to her? And can you see parallels between her life and those of women today?

2. E. L. Doctorow famously said: 'The historian will tell you want happened. The novelist will tell you what it felt like.' What is the novelist's role in bringing history to life and how do you think Annie Garthwaite does it?

3. The book's cover describes Cecily as wife, mother, politician, traitor, fighter and survivor. Which of these aspects of her life impressed you most – and did you ever feel they were in conflict?

4. Cecily's marriage to Richard was arranged by her parents and made for dynastic reasons, yet they seem to have achieved a strong partnership. Is *Cecily* a love story? And what did you find most surprising about Cecily and Richard's relationship?

5. Is Cecily politically ambitious in aiming for the Crown, or is she simply driven by necessity in order to protect her family?

6. Richard's father died a traitor. How does this affect both Richard's personality and his political motivations? And do you think he wanted to take the throne?

7. *Cecily* is set during a period when England was almost constantly at war – either with the French or with itself. Do you get a sense from the novel that this constant, brutal fighting has shaped the personalities of the characters?

8. *Cecily* juxtaposes events in the national sphere (war, politics, regime change) with the domestic (marriage, motherhood, loss). What does this juxtaposition bring to the novel and does it make you think of history differently?

9. At the beginning of the novel, after the burning of Joan of Arc and the coronation of Henry VI as King of France, Cecily observes that 'the will of God, which has called all things into being, might turn a child into a king, a girl into a warrior, or a body into ash. And that any man – or woman indeed – may, according to their courage, shape His will to their purpose.' How would you describe Cecily's relationship with God and how far does her belief in Him drive her actions?

I learned to read long before I went to school. Mum taught me. When my older brothers had been bundled off to school and whatever housework that needed doing had been done, she'd sit down with me for an hour or more. 'Our time,' she called it. I spent my mornings in anticipation of that hour's arrival, my afternoons pining that it was gone. Soon enough though the boys would be back, Dad would come home and Mum would be pulling on her coat to go work a twilight shift at the local factory. The boys would watch telly then, or go out to play in the street. Or not play, as they got older. I'd head back to the settee and carry on turning pages.

Mum started me on picture books, but eventually words took over. We progressed beyond children's books quickly enough. By ten or so I would just read whatever she was reading. Catherine Cookson for a long time, I remember. Story after story in which indomitable working-class women overcame adversity through relentless effort, sustained only by thick black tea, drunk caustic and scalding. It was an authorial indicator of rare good times if there was a penny to spare for a pinch of sugar to sweeten it. In my mind's eye I see those women still: tight-jawed, sleeves rolled, ploughing up cobbled streets to the defence of their men or their children. Towering matriarchs, every one. They'd take on all comers.

When it wasn't gritty family sagas, it was romantic histories. Jean Plaidy, Georgette Heyer, you know the drill. When Dad was on night shift we'd curl up in Mum's bed and read long into the night, turning page after page to find out whether Lady this or

Queen that would find freedom, or justice, or peace or, well, love, mostly, if I'm honest. We'd fall asleep with sentimental tears still wet on our cheeks. She wasn't above sentiment, my mum. Sometime factory worker, shop girl or cleaner, a nurse early on, obliged to give it up when she married. She knew the way the world worked, but would indulge a bit of romance. A pragmatist come morning though. If I was still swooning at breakfast, she'd give one of her wry smiles, put hot tea in front of me and say, 'Yes, well, don't get too caught up in all that.'

Ultimately she gifted me with a love of reading and an untutored conviction that storytelling and history were two sides of the same coin. Later, I met a history teacher who seemed to share that conviction.

The Manor wasn't a terribly progressive school back in the 1970s. A secondary modern on a north-eastern council estate, it went comprehensive the year I passed the Eleven Plus. It typically churned out boys for the steelworks. The girls would go to the chicken factory or build telephone exchanges for Siemens. Women's work, you see. Nimble fingers. We lived across the road, so geography dictated I had to go. Mum wasn't best pleased. 'She should be going to the grammar.' That was one fight Dad wouldn't back her in. A union man and a socialist from cap to boot soles. Anyway, she knew he was right. I think so, too.

It worked out well enough. Keith Hill taught history like it happened yesterday, and fanned the flame my mother had ignited into a consuming blaze. I think he was just glad to have an interested pupil and would rattle on as long as I'd sit and listen (which was a long time) in class, after school, in break times. He'd bring in extra-curricular books and lob them across the desk at me. 'You might take a look at this,' he'd say, knowing I would. History textbooks mostly. Novels occasionally. It was the Wars of the Roses for A level and my head was alight with vicious rivalries, breathtaking treacheries, unlikely triumphs, fearful fates. And towering characters! Edward IV, the golden boy who avenged his father and hacked through swathes of enemies to reach the throne. Earl Warwick, king-maker, showman, faithless traitor. Hapless Henry VI, the mad heir of Agincourt. And the women were no less seismic than the men. Marguerite of Anjou, who put on armour and rode at the head of an army with her five-year-old son. Elizabeth Woodville, the impoverished widow who denied the King her body till he married her to get it. Margaret Beaufort, who lost her only son to exile, but conspired lifelong to bring him home and make him England's first Tudor king.

'So why do you think she/he did that?' Keith Hill would ask. 'What was in his/her mind when . . .?' My final exam mark wasn't that impressive. I was a bit woolly on dates and politics, but *very* strong on character motivation.

If you ask who was the stand-out figure for me then, I'd have to say Richard III. The hunchback, the tyrant, the child-murderer. I'd been about to write him off. 'But was he?' Keith Hill asked, eyes closed, leaning back in his chair. 'Who says so?' And that was the moment when the story/history penny decisively dropped. The past, I realized, isn't fixed, definitive or singular. It's the raw material of story, open to interpretation, investigation, retelling. 'Read that,' he said. The next book he tossed my way was Rosemary Hawley Jarman's novel *We Speak No Treason*, and it had me entranced. It gave me a new Richard. Not a murdering tyrant, just a man making hard decisions in tough times. A hero, actually. Keith Hill was out of the stalls like a greyhound. Revisionist histories came flying thick and fast. The other side of Richard. The history Shakespeare didn't write.

Now. Shakespeare. There's another thing. Keith Hill had his match in Bob Martin, the English teacher. The A-level text was *King Lear*, but it was hard to get him to stick to the point. He'd come into class with stars in his eyes and say, 'Now, I was reading *Othello* last night, listen to this.' And the hour would pass in Desdemona's bedroom, or Lady Macbeth's hall, occasionally on the blasted heath, revelling in language and the alluring alchemy of words. One day I remember saying to him, 'It's just beyond beautiful, isn't it?' The smile he gave me was the widest I've ever seen on anyone. 'Yes,' he answered. 'It absolutely is.'

It was a perfectly imperfect education. I left for university – the first to do so from the Manor, I believe – knowing that whatever happened next, story would be my sustaining tea, language my penn'orth of sweetness.

History remained a passion, Richard III an abiding interest. Nearly ten years ago I found myself staring into a grubby hole in a car park the day after his body had been exhumed from it. I followed his hearse to Bosworth, stood in the rain outside Leicester Cathedral to watch his funeral on a big screen, laid my tribute of white roses. It was part apology, really. When I left school I had imagined I'd one day write a novel and it would be about him. In honesty though, and long before Richard emerged from the car park, my interest had shifted.

Richard's life was entwined with those of so many strong women, and I'd met most of them in my reading. But I couldn't escape a nagging sense that one was eluding me. Where was Richard's mother? The bare bones were obvious enough. She was Cecily Neville, granddaughter of John of Gaunt and his mistress-come-wife Katherine Swynford. Her own mother, Joan, though born their bastard, rose to become a countess. I knew Cecily's children's stories like the back of my hand. Her parents' and grandparents', too. But in all the novels and biographies I'd read – so many over the years – I'd never really encountered Cecily. *Why?*

Well, you might say Shakespeare 'did for Cecily', no less than he did for her son. Her appearances in his history plays are brief. She has no political agenda, exercises no power and serves no dramatic purpose other than to curse her misbegotten offspring. Shakespeare's summation of Cecily is simple: old, pious, embittered and dull. No wonder historians and novelists marginalized her for 500 years. There were more interesting women to write about. Bigger fish to fry.

Really? Who says so?

Cecily lived through eighty years of tumultuous history, never far from the beating heart of power. She mothered kings, created a dynasty, brought her family through civil war. She met victories and defeats in equal measure and, in face of them all, lived on. Last woman standing. There *had* to be a story there, surely.

It was the 1990s by this time, I suppose. I'd regretfully given up an early career in publishing because I simply couldn't make a living at it. I was now in my thirties, heading up European communications for an American multinational. I remember no other women at my managerial level, few enough in the company at all. I was learning first-hand how women exercise power in environments dominated by men. Cecily seemed to be getting closer. Within a few years I'd leave to set up my own business, which I ran for twenty years. But I'd made myself a promise. For now I had to make my way in the world. Once that was done, I'd find Cecily's story and I'd set it down. I set myself a target. At age fifty-five I'd stop work. I'd write.

All was going splendidly to plan until, nine years out from that target date, a combination of the financial crash and a fraudulent financial advisor wiped out my pension savings and left me deep in debt. It looked like early retirement was out of the question; I'd be working till I dropped. But by then, perhaps, I'd imbibed a bit of Cecily's resilient spirit. 'Don't worry,' I remember a friend saying. 'There'll be light at the end of this tunnel.' Only if I switch the bloody thing on myself, I thought. So I redoubled my efforts, worked harder, took no holidays, abolished weekends and, when not working, pursued compensation, justice, redress. Gradually I paid off the debts, rebuilt the savings, got back on track. When at last I could lift my nose from the grindstone, low and behold, a light.

So, in 2017, at age fifty-five, I stopped work and started a creative writing MA at Warwick University. I gave myself two years to bring Cecily to the page.

At the same time – serendipity – the historian and specialist in medieval women Joanna Laynesmith published a biography of Cecily. I read it and begged her to have lunch with me. We talked through to dinner. I compared what I'd long suspected about Cecily to what she knew. Matched my storyteller's intuition to her meticulous scholarship. In the days that followed, the shadow figure of Cecily came gradually into focus. Here was someone who could give any of us a lesson in how to operate as a woman in a man's world.

I'd long understood that the journey towards female emancipation hasn't been a steady upward progression. Medieval women, especially those of the aristocracy, or in what we might think of today as the middle classes, had freedoms their Victorian counterparts, or even our post-war mothers, could only dream of. They could own property, run businesses, take up trades. Widows, especially, could achieve significant economic independence. Men ruled, certainly, but in the margins women could exert agency, assume authority, push boundaries. Women of Cecily's status, with huge households and vast estates, would be responsible for enterprises similar in size and complexity to mid-sized FTSE companies. They would be highly literate, understand finance and the law, have a firm grasp of politics. They were, in short, women of business.

At the same time, they'd be expected to support their husband's political career and advance their family's interests within intricate and hierarchical social networks. Above all, they were expected to breed. Children, ultimately, were the measure of their value. If they failed in that regard, nothing else counted. Come now, did you think it was only twenty-first-century women who were expected to 'do it all'?

Cecily excelled on all these fronts. But that was just the start of it. She not only *lived* through seismic political and historic events, she *shaped* them. A lifelong dynast, she engineered her husband's bid for the throne and, when that failed, her son's. She was brazen enough to maintain a cordial exchange of letters with Henry VI's queen while, at her husband's side, planning a rebellion. Bold enough when defeated to barter for her children's future with an enemy king. In the aftermath of her husband's death, it was her London home that became the centre of Yorkist planning as her son fought his way across England to claim his crown. And, when he left the city to fight again, he had the good sense to leave management of his kingdom in no one's hands but hers.

Old, pious, dull? I don't think so.

I could see her clearly now, at last. Striding the fifteenth century's corridors of power with her sleeves rolled up, knocking on doors she had no business to enter, defending her own against all comers. Here was *my* matriarch.

History has given us few visual representations of Cecily, but I found one that revealed her character to me. It's in a book of hours in the French national library. It was likely commissioned by Cecily the year she watched Joan of Arc burn. She was sixteen. In it Cecily's parents face each other across the page, flanked by their sons and daughters. Below, a series of armorial shields displays the status of each parent and child. Though the youngest of the daughters, Cecily has placed herself in the first rank, kneeling almost on her mother's black hem. She has dressed herself in the richest colours, the finest jewels. Behind her, her sisters, countesses and duchesses in their own right, become a pale crowd, muted, shadowed, plain. The men opposite are smart enough, I suppose. 'Me first,' says Cecily. At sixteen she understood what it took me years to learn: that in order to exercise power in a man's world you have to assume it. You must look the part and turn the language of power – images such as this, in Cecily's world – into your own propaganda.

Cecily was a woman of the fifteenth century – of a pre-reformation, pre-feminist, Catholic, male-dominated world. She is also a woman we can feel kinship with today; fighting with words when swords were denied her, exercising whatever power was given to her, pushing for more, testing boundaries, holding her own. She faced the questions women still struggle with in our own times. What comes first, love or ambition? Which family commands our first loyalty, the one we're born into or the one we make? How far will your courage take you?

I spent my childhood in Richard III country. As his brother Edward's loyal Lord of the North, he kept the Scots at bay. In my teenage years I trailed his border castles, narrowed my eyes, as he would have, to watch the weather roll across Yorkshire's dales. On the day of the Queen's silver jubilee my mother took me to his principal seat, Middleham Castle. In the inevitable gift shop she bought me a replica of his royal seal. It sits on my desk as I write. Today I live in Cecily country, close to the Welsh border, and to Ludlow Castle where she and Richard's father ruled supreme for a time, and where, on the darkest of days, she faced down an army alone. I go there often. I stand at the foot of the castle steps as she did and imagine her enemies coming up through the town, bladed and bloody. I square my shoulders, lift my chin. Let them come.